That Girl from Wagga

The True Blue Editon

David Parker Ross

Contents

From the Office of Captain Stacefield E. Grant, OSC, MoV.

Is this thing working?

It is?

Okay. Thanks, mate.

No, I'll call you if I need anything.

Okay, where to start?

The success of Phelk's book "Jenna Plural Wants You!" surprised a lot of us. The result was that both Jenna and Phelks thought it would be a good idea if I told you my story. I have no idea why.

Write a book? Fuck, I don't even remember the last time I read one. Even with Phelk's book about Jenna, I listened to an audio version. However, in a moment of weakness, okay, I was drunk, I agreed. But I'll be stuffed if I'm gonna sit here and type.

So, I'm just gonna ramble on in this recorder.

Phelks is supposed to have that eidetic memory chip, but I'm calling bullshit on a lot of what he said and will severely challenge its accuracy. After I listened to his book, I asked him about it, and he claims that he doesn't always have it on because it's too intrusive. So, I'm going to set some of the record straight here.

And I know some of you perverts out there are just gonna skip to my version of events with him.

So, let's get on with it. My full name is Stacefield Ellen Grant, but I prefer to be called Stacey or Stace. I was born in Melbourne and moved to Wagga Wagga when I was ten years old. Yes, Wagga Wagga is a real place, and no, it's not made up. If I had a beer for everyone who questioned that, I would... well ...I'd be a very happy girl, but I digress.

My mum was industrialist Marcia Grant, who pretty much ditched my dad, brother, and me. Dad raised us to the best of his ability, working two jobs to support us. He died when I was sixteen, leaving me in the care of my brother. He died a year later, serving in the Australian army on some insignificant moon of Jupiter that doesn't even have a name.

They tried to put me in state care, but I went on the run 'til they caught me and put me in Juvie. Play your cards right, and that's a story I might tell you someday. At eighteen, I joined the Australian Air Force. I started out working in intelligence, and two years later, I got my wings.

It was another two years later when I met Jenna Plural, and this is how that happened...

Chapter One

The Battle of Cape York

Vince Pascal slammed me against the wall, and I gasped as the force of it winded me. I smiled, biting my lower lip and looking into his eyes as he pushed his body up against me. I could smell the beer and cheap cigars on his breath as he moved in to kiss me. His arm slid around my waist as I slipped my own around his neck. I pulled his head to mine and kissed him hard as he slid his hands up to molest my breasts like some wild animal. We were alone in the barracks; we had snuck away from a squadron boozer. Although I was horny, I was also pissy and unsure if I wanted a root or a blue. When Pascal kissed me with his slobber, it felt like I was snogging a puppy. I love puppies as much as the next girl, but I don't want to smack face with one. It was such a turnoff. "You'd better have something down there to make this worth my time, Pascal," I said provocatively.

He pulled his head back and grinned. "Oh, I got what you need, Stace."

"Let's just see about that." I slipped my hand down the front of his chest, along his waist, and then cupped his crotch through his combat pants. He was a full mast. I couldn't help the feeling of disappointment. "Seriously?" I frowned. "You brag about your size, and this is all you've got for me?"

The smile disappeared from his face instantly. He pushed himself back away from me and stared angrily into my eyes with his hands on my shoulders. "You bitch," he said, glaring at me.

I just smiled and shrugged. "What can I say? Those little girls who told you size doesn't matter were all lying." I expected him to be embarrassed, not in a rage. Oh. How wrong I was. I suddenly felt a stinging pain and momentarily saw stars, and it took me a moment to realize what had just happened. Pascal had struck me with the back of his hand—big mistake. I brought my knee up into his groin. I'm not exactly a well-built girl. However, I know how to take care of myself. My bony knee collided with his balls with as much force as I could muster. Tears sprang to his eyes as he doubled over toward me. I was not done, and I head-butted him in the face, hearing the crack of nasal cartilage as I did. I then ran my ankle behind his and kicked his feet out from underneath him, and he went down on his back.

In the confusion, he didn't know whether to grab his swollen balls or clutch his bloody, broken nose. "You're an arsehole, Pascal," I said, thinking it was all over. Suddenly, I felt him as he grabbed my ankle and flipped me over as I stepped over him. I went down, face-first, landing on my chest, winding me momentarily. I quickly turned over onto my back and tried to get up, but he was on me in a moment. He sat astride my waist, grabbed my wrists, and stared angrily at me. He shimmied up until he could hold my arms with his knees. I tried to buck him off, but there was not much hope with ninety kilos of air force pilot on top of a fifty-five-kilo girl. "So, you think you can be a little prick tease then humiliate me, do you, Stace?"

I spat up into his face, and, holding both my wrists in one hand, he slapped me again. His eyes dropped down to my breast, and he ripped open my shirt. "Don't even think about crying rape. Everyone knows what we came in here for."

"You are one dead motherfucker, Pascal," I said, trying to bite his hand.

Someone grabbed him by the hair, pulling his head back, "Didn't anyone teach you, Pascal? No means no." It was my friend, Harper Davis. We hadn't seen or heard the door open. Pascal tried to turn and knock her aside, but she brought one of her skinny knees into the side of his head. Now, Harper was that skinny girl everyone knows who makes tight clothes look baggy. Her action was enough of a distraction for me to slip out of his grip. I interlocked my fingers and slammed a double fist into his face. Harper landed another kick to the side of his head. He fell to one side, and I managed to get up to my feet.

He would've had to be carried out if Harper and I had our way that day. Who knows, maybe that would have saved his life. However, it was at that moment that the sirens went off. The urgent voice came over the public address system. "All crew to their positions. Pilots to their aircraft. Prepare for immediate takeoff. This is not a drill." Harper and I looked at each other, then raced to our lockers. The two entrances to the barracks opened, and the other pilots rushed in as we pulled out our flight suits. Pascal was also up and at his locker. We had trained for this many times, and on many occasions, we had had to do it in an emergency. It was less than a minute or two, and we were in the orange flight suits, helmets in hand, and racing out to our craft.

I flew a ZZP Interceptor with Harper as my rear gunner. She was coming to the end of her rookie year. She had proven to be an excellent gunner. She was a good kid, nineteen years old, and had that hungry look. She wanted to be a pilot so badly. She had been assigned to me just under a year ago and had become a permanent fixture on my hip. For my life, I don't know why, but Harper idolized me. I have a rep for being a good pilot, but I'm certainly no role model. She'd dyed her long hair pink like mine was back then. What can I say? It was all the rage. She was taller and skinnier than me and had virtually no tits. Shit, she still had to show ID to buy alcohol because she looked like a kid. Fuck! She *was* a kid.

We raced across the tarmac under the blazing summer sun as the ground crew scampered around like ants when the nest was under attack. At first, we thought it was just a simple bombing raid, so common in the last year. I had no idea the Peons were spearheading a full-scale invasion of the Australian mainland. As I reached the craft, I saw Bitty. I'll always regret not knowing her real name, even though I'd worked with her for over two years. She was the head of my ground crew and prepped my kite for launch. The engine was already running, and smoke filled the air as the aircraft all down the line powered up, ready for the fight. I pulled on my helmet and closed the visor. "Good to go?" I asked her.

"Everything is tickety-boo, Ma'am," as she raised her hand, and we high-fived. That was the last time I saw her. To this day, I don't know if she's alive or dead. I just wish I knew her name.

I climbed into the cockpit of my craft and slid into the seat that'd been specifically designed for me. Harper climbed into the back, facing the rear as my tail gunner. We quickly ran through the checklists and waited until we got the order to taxi to the runway. "What the hell was all that with Pascal?" Harper asked me.

"I thought it would be a bit of fun, but I changed my mind. He didn't like that." That wasn't quite how it was, but what the fuck? She didn't need to know the details.

"Men are bastards," Harper said, annoyed, before cheerfully adding, "You should find yourself a nice girl. You know, like me."

I chuckled at this. "I don't think I'm ever gonna swing that way, Harp. Anyway, how are things with that girl from the canteen you were seeing?"

"Becca? Yeah, ah, well. We broke up," Harper said with a slight edge of dejection in her voice. "She kept worrying about that whole fraternization thing and got so whiny."

I laughed at that as I watched the other Raptors taxi and take off. "She's a bloody civilian. You can definitely fraternize with a civilian."

"Yeah, she was pretty dumb. But she's got a real nice ass. Not as nice as yours, though, Stace. "

"Give it up, Harp. It ain't ever gonna happen," I shook my head and chuckled at her persistence.

"Oh, you don't know what you're missing."

Suddenly, the radio came online, and the voice of our Squadron Leader, Allen Conroy, boomed out. "Gamma squadron, check-in."

Each squadron member counted off until it reached us, "Raptor Twelve ready and standing by."

Allen then came back. "Move on out, Gamma." In call sign order, we taxied to the runway. Then everything moved fast. We launched just seconds behind Raptor Eleven, who hadn't even taken to the air before I was following behind his exhaust. "Yeeee haaa," Harper cried out as she always did when we took off.

We formed in the sky above Cape York and headed out to sea. Allen quickly briefed us. "It's what we feared, ladies and gents. A full-scale invasion of our country has begun." My heart skipped a beat as he said these words, and my blood ran cold. I could hear Harper mutter, "What the fuck?"

"Don't worry, Harp," I told her. "No Peon's gonna set foot on Oz."

"Ain't that the truth!" Harper responded determinedly.

But as I looked down at the scanner in front of me, I saw a fleet of ships coming in from the ocean, as well as a wall of aircraft coming straight toward us. Ben, one of my wingmen, came in over the line. "Jesus! We're outnumbered ten to one."

Allen came back quickly, "Stow it, Raptor Seven. All that means is you have to shoot down eleven, but if you shoot down fourteen, you'll beat Stacey's record."

"And let's just say on this occasion, I really don't mind anyone beating my record," I responded, and I heard Allen laugh.

"Come on, Redbacks. Let's send the bastards to hell," he cried.

"This'll be remembered as the greatest day the Australians have ever known as we beat those bastards back into the sea," Trisha McFarland, the second in command, came over the radio. And then I saw them with my own two eyes. The sky was filled with enemy aircraft, specifically German Hawks. They were designed to intercept enemy aircraft and gain air superiority. I clenched the control stick harder and gritted my teeth, and if I'm real honest, I didn't expect to live through that day. But one thing I was sure of, I was gonna take down as many of those motherfuckers as I could before my end came. As we drew closer together, I could almost feel the tension rising among my colleagues. With the other squadrons having launched, at least two hundred of us were now in the sky over Cape York. But that was nothing to the incoming enemy.

And then the sky lit up as the enemy fired thousands of missiles straight at us. "Break and engage, break and engage," came Allen's urgent voice.

I spun the Interceptor in a circle, and Harper engaged missile countermeasures, sending out a pulse that would prevent the missiles from locking onto us. That would not stop us from running into one, and I had to bank and curve to avoid becoming one of the first victims of an invasion. I tried to ignore the sounds of several of our aircraft igniting into flames and plummeting to the ground. I tried not to think about which of my friends had just died as the second wave of missiles was launched; another volley rained down on us as the second line of the enemy fleet entered striking range. We were out over the ocean, and I took my craft into a steep dive, skimming along the top of the water; a wake rose behind us, hampering the enemy's projectiles. Harper sent out another pulse, which made them explode harmlessly underwater. My maneuver meant that we were now too close for the enemy missiles to attack, and as I pulled up directly underneath their front line, I let my guns rip. I had set my guns to wide spray and watched as the undercarriages of at least three aircraft disintegrated in front of me. Then, in a move they weren't expecting, I flipped my craft upside down and pulled away, narrowly avoiding a plane plummeting down on top of me.

Harper and I now found ourselves behind the first line of the assault as they attempted to launch their mines at us, but Harper was prepared and activated our counterstrike systems again. This time, when she enabled the system, it projected a phantom image of our craft. Their mines locked onto this instead of us and attacked it as I opened fire on the enemy craft's rear, but they broke formation after realizing my duplicity, and our attack strategy became much harder.

"Someone help me out 'ere. I can't shake this fucker," rang out Pascal's voice, and in the heat of warfare, any grudge I might've had vanished as I spun my craft toward his Raptor Three and opened fire on his pursuer. I missed, so I swept my craft right before his nose. A dangerous move, one that many would call foolish, but one I had done many times. It was effective at scaring the shit out of the enemy pilot, and I was not disappointed as he swung away so fast he nearly lost control. As he struggled to right his craft, Harper launched a limpet mine onto the side of his wing, and as I pulled away from him, she sent the signal for it to explode, and he fell, spinning down into the ocean.

It was almost a struggle avoiding each other in the air, let alone trying to battle enemy craft, but I came up with an idea. I waited until there was a near miss and sent my craft spinning toward the ocean as if I'd been hit. The intent was to take the attention away from me just long enough to try something. Harper instinctively knew what I was doing, and suddenly a burst of explosive flak fired out of the rear of my craft, and several enemy vessels flew straight into it and were ripped to shreds as the flak ignited against their hulls.

I looked down, checking the readouts of my squadron. I couldn't stop the audible gasp that emanated as I saw that two-thirds of us were gone after just six minutes in the air. Pascal's radio was still transmitting when the enemy finally lit him up, and I heard his screams as he died. He was an asshole, but he was also a longtime comrade; I don't want him remembered only for the incident I described earlier. In truth, I only started with that to piss off Jenna for a laugh.

There is no time for grief when you are out there in the sky. You can't think about your friends coming to the end of their days. If you do, you'll bloody end up like them.

I quickly had a bogey on my tail, and he or she was doing well as I struggled to shake them. They evaded all of Harper's exceptional gunnery skills, and I had to call out for assistance. "I got your back, Stace." I heard Trisha respond as she came up from underneath my tail. I dropped us into a nosedive as Trisha gunned away the rear end of my opponent. There were so many on me now. All I could do was continue ducking and weaving out of their way. I desperately looked for a target to lock onto, but the minute I did, I became the enemy's target when I got into firing position.

Trisha came back on the line. "Retreat on my mark."

I was confused by the order and responded, "Repeat your command. You aren't Squadron Leader. Repeat command."

"Al's dead, Stace. I'm Squadron Leader. Retreat on my mark."

Retreat? What the fuck? I looked down to where she transmitted the direction we were to follow. "Confirm your mark, Raptor Two. That's out over the ocean." Of course, this was not just a casual conversation. I still had to maneuver and watch out for incoming craft that now swarmed around me like bees. It was only a matter of time before sheer, massive firepower would take me down, and no amount of skill in piloting would help me then.

"Mark confirmed, Stace. Now, move it."

"We're running away?" I screamed.

"Look at ya scanner, Stace. We're the only two craft left, and Scherger's stopped broadcasting. I don't know what the hell happened, but the battle's lost."

Eight minutes, that's all it took. Eight fucking minutes to bring down the air power of the greatest fucking country in the world. My blood ran cold, and the anger welled up inside me. I couldn't think straight; the idea of abandoning Australia was beyond anything I'd ever considered. Then I spotted the aircraft carrier Berlin, and I pointed my craft toward it, determined I was gonna take it out with my own life if I had to.

"What the fuck are you doing, Stace?" Harper shouted. "You might have a death wish, but I don't. You can get us safely out of here, but if you don't wanna do that, tell me now, and I'll eject."

Anti-aircraft fire from the Berlin began firing, shredding our fuselage. Swearing blue murder, I pulled up and hit the throttle. I could take my own life in a desperate act, but I had no right to take Harper's. I flew back down to water level and weaved in and out between the European fleet, knowing no aircraft would fire upon us and risk hitting their own ships. Trisha saw what I was doing and fell in behind me. "Nice move, Stace. Hopefully, they won't consider us worth following." I didn't reply. I tried not to think about the friends I had just said goodbye to, or rather hadn't had the chance to say goodbye to. What I really needed to know now was what the hell was going on in the rest of my country and, more importantly, what I could do to help. Eventually, our pursuers pulled away, and we were free from enemy fire. "When are we gonna turn back to Oz?" I finally asked Trisha.

"We're gonna head east, then north, and make for Japan. It's the only allied territory that's open to us."

"Trish, we gotta get back to Oz. Even if Cape York has fallen, we could make for another base and join up with another force," I retorted.

After a long pause, Trisha replied. "They've completely overwhelmed us, Stace. Every major coastal city is reporting attacks. Casualties are already in the thousands, and the enemy has air superiority. There's nothing we can do. All forces that can retreat are retreating."

"You're bullshitting me," I shot back in disbelief.

"We've no choice, Stace. We have to make it to Japan while we still have power. It is just a tactical withdrawal to regroup. This isn't a surrender, Stace." I didn't reply. I just looked down at the damage readouts to my fighter. There was considerable damage to the wings, engines, and the D.E. compensator. This was gonna be a rough trip.

Chapter Two

Burn Up

"Are we going to make it?" Harper asked solemnly.

"To be honest, I don't know," I said just as one of my engines quit. "But I'm gonna give it a red hot go."

"I guess if anyone can do it, you can," Harper responded, but without conviction.

"You've been flying with me for over a year now. Have I ever let you down?" I said, trying to sound reassuring.

"Not in the air," she replied after a short pause.

I chuckled; humor had always been my release for stress, and I was more stressed now than I'd ever been in my life. "Now we hear the truth? What have I done to you?"

"You're the reason for the fourteen demerits on my record."

"Hey," I responded defensively. "Anything you did with me, you did off your own back. No one ever forced you to follow me into some of my stupidity."

"You're the closest thing I have to a best friend, Stace. And for the record, there was a lot of peer pressure keeping up with you."

I fell silent as I pondered her words before finally responding, "You're my best friend too, Harper. I'm sorry if I am not exactly a role model for you, but I never pretended to be."

"You're considered one of the best pilots in the Australian Air Force. Correction, you *are* the best, and you cop a lot of slack for that. I don't. I just get the demerits."

I started to feel a little irritated, and as I watched a second engine go out, I sighed. "I'm not your mentor, Harper, nor am I the holder of your virtue. If you don't wanna hang out with me after this, that's up to you. But right now, all I'm worried about is getting this beastie to the ground with us both intact."

Before Harper could respond, Trisha came on the line once more. "How are you doing there, Stacey? I can see you've got two engines out."

"I like to think of it as I still have two engines working – glass half full and all that."

"Well, you're D.E. rated. Switch to your dark energy compensators if you need to."

"No can do. The D.E. compensator is out of action, too."

"No shit, Stacey, you gonna make it?" Trisha asked earnestly.

"No clue. But here's hoping."

"If you're gonna ditch, you can eject."

"If I ditch, I'll eject Harper; I'm not ejecting myself. "

"D'you wanna die some sort of martyr?"

"Maybe one day," I laughed, but then said thoughtfully, "I've already ejected three times in my career. A fourth time means I'll get permanently grounded. There's no way I'm gonna be grounded when those fuckers are back in Oz."

"Being grounded doesn't mean the end of your career, Stacey. Being dead does. You can do more than just fly a fighter," Trisha implored.

"That's bullshit," I snapped back. "I fly; it's who I am. I'd rather chance the landing than lose my wings."

"Hold on. I'm getting a call from the Japs." There was silence as my third engine cut out.

"Oh shit," Harper muttered behind me.

"One engine is better than no engine, mate," I responded casually.

Trisha came back on the line, "Okay, the Japs don't want us coming in loud. They want radio and radar silence so your destination can't be tracked."

"Activating radar silence now, and stealth mode is engaged." Now I know you might be wondering why we didn't do that back during the fight. Hiding from radar doesn't mean to say you can't be seen out a window, and you can't engage in a battle where you can't see or be seen.

"It means I'm going to have difficulty following you in. If we lose line of sight, I won't know where you come down if you don't make it to the base."

"Don't worry about us, Trish. We'll make it." And with that, we deactivated the radio. "It's just you and me now, Harp."

We sat in silence for a few minutes. The only sound was the single engine struggling to maintain power.

"Do you believe in God, Stacey?" Harper asked in that tone she always had when she was about to say something deep.

I pondered this for a moment. "Sometimes I do, sometimes I don't."

"I do. What do you think heaven's like?"

I chuckled and replied, "I don't know, a place with plenty of beer and well-hung men."

"You are so crude," but she laughed. Her laugh trailed off when the last engine cut out.

"Okay, mate, we're gonna make landfall the hard way. My ability to maneuver this beastie onto a runway or even a road is highly unlikely. But I'm gonna eject you just before we hit the ground, okay?"

"Please eject with me, Stacey," Harper implored.

"Sorry mate, I can't do it. If I can't fly, what's the point?"

"The point is those who care about you. Doesn't that mean anything?"

"Most of them died back there, and seriously, without a pair of wings and the chance for payback, I'd rather take my chances ditching."

As we began to slow down, the craft started to descend. I struggled to keep it from flipping and looked for signs of a road or just some relatively flat land, but would you believe it, we were over a fucking forest.

"Okay, Harper, brace yourself." I didn't give her the chance to argue, and I hit her eject button. Nothing happened. I hit it again, but still nothing. "Shit, shit, shit. Harp, eject yourself!" I shouted.

"Already tried," Harp panicked. "The damn thing's jammed."

"Then really brace yourself," I sighed.

We started to skim the trees, which slowed us even more, bringing us down even faster until, finally, we were smashing through the undergrowth. The canopy in front of me cracked and splintered. I checked the seal on my visor to ensure it wouldn't rip my face apart if any glass broke through. The wings went next, the first one, snapping against some trees, causing us to spin around. The next wing came off as branches came through the front of the canopy, pinning me to the back of my seat, but they, too, snapped off as we span and tipped, and then we flipped over. I saw something dark coming toward me. I can only assume it was a tree because seconds later, the last thing I remember hearing was the smashing of the front of the canopy and then complete darkness as I fell into unconsciousness.

I don't know how long it was before I came to, but the first thing I was aware of was pain; most of it was concentrated on my right eye. I managed to reach up with my left hand to feel it caked in blood. I managed to wipe it from my left eye, but couldn't seem to get it out of my right. The next source of pain was in my gut, and I reached down to find a shard of glass sticking out of it. I gripped it and pulled it out, and instantly regretted it. As I went to scream out in pain, my mouth filled with blood. I coughed and spluttered as I managed to gasp in a lungful of breath before quickly drowning in my own blood.

I couldn't see, and I couldn't move beyond what I could reach with my hands. I could feel the blood running from my stomach, and I knew that I had made a colossal mistake yanking that shard out. I carefully pulled down the zipper of my flight suit and ripped my shirt, which, thanks to my encounter with Pascal back in Cape York, was already undone. As I pulled and tugged with my limited reach, it couldn't tear it free, so I reached inside the sleeve of my flight suit and retrieved the knife I kept there... just in case. I cut part of my shirt away, and I stuffed the rag into the hole in my stomach. It hurt like a sonofabitch, but it seemed to do the trick. But that pain... It was enough to make me nauseous. I reached into my sleeve again and pulled out a stim. Usually, it would go into the arm, but I wasn't in a position to remove the flight suit, so instead, I thrust it into a bare area of my stomach and hit the plunger. I then lay still, waiting for it to take effect. While the pain wasn't completely gone, it became bearable enough for me to think and work out what to do next. There was still blood coming out of my left eye, and I cut away at the sleeve of my flight suit and wrapped it around my head, covering my eye. Once tied up and the blood flow stemmed, I wiped my left eye again and blinked. I was looking up into a canopy of trees, just able to make out a crescent moon above. I hadn't only been thrown from the craft, but I wasn't even in my flight seat. I coughed again, checking if I was clear of blood in my mouth. I realized that it was blood from my wounded eye that had filled it. Thankfully, there wasn't an internal injury causing it. As the stim took a more significant effect, I managed to lift myself onto my elbows and was horrified to see my right leg twisted in an unnatural position; the leg snapped in two. I was lying in soft, wet mud when suddenly I thought of Harper, and I looked around me frantically. I could see the devastation the plane had wrought through the trees. It had moved some distance even after I was thrown from it.

Debris from it lay all about me in such a state of destruction that I couldn't recognize any part of it until I saw the twisted E from my name, where it had been painted on the side of my craft. I tried to call out Harper's name, but I barely got it out in a rasp. I coughed again. Again, I tried calling her name, a little louder this time. It was only then that I noticed the canopy's remnants appeared far away, but it was hard to judge the distance with my missing depth perception. Thinking back on it, it couldn't have been that far, as I wouldn't have seen it in the dark night. I couldn't tell, but I felt sure I could see Harper's seat was still intact, but it was pitched at an awkward angle, and I couldn't see the girl in it. I looked back down at my leg. I certainly wasn't going to be walking over to her. I managed to reach out for some twigs and sticks, and slowly I turned my leg to the proper position, but the pain got the better of me, and I'm pretty sure I blacked out again for a few minutes. I came to once more and hit myself up with another stim. I had to be careful. Too many of these, and I'd start to get high. I cut off my right sleeve and tied it around the sticks on my leg. I knew I wasn't going to walk on them, but I was trying to ensure that it stayed splinted in position.

Turning my back to the canopy and using my hands, I shuffled my backside slowly through the mud toward the only recognizable remnant of my craft. To this day, I can't tell you how I made it. It took me almost two hours to move the distance, as I had to stop to navigate past undergrowth that hadn't been completely flattened. I can't explain how I did it, except that sheer willpower to get another kite and get back in the fight pushed me onwards. I didn't know if Harper was dead or alive, but even if she was dead, the survival packs in the canopy could help to keep me alive until help came. And I may have my doubts about the existence of some holy deity, but right then and there, I prayed to God, Allah, whatever the Hindu guy was, and everyone I could think of. And to be honest, my sanity at that point couldn't cope with the idea of Harper being dead, too. Eventually, I made it there, but the canopy was stuck a few feet above me, wedged within the trees. Not a problem if I were standing, but I was sitting down on my arse, covered in mud, getting wetter and colder as time went on. It seemed like an insurmountable problem. I knew it was urgent to get to Harper, but I had no choice but to rest, and I sat there for, I don't know how long. It could have been ten minutes. It could have been an hour. I'll never know. I knew I'd have to force myself to get up there. So I pulled my third and final stim from my pocket and thrust it into my broken leg as if that would bring the pain-reducing chemicals right to the root of the problem. I don't know if it helped, but after a minute, I tried to get up on my good leg. I can't imagine what the pain would have been like without the stim, but it hurt like fuck. I turned and looked into the canopy and saw her lying in the seat. Her body twisted and hung at an awkward angle. I was confident she was dead, and when I felt for a pulse, I couldn't find one. But as I was about to give up and let myself fall back to the ground, her eyes flickered momentarily and opened. She looked at me with sheer terror, unable to move. I reached up and felt her neck. Her spine was broken. I knew I could not move her, or it'd kill her. "It's gonna be okay, mate." I patted her arm in a way she could see it; I knew she probably couldn't feel it, though.

"You got me in trouble again." Her voice was raspy, and I was surprised that she could talk.

"Yeah, well, it's me that's gonna get the demerits this time," I grinned.

"Wow, Stace, you look so fucked up I can barely recognize you," she rasped.

"Yeah, I left my lippy back in Oz," I replied, and she laughed silently.

I then checked her over for other wounds, and despite hers being considerably more serious than mine, it appeared the broken neck was all she had encountered beyond some mild bruising. "It's getting cold. Let me find your blanket."

"I can't feel anything, so I wouldn't worry about it," she managed to smile.

"Yeah, well, the fact you can't feel it won't stop you from getting hypothermia." I reached behind her seat, hoping that the survival kit hadn't been lost. Fortunately, it hadn't, and, undoing the zipper, I pulled out a blanket, one of those funny silver foil hypothermic ones. I don't know what they're called. I covered her in it, and she thanked me."Okay, so here's the sitch. Trish is gonna have them looking for us, but I don't know how long it's gonna take. I've just used the last of my stims, and they're gonna wear off eventually. When the pain comes back, I'm gonna be as useless as a baby in a wet nappy. But we're gonna get out of this, I promise you." I wasn't as confident as I sounded, and it was a hollow promise, but I think she needed to hear it.

"Well, take my stims, ya moron. I don't need 'em."

I laughed weakly and said, "Good point." I carefully reached into her flight suit and pulled her own out of her sleeve. I slipped them into my pocket. "Okay, mate, I have to sit down now. You won't be able to see me, but I'll be here." I dragged the rest of the survival kit out from behind her and let it fall to the ground.

"I can still hear you. You can talk to me."

"You bet, mate. You bet." I lowered myself back to the ground as gently as I could and pulled another blanket from the pack.

"What are you gonna do when we get back to Oz?" I asked as I pulled the blanket around myself.

"Kill some fucking Peons," she rasped out in a light laugh.

"You got that right, mate," I said, praying that I could still get flight clearance when we returned to our homeland. We fell silent for a few minutes, and I turned my attention to the contents of the survival pack. There was a lighter and some oil, and I pulled it out and gathered more twigs and dry leaves, managing to start a small fire, which also helped light us up. We talked for about an hour about the things we loved back in Australia. The barbecues, going down to Bondi Beach for some surfing in the summer. Christmas in the backyard with a cold beer in hand. Stupid stuff like that. I felt sleep overcoming me, and I told Harper this. She told me to go ahead and sleep. Little did I realize it was my body shutting down, and when I closed my eyes, it could have easily been for the last time.

The next thing I recall was opening them and seeing Japanese men and women rushing around me. I was lying on my back, strapped to a gurney. A cable ran up to a craft that hovered silently, clearly something with a D.E. engine. I couldn't understand what the men were saying, but one of them spoke to me in reassuring tones. Then he pressed some buttons on the side of the Gurney, and I felt that peculiar effect of gravity disappearing. The cable didn't lift me. It guided me to the right place. Once again, darkness overcame me.

Chapter Three

Jenna Plural

They took me to a hospital in Nagasaki. I didn't wake up for another three days. My first concern was finding out about Harper, but the nurses couldn't speak English, and I couldn't speak Japanese. I was in a white room on my own in a hospital bed. My leg was fixed while I had been out of it. Bones are such simple fixes. Even field medics set them during ground battles. Even my stomach wound had been healed. All that was left when I felt was just the faint puckering of a scar where I had been impaled.

As I reached up to feel the bandage covering my right eye, I was confused about why they hadn't fixed that. It was frustrating to be able to see out of only one eye.

Eventually, I did get to see someone who spoke English, albeit a somewhat different version – she was American. The woman who entered wore the uniform of the United States Marines. Under normal circumstances, I would have wondered why the Americans wanted to talk to me. However, I found myself very distracted because she was the most beautiful woman I'd ever seen. I'm talking so hot that even I considered giving up my heterosexuality. Genetic modification was always outlawed in Australia. Hey, we are pretty much perfect, so who needs to mess with Mother Nature, right? It was only used to correct genetic conditions and potential health problems before birth. But this woman was the epitome of American perfection, the kind the Yanks seem to be obsessed with. Perfectly straight white teeth, a perfectly proportioned nose, large blue eyes that sparkled, and thick, long, light brown hair, the average girl in Wagga would kill for.

She stood by my bed, arms behind her back and legs apart, in a proper military bearing. "How are you feeling?" she asked, but the tone didn't have any warmth.

"Pretty much like I just fell outta the sky in a big plane," I replied.

She smiled back politely, but it was clear my joke didn't particularly amuse her. "Well, you've certainly been through it, Lieutenant Grant. My name is Jenna Plural, and I'm a Lieutenant with the United States Marine Corps. My companion here is Lieutenant McKenna Anderson of Army Special Forces, currently seconded to my unit."

It was only then that I noticed that Jenna wasn't alone. I hadn't been able to tear my eyes away from the gorgeous Marine to see that there was another person. Standing just behind her was a dark-haired woman in the casual attire of jeans and a leather jacket

"G'day," I said, giving her a nod.

"A pleasure to meet you, Lieutenant Grant. I understand you are quite a legend in Air Force circles," Anderson smiled. She had a southern twang, but the classy kind that reeked of old money. She was actually kinda cool once you got past her ruthless ability to kill people with her bare hands. We became pretty close over the coming years until it all went wrong, but I'll get to that; that was sometime after these events. For now, I merely shrugged. She was kissing my arse, and that's a bloody red flag right there. "Well, modesty forbids, you know," I looked back at Jenna. "Can you tell me what's going on?"

"What do you want to know?" She replied casually.

"What's happened to Oz? Is Harper still alive? How is she doing? When am I gonna get out of here and get back in a kite? And what the fuck do you want with me?"

Jenna sighed, "Okay, well, first of all, Harper Davis is fine and doing well. She had surgery on her broken vertebrae and was released from the hospital yesterday."

"So, where the fuck is she?" I asked, irritated that I'd been lying here for several hours with no sign of my supposed friend.

Jenna clearly did not know the answer. She looked back at McKenna. "She was by your bedside for the last twenty-four hours but has gone into town for I don't know what activity," McKenna told me.

"For your next question," Jenna now tensed and fixed her eyes rigidly upon me. I knew that I was not about to hear good news. "Canberra officially surrendered to the European high command yesterday. Australia is out of the war."

I stared blankly at her then. Sitting up, I shouted. " You fucking liar!"

"No, I'm sorry, Lieutenant Grant, I am not," Jenna responded, unfazed by my reaction.

"You are telling me that it took two days to take over my country? That's bullshit. It's not remotely possible that they have every town or community. Somewhere we are fighting back."

Jenna nodded. "The odds were overwhelming. They threw everything they had at you."

"So, where were you? We always had your back. Why didn't you have ours?" I accused.

Jenna stiffened slightly, but her face remained impassive. "I am sorry, Lieutenant Grant. It was over before we could respond."

"So, what are we doing about taking it back?" I let myself fall back down on the bed but kept my eyes, or rather eye, fixed upon Aphrodite.

"Nothing directly. We simply do not have the resources to launch an invasion of Australia right now, but we are working toward it."

"And how long is that gonna take?" I probably sounded like a sulking child now.

Jenna sighed, "I want to be honest with you, Lieutenant Grant. It could be months, even years, but the fight for Australia is not over. I promise you we will eventually get your homeland back."

I studied her carefully before saying, "I get the impression you're not here just to tell me stuff the Japs can't."

"I am, indeed. Many allies are incorporating Australians into their forces, leveraging their specialized skills. To be honest, I want to recruit you before any of our other allies get to you."

"What do you want me for?" I asked unenthusiastically.

McKenna Anderson took a step forward, "Lieutenant Grant, you are not just one of the best pilots in the world; you are one of the best pilots in the whole damn solar system. We want you on our team."

"If it's all the same to you," I said coldly. "I'd prefer to stick with the Australian Air Force."

"There is no Australian Air Force. Not anymore," Anderson stated quite calmly.

"Fuck you, Mac. As long as there's an Aussie who can fly, there'll always be an Australian Air Force."

Jenna returned to the conversation. "There may not be an Australian Air Force, but there is the start of the Australian Free Forces. They are giving their talents to the allies to work toward their return to their homeland."

"Forget it. I'm True Blue, and there's only one flag with stars on it that I'll stand under."

"You may be working for the United States military, but we won't forget you are an Australian."

"I am not about to salute a Yank," I stated almost aggressively.

"And I'm not about to ask you to. What I'm asking you to do is to kill Europeans," and she smiled ruefully at me.

Anderson spoke again. "We want you for an extraordinary mission that can seriously turn the tide of this war."

"They usually say that about very high-risk missions," I almost sneered. "Next, you're going to say I'm the only one that can do it."

Jenna smiled and shrugged. "The mission is high-risk, and we think you are the only one who can do it."

I pondered the words. I wasn't sure what to make of these two. "Look, I don't know how long I'm gonna be in here. They don't seem to be doing anything about this," I pointed at my bandaged eye. "So I can't see myself sitting in a kite anytime soon."

Jenna frowned slightly and shifted uncomfortably from her rigid stance. "Have they not told you about your eye?"

My eye met hers nervously. "Told me what exactly?"

Jenna glanced at Anderson, then back at me. "You lost your eye. It was destroyed in the crash and could not be reconstructed."

This hit me like a brick. Whoever heard of a one-eyed pilot? I lay my head back on the pillow and closed my one good eye.

"It can be replaced," Anderson said, trying to sound positive. "In fact, we can make it better with modern technology."

"Or you can just have an ordinary organic replacement," Jenna added.

"Organic replacements are never perfect," I muttered.

"An artificial one can be twenty-twenty and even better. A military-grade one can have additional features," Anderson tried but failed to reassure me.

I opened my eye and stared at her, smiling mirthlessly. "Oh gee, but I won't be pretty enough for Brad to take me to the prom," I said sarcastically, trying to sound like a Yank.

Jenna raised her exquisitely shaped eyebrow. "Was that supposed to be an American accent?"

I flushed slightly, "Um, yeah."

"Please never do that again," she said, and I wasn't sure if she was joking or not. "Look, Grant, I know you have been dealt a bad hand recently, but I'm offering you the chance to give the Peons some payback. There is a place for you on my team if you're interested. We need your particular talents. Take some time to think about it, and I'll check on you in a few days."

My response was just a noncommittal shrug as I said, "I make no promises." With that, Jenna Plural and McKenna Anderson left me to my thoughts.

I didn't know what I wanted to do. I sat up; my head spun for a moment, but it quickly went away. I winced as I put my bare feet on the cold floor. I was dressed in one of those hospital gowns that tied up at the back, but I wore nothing else. I looked about to see if my clothes and flight suit were around, but they were nowhere in sight. Considering their state, they'd probably been disposed of long ago. An almost claustrophobic feeling came over me because I couldn't just walk out. I never liked the feeling of being trapped, even when it was situational rather than physical. But I couldn't just sit in that bed.

A young nurse came into the room and chattered away to me in gibberish, otherwise known as Japanese. I would learn the language a year later, thanks to developing an anime addiction while in this country, but I couldn't even say hi back then. He was annoyed that I had gotten out of bed. He indicated that

I was to get back in, but I pointed to the gown I was wearing and then ran my hands up and down in front of me, meaning I wanted my clothes. He shook his head.

"Oh, fuck you," I muttered irritably, but his face turned grim real fast. Apparently, the word 'fuck' is pretty universal. He turned on his heel and headed out the door swiftly.

I walked over to the mirror and was shocked. Despite no pain, my face was black and blue with bruises. I touched the bandaged wadding where my right eye had once been.

"Bloody hell, you look like shit." I turned quickly to see Harper coming in through the door, a big grin on her face and a shopping bag in her hand. She had no injuries and was just in casual jeans and a T-shirt.

"I still look better than you," I muttered.

Harper chuckled and tossed the bag down on the bed. "I didn't know your sizes, so I had to guess."

I glanced at the bag and then back at her. "They're discharging me?"

She shook her head, "No, but I know you're not gonna stay here, and I don't think the Japs'll appreciate you running around Nagasaki starkers."

I grinned, and I stepped over to open the bag. I pulled out a pair of jeans and a T-shirt similar to hers and placed them on the bed. As I pulled out undies and a bra, I looked at her with raised eyebrows. I held out the end of the bra strap between my thumb and forefinger, "Do you really think my tits are that big?" I sneered and tossed the useless garment aside. I never liked the damn things anyway.

Harper just smiled and shrugged, "I guess I was living the fantasy."

I pulled off the gown and started to pull on the undies, but as I got them up over my hips, I looked up to see Harper looking at me admiringly, "For fuck sake, Harp. Turn around, ya bloody perv!"

Harper grinned and turned her back to me. "Ah, you're no fun, sweetie."

"Keep trying; I'm still not into girls." I pulled up the jeans and added, "Although, did you see that Jenna Plural?"

Harper gasped. "Bloody hell, did I ever. I wet my undies. That is one amazingly genetically designed piece of arse."

Her reaction made me chuckle as I fastened the slightly tight trousers. "Yeah, she nearly turned me."

"No way, mate, you either have it in you, or you don't," Harper sneered reproachfully.

"If that's the case, why do you keep hitting on me?" I laughed.

"Because I have excellent gaydar, Stace, and I know you're just in denial," Harper chuckled.

"Dream on, ya idiot," I laughed as I pulled the shirt over my head and turned to look in the mirror. I looked like a badly dressed teenager who'd been brawling. I turned back to the bag with a sigh and pulled out a pair of runners. "Fucking hell, mate, do you think I'm a bloke?" They were two sizes too big.

"Quit your whining. We can go to the shops, and you can get whatever you like."

"Oh, and how did you suddenly come into a lot of yen?"

She slipped a credit card out of her back pocket and waved it in the air, "United States military expense account."

"The Yank bastards are trying to get you to sign up, too?" I sneered.

"Nope. They're trying to get me to get *you* to sign up. I'm just your average gunner, they don't have any interest in me, mate."

"Bullshit. We are a package deal. I go, you go," I said honestly.

Harper turned back to me with a beaming smile on her face. "I was hoping you'd say that."

"Hell, I don't know if I'm even gonna go," I shrugged, "What do we owe the Yanks? Bunch of fucking morons, if you ask me."

"What other option is there for us?" Harper said dejectedly. "There's no Air Force anymore, and we can't go back Down Under. Not yet, anyway."

I sighed dejectedly as I sat down on the bed and tied up my shoelaces. "We're definitely stuck in a shit storm, that's for sure."

Harper tilted her head and eyed me suspiciously, "Stace," she said softly, and I looked up when she fell silent. "You're not going to cause trouble with the Yanks, are you?"

I couldn't stop the grin that stretched across my face. "What do you think?" Then something occurred to me, "What happened to Trisha?"

"The Yanks have already got her to sign up. She didn't hesitate. They're shipping her out to the States next week. Apparently, they'll set me up with a job somewhere if I persuade you to join up."

"Otherwise, they'll just leave you here in Japan?"

"That's about the size of it."

"Bastard, motherfuckers," I muttered. "Our so-called allies only wanna help us if we've got something to offer them back!"

Harper's face fell. "There are thousands of Aussie refugees, mate. Some escaped the fall of Oz, and others weren't at home when it came. Ships are coming in from the outer planets with nowhere to land. The Yanks are holding up their convention but sticking to its letter, only letting a certain number into the States. So, naturally, they're giving preferential treatment to skilled people."

"So we're scattered across the world and the solar system?"

"Yep. The Yanks were even taking over our colonies in case we decided to follow instructions from Canberra and turn them over to the enemy. We're pretty much wasted."

Anger welled up within me, but I resisted spouting more rhetoric and simply said, “Did you bring any tucker? I could eat the arse of a low-flying duck.”

Harper chuckled and reached over and picked up the now-empty bag. “Nope, but we can go get some sushi.”

“Bloody hell, I want a burger, not some raw fish.” My thoughts behind my words belied my mood. I wanted to cry, but fuck it, I couldn’t. Slipping my arm in hers, we headed out of the hospital.

Chapter Four

Dreamland

We stayed in Nagasaki for about a week. The Yanks put us up in a fancy hotel, all aperitifs and fancy shit like that. Not exactly my cup of tea, but it'd do in a pinch. I spent most of the first half of the week watching the news about the fall of Australia. There was no mention of Wagga, but I watched Sydney, Melbourne, Adelaide, and Canberra all burning until, on the third day, I could stomach it no more and found some Anime cartoons to watch.

My first course of action upon leaving the hospital had been to go shopping; I couldn't stay in the shit that Harper had got me. I had my style, and I preferred skirts to trousers when it came to civilian dress. I also had a penchant for dressing in white. I got myself a lovely short leather skirt with white tights, a rather nice pair of white knee-high boots, a T-shirt, and a leather jacket that came down to my knees. I kept the stuff Harper got just to wear hanging around the hotel room.

Jenna Plural or one of her reps often visited us to see if I'd made a decision. I had. But I enjoyed leaving them dangling on a hook. I was almost challenging them to withdraw their offer, which would have wound up Harper considerably. I'd already decided that Harper's fate was the deal-breaker – no Harper, then no me.

Several days later, I was escorted by this cute little Marine guy who took me up to a U.S. Embassy building. I'd almost forgotten Jenna's Aphrodite looks as I entered the office. She was seated behind a large walnut desk and gestured to the seat in front of her. "Have you made a decision, Lieutenant Grant? I have to return to the U.S. It's make your mind up time."

"That really depends on you, Lieutenant Plural," I replied, taking a seat.

She raised her eyebrows questioningly. "Enlighten me."

"Harper Davis comes with me. She remains my flight partner on whatever mission we undertake."

Jenna mulled it over, then looked back at me. "You can take her to the U.S. with you. We will find her a position within the United States military. However, I can't agree to allow her to go on the mission with you. She is not qualified, and there is limited space for team members. She will be a liability to the mission. If you can't accept that, then our conversation is over."

So, the bitch was playing hardball. Sure, I could live with that. However, it was mainly Harper's safety that I was interested in, so I nodded. "Fine, I'll accept that," I said begrudgingly.

"Anything else?"

"Just one thing. Suppose there is an assault to take back Australia; whatever you got me doing stops. I wanna be on the frontline of any liberating force."

"Agreed," Jenna didn't hesitate on that one.

"Another thing."

"I thought you said 'just one thing' with your last condition!" Jenna frowned and sat back in her chair.

"Yeah, well," I shrugged. "What can I say? I'm fickle. I don't wanna have to follow all the formal military customs of Americans. None of this, sir or ma'am, bullshit. You can call me Stacey, not Lieutenant Grant. "

"That is probably the dumbest request I have ever heard, and I have been around quite a few years," Jenna narrowed her eyes and arched her fingers.

"That's not an answer, mate."

"Could you give me a few minutes to check your qualifications again?" she said.

"Well, I never. The sexy GenMod has a sense of humor," I raised the one eyebrow I was still able to.

She fixed me with a cold stare. "Don't ever call me that again."

"What? Sexy or GenMod?"

"Either."

"You agree to mine, and I'll agree to yours."

"You are quite serious about this?" and she sighed when I gave no reply. "The truth is, we need you more than you need us. I see that. So, although it is against my better judgment, I will agree to your uncouth terms."

"And six bottles of Portobello Brandy for good measure," I threw that one in for laughs, but I decided to hold firm on it when Jenna responded thoughtfully.

"Australian Brandy is not exactly easy to come by now. Never mind that it cost a fortune even before the occupation," even her frown was perfect.

"Well, you shouldn't have told me you need me more than I need you," I shrugged and grinned at her.

"Touché, Lieutenant Grant," and Jenna actually smiled.

"Ah, it's Stacey. Remember?"

"Well, *Stacey*," she said, emphasizing my name. "I cannot get you Portobello, but I can get you the next best thing."

"Nope, Portobello is distilled by my family, and I want a little piece of home," I responded seriously, although I was laughing inside. I didn't really give a shit about my mother's side of the family.

"Very well, here's the deal. If you come back from this mission successfully, I'll get you your bottles of Portobello if there are any left in the USA. Now, is that it?"

"Yes, mate. You've got yourself a deal," I smiled smugly.

"Eventually, we will find you a position in the Navy or the Air Force, but, for now, you are officially a civilian contracted to intelligence," she said, typing something into her tablet, which sat on the desk.

My eye widened in surprise. "Intelligence?"

A slight smile crossed Jenna's face as she looked back up at me. She sat back in her chair and arched her fingers again. "Yes, I know that feels like an oxymoron in your case, but we will do the best we can with your input."

"Well, well, well. Another funny from Aphrodite."

"Don't call me that either. You are dismissed. You will be contacted with your shipping orders in the next hour or two. I suggest you gather whatever belongings you have and be ready."

I reunited with Harper back at the hotel and told her the situation. She wasn't happy about the idea that I'd be going on a mission on my own – without her – she fell into a rather sullen mood. I looked around for what to pack. I didn't have anything besides the few clothes I had bought. I stuffed whatever I wasn't wearing into the bag Harper had brought to the hospital with her stuff. I decided to get some sleep while we waited, but was woken less than an hour later by a sharp knock at the door. Two Marines, one cute, the other not so much, came to pick us up, and we said goodbye to Nagasaki.

The flight to the U.S. was pretty uneventful, even though we had first-class accommodations, and it lasted less than 15 minutes. Fortunately, we headed straight over the Pacific, avoiding the need to detour through any neutral or enemy countries. It took us about twelve minutes to arrive in Los Angeles.

Landing in LAX is not something I'm ever gonna forget. Harper and I weren't the only Australians there. Thousands had escaped the country, and worldwide, they were seeking sanctuary in every allied nation. Even Britain took us in, even though they'd never forgiven us for leaving the Commonwealth and becoming a republic. Lost and utterly desperate people who wanted nothing more than to go home, having to beg to be let into another country. I only had one eye to cry with, but that was too busy checking out what we needed to do next.

Harper and I found ourselves in front of an officious-looking little prick. You know the type – stick some dipshit in a uniform, and he thinks he can intimidate a couple of poor little Aussie girls.

Yeah, right, wanker!

Okay, so yeah, Harper felt intimidated as he looked at his tablet and then stared at her. She didn't like being around blokes at the best of times.

Even though we'd been invited, we still had to undergo arduous (read pain in the arse) security checks. He took our fingerprints, retina scans, and a DNA sample extracted from the sweat on our fingertips. I don't remember this bloke's name, so we'll just call him Dick. Dick was staring at the tablet in his hands, then up at me, and then back at the tablet.

He muttered something I didn't quite hear, so I leaned over the counter. "What?"

He looked up and said loudly, with a patronizing tone in his strong, Midwestern accent, "Don't you understand English?"

"Well, when I hear you speak English, I'll tell you if I understand it, mate," I said, getting seriously pissed off.

"I asked you to tell me your full name," he said, glaring at me.

I looked down at the tablet, where my name was clearly written, having been picked up by the retina scan. "It's right there," I pointed.

"Just answer the question," he said impatiently.

"Can't you read, you moron?" I snapped.

He put the tablet down and folded his arms. "Full name."

Harper nervously nudged me, and I sighed and rolled my eye, which was now covered by a patch, "Stacefield Wallaby Grant." Harper nudged me harder, and I pushed back this time. "Fine! Stacefield Ellen Grant."

Dick looked back down at his tablet. "Date of birth?"

"May the second, sixty-nine."

"Nationality?"

"True blue Aussie, mate."

"Are you applying for refugee status?"

"Fuck no," I said sharply.

He looked at me, confused. "You can't come in without declaring your status."

"Fine by me," I shrugged. "When's the next shuttle back to Oz?"

To this day, I dunno what caused him to snap, but boy, did he. "I am sick and tired of dealing with Australians. You're like damn vagrants coming over here and expecting us to support you."

I didn't move. I didn't speak. I didn't even change my expression. Of course, Harper instantly saw the warning signs. She grabbed the sleeve of my jacket and pulled my ear to her mouth. "Don't, Stacey. Please." She only ever called me Stacey, not Stace, when she really wanted to get my attention. She didn't get it; Dick had my complete and undivided attention. Oh yes.

"Maybe if you stayed and fought for your country, you would not be here on your knees...." Dunno what he was gonna say next because I pulled myself out of Harper's grip and was over the counter before he'd managed to get out another word. I gut-punched him hard enough to make him double over. I held his head down by his hair and brought my knee up into his face. I ruined a perfectly good pair of tights on his teeth. Even with modern-day technology, bloodstains were still a bastard to get out.

I don't exactly remember how many American security personnel ended up on top of me. Within seconds of my actions, I was facedown on the ground, my arms and legs pinned, and a knee in my back. Shouts and screams came at me in all directions, and I couldn't distinguish one from another. My wrists were uncomfortably cuffed behind my back, then silence fell, and all I heard was clip-clop, clip-clop, clip-clop.

"Do we have a problem here?" I heard the voice of a woman with a surprisingly British accent.

"Ma'am, please step back. This is none of your concern," a security officer said, and there was a long pause, which I assume was filled by the new arrival showing him her credentials before he continued, "I see. How can I be of service, Ma'am?"

"Miss Grant is a guest of the United States, Sergeant. Please release her immediately," her voice had the sophistication of the country club set.

"Respectfully, Ma'am, but she just assaulted one of my officers. I intend to bring her up on full charges."

"That would be most inconvenient for me, Sergeant," the woman sighed.

"Sorry to hear that, Ma'am. But I can't just let people go around attacking my staff. It's standard procedure to bring down full charges, no exceptions."

The response was cold, sending a shiver down my spine. Which, incidentally, now hurt like fuck from some bastard's knee pushing down on it. "Sergeant, look at my face very closely. Does it look like I give a fuck what your procedure is?" It was hard to laugh with your face pushed down onto the floor tiles, but I gave it a good try.

There was a long silence before the officer said, "Let her go." Those holding me down were not impressed with this idea, and I was raised to my feet most uncomfortably. The cuffs were removed, and I rubbed my wrists. I looked over at the man I had hit. He held a cloth over his bloodied face, and I gave him a wink. I don't know if the look he gave me was fear or anger, but he definitely looked shocked.

The woman who rescued us didn't look like a government rep. She sported a short black designer dress, matching stockings, and three-inch pumps. She would have been taller than me in thongs, so imagine how intimidating she must've seemed in heels. "I would like to apologize on behalf of the United States government, Miss Grant, and Miss Davis. This incident shall be investigated," she said, shaking first my hand and then Harper's. "I am Charlotte Kensett, political officer to the Central Intelligence Agency and your escort to where you'll be briefed on your assignment and find your accommodation."

"G'day, Charlie," I smiled and was surprised at her lack of reaction at being called that. This ice queen was a real pro, and I knew right then I'd better watch my back around her. I gave the sergeant a cold stare. "If you worried more about how your people treat my people, this wouldn't have happened, mate."

He made to take a step toward me, but Charlie placed a hand on his arm, and as he looked back at her, she shook her head. "Do you require any further information from our guests?" she asked the sergeant coldly.

He made as if he was going to speak again, but instead, he let out a weary sigh. "They can go."

As Harper and I fell in step with Charlie, I could hear the babble of complaints the sergeant's security team inundated him with as we left the immigration area.

A limo was there waiting for us, and as we climbed in, Charlie said, "Welcome to America, ladies."

The driverless limo automatically fired up, and we headed out into the busy L.A. streets. The ride didn't take long as we headed out of the city and onto the highway, quickly entering Nevada. Although I didn't know it, we headed down a road that didn't appear on any map. We eventually reached a mountainous area and a small, derelict-looking base. Charlie showed her ID to the gate guard as we pulled up outside the three-story complex. Harper and I felt like VIPs, and it made my stomach turn. I've always preferred people to act naturally – I hate pomp and ceremony – but nevertheless, we carried on and followed Charlie into the building. We went through various scans, checking us for explosives, chemicals, weapons, and whatever else the Yanks were always so paranoid about.

The inside of the building belied its tatty exterior, and serious tax dollars had been spent decorating it with chrome-colored walls and hidden lighting. We stepped into an elevator and were taken up to the third floor. When we got off, we found ourselves in what looked almost like a hotel hallway. She began directing us to two different rooms, but I shook my head, as did Harper. "Sorry, Charlie. But we stay together."

Charlie simply smiled and said, "As you wish."

She showed us into what looked to be a suite; it was even bigger than the hotel rooms we'd had back in Nagasaki. I looked at her and frowned. "Look, we didn't come here to hang around another hotel room. Can we just get on with this?"

"Lieutenant Plural told me to give you time to freshen up after your journey."

"It's been two hours since we left Japan, and while I agree hygiene is important, I don't feel the need to shower every few hours."

"Then I'll let Lieutenant Plural know that you are ready," and with that, she departed.

"For fuck's sake, this is starting to really grind my gears," I said, sinking onto a sofa and throwing my head back.

Harper walked over to the window and stared out. Her hands parked squarely in her back pockets, and she swung her hips side to side. "What is this place? It feels like it's some sort of undisclosed black ops base. I mean shit, we're in the middle of the fucking desert."

"You've been reading too many cheap novels, " I said with a laugh. "What would a black ops operation want with someone like me?"

Harper shrugged and turned back to me and said, "Who knows with Americans? They're kinda weird about that sort of thing."

"Are you sure you're going to be okay? " I asked, looking up at her with concern.

"Considering I have no idea if my family's alive or dead, and I don't know if I'm ever gonna go home again. I mean, apart from those minor details, I'm just ticketyboo," she shrugged.

I have to admit that I hadn't given my family one thought since everything had happened. "We're gonna be okay, Harp. I promise." The truth was, though, I didn't know if I believed that.

Chapter Five

Operation Pallas

Our next visitor was a doctor, an eye specialist. I don't remember his name, so we'll just call him Doc. He came to our door wearing a white coat over his clothes, telling me he was here to discuss my eye. "Lieutenant Plural has given me the authority to discuss all the possibilities we can give you."

"Who's paying for this?" I asked casually.

"The United States government," he responded.

"Then I want the most expensive," I said confidently and shrugged as I looked at Harper.

He appeared to be taken aback by this and stammered out his response. "You don't want to discuss the options and upgrades that we can put into it?"

I gave a deliberate look of fake pondering and then shook my head. "Nah, mate, let's just go ahead and whack in the most expensive."

He looked quite nonplussed, shaking his head slowly. "As you wish, Lieutenant Grant. We will prepare for surgery this afternoon. It will take about 4 hours, but you'll be placed in suspended animation. Should everything go well, you should be up and about immediately afterward."

"That sounds like a plan, mate."

"Why do you enjoy provoking the Americans so much?" Harper asked after he'd left, flopping down into a seat beside me.

I shrugged. "There aren't any Poms to pick on?"

Harper laughed at this and jumped back up to look for some food in the fridge. That girl could never stay still.

"Fuck yeah!" she called out from the kitchen.

"What is it?" I called back.

"They've got grog in here. Wine, beer..." she paused, and I heard another gasp. "There's even a cupboard full of spirits above it."

"Now you're talking," I said, jumping up and heading into the kitchen. I studied the rows of different bottles and picked out some fancy little liqueur. I don't remember what it was. Sure, they had the regular stuff: vodka, whiskey, etc., but this little bottle looked so cute I couldn't resist. I carried it back into the living room without a glass. Harper followed me with a bottle of genuine top-shelf vodka. Slowly but surely, we got well and truly munted.

We laughed and joked like a couple of high school girls who had raided their dad's liquor cabinet. And when a nurse came up to tell me that they were ready to take me down for my surgery, it was promptly canceled. They couldn't do surgery with a half-gallon of alcohol in my system, but I didn't really care. You see, behind the jokes, behind the displays of bravado, I just wanted to curl up and cry. I didn't want to be here. I didn't want to work for the Yanks. I even considered reneging on my agreement with Jenna Plural. I just wanted to go back to Oz. But eventually, I passed out and had some disconcerting dreams, which, fortunately, I couldn't remember the details of when I woke up.

I had one hell of a hangover the following day. When the nurse came to get me, she shot me up with detoxifiers and led me down to the second level. It was as if they were hurrying, so I didn't have time to start drinking again. I was led into a sterile room where a strange bed-like contraption stood upright but on a slight incline. The nurse gave me another one of those stupid gowns and told me to change into it. Once that was done, I then stood on the small ledge of the bed-type thing and leaned back. The doctor came in, and he clearly had no patience to talk with me anymore. He simply hit a button on the bed device, and the world blinked out, then, from my perspective, immediately blinked back into existence. I felt the bandages were now gone from my head, and in their place, there remained something hard. I reached up and felt the metal rim that ran around my eye socket and then tapped the lens in the middle. Righto, what exactly was I now? Some sort of cyborg from one of those dumb arse sci-fi movies. What concerned me the most was that I could still not see out of it, and as I looked about the room, I saw the doctor observing me.

"I'm about to activate the device. It may feel a little unsettling at first, but you will get used to it quickly." He reached up to me with what looked like a tiny metallic wand and touched it against the side of the device. Suddenly, a blinding light appeared, and everything turned white. I closed my one real eye, but the other seemed permanently open. "Relax," the doctor said firmly. "You cannot close that eye in the conventional sense, but you can turn it off in the same way you would unconsciously do things with the rest of your body. It just takes time to adjust. Until you master that, though, you'll have to concentrate," and he stepped away from me. "There are already some inbuilt automatic functions like night vision, which will activate when you are in darkness. It works in the same way as any light-intensifying device does. If there is no light at all, there's nothing to intensify, and it would still be just as dark as anywhere else. If you want to focus on anything at a distance farther than normal, just close your left eye and concentrate on the object. If you need to use any of the functions, just think about what you want to do, and it will turn on."

"Does it pick up cable?"

The doctor sighed wearily, "Grant! If you don't want to take this seriously, I have better things to do."

I shrugged. "Fair enough, Doc. Might come and pick your brain later."

"What?" he snapped at me.

"Well, you said you had better things to do if I didn't wanna take this seriously, and, to be honest, I don't wanna take this seriously. So, we done here?"

"Are all Australians this impossible?"

"Hmm, probably. But we're also quite lovable when you get to know us," I quipped as I gave my best sweet, most patronizing smile.

"Indeed," he sighed. "Well, I can't force you to take this seriously. You are free to go, Miss Grant."

"Doc, I wasn't waiting for permission to leave," I said, stepping down from the strange bed-like thing and grabbing up my clothes. "Now, unless you're planning to perve on me as I get this gown off and get dressed, I'd appreciate it if you left."

The doctor just glared at me and muttered something under his breath. There may or may not have been profanity.

Thinking back on it, I have to admit that I was a bit of an arse in those days. The truth was, I simply didn't care about anything. I was broken. I just wanted to go back Down Under. I'd never considered myself very vain; I'm not particularly beautiful even to McKenna Anderson or Charlotte Kensett's standards, let alone Jenna Plural's, but I wasn't exactly beaten with the ugly bush. I had a prominent overbite to the degree that my teeth were almost always visible, something that would severely bother an American, and I'd never once considered getting it fixed. So, I was surprised by how much having the artificial eye bothered me. It was grey and ugly, covering my face from just below the eyebrow to the cheekbone. The eye itself was a lens that moved in conjunction with my left eye. It bothered me enough that I would eventually change my appearance. I grew my hair out so that it fell over the right side of my face, completely obscuring it from view. Surprisingly, having my hair over it didn't obscure my vision, even after applying plenty of hair product to keep it in place.

I dressed quickly, and when I stepped out of the room, I found a guard waiting for me. This didn't sit well with me. I knew where my quarters were, but it felt as if I were a prisoner, needing an escort. "G'day, mate," I smiled up at him. "You the stripper we ordered?" The look of confusion on his face was priceless.

"No, ma'am, I'm your escort."

I grinned. He was like a lamb to the slaughter. "Wow, Jenna's now providing us with escorts. Let's get back to my room and get your gear off." The big moron blushed, and I gave myself a mental high-five for that hilarious joke.

"Ma'am, I'm not that sort of escort."

I let the façade drop. "I know, you moron. So, fuck off and tell that Jenna Plural I don't need a guard to walk from room to room." I headed over to the lift and pressed the up button, and he fell into step behind me as the door opened. I stepped inside and turned around; I didn't move to give him room to join me.

"Ma'am, I need to come with you. Could you please let me in?" As the door began to slide closed, I grabbed his hand and pushed it out, and as he moved to stop it again, I fixed him with a steely gaze. "Touch that door, and I'll start screaming."

He was so startled that he let go of the door as if it had burnt him. I gave him the one-finger salute as the door closed.

Back in my room, I found Harper wasn't there. I wasn't concerned at first, but as time passed, my concern grew. Then my phone rang, and I answered it.

"That guard you ditched was there to show you where to go for a briefing. He wasn't guarding you," McKenna Anderson told me coolly.

"Well, I guess that makes me a bit of a wanker then," I said, glad she couldn't see my face flush.

"Indeed. He is waiting outside your door, unwilling to knock or enter for fear of your rape allegations."

"I just said I'd scream. I didn't say anything about screaming 'rape,'" I said meekly, "I'll be down in a sec."

I hung up the phone and stepped outside to where the guard nervously stood with what was possibly abject terror in his eyes. "You could've told me what was going on, mate."

"You didn't exactly give me the opportunity to do so, Ma'am," he replied, pressing the button for the lift once more. This time, we stepped in together.

I ended up in a large meeting room with a big oval table and about a dozen seats arranged around it. Only four of the chairs were filled. Jenna Plural sat in the center seat, and next to her, on one side, was that creepy CIA intelligence agent, Charlotte Kensett. She was in yet another designer suit, and I couldn't help but be a little envious of her government expense account. To one side of Jenna was McKenna Anderson in casual Marine fatigues. On the other side of her sat a man I didn't recognize. He was quite elderly, wearing a U.S. Marine Corps uniform with the insignia of a general. Jenna indicated a seat as I entered, so I sat somewhere else.

The elderly man arched his fingers and stared at me, clearly disapproving. "Miss Grant," he said quite grimly. "I am aware of your record of insubordination within the Australian Air Force. The Australians may tolerate that, but Americans do not."

This brought the hackles up on my neck, and I rose to my feet. "Listen here, mate..."

"Sit down, Stacey," Jenna interrupted. "I am sure the General intended no offense." The look on his face indicated otherwise. I sank back down into the chair slowly and deliberately, keeping my eye fixed upon his, and in turn, he kept his fixed squarely on me. "This is General Adrian, my commanding officer. He's here to sign off, or not, on the mission we have planned. All I ask is that you refrain from comment or interruption while we lay out the particulars of the operation to you."

"As long as this clown keeps his mouth shut about my service and my superiors, I'll keep it zipped." I thought I saw steam coming out of General Adrian's ears.

"Plural, I have never questioned your decisions before, but I think I might be about to," he said with evident irritation in his voice.

Jenna sighed, clearly frustrated. "General, you may have seen her record of insubordination, but you've also seen her mission record. She has faced and survived more combat than any of our pilots. She has taken aircraft through landscapes we have deemed impossible to navigate at those speeds. It is my judgment that whatever Stacey Grant's failings are, she is the only one who can complete this mission successfully or who even stands a chance of coming close."

I smiled at Aphrodite. "Ah, Jenna. I love you too."

Jenna rolled her eyes despairingly. "Stacey, do me a favor and just shut up." I gave her a half-hearted salute and ran my thumb and forefinger across my lips in a zipping motion. Jenna turned to Charlie, "If you please, Miss Kensett."

Charlotte Kensett rose to her feet and, with the clip-clop of those damned expensive shoes, walked over to the large monitor built into the wall. I picked up a remote control and turned it on, and what I saw made my jaw drop. There on the screen was a craft, a fighter, but larger than anything I had ever seen, all gleaming white and with the most beautiful curves any woman would be envious of. But what stood out was the glistening array of weaponry. Missile rack upon missile rack, forward guns, port guns, starboard guns, ray guns... Okay, so no ray guns because they don't exist outside of science fiction, but you get the point, right? This one craft appeared to have the firepower of an entire squadron. It was a motherfucking beast.

"You want me to fly that?" I said, unable to hide the eagerness in my voice and unable to tear my eye away from it. Damn, I think I was drooling.

"It's a little more complicated than that, Stacey," Jenna said so uneasily that I finally tore my eye away from it and looked back at her. "We want you to steal it."

My face fell. "Bloody hell, Jenna, you got me all horny, and you're now telling me it's not even ours."

Jenna grinned. "Well, we're hoping, with your help, it will be."

"This is the prototype of a Peon craft they've named the Starbourne," Charlie stated. "If it goes into production, it will be game over for us throughout the colonies."

"We plan to steal that vessel and study it to ensure that we have counter-measures ready before it goes into production," Jenna added.

"So, somehow, you're going to get me into Europe?" I said, raising a skeptical eyebrow.

"No, Miss Grant," Jenna advised. "This vessel is not in Europe. It isn't even on Earth. This ship is in one of their colonies on Pallas."

I sighed and shook my head in disbelief. "Pallas is a fortified research base. That's a bloody suicide mission, mate."

"Possibly," Jenna stated. The one thing I love about Jenna is that she never lies to you unless absolutely necessary. "However, an essential one. The team will be led by me, with Anderson here. And a team of Marines handpicked by me."

I slowly shook my head. "That's all?"

Jenna nodded. "We need to keep the numbers small to minimize the risk of detection."

"Then you're all a bunch of stark, raving lunatics," I sighed. "That ship requires three people. I can pilot it out of there, but it takes two others to man the weapons systems. Unless you think the Peons are gonna just let us fly off with it without a fight, then we're fine."

"What makes you think it requires three people?" Charlie asked disbelievingly.

I sighed and shook my head again. Standing up, I walked over to where the image was. "So here is the cockpit. This is where yours truly will sit, but there are two more cockpits if you look down here."

"Yes," said Anderson. "They're for co-pilots. We're going to have to do without a co-pilot."

I grew frustrated. "Bloody hell, you really *are* a fucking moron. Look carefully. One is facing port to rear, and the other is facing starboard to rear." I pointed to each in turn. "I've never heard of a co-pilot flying backward." All four stared blankly at the screen. "Oh, for fuck's sake. They're for gunners. So, if we're going to get out of there alive and intact, I'm gonna need two professional gunners."

The silence was deafening as I returned to my seat. Jenna shot a dirty look at Charlie, then glanced at Adrian, who had steam coming out of his ears. "I will start looking into our personnel immediately and see if I can come up with anyone," she finally said, annoyed at her intel rather than me.

"No. The Gunners are gonna be Harper Davis and Trisha McFarland," I said pointedly.

General Adrian snorted. "How convenient. Both of your choices are Australian."

I stood up, and all eyes were on me, wondering what I was doing. I fixed both of my eyes on General Adrian this time and leaned on the desk with clenched fists. "Listen here, mate. I know you Yanks are full of yourselves, but let me paint you a little picture. It's not a pretty picture, but it is a clear one. Where were you at the Battle of Cape York? Where were you when the enemy marched into Sydney, Melbourne, or Perth?" I turned my gaze to Jenna, who looked down. "I'll tell you where. You were here sitting on your arse while I watched my country burn. I lost my home, my state, and my nation." I looked up at Charlie, who remained stoic and impassive. "I watched my mates die one by one as they were shot out of the sky. I dunno if my family is alive or dead. I have nothing, and I owe you nothing." My eyes returned to Jenna. "You want me, not the other way around. Now, here is what you are going to do. You're going to sit there and very respectfully convince me why I should give a fuck and not give you the finger, tell you to shove it up your arse, and turn around and walk right out that fucking door without looking back." I sat back down, crossed my legs, and folded my arms.

Jenna fixed her gaze on me, and our eyes locked like two bitches in a pack of dogs about to square off. "McFarland's already been shipped out on the U.S.S. Nevada. She isn't even on Earth. And I keep telling you Davis isn't qualified," Jenna said coldly, but she was not going to win this argument.

"Davis is more qualified than anyone you can offer. She has worked with me for a year. She is familiar with my tactics and responds to them efficiently. Ask any of your Air Force people, and they will say that's the kind of relationship you need between a pilot and their gunner. As for Trisha, she's flown with me more than anyone else, and I paused and added. "Well, she's about the only one still alive. If this mission is this important, you'll find a way to bring her back."

"Agreed," said Jenna after another long silence hung in the room.

General Adrian harrumphed. He rose to his feet and headed to the door. "Come see me when you're finished here, Plural."

"Wow. That guy *really* needs to get laid," I said as he exited the door, making sure he heard me.

"Well, on that charming note, Stacey, I believe we're done here. Our job will be to get you there; your job will be to fly the craft."

"From what I hear about security on Pallas, your job is gonna be a lot harder than mine," I said, rising to my feet. "So, tell me, what do you guys do for fun around here?"

"There is a general mess which you are free to use. I am sure Anderson will be happy to show you the way." At the look of horror on Anderson's face, I grinned. "I'm sure I can find my way, Jenna."

It turned out that Harper had already found it. That was where she'd been while I was in the meeting. It was early afternoon, and no one else was in there. Their general mess was a low-lit bar with a couple of pool tables, a dartboard, and various tables seating four to six people.

The barkeep was an elderly man. He was one of those veterans who'd retired but still lived vicariously through the troops who came in to drink. Pictures of himself in uniform dotted the back of the bar in between the optics. He was polishing glasses as I entered and chatting to Harper, who was sitting on a stool in front of him. "Hey there," he greeted me with a half-moon smile and a thick Texan accent. Harper looked startled as she turned around and saw my cybernetic eye staring at her.

"Bloody hell, Stacey. You look like you just stepped out of a Hudson Grainger movie," she said, referring to a popular sci-fi action movie star.

I touched it again. "Yeah, I think I'm gonna grow my hair over it. It really doesn't do a lot for my overall sex appeal."

Harper grinned. "I dunno. I think it looks kinda sexy."

I raised the eyebrow above my artificial eye and looked at her incredulously. "You are seriously fucked up, girlfriend," I said, slipping into the seat beside her.

I turned to the barkeep, still waiting patiently for my order. "Scotch, make it a heavy pour. An Australian heavy pour, not one of the pansy small American pours."

The barkeep just grinned as he got me my drink. "I was just telling your friend here. I served with the Aussies back in the day; it was during the Congo campaign. They introduced me to the Anzac Day celebrations. Damn, that was a wild day."

"I bet it was." I had met his type before. Old veterans who had made the military their life but now felt redundant, unable to continue their careers. They're often made fun of as they rehash their old war stories. This was one type of person I didn't make fun of – this guy had my respect. In my book, he was a bloody hero, and I happily listened to him as he retold his adventures in one of the bloodiest fighting arenas in history.

As we chatted and drank, steadily getting munted. The afternoon turned into evening, and our companion's attention turned to others who'd started to come into the bar. Mostly U .S. Marines, but some regular army, and the noise of chatter and slamming of pool balls took away the quiet of the afternoon.

We weren't the only women present, but we were the fresh meat, dressed in civvies. We must've looked like fair game. A tall guy with shaved blonde hair and the type of chiseled body that you just wanted to lick approached Harper; they always went for her first. She was the better-looking of the two of us, and guys seemed to love that doe-eyed innocent look.

I love watching guys hit on Harper, who is as likely to date a guy as a cat is to date a dog. "Well, hi there, it's nice to see a new face here." He was cautious, not knowing who we were, but his face brightened up as soon as Harper responded, "Well, g'day there."

He grinned. "Australian?

"True blue," she replied.

"Well, that must make you Davis and Grant?"

I was curious to know exactly what this guy had heard about us. "Yep, but you can call us Harper and Stacey. I'm Harper. She's Stacey."

"G'day, Sergeant," I said, checking out the chevrons on his uniform.

He proffered a hand to Harper first and then to me. "Joshua Timberlake, United States Marine Corps. And I believe we will soon be working together quite a lot."

"You may be working with Stacey, but I have no idea what they're gonna do with me yet," Harper said dejectedly.

"Oh yeah," I said quite bashfully. "I forgot to tell you. We're going to Pallas."

Harper turned on me, eyes wide with a mixture of joy and trepidation. "Seriously?"

"Yeah, seriously. It turns out they now realize you're the best gunner a girl could ask for."

"Yeah, yeah. You made them take me," Harper smirked.

"Ladies, you realize you're discussing a classified mission here," Josh said in a low yet urgent voice.

"Oh, lighten up." I snorted at the Yank. "I haven't said anything about your precious mission." I turned away from him with my drink and made it clear our conversation was over. This was probably a suicide mission, and I had just realized that I didn't care. It was not like I had a death wish or anything, but if the end came, would it be such a bad thing? Although it would be good if I could take out as many Peon bastards as possible before I went.

"I'm sorry if I offended or upset you, Miss Grant," Joshua said to me.

Interrupted from my thoughts. I looked at him, "No worries, Sarge, you didn't." I slipped off the stool and told Harper I was heading back to my room. She decided to stay a while longer.

I couldn't sleep that night. All sorts of things were going through my head, and I couldn't turn off the artificial eye. In the end, I just stuck a plaster over it. I heard Harper return, banging and crashing as she stumbled about, truly munted. I gathered that she had a good time, but I didn't get up to talk to her. It was around 3 am when I finally fell asleep, pondering the journey ahead.

Chapter Six

John F. Kennedy

We were on board the U.S.S. John F Kennedy about a week later. At that time, it was the flagship of the U.S. Navy. The U.S.S. Constitution was still under construction in a secret dockyard unbeknownst to almost anyone. With a crew of nearly two hundred, it was three times the size of any other vessel currently in the fleet. It was too big to land, so we had to take the shuttle up to it. Phelks has already explained how complicated leaving Earth is, but unlike the occasion he recounted, we didn't have quite as many issues. Onboard the shuttle, apart from the flight crew, there were Harper and me, along with Jenna, Anderson, Timberlake, and two other Marines. It was an uneventful ride, and we docked in the largest docking bay I had ever seen, with more crew running around for our little shuttle than we had for our entire squadron back in Cape York.

As we stepped off, Harper looked around, her mouth open in awe at the size of everything. "Bloody hell, this bugger is a beast."

Jenna gave her a wink and grinned at her. "She's the pride of the fleet."

"Yeah, well, size isn't everything, as I recently made clear to someone," I muttered, but I have to admit even I was impressed – she was a beaut. We were approached by a small entourage led by a tall woman in a Marine officer's uniform, bearing the markings of a second officer. She stood in front of us at ease and smiled warmly, telling us, "Welcome aboard the U.S.S. John F Kennedy. I hope you enjoy your stay." Like it was some fucking pleasure cruise, and she was our cruise director.

Jenna saluted sharply along with the other Marines, and then Harper, and then I gave a more half-hearted attempt. "I'm Lieutenant Stephanie Morris, second officer." Yep, future First Officer of the Chesty. Executed by Jenna after she fucked us over. "Captain Dale Rodriguez currently commands the ship. Unfortunately, she is unable to be with us at this moment, as we need to prepare to get underway before we are detected in the Earth Area System. The Peon bastards would like nothing more than to catch the flagship, where they keep most of their fleet. The Kennedy would be quite a coup for them. My aides here will show you to your quarters to settle in."

"We're staying awake for the entire trip to Pallas?" I asked unbelievingly. "That's going to be months."

"Only for the first couple of weeks," Jenna advised us. "We're going to run mission prep to make sure we're ready for what we encounter."

At this point, we were separated from Jenna and the Marines, who were heading toward military quarters. Harper and I were taken down to what they called the guest quarters. I was not too impressed by the feeling that the Aussies were getting treated differently once more. "You'll have the run of this ship level," the steward told us. "There are recreational facilities and even a movie theater and gym if you're interested. All other decks are off-limits unless authorized by your commanding officer or appropriate personnel."

Harper looked at me and shook her head as I grinned at her. We walked behind the steward, so he did not see my reaction. Harper knew full well that being told that I couldn't leave this deck meant that I would, in fact, leave this deck. Once again, we were left alone to our own devices. "You know, Harp. I'm getting so tired of these Yanks not treating us as equals."

Harper sighed and gave me a judgmental look. "Bloody hell, Stacey, please don't go causing trouble."

I looked at her innocently and pointed to myself. "Who me?" Yeah, it was cliché, but it was still funny to me.

She simply rolled her eyes and went to check out the other rooms. I took the opportunity to slip back out the door, knowing she would try to stop me. I found an elevator, but it was palm-activated and, obviously, not keyed to me. Which was most unfortunate, but that wasn't going to stop me. All vessels had emergency ladder access. A quick hunt around, and I found it in a hatch in the floor. It was alarmed, of course, but you don't grow up on the streets of Wagga without knowing anything about an alarm or two. A couple of disconnected wires later, I opened it and slid down it, fireman-style.

I didn't even know what deck I was on. The best way not to be noticed is not to try to go unnoticed. I strode purposefully down the corridor, passing several naval personnel who glanced at me in my civilian wear. Still, I must undoubtedly be authorized to be there due to my confident demeanor.

There was no way the crew knew the purpose of our mission. You don't discuss that with two hundred enlisted grunts who run a ship. Most would probably not even realize we were on board. Trouble would come if someone spoke to me. I couldn't sound like an American if I tried. Fortunately, no one talked to me, and as I headed further down the deck, I realized that I was passing through crew quarters. Disappointing. I wanted to be somewhere they desperately did not want me to be. Don't ask me why, beyond the fact that it's fun. I had nothing to lose. If they pulled me off the mission, they had no mission. Unless they hoped Trish could pull it off. Now, don't get me wrong. I'm not knocking, Trish. She's a damn good pilot, and I'm not being arrogant, but it is simply a fact that I was better. Everyone was surprised when she got second in command of Epsilon Squadron instead of me. Everyone except me, that is. I'm not too fond of rules, I don't particularly appreciate being told no, and I don't like doing what is expected of me. Unless you expect me to play up, then I'm your girl.

"You know the Captain can order you locked into those quarters?" I spun about and found myself face-to-face with Jenna Plural. She stood staring at me with her head to one side, looking at me questioningly.

"A ship the size of fucking Melbourne, and I still run into you," I stated dejectedly.

Again, I saw a rare smile. "You're proving to be quite a challenge to me, Stacey."

"Well, they say the United States Marine Corps is up to any challenge," I smiled.

Jenna rolled her eyes. "You are not as amusing as you think you are. Do you really want to see this ship?"

"This is the fucking Kennedy. What d'you think?" I said, like it was a stupid question.

Jenna smirked and nodded. "Come on then, let's go see what you really want to see."

"Oh, and what do you think that is?" I asked smugly.

"The flight controls on the bridge," she smiled, stepping past me.

"Good guess, boss lady." I grinned to myself and turned around to follow her.

As we stepped out of the elevator onto the bridge, it was like something out of some old Space Ranger movie: shiny panels all around, soft leather seats for the pilot and co-pilot. The Captain was on the deck and turned to us as we entered. She smiled at

Jenna, and instead of saluting, they shook hands. "Good to see you again, Plural. What's it been? Twenty years?"

I turned to look at Jenna with wide eyes; she barely looked old enough to vote. I was even more shocked when she replied, "More like thirty."

The Captain turned to me, "And you must be Lieutenant Grant of the Royal Australian Air Force?"

"You got that right, mate."

The Captain looked startled for a moment and glanced at Jenna. A wry smile crossed Jenna's face, and she glanced away for a moment. I realized Jenna had deliberately brought me to the Captain for her own entertainment.

"Yes, well, it may be lax in the Australian military, but there's a certain formality that we adhere to within the U.S.," her voice trailed off as she noticed Jenna urgently shaking her head at her, but it was too late.

"We got a certain formality in the Australian military, too. One that means we don't take lightly to anyone dissing Australia or the Australian military. So, with respect to your rank, I'm not gonna ask you to step outside but simply remind you not to make any derogatory comments about my country."

I noticed the entire bridge had fallen silent. Everyone was watching us with rapt attention. There was a moment of tension, which Jenna broke, "I can assure you, as can Stacey here, she is not exactly representative of her peers in the Australian military."

I turned on her to protest, but as I thought about it, I simply shrugged and acknowledged, "Good point."

"I see, " Dale said and moved on as if nothing had ever happened. "Have you ever piloted an interplanetary ship before?"

"Fighters and shuttles, but nothing in this class."

Dale nodded and turned toward the pilot. "Would you care to give up your position to Lieutenant Grant for a while, Mr. Helmsley?"

Helmsley smiled and nodded, "Yes, ma'am," he said, climbing out of his seat. He was a good-looking bloke with blonde hair and a chiseled jaw, which made me weak at the knees. He indicated the seat to me.

I looked up wide-eyed at the Captain, "You serious?"

Rodriguez smiled and nodded to the chair. I didn't hesitate. I slipped into the luxurious chair and looked down at the controls. They were a standard American configuration with a few extras whose purpose I didn't know. I had studied the layout back in basic, but that was a long time ago, and I prayed that I wasn't about to make an arse of myself. "Would you lay in a course indicated on your readout, Miss Grant?" Rodriguez ordered.

"Aye-aye, Ma'am," I frowned curiously at the coordinates. It was for a location smack dab in the middle of nowhere, but not too far away from us—a few days at most. I plotted in the course. I thought that would be it, but then she commanded, "Bring her up to standard by three."

I glanced over my shoulder with a raised eyebrow, but she just stared at me, waiting. "Aye-aye, Ma'am," I said and turned back to the controls with a huge grin on my face. I glanced at the co-pilot next to me, a cute little thing who smiled back at me. My hands started moving over the controls, and the slight humming of the engines powering up got my adrenaline racing. I was in control of what was considered the most powerful ship in the Pacific Alliance. I slowly brought her up to speed; looking up at the rearview screen, I saw the Earth disappear as I banked to starboard during the routine scan for Earth-orbit debris. Yeah, that was it. Probably not exciting to you as you sit on your couch with a nice cup of tea, but as a pilot, this sort of thing just wets your knickers. I ran my hand lovingly over the edge of the console. I glanced up at Helmsley as he moved to my side, wanting his seat back. "Just give me a minute, mate."

He chuckled lightly, "Sure."

I waited about another minute before reluctantly slipping out of the chair with a sigh. I offered my hand to Helmsley, I thanked him, and turned back to the Captain. "Thank you, Ma'am."

Dale grinned back at me. "You are most welcome, Miss Grant."

As Jenna and I left the bridge and the elevator doors shut, I looked up at her, "You certainly know your way to a girl's heart."

"I have had quite some time to understand people and how they react to things." She turned to face me, "We're on the same side, Stacey. Yet my people are arrogant and paranoid. You will always be a foreigner to many, but I wanted you to know that I consider you one of us. I will be there for you for as long as you are there for me."

Silence lingered between us as I mulled this over before answering. "You got it, boss."

Jenna grinned and looked at me, realizing that that was the closest she would get to a title of respect for her rank on this mission.

And just like that, a bond of friendship was established that would only deepen over the coming years.

The following week was a bunch of body-bashing drills led by Timberlake. The idea was to get us used to each other and work as a team. An assault course had been set up in the cargo bays, and I had not undergone such a grueling physical challenge since basic training four years prior. The only break we got was a few days later when I found out the course I had set was to rendezvous with the U.S.S. Nevada. Harper and I were reunited with Trisha McFarland, who was as pleased to see us as we were her. She was a tall, chunky girl and was a little older than me, with a red, rosy face and those dimpled cheeks that you just wanted to pinch. Out of all of us, she had had the most space-time experience, having piloted a frigate between Mars and Earth before switching over to being a fighter pilot. She had logged fewer flight hours than me as a pilot, but had moved ahead of me in rank due to our differences in, let's just say, extracurricular activities that landed me with demerits and her with merits. We met her at the airlock when they crossed the umbilical with the Captain of the Nevada and his entourage. She thanked him, and they shook hands. I could not help but comment on her wearing the United States Navy uniform. "I never thought I'd see an Aussie done up like a Yank."

She grinned and turned to show me the patch on her left arm. It bore the Australian flag, featuring a ship in flight flying between the stars, and bore the words' Australian Free Forces'. "I want one of those," I told Jenna, like a child who'd been left out.

"I'm surprised you don't have one and that you're not in uniform," Trisha said as we headed back toward our quarters.

"We haven't signed up with them yet. Not sure if I'm going to," I informed her. "I've just agreed to do this one mission for them at the moment. To be honest, I can't bring myself to admit that the AAF is no longer a thing. "

"Yeah, I get that. By the way, I like the new face jewelry." Instinctively, I raised my hand to touch the artificial eye.

"Yeah, I'm a robot now," I muttered.

"Isn't it kind of odd?" said Harper. "That the primary personnel in an American mission are Australian."

I looked at her and grinned as we entered our quarters. "Crikey love, only the true blue can show these Yanks how to wrestle a croc," I said in my best stereotype Australian.

My companions laughed at this as Trisha dropped her duffel bag onto the couch. "Well, here we are," she said. "Epsilon Squadron back together again. Well, what remains of it anyway."

Chapter Seven

Coitus Interruptus

As the days passed, I started to resent Timberlake. Not because he did anything wrong. He was doing a damn fine job, but the rigors of his training program were killing me. Each day would end with discovering more muscles that I was sure were only there so they could cause me pain. About two days after Trisha joined us, I was determined not to end my evening asleep in bed at 6 pm. I felt the need to get fucked up, and I wanted to do it with my two sisters. Harper whined so much about being tired that, in the end, it was just me and Trisha who made our way down to the little bar that was on our level. You'd be surprised to know that it was our first time there, but we were far from happy when we discovered that this bar was for passengers only, and we were the only ones. The room stood empty, and there wasn't even a barkeep; it was a self-service bar, apparently. So, we did. I took a bottle of scotch, and Trisha took a bottle of rum, and we went down the ladder to the crew deck. Once again, no one questioned us, even when I asked them where the crew mess hall was. Following the directions we were given, we walked into what appeared to be a loud party. There was a celebration going on for some Sheila who had been promoted or something - I honestly don't remember. So, technically, we were crashing a party, but no one seemed to mind as Trisha and I found a table in the corner. Trisha looked at me in disgust as I picked up someone's used glass, drained out the dregs, and poured myself a glass of scotch. "Stace, that's just gross."

I shrugged. "It's alcohol. It'll kill any germs that are in there."

"Even so, Stace. Even so," she said and headed through the crowd to get a glass from the bar.

Shortly after she left, I noticed Helmsley across the room. I raised my glass to him in a cheers gesture. He grinned and headed over to me. "Hey, Miss Grant, good to see you again."

"Hey Helmsley, pull up a chair and call me Stacey," I said, kicking out the chair and pouring him out a drink, not telling him that it was someone else's glass.

He smiled and sat down by my side. "My name is Gregory."

I wrinkled my nose into a sneer. I looked at him, "I am not calling you Gregory. That's a poofter's name."

He frowned at me. "That's a rather homophobic comment."

I shrugged that off. "I don't mean it like that. It's just, I mean, Gregory is not a very manly name."

"Well, you can call me Greg, but I don't particularly like it."

"Well, if you don't like it, I'm not gonna call you it. How about I just call you Helmsy?

He laughed and shrugged. "If that's what makes you happy, Stacey, you can call me Helmsy."

I downed a shot, and as I refilled my glass, I looked at him and said, "It does." I looked over to where Trisha was at the bar and saw her talking to a guy who was flirting with her. Good, I had this guy to myself. I was feeling horny, and this guy was hot. "Tell me about yourself, Helmsy, and don't make it boring."

He chuckled. "Well, I don't really have anything exciting to tell you."

"Naa, naaaah," I said, imitating a loser buzzer for a quiz show. "That's not a good way to start a story. I'm losing interest already," and I sat back and grinned.

He smiled, leaned back in his chair, and folded his arms. "I fly the most incredible ship in the American fleet and have taken her into combat multiple times. "

"That's better. But it's something I already know, so naa, naaaah."

"I was Captain of my high school football team back in Flint, Michigan."

I shrugged, "I guess you have never seen Australian footy. It's real football without all that pansy-arse body armor."

"You don't seem to have a very high opinion of Americans."

I shrugged and sat back in my chair, "Americans are okay. There's only one thing wrong really with them."

"Oh, and what's that?"

"They're not Australians," I grinned.

Helmsley laughed and drank the scotch down. "I have never been to Australia. I've never left the U.S.A. when it comes to going to other countries. Ironic considering how many moons and planets I have visited."

"It's funny. I'm quite the opposite. Apart from the occasional jaunt to the moon, I have never traveled this far away from the homeworld. "

"It's not that exciting. Well, not the travel. And even the battles up here are a lot slower than you would be used to. You can't close in on another vessel easily and have to try to board it. As you know, we can't lock missiles on the ranges, and it's more like seventeenth-century pirate battles. As a pilot, my job is just to keep us from letting an enemy vessel get close enough."

I deliberately yawned. "I may not have been out here, but I am a trained pilot, and I know what goes on. I hope you're better in bed than you are at making conversation."

I grinned as the big drongo positively blushed. "Well, I can't possibly comment on that. Though I've never had any complaints."

I stood up and held out my hand to him. "Come on, let's go find out." He took my hand and stood up, looking very nervous. As I led him to the door, several of his friends sent wolf whistles in our direction. I glanced over at Trish, and she rolled her eyes at me, but then returned her attention to her own man. I led Helmsy back to our quarters and was relieved to find Harper had gone to her room and was probably asleep. I took him into my room, and once inside, I kicked the door shut and pulled him toward me. I threw my arms around his neck, pulled his face down to mine, and kissed him hard. His hand slipped around my waist, and I pulled him back onto the bed, bringing him down on top of me, still locked in the kiss. My hands fumbled at his belt as he began to unbutton my shirt. Our breathing grew heavier with more resolve, and our hands started to move faster as our lips remained locked and our hands roamed freely. When the intercom buzzed, Helmsley made to pull back, but I pulled him back down on me. "Ignore it," I mumbled with my face still attached to his. He complied, running his hands over my breasts. The intercom buzzed again. He hesitated again, but this time, I said nothing as I unzipped his fly and started to pull up his shirt. "Intercom override." Although it sounded human, it was the familiar voice of the computer that appeared on nearly every American ship or base. The following voice was Jenna's: "Stacey, are you there?" Helmsley froze, as did I.

"Fuck off, I'm busy," I shouted a few moments later.

"Well, get unbusy. I want to see you at the Tech Center pronto," Jenna responded curtly.

"For fuck's sake!" I snapped back and gently pushed Helmsley off. I sat up, rapidly refastening my buttons as he did up his belt. "What's happened? Is someone hurt?" I said to the intercom, concerned about Trisha, who was the only person I cared about that I couldn't account for.

"Just get down here. We have an issue we need to deal with." The intercom switched off, and I sighed.

I turned to Helmsley and shrugged, "You can wait for me here if you want," I said noncommittally. We both knew the moment was gone.

Helmsley shrugged, "I'd best get back to my quarters. You may not be American military, but you're still military. I'm not sure what the fraternization rules are between us."

This kind of irritated me. I shrugged again and just said, "Whatever. Perhaps you could show me the way to the Tech Center."

He smiled softly and placed a hand on my arm, "Maybe another time?"

"Tech Center?" I said it again, and he nodded as we silently walked down the hall together. He opened the elevator, which took us up two levels, and he indicated the Tech Center.

"Maybe we can meet up tomorrow?" he asked.

"Well, only if your commanding officer lets you come out to play," I replied snarkily.

His smile faded. "Yeah, well, it was nice to meet you, Stacey." There was irritation in his voice as he took the offense that I intended. I felt guilty, just a little. It wasn't his fault we'd been interrupted, but I was frustrated, not just sexually, but by the whole situation. I wanted to spend the night with him and just forget everything, get it all out of my system. To just have a moment when I was not thinking about what was happening back Down Under.

I watched him go back into the elevator, tried to smile as he turned to face me, and as the doors closed, the smile eluded me. I sighed and turned to enter the Tech Center.

Jenna Plural was there with a tall, skinny redheaded girl. Obviously, I had no idea who she was. She was dressed in jeans and a cream hoodie, looking like some college kid. "Come in and take a seat," Jenna instructed. I did as I was told, and the three of us were seated at a small desk. "Stacey Grant, please meet Sergeant Helen Tracker. Across the desk, we both reached over simultaneously and shook hands. "Tracker is our tech wizard. She'll be coming with us on the mission."

"Okay, but what's so urgent that you needed to interrupt me tonight?" I asked irritably.

"It's your new eye," said Helen, her voice soft and gentle with the hint of a New York accent.

"What about it?"

"The doc back in Nevada gave you a state-of-the-art military replacement. You'll be going on to Pallas as a civilian worker who couldn't possibly afford such a device. It will instantly draw attention."

"So you want to remove it? I can't fly kites without two eyes," I snorted.

"No, not at all. I do, however, want to adjust it. It's far too useful for you to give it up in the current circumstances. The adjustment will give a false reading if anyone tries to scan it, and it will also disable the additional functions, so they don't register on the scan either."

I rolled my one good eye, and the lens in the other followed suit. "And this couldn't wait till the morning?"

"No," Jenna said. "Timberlake has reported that he thinks you're ready, so the Captain is getting us ready to upload to the M.E.T."

"I can't be uploaded," I pointed to the eye. I can't have anything non-organic when I go through the zapper."

"Oh, you can take it out simply enough. It bonds to your neurons with an energy matrix," Helen told me. "Didn't the doctor explain all of this to you?"

"No, he didn't."

"Well, from the report I got, you didn't exactly give him the opportunity," Jenna intoned severely.

I shrugged and stared down at my feet like a naughty schoolgirl who the principal had reprimanded. I then looked up to see Helen grinning. "You just press the left and right sides simultaneously, and it'll pop right out. It auto-sterilizes, so you don't have to worry about cleaning it or anything like that."

"Well, isn't that just dandy?"

"The procedure to adjust it takes about thirty minutes. Do you mind if we do it now?" Helen asked.

"Honestly, I don't care if she minds or not. She should have done this back on Earth. It will be done now because it's the only opportunity before we upload in the morning," Jenna said.

I was about to backchat her with a sarcastic comment, but the look in her eye was quite severe, and I backed down and complied. It was disconcerting seeing metal tools brought up to my eye and Helen Tracker's face so close to mine that I could clearly make out the freckles on her nose. There was mild discomfort, but otherwise, the procedure went as planned. When she finished, she showed me how to remove it; It did slip out easily, but I made the mistake of looking toward the mirror and saw the ugly hole in my head. It was this sunken, weirdly sunken divet, surrounded by skin, where the connectors made contact with my nervous system. I gasped and felt physically sick, but Tracker quickly stepped in between me and the mirror. "You'll get used to it," she said. "But you'll only ever need to take it out for things like the M.E.T."

"Yeah, yeah," I muttered, not believing her, but she was right. I did get kind of used to it in time.

As I returned to my quarters, I heard grunting and panting coming from Trisha's room. I paused and hesitated outside the door, then went and grabbed up a bottle of whiskey and headed to my room. "Lucky bitch," and I slammed the door behind me hard enough for them to hear.

Chapter Eight

Hangovers and Other Headaches

If you've ever considered going into the M.E.T. with a hangover, don't. That bastard comes out with you on the other side, no matter how long you've been in there, and the effects from the process make it ten times worse than when you went in.

Timberlake woke us early, and we followed him down to the M.E.T. room. You know what the one on the Lewis Puller was like. Well, there was a hell of a difference on the Kennedy, with large, beautifully designed locker rooms for changing in privacy. The whole team was there: Jenna, Anderson, Timberlake, Tracker, three other Marines I won't need to introduce you to, you'll see why, and of course, us Aussie girls. Timberlake first supervised his Marines as they went up, and we followed them when it was our turn. We stripped off, but I hung back. I didn't want Trish or Harper to see me take out my eye. "Is it safe?" Harper looked back at me – she was referring to the M.E.T.

"Safer than a dogfight, you drongo," I said, pushing her ahead. "You can't sit in the back of a kite with me doing Mach 5 all fine, but *this* has you quaking in your boots."

"Well, I'm not in control of this," she whined.

"Bloody hell, Harp, you're not in control in the cockpit either. I am," I said incredulously.

"Can we move it along?" I heard Jenna say.

"You're going to be perfectly safe, don't worry," Trisha said. "Look, I'll go first. You'll see it's okay."

Trish stepped forward and held her hands out by her sides. She gave Harper a wink and disappeared. Harper glanced back at me again, then nervously stepped up. She was about to say something, but the operator didn't give her a chance, as she, too, disappeared. I popped the artificial eye out of its socket, and I turned to see Helen Tracker as she smiled and took my eye from me. "I will see that it gets into your locker."

I nodded my appreciation and turned to Jenna. "Hey, Boss, do me a favor. Have them wake me up before the others. I don't want them to see me like this."

Jenna smiled at me and nodded. I then stepped forward and raised my arms. The flash of light blinded me in my one good eye.

"Welcome back, Lieutenant Grant. Please step down," the same technician who uploaded me appeared to be still standing in the exact same position. But I knew some time had passed. "How long?" I asked.

"Forty-three days."

I arched an eyebrow at him. "Which means we haven't reached our destination. Who ballsed it up?"

"Sorry, Ma'am, I can't make any comments. Please move along so I can download the others."

As I stepped out, I saw Jenna buttoning up her tunic. "We're still a week out from Pallas." McKenna Anderson overheard me. "We're changing ships."

There was a flash behind me as I asked, "Why?"

"You didn't think we were going to fly into a Peon base in the flagship of the United States Navy, did you?" Jenna responded.

I grinned as I stepped over to my locker. There was another flash behind me, "Call me a moron, but no, as it happens. I guess I never really thought about that part of the mission." I grabbed my eye from the locker and tried to get it in before the two women behind me caught up. Only then did I glance over my shoulder at Harper and Trisha.

"We are meeting up with a Norwegian frigate that trades with the Peons," Jenna continued as we dressed.

"The Norwegians are neutral," Trisha pointed out.

"Technically, yes, they are. But this is an independent ship, and the Captain is receiving a large sum of money to get us onto that base."

"You've entrusted our lives to a mercenary?" I asked with some incredulity.

"Yes. It's a risk," Jenna agreed. "That is why we will spend the remainder of the voyage downloading."

"Bloody hell, Boss. They could just as easily be taking extra money to turn us in," I said, blinking my artificial eye to ensure it still worked.

"We have used these people before – they have always been reliable. I have no reason to believe they will betray us now."

"Why didn't you tell us any of this?" asked Harper.

"Need to know. The fact is, it wasn't necessary to tell you anything until now. Very few people are aware of this rendezvous. Even Timberlake and his people don't know our goal." A klaxon sounded, and we turned back to the tech battling at the M.E.T.'s controls. I saw Captain Dale come in and rushed over to him. Jenna wasn't far behind. "I'm getting a diminishing signal on the next two personnel," the tech told them.

"Pattern degradation or system failure?" Rodriguez tried to clarify.

"I can't tell, Captain," he paused. "Pattern degradation, confirmed," he said dejectedly,

"My people?" Jenna asked solemnly

The tech sighed and let his hands drop to his side. "Yes, Ma'am. I'm sorry."

"Who?"

"Timberlake and Smith." He didn't actually say Smith, but I can't remember the other person's name for the life of me. Hell, I couldn't even tell you if they were a guy or a girl.

"Let me take a look," Helen Tracker stepped up. The tech glanced at his Captain, who, in turn, glanced at Jenna, who nodded. As the Captain nodded to the tech, he stepped aside.

Helen's hands darted over the controls like a seasoned pro. "I can reimage Timberlake, but I've lost Smith. However, he's going to be seriously messed up. I don't even know if he'd survive," she said as she looked up at Jenna.

Jenna shook her head. "You have to give me more than that, Helen. You're asking me to make a call about a man's life."

Helen let out a heavy breath and said, "I can't guarantee that Timberlake will survive, Ma'am, and if he does, he'd be severely disabled. I can only reimage about 90% of him." There was a long silence, and then Helen said, "The decision has to be made now."

"Let him go," Jenna said softly. "I've seen people come out of these things messed up. I can't in good conscience do that to him." With that, Helen stepped away from the M.E.T. controls.

Harper spun around and, through gritted teeth, spat out, "It's safe, huh?"

I didn't respond. Instead, I just glanced at the ground.

Jenna turned to Rodriguez, "Give it a few weeks, then send my condolences to Timberlake's and Smith's families. Tell them they died in the line of duty, but don't go into details." Dale simply nodded in response. Jenna turned to McKenna. "Where does this leave us?"

McKenna sighed. "We're pretty screwed." She looked to Helen Tracker. "We still have two more Marines in there. Can we download them?"

"Their signals are still strong. One hundred percent patent clarity," Tracker replied.

"Do you know what went wrong with the device?" Jenna asked.

"Just the standard pattern degradation – a 1 in 100 chance. Unfortunately, the technology isn't perfect."

"You're sure that you can download the other two without a problem?" Mac asked.

"As certain as I can be," Tracker shrugged.

Jenna pondered a moment before she replied. "Leave them there for the moment while we assess the situation." She turned to Rodriguez. "Have you got somewhere we can sit down and discuss this?"

"Follow me," Rodriguez said, and we fell into step behind her as she led us down the corridor to a small briefing room used by N.C.O.s.

Disspirited, Jenna collapsed into a seat as the group assembled around the table. "Give it to me straight, Anderson."

"It's pretty much mission scrubbed. The chances of us *not* getting into a firefight are next to nil. Our flight crew here," she indicated to us, "likely possesses little more than basic combat training, which is only slightly more than what Tracker here has. That leaves you and the uploaded Marines as the only effective fighting force we have now. And let's not forget that Timberlake was the only one who could speak fluent French."

Jenna shook her head. "Scrubbing the mission is out of the question." She turned to Rodriguez, "I assume you have a contingent of the army or Marines on the ship?"

"Of course, but none of them are mission-ready."

"Well, this is the flagship. Surely you must have some men and women ranked as the best?"

"You know this isn't our only mission?" Rodriguez said curtly. "I haven't got a clue what your mission entails. All I know of my part in your mission is that I'm to drop you off so that you can rendezvous with the Norwegian ship. We have our own mission to fulfill after that. I will need the best."

Jenna managed to smile. "Well, there's the rub, isn't it? Neither of us knows each other's mission plans, so we can't decide which one is more important. I am only asking for two people. A sergeant and a grunt who are capable and deadly. And preferably someone who can speak French."

Dale pondered a moment before replying, "I'll make sure you have them."

"If I may say something," I said, unable to hide the curtness from my voice as all eyes turned to me. "Frankly, this is bullshit. We've been training with *this* team, and now you're saying that we're just gonna replace the Marines and the sergeant in charge of them?"

"I would be most interested to hear your solution, Stacey?" Jenna asked curtly

"Well, I suggest we turn around, go home, open up a couple of tinnies, and forget this whole bloody idea."

Jenna looked around the room, "Does anybody have a sensible suggestion?" I felt my face redden, but I didn't know whether it was from anger or embarrassment.

But no response came, and Jenna said, "Very well then. We will proceed as planned, and the Captain will supply us with two new troopers. You are all dismissed until I call for you again." As we got up to leave, she turned to Tracker and added, "I would like you to oversee the download of the remainder of our personnel."

As Helen nodded, I was already headed out the door.

So now you know why I didn't introduce the rest of the team earlier. First, there wasn't any point; second, I just don't remember their names. The whole thing was a complete clusterfuck. We went alone to a small mess hall away from the others, and the steward served us breakfast. None of us spoke as we sat there, lost in our thoughts. I was pretty annoyed at myself for being irritated that there wasn't any sugar on my porridge. I pushed my bowl aside, and rather than asking for sugar, I called over to the steward, "Got any Vegemite, mate?"

"Pardon me, Ma'am? I don't know what that is," he said.

"Never mind, " I pouted.

"This is bullshit. Total and utter bullshit," Harper muttered under her breath as she stopped eating and tossed her fork onto the barely eaten plate of eggs. Neither Trisha nor I replied. I just sat there staring off into space, clutching the mug of coffee in my hand. This only seemed to irritate Harper even more, and she glared at each of us in turn as we ignored her. Finally, she snapped. "Don't either of you have anything to say about this situation?"

"What the fuck do you want me to say?" I snapped back.

"I dunno. Something. Anything."

"How about 'shut the fuck up, Harper'?"

"Both of you, just calm down now," Trisha said. Technically, she was still our commanding officer, I guess. All of that had kind of gone out the window since the fall of Oz. We fell silent again, and I returned to my coffee.

"The mission should be scrubbed," Trisha finally said.

"That's not our call," I responded. "It's up to Aphrodite to make that decision."

"Of course, it's our call. We aren't Americans. We're under no obligation to take orders from the American military. If we say no, then it's no."

"And then what are we supposed to do? We certainly won't get a place in the U.S. military, and bam. There go our chances of being a part of the spearhead back into Oz."

Trisha sighed, and once more, silence fell over the room. The silence was deafening. I really can't explain what I mean by that. It just was. You either get what I mean, or you don't. But I guess it's not really important. The silence wasn't broken until Jenna entered the room. "We are fourteen hours out from meeting up with the Norwegian ship. I have asked Dale to try to delay it for as long as possible to give us more time to ready our new personnel."

"Woopie-fucking-do!" Harper sneered quietly. "Yanks are so brilliant they can train for a mission they know nothing about in just a few short hours."

I glared at her, then looked up at Jenna. "I think maybe you need to look for a new gunner, too."

"Fuck you, Stace. Fuck you to hell," Harper screamed at me.

Jenna slammed a fist down on the table. "Will you stop bickering like little schoolgirls? I am not scrubbing this mission. It is too damned important to the war effort. But you are seriously making me question whether or not you three have the chops for this. So tell me now, can I rely on the three of you?" There was silence, and she banged the table again. "I want an answer, and I want it now, damn it."

We all stared up at her, like the naughty schoolgirls she likened us to. Trisha spoke first, "You can rely on us. Don't read anything into our behavior or how we talk. I, for one, trust both these sheilas with my life."

"Ditto," I said and took another sip of my coffee.

"I respect your passion for your country," Jenna said, her voice still filled with aggression. "I really do. However, you are now in the United States military, whether officially or unofficially. I expect you to act like members of the U.S. military.

You are under my command, which means your lives are my responsibility. I can't promise to do my best to keep you safe unless you promise to follow orders and behave in accordance with military protocol."

I was about to comment that we'd agree that I didn't have to follow military protocol, but she anticipated it. "Stacey, for the sake of all our lives, I want you to put aside what we discussed until the conclusion of this mission."

I considered declining, but the part of me that relished rebellion was silenced by the rare appearance of my common sense. I looked up at her and said quietly, "You're the boss, boss. At least until the mission is over."

"Thank you." She then forcibly calmed herself and discussed the mission itself. "When we transfer, I do not want you to have anything on you that could identify you. That means nothing that can connect you to either Australia or the United States. This mission is under the remit of plausible deniability. If any of us are captured or killed, the United States government will deny any knowledge of our activities."

I grinned as something dawned upon me as I looked up at her. "That's why you wanted me. So the Americans can't get blamed for anything that goes wrong."

"I will admit that did draw Anderson to your file, but that was not the final deciding factor. We still believe you are the best pilot for this job."

I chuckled and shook my head, but managed to restrain myself so that all I said in reply was, "Okay, Boss."

"Stacey, I need you to trust me. Everything hinges on your comfort under my command. I am not lying to you." Of course, I know now that she wasn't lying to me. She did have faith in me, and to this day, she still does. Although I was starting to trust her a little bit, I still doubted her.

I decided to be honest with her. "I'll try, Boss."

We were on the bridge when the procedure to dock with the Norwegian ship was in progress. Helmsley was guiding us in; neither of us acknowledged each other. I was busy staring at the wreck of a ship in front of us. It was old and battered, which made me uneasy. The procedure for docking the two very different ships was not easy. It took a couple of hours to line us up so the transit tubes could be extended across the vacuum of space. Someone came over the communications channel speaking Norwegian, and I assumed it was because everything was ready, as Helmsley simply acknowledged it and turned to the Captain, nodding.

We headed down to the airlock, and it was bizarre to see everyone in civilian clothes. Jenna looked pretty hot in a skirt, a button-up collared shirt, and a leather jacket. Tracker was more casually dressed in jeans and a hoodie. McKenna wore jeans, a T-shirt, and a caramel jacket. Everyone wore jackets, and I thought that was odd; they weren't necessary on a climate-controlled craft. But when Jenna started handing out snap guns in holsters designed to go under the arm, I realized why. "Are we expecting a problem?" Trisha asked

Jenna hesitated. "Well, there is an aspect to this mission that I have kept from you until now. The Norwegians don't exactly know the actual location of where we're being transported."

"For fucks sake! What do they think is gonna happen?" I asked, irritated.

"They think they're just transporting us to an American base," said McKenna.

"So, they're not exactly going to be willing to infiltrate the Peons?" Trisha rolled her eyes.

"No, not even a civilian vessel would be willing to break the neutrality of Norway," Jenna said.

"So what you're saying is, we're gonna have to take this ship by force," I put in.

"Exactly," said McKenna as she chambered a round.

"Boss," I said quietly. "It's tough to trust someone when that someone is shoving a pineapple up your arse. I wondered why we needed plausible deniability to attack a Peon base in the middle of a war. It's because of this, isn't it? We can't be seen to be attacking the Norwegians."

Jenna simply checked the magazine in her snap pistol, then holstered it. She looked at me and said, "You ready to go?"

Chapter Nine

Norwegian Air

I couldn't help but feel a pang of guilt as the airlock opened and the smiling face of a young woman welcomed us aboard in very broken English. I was surprised by how easily Jenna responded in a very relaxed manner. "Thank you very much for helping us out here. We had no idea how to continue our journey after our ship broke down. The Captain of the Kennedy did us a great favor getting us this far, but this is above and beyond."

"We are more than happy to help," she smiled as we entered the Norwegian ship.

Now I know what you're thinking. Openly confessing to attacking a Norwegian ship is gonna bring the Norwegians against us now. So, let me clear this up right now: this was not a Norwegian ship; I'm only using 'Norwegian' to provide a frame of reference. I'm not gonna divulge which nation's ship this actually was for obvious reasons.

This was probably the worst ship I had ever seen until I boarded the U.S.S. Lewis Puller. It was a reasonably large freight carrier, but most of its capacity was allocated to cargo, and the crew consisted of just six people. I realized then they didn't stand a chance against us, but I thought we could take them alive and upload them into the M.E.T. I soon found out they did not have any M.E.T. to upload to, so their fate was sealed. War brings out the worst in people, and I can't exclude myself from that truth. Whilst I carry many regrets, that doesn't alleviate my guilt for participating in various events over my career that I should never have been part of in the first place. But trust me, when you lose your country, you lose everything except the bitterness and anger you hold for the enemy.

The girl's name was Lucy, and she was a regular crew member who made her living hauling minerals between Earth and Io. There were too many of us for her to take up to the small bridge, so Jenna decided that it would just be her and McKenna. I followed along and glared at Jenna when she was about to protest.

As they walked onto the bridge, there stood an elderly man in command. He was past retirement age and had a cheery smile and bright eyes, but all that changed when Jenna casually pulled out her snap pistol and shot him in the chest. Lucy screamed as her commanding officer fell to the ground, gasping for breath – he expired shortly after. The scream didn't last long as McKenna stepped up to her; I couldn't see what had happened, but Lucy gurgled, her eyes staring wide-eyed before falling to the ground. I saw the blood as it spread across the front of her shirt. McKenna had stabbed her. I was disgusted with McKenna Anderson. Even now, I'm surprised by how close we would become later on.

The pilot scrambled from his seat, but he didn't get very far before Jenna shot him, too. She then appeared to activate a communicator in her ear and said just one word, "Go!" She then turned to me and asked, "Can you fly this thing?"

I stared at her in disbelief, my eyes wide with shock. "Hell, Jen, you're seriously one heartless motherfucker."

"Can you fly this thing?" she repeated.

I stepped over the controls, ignoring the body on the ground just in front of them. "Sure, you'll just need to give me two years to learn Norwegian. These aren't even remotely similar to either the American or Australian designs."

"Could you do it if we could change the language?"

"Sure, as long as it's English." Again, I turned to humor as my refuge from stress.

Jenna once more concentrated on her internal communication device. "Tracker, get up here."

Not having one of these American internal communication devices in my ear, I didn't hear her reply. Still, Jenna indicated that she was on her way, and about a minute later, Tracker entered the bridge.

"How's it going out there?" Jenna asked.

Tracker looked as sick as I felt before replying. "All objectives are being met without resistance."

Jenna simply nodded and said, "We need you to work on the computer system and switch it over to something Stacey can understand."

"On it." Tracker glanced down at the body and winced. I don't know why I was so concerned about her squeamishness when my own was running rampant.

McKenna rolled her eyes and came over to us. She grabbed the body by the collar and dragged it away. I switched on the mental autopilot I used when colleagues were killed. That "couldn't care less bitch mode" was necessary for survival in extreme situations. Tracker slipped into the seat next to me and tapped away at the console. Putting a small device from the pouch on her belt into some slot, she sat back. "It'll take a while for my program to hack the system. It was designed predominantly for European vessels, but I didn't have time to convert it to Norwegian."

"We have time," Jenna stated.

I didn't know what to think. Fuck! I wanted a total genocide of every European as payback for each and every one of the Australians they had killed. Surely if this was the cost of achieving that ultimate goal, maybe... Ugh, maybe I don't fucking have the answers. I mean, what do you expect from me here? I'm no psychologist or philosopher. I can't explain the human psyche. All I can tell you is what happened and how I played my part.

I pulled myself from my thoughts and turned around to see that Jenna had left the bridge with Anderson, and it was just Tracker and me. I went to say something to her, but the words never came. Eventually, I just slipped out of the chair and slunk out of the bridge with my tail between my legs.

Harper was in quite a state when I found her. She was sitting on the floor in a small storage room, her knees drawn up to her chest. It took almost an hour to find her, and I admit I was a little pissed off that I had to search. She looked up at me as I entered with tear-stained eyes. "They weren't even armed, Stace."

"I know," I said, sliding down on the floor against the wall in front of her.

"They just shot them," she said, her voice weak and trailing off at the end.

"I know it doesn't make it any better, but we didn't have a choice. If we kept them as prisoners, we'd be detected when we landed on Pallas, and our cover would be blown before we had a chance to complete the mission."

"Fuck the mission," she muttered.

I let out a long sigh, rested my head against the wall, and closed my eye. "If we don't keep going, then it was all for nothing. I know that doesn't make it better, and I know you wish you could have done something to stop it. I do too, but I think it means we have to make sure this mission counts for something. Think about the lives we could save instead of the ones we've lost." At the sound of her sobbing, I opened my eye, got up, and slid over beside her. I placed my arm around her shoulder and pulled her to me. She rested her head on my chest as her body convulsed. "Just let it out, mate, and move on." We remained there for about thirty minutes until a ship-wide announcement told me to return to the bridge. I got up and held my hand out to Harper. She took it, and I helped her to her feet. Hand in hand, we went back up to the bridge, only letting go before we entered.

Tracker looked delighted with her work as I slipped into the pilot seat. Jenna looked at my companion. "Are you not going to take your seat, Miss Harper?" she indicated the co-pilot's chair.

"I'm a gunner, Lieutenant Plural," she said sarcastically. "Not a lot of point sitting in that chair, considering this vessel doesn't have any weapons.

"Sorry, I forgot. I'll call McFarland."

"That won't be necessary," I said as my hands darted over the controls. "I'm already locked onto Pallas if that's what you wanted."

"It is."

"Then I'm ready to engage thrusters at your order. Stand by for the maximum speed this hunk of junk can achieve."

"Kindly proceed, Miss Grant."

I set the controls to engage. The acceleration took several days to reach maximum speed, so it took another couple of weeks to arrive at the dwarf planet.

"Course laid in. We're on our way." I turned to face Jenna, "If this ship was never scheduled to arrive at Pallas, how are we meant to explain its arrival?"

Anderson replied, "I won't go into details, but Charlotte Kensett made arrangements to supply the Peon base via one of her spooks. She's successfully faking this ship as the source – the crew doesn't know it, but the Peons are expecting them."

"Quite the devious little sheila, ain't she, Mac?" However, McKenna gave no response – neither verbal nor otherwise.

The one thing that pleased me was that the Americans never expected us to deal with the bodies. I have no idea what they did with them to this day. I can only assume they did what they always did with enemy combatants: threw them out of the airlock. There aren't exactly many places on a ship for storing bodies. However, we do our best to retrieve our fallen so we can give them a decent burial.

We kept ourselves to ourselves. The only difference this time was that Trisha took a separate room from Harper and me. The only reason I shared with Harper again was that she didn't want to be alone, but we had to share a bed because there was only one in each room. I know what you're thinking, but we just slept together... Wait. That doesn't sound right. Oh fuck it, ya dirty-minded bastards, you know what I mean. This one night, she was snoring so loudly that I couldn't sleep, so I gave up and headed off to the small mess hall. It was about the same size as the one on the Lewis Puller. The most irritating thing, though, was that there wasn't a drop of alcohol on this ship. What the fuck the Norwegians did for entertainment, I'll never know. So, instead, I made some coffee, sat down, and stared at it. I was probably there for about 20 minutes when someone else came in; Jason Richards was one of the last-minute recruits from the Kennedy. An army sergeant to replace Timberlake. "Oh! Hi, I wasn't expecting anyone to be in here."

"Well, mate, that's a coincidence because I wasn't expecting anyone to come and disturb me."

"I can leave if you want," he said without a hint of malice.

"Don't let the door hit you in the arse on the way out," I replied.

"Ah, well, now I feel a little bit awkward."

I looked up at him, wanting to wipe that smile off his face. "What?"

"Well, I was only being polite when I said I'd leave. I had no intention of leaving."

Now that was actually funny. This bloke had a sense of humor like mine. I chuckled and smiled back at him. "Don't just stand there like some giant, fucking lump. Get yourself a coffee and sit your arse down."

He grinned back at me and went to pour himself a cup. "Well, I can tell you're one of the Australians. Sorry, I don't know which one you are, though."

"Well, aren't you just a regular old Sherlock Holmes? I can only assume it was my good looks that gave away I'm Australian."

He chuckled lightly. "You're Stacey Grant, I presume?"

"Well, color me impressed. But I mean, you did have a one in three chance of getting that right."

"Well, my odds were a bit better than that. There was a lot of talk about a mouthy Aussie called Stacey Grant, and well...."

I laughed so hard I snorted embarrassingly. "And what, I'm the only mouthy Aussie bitch you've encountered?"

"Well, I wouldn't have put it quite so indelicately," he grinned, sitting down at the table opposite me.

"To be honest, mate, I'm not exactly great company at the moment. But it's up to you if you wanna hang out."

"I'm just here for the coffee, which you made too weak, by the way."

"What did your last maid die of? Make some your bloody self if you don't like it."

"No, this will do."

"Then stop whining, ya sook, and just bloody drink it."

He took another sip while studying me carefully. "There's one thing I am curious about, though."

"What?"

"What the hell is a sook?"

"Umm, it's another word for a crybaby," I replied.

"An interesting culture you have," he smiled

"Are you taking the piss?" I said, narrowing my eyes at him.

He raised his hands toward me in surrender. "Not at all."

"I think I might like you. But listen here, if you want to stay in Auntie Stacey's good books, make sure you don't."

"I'm half Australian," he said, taking me completely by surprise.

"What?"

"It's true. My mom is from Alice Springs," he insisted.

"Well, you sound red, white, and blue to me," I responded doubtfully.

"I am. My dad's from Chicago, where I was born and raised. Never once set foot in Oz."

"Why not?"

"I don't know, just never got around to it, I guess. I lost my mom when I was a kid, so I never really knew her."

"Aww, sorry to hear that, mate. I grew up in Wagga Wagga with my dad and brother. He was divorced from my mom, who lived in Melbourne."

"You're kidding me, aren't you?" he laughed.

"Kidding? About what?"

"*Wagga Wagga*. Surely that isn't actually the name of a real place."

"Fuck you, mate. Wagga is the best place on Earth. I'd rather live there than anywhere else in the bloody solar system."

"Sorry, that's just a very unusual name."

I shrugged. "So I've been told. But where I come from, it's pretty normal."

The intercom came online before anything else could be said. "Sorry to wake you, Stacey. You're needed on the bridge."

I sighed and put my coffee cup down. I walked over and hit the intercom button. "No worries, Boss, I was awake anyway.

I'm on my way up." And I turned back to Richards. "It was really nice talking to you. Maybe we can do it again sometime."

He smiled up at me, and there was a twinkle in those blue eyes. "I think I'd like that too."

I nodded and headed up to the bridge, where I found Jenna and Anderson. Anderson was looking as passive as ever. Meanwhile, Jenna was looking concerned. "The ship's system has alerted us that a Peon ship is in the vicinity. Not entirely unexpected, considering we're in European-controlled space. However, it's changed course and headed in our direction."

I slipped into the pilot chair to confirm her information for myself. The frigate was about six hours out. "It might have been a smart move to bring someone who could speak French to at least try and bluff them," I said in a somewhat condescending tone.

"Give us some credit, Stacey. We have a fluent French speaker."

"Who?"

"Sergeant Jason Richards. His mother is French, and she lived in Louisiana when the war started."

Chapter Ten

Parlez Vous Anglais?

Turning back to the ship's controls, I tried to work out why Jason had just lied to me. I mean, it's not that it was some life-altering lie or anything. I was just irritated that he felt the need to lie at all. I turned my attention back to the task at hand and began sending scans. I felt a hand grip my shoulder, and I spun around. "It's against Peon law to scan the military vessels. You are drawing unnecessary attention to us," McKenna snapped.

"Look, Papa Grant didn't raise no idiot. I sent it out behind a tachyon field, so it appears we have a very minor and completely harmless leak, as far as the Peons are concerned. And if you don't take your meaty paw off my shoulder right now, I'll break it off and beat ya with it."

"I'm sorry," she said, embarrassed, and then she stepped back. I looked up at Jen, who grinned at me.

"What have you got for me, Stacey?"

"Well, we certainly mistook the model. It looks like a Lyon-class frigate, but it's just a scout ship, part of the military. Its job is simply to search for hazards in heavy-traffic areas. It's unarmed with a crew complement between eight and twelve."

Jen frowned. "How could you possibly know all of this just from a scan?"

I laughed. "I don't. I know from the scan that it's a B-class scout ship, and I know what a B-class scoutship is from my time working with the A.S.I.S."

"You were in intelligence?" McKenna asked in surprise.

"For a couple of years," I winked. "Until I got my wings anyway. "

"So, why is it coming toward us then?" Jen asked

"Probably just checking us out. If we don't do anything, it'll probably just pass on by. The real danger is if they decide they want to say, 'g'day.'"

Jen turned to McKenna for her input, and she replied, "I concur. The only real danger to us is if we screw up contact. If we do, there's not much they can physically do to us, but if they tell their friends about it, then we're in real danger. If we raise even the slightest suspicion, it's game over."

"And in this old bucket of bolts, there's no way we'd get back to Earth or even a safe base before they sent something up from Pallas to catch us," I added.

Jen hit the intercom on the wall, "Sergeant Richards, would you come to the bridge, please?"

Minutes later, Jason Richards entered and raised a questioning eyebrow at me as I glared at him. Jen quickly apprised him of what was happening. With a nod of understanding, he slipped into the seat next to me. "Okay, how do I turn the inter-ship communication system on?"

I reached over, flicked a couple of switches, and tuned to the Peons' frequency. I was unsure if I imagined it, but I swear I felt him sniff my hair as I reached past him!! I sat back, nodding to him. A beaming smile spread across his face as he looked ahead at the stars out of the forward window. "Bonjour, mon ami." That was about all I understood as he gabbled away cheerfully; an equally cheerful voice responded to him, and he spoke some more, and then they both laughed. This carried on for six or seven minutes as we waited tensely for the conversation to end. Finally, he nodded to me, and I disconnected the communications. He spun around in his chair to face Jen."They were concerned because we were off our recorded course, but when they detected a tachyon leak, they concluded we must have an engine problem. They offered to come aboard and help, but I told him that our engineer was working on it and not to worry. It was only minor."

"Why would he think we were off course?"

I fielded this question. "The Norwegians probably had a specific flight plan that was logged with E.U. Command so that people can't do what we've just done."

"There has clearly been a failure on behalf of our intelligence," McKenna freely admitted. "My apologies."

"No worries, mate," I smiled. "It's only a mistake that could have gotten us all killed. Nothing to worry about at all."

"That's enough," Jenna interceded before McKenna could reply. "The only one here with authority to chastise anyone for mistakes is me." She looked at Jason, "So what's our status, Richards?"

"We are all clear. They've even logged our current course as the new flight plan with E.U. Command. We've been given clearance to go through their security perimeter."

Jen grinned. "Nice work, Richards. I'd give you a damn medal, but I don't have the authority to."

"Well, it's thought that counts," Richards grinned.

"I can confirm that the scoutship has resumed its original course," I informed them.

"We could go and finish that coffee now, Stacey?" he smiled with those damn sparkly eyes.

I slipped out of my chair, looked him dead in the eye, and I said, "Gee, thanks, Sarge. But I think I'd rather shit in my hands and clap."

I strode out of the room under a look of utter bewilderment from Jenna and headed down the corridor.

"Hey, Stacey, wait up," I heard Jason say behind me as he chased me down the hall and caught up. "What's the matter? Did I do something wrong?"

"Why don't you go and ask your mother that question?" I said without turning around, then continued striding down the corridor. "I think you'll find her in New Orleans or some other town in Louisiana... Where she lives."

"Ah!" he said softly. "The penny drops."

"Then it should come as no surprise when I tell you that you can fuck off."

"Stacey, I'm sorry. But you were being pretty cold toward me, and I just wanted to find a way to get you to like me. It was wrong, and I'm sorry, but ...."

I stopped and turned, looking up at him with disdain. "So what you're saying is that you're telling me about your dead mother was your smooth move to get into my undies? You really are a moron." Before he could respond, I turned back around and continued my stride until I reached outside the elevator and hit the button.

"I know, I know. It was really stupid of me, but please, just hear me out."

The door opened, and I stepped in, and just as I had done with the guard in Nevada, I blocked his entrance. "Come on, Stacey, give me a chance."

As the doors began to close, I said, "You can start to make it up to me by making me breakfast in the morning and coffee the way I like it," and I caught sight of his grin as the door shut.

For the first time since Cape York, I slept well and had some quite pleasant dreams. I woke late, but it was to the sounds of screams from Harper. I ran out of my room in nothing but my underwear and the snap gun Jen had given me in my hand.

Harper stood there shouting at someone in our small kitchenette; she, too, was in nothing but her undergarments. As I raced to her side, I heard the distinctive voice of Jason Richards. "I'm sorry, I'm so sorry. I didn't know Stacey shared a room. I was just trying to make her breakfast." That's when I smelled bacon and eggs cooking on the stovetop.

I dropped the gun to my side and stood in the doorway, staring at him, half amused. "I meant in the mess room, not my quarters."

"I'm sorry," he blushed.

"You know this pervert?" Harper asked me incredulously.

"Yes, unfortunately. Harper, meet Richards. Richards, Harper."

"Hi," he said weakly and gave a little wave.

Harper just glared at him. She then turned to me and said curtly, "I'm going to take a shower and put some clothes on."

I chuckled as she stormed off. "You are such a bloke," I said and walked off to my room. I quickly pulled on some cargo pants and slipped a T-shirt over my head. Not my usual style, but it was quick. When I returned to the kitchenette, I noticed that he had the good sense to make a third place setting. He looked at me with puppy-dog eyes, which I found strangely attractive. As a general rule, he was so not my type; I preferred my men to be muscle-bound and hung like horses. I mean, it wasn't that he wasn't well built; he was, but that babyface was hard to get past.

With his sparkling blue eyes, he had that surfer boy look with a touch of innocence. He was certainly attractive, but did he attract me? I wasn't so sure. He had his back to me, tending to the frying pan when I re-entered. I leaned on the counter and just watched him for a moment. I pondered whether I wanted to fuck him or not. To be honest, I didn't look at him the way I looked at most guys. I liked him for sure, but I felt like I wanted more than just a good rooting from this guy. I've never really felt that way before. For all but the first four years of my life, we'd been at war. My entire adult life has been spent at war. The men I lived and worked with died or risked dying every single day. Relationships were just too risky. Heartbreak was just a bullet away. It simply wasn't worth getting into anything too serious. He was startled to see me standing there looking at him as he turned around with the pan. He smiled and began dishing out the contents onto the plates. "There's some disgustingly weak coffee in the pot over there if you want to go get some."

I grinned at him as I stepped over and poured a mug for myself. He noticed what I'd done and just rolled his eyes. We smiled at each other as I climbed up on the stool in front of the counter. He pushed a plate toward me, and as he stood on the other side of the counter. I picked up the fork he had laid out for us and started playing with the food.

"Eat it while it's hot," he said, pointing to my plate with this fork. I placed my fork back down and picked up a rasher of bacon with my fingers. It was dry and crispy. "American-style bacon. "

"Bacon's good. However, you cook it."

I took a bite. It wasn't bad, but hell, if I was gonna make it easy for him. "Meh, if you say so."

He didn't rise to the bait, which made him all the more endearing. "That's fine. More for me, I guess," and he reached over to take the bacon from my plate. I slapped his hand hard, and he pulled it away sharply.

"I didn't say I wasn't going to eat it, did I?"

Before he could say anything, Harper reappeared dressed in a tracksuit and flopped down on the seat next to me. "Good. Breakfast," she said, and grabbed up a fork as if having a total stranger see you half-naked in your own quarters was completely normal. Or inviting yourself to have breakfast with two people who clearly had made plans to have breakfast alone was also normal. We both stared at her in disbelief, then looked at each other and grinned again. She appeared to be clueless that the decent thing to do would be to leave us alone, but I knew better. Harper had a thing for me, and those feelings weren't going away anytime soon. She was completely jealous, and she used that jealousy to be an ever-present cockblocker when it came to guys and me. So we played along with her game. There wasn't anything we could do about it anyway. We were all set to enter Peon space any minute, which meant it would be all work and no play from here on out. If anything happened between Richards and me, it'd have to happen after the mission. When breakfast was over, I left Harper and Richard talking and went to take a shower. I changed into my usual white skirt and boots, paired with a matching pullover, before rejoining them in the kitchen.

The three of us headed up to the bridge. Even though Harper wasn't required, I brought her along anyway. Jen was there, as always. It was as if she had never left the bridge.

"We just entered Peon restricted space. We should be hearing from them any minute," she told us.

I slipped into my seat, and Jason sat in the seat next to me. Harper went and stood beside Jen.

It was still impossible to see Pallas with the naked eye, even at this close range. The asteroid was barely a thousand kilometers across. The closer we got, the more Peon ships entered our radar range. Most appeared to be freight vessels, and there was the usual contingent of military vessels securing the space around one of their colonies. The tension on the bridge was so high that barely a word was spoken during the next couple of hours. The only thing that broke the monotony was when Jen called down for coffee to be brought up to us. I'd barely taken a sip when the intercom beeped, and we all sat up. I looked to Jason, who nodded, and I switched on the intercom. He didn't have time to speak before a flurry of words I didn't understand came at us. It was harsh and more formal this time, but Jason maintained his cheery Peon persona. He blathered away, his face giving nothing away about how it was going. Eventually, the radio went off again, and I disconnected our communications. Jason sat back in his seat and took a deep breath. "Clear skies," he grinned. "We are cleared to proceed, and we don't need to pass any more checkpoints until we prepare for landing on Pallas." We all breathed a collective sigh of relief.

"Excellent. I want everyone to meet in the cargo area to discuss our next steps." Jen turned to Harper, "I need someone to stay here and maintain a listening watch. Would you be willing to do that, Miss Harper?"

"Yes, Ma'am," she replied, although she looked a little put out by being left out of the meeting and glanced at me. I just shrugged in response and followed Jenna.

She turned the meeting over to McKenna Anderson in the cargo area. "The most dangerous part of our landing will be getting out of the port. We will be expected to begin unloading cargo. This is something we will do just as if we were a freighter, so we don't raise any suspicions. The problem will come if anyone tries to speak to anyone other than Sergeant Richards. If they do, do not panic. We're supposed to be Norwegian, and English is the common language. If you're spoken to, give simple answers or indicate that you don't understand if you can't. Even the trace of an American or even Australian accent, and it is game over. I cannot stress the seriousness of the first few hours in Pallas. If we're rumbled before we get out of the docking area, we won't survive. You all need to go through the former crew's clothes. "Dress appropriately, as if you were a laborer ready to work."

Trisha wrinkled up her nose. "That feels a little ghoulish if you ask me."

Jen actually smiled and cracked a joke. "Then it's a good thing I didn't ask you. Trust me, a lot worse will happen on this mission before it's over." When she said those words, I had no idea how accurate they would be.

McKenna continued. "Once the cargo is off the ship, we will not be expected to return to it until tomorrow and will be given free use of the facilities provided. That's when we will make our escape from the astrodome and into the base. We will be doing it in separate teams. I'm sorry, Stacey and Trisha, but I will have to separate you. We need to ensure that at least one of you survives to pilot the Starbourne."

Several hours later, we were back on the bridge. I was dressed in a pair of skinny jeans, a tank top, sneakers, and a baseball cap with the ship's name on it. Once more, Jason went through the communications with Pallas as I started to bring the ship down to the small planet. They were giving him instructions, and he typed them out on the screen in English for me to see.

I set the landing coordinates. I took us into a low orbit until we reached the large base. I then depowered the engines and switched over to the D.E. compensators. This allowed us to drift down rather than use retro jets. Slowly, beneath us, a large dome began to open, creating a large donut-shaped area of buildings with a central space for me to land. The whole procedure took about an hour – the approach would have been much faster in a modern military vessel. It all became too real for us, and finally, the buildings ahead came into view through the window. The ship shuddered slightly with a bump as we reached the ground. A whole bunch of jibber-jabber started up again on the comms.

"We have to wait for them to flood the bay with enough dark energy to simulate an Earth-type gravity," Jason informed us.

I sat back in the chair and stared out the window. Well, we had made it this far. We'd made it to Pallas and were sitting inside the enemy base.

Chapter Eleven

Exposed

I was the last to go down to the cargo bay to start the unloading. It was my job to open the ship's rear hatch from my bridge controls. So, by the time I arrived, everyone was already using D.E. lifters to transport huge mineral containers in gravity-defying fashion. I pulled my cap down low over my eyes, not because I was expecting someone to recognize me. Rather, I wanted to ensure I didn't draw attention to myself by looking at someone. Jason stood near the entrance, barking out commands as if he were the boss. Jen and Mac stayed near him, blocking access and preventing any Peons from getting close to us. A couple of Peon troopers with rifles came up, checked us out, showed little interest, and then wandered off. Port workers came to help us secure the containers and pulled them out into the bay, where others would pick them up and transport them to their designated storage locations. It was an intense two hours of labor, adrenaline pumping through our veins every minute, exhausting us as we feared we'd give ourselves away. One guy tried to flirt with Trisha, and she feigned not understanding until Jason came over and chased him out; we then managed to relax a little. Eventually, the cargo bay was empty, and Jason had to go up into the Control Center and sign off on the paperwork. Those next few minutes felt like hours as we half expected him not to return or see Peon troopers running out and gunning us all down where we stood.

When we saw Jason emerge from the doorway, we breathed a sigh of relief. "How did it go?" Jen asked quietly.

"All's well except for one minor snag," he replied reluctantly.

"Which is?" Jen narrowed her eyes.

"The sector chief wants me to meet her for drinks tonight," he said as he looked suitably embarrassed.

"And you didn't decline?" Jen asked incredulously.

"I didn't have an excuse to. I'd just asked her if we could use the recreational facilities. She knew I wasn't busy when I asked that. I couldn't exactly risk pissing her off by turning her down and embarrassing her."

McKenna shrugged. "Okay. Well, this is as far as Jason goes. However, it could be a good distraction. Do you think you can get her into bed?"

"Wait on a minute," Jason's eyes narrowed. "We plan to leave this planet on the Starbourne. If this is as far as I'm going, are you telling me I'm not leaving with you?"

McKenna shrugged, "I see no alternative."

"Whoa there," I said, stepping up to them. "That is not going to happen."

"I don't think that's your call, Miss Grant," McKenna said curtly.

"So you don't wanna hear an alternative," I argued aggressively.

"Go for it, Stacey," Jen instructed.

"Let him go on this date and then have his wife turn up."

Jason cursed. "Damn it. I should have said I was married, but she took me by surprise."

"And who exactly is going to be this wife?" McKenna said coolly. "You? You can't speak French."

"As you already pointed out, I don't need to," I said in my best Norwegian accent.

"Do you think she'll pass?" Jen asked Jason.

"Hard to say, but I prefer this option over Mac's."

"Fine, we'll give it a go," Jen said, albeit reluctantly.

As the rest of the team prepared to head out of the ship, McKenna came over to me. "Would you come with me a moment?" she asked, and with considerable curiosity, I obliged. She took me to her quarters, lifted a small duffel bag she had brought with her, and reached inside. She removed a compact little gun, even smaller than a snap pistol. "I don't want you to go in there unarmed," she said and handed me the weapon. It looked and felt unusual – all white and shiny. "It's made of porcelain and only holds three point 22 rounds. It won't show up on the detection systems."

I studied the weapon carefully, then slipped it into the folds of my jacket sleeve. "Thanks, mate. But why the sudden nervousness?

McKenna shrugged and shook her head. "I don't know. I can't put my finger on it. It's just that something doesn't feel right, and I have learned to trust my gut instincts over the years. Hopefully, you won't need to use it, though."

I thanked her again, and we returned to the others.

Jason and I stayed behind. I relaxed a little as I returned to the bridge and closed the vessel's back door. Jason joined me a few minutes later with a pot of coffee and a sandwich. "Hell yeah. Thanks, mate, I'm starving," I said and stuffed half the sandwich into my mouth. He poured me a cup of coffee and then sat down in the co-pilot seat. "So what do you think, Stacey? You think we're going to pull this off?"

"We don't have any other choice, mate. I intend to be on the frontline of the counter-invasion of Oz," I shrugged and took a mouthful of my coffee. "I can't very well do that if I die in the back end of space."

Jason laughed. "Well, that would certainly be inconvenient. It'll be interesting to see you piloting with such an advanced fighter."

Something about what he said didn't sit well with me, but I couldn't put my finger on why. Something in the back of my mind made me think what he said was odd, but I shrugged it off, putting it down to the tension of the current situation.

"You'll probably regret it. They're gonna send everything after us." I finished the sandwich, and we chatted casually for the next couple of hours until evening drew in. Well, I say 'evening,' but places like this operate on an odd day or night schedule, following Earth time. In this case, we were running on Paris time. The time for his date arrived, and he headed out. "I'm gonna give you an hour before I come in protesting about where my husband is," I told him.

He smiled back at me, then he took a step toward me, and before I knew it, he was kissing me. Not that mad passionate type of kiss you'd get with an impending rooting, but gentle and caring. I felt my heart beating faster and the weird sensation of butterflies in my stomach. He then pulled back, gave me a wink, and headed out of the airlock without another word, leaving me speechless. A sensation I was none too familiar with.

An hour later, I stormed out of the airlock, shouting and carrying on with my fake Norwegian accent, enjoying the attention of those around me as I headed to the Command Center. A guard blocked my way, but was startled when I launched a tirade of expletives and cries about my cheating bastard of a husband. He got onto his radio and called up to the commander, but instead of a berated-looking Jason coming out, the guard told me to go inside. To my surprise, as I stepped inside, I found myself surrounded by guards with their rifles aimed at me. Slowly, I raised my hands, realizing something had gone terribly wrong.

They led me up to the commander's office, where she was seated at a desk, Jason Richard standing at her side. At the commander's wave, the guards departed, a decision that would turn out to be the biggest mistake of her career.

"I'm sorry, Stacey," Jason said disingenuously.

I was confused for a moment, but as I saw the smile on the stern-looking commander's face, it all sank in. "I am one dumb bitch," I muttered.

Jason shrugged and smiled at me. "Not as dumb as Harper."

I rolled my eyes. "What did she do this time?"

"She told me of your intent to pilot the Starbourne while you were in the shower." He grinned.

"Right. I knew there was something odd when he talked to me about that. You gave yourself away, and I didn't even notice. Jenna's 'need to know.' You only need to know how to get up there and protect us. You didn't need to know what we intended to do while here. Yet, clearly, you did."

"Well, Grant, we've known for some time the Americans intended to infiltrate Pallas," intoned the commanding officer. "We thought your plan was a simple act of sabotage where you were intended to blow up the Starbourne. We never thought the Americans would have the audacity or the courage to try and actually steal it."

"Well, they probably couldn't do it on their own, which is why they needed us Aussies, mate." I looked back at Jason. "So what's in it for you?"

"What can I say?" Jason narrowed his eyes. "They arrested my French mother and put her in an internment camp. Let's just say my loyalty to the United States has severely diminished."

"But you weren't even on this mission. You were back up."

"It was easy, really. When E.U. Command learned that you were going to attempt to land on Pallas, I simply rigged the M.E.T. to degrade the pattern of the only two members of your team who could speak French. And as luck would have it, that left me, the only Marine in the Kennedy crew who could speak French. I was the obvious choice for replacement."

"But that doesn't make sense. If you knew we were coming, why didn't you just stop us before we got here?"

"Because we didn't know when you were coming," the commander said, sounding quite smug. "We found out about a year ago that you were considering this, so we just played the waiting game. Plus, there's Jenna Plural."

"What about her? She's just some Lieutenant."

Jason laughed at this. "Is that really what you think? Jenna Plural is a United States Marine Corps veteran who has served for over a hundred years. She currently serves with the Department of Intelligence. She's a veritable walking encyclopedia of classified information. We knew if we let her land here, we'd have the perfect opportunity to capture her."

"So, all that hitting on me was just to find out information," I asked coldly.

"Sorry," but his grin clearly showed he was anything but sorry. "It could have been a whole lot worse."

I narrowed my eyes. "How?"

"I didn't have to sleep with you like I thought I would. Who knows what diseases you have up there, considering your reputation as an insatiable slut. I have to thank Harper for that when we pick her up."

I laughed, but inside I was seething with anger. He had played me for a fool, and now he'd just insulted me. "You are a funny man, Jason Richards. Do you wanna know something even funnier?"

"And what pray tell is that?" he said confidently.

"You don't fuck with a girl from Wagga," I reached into the sleeve of my jacket and drew the small, undetectable porcelain firearm. I shot the commander straight between the eyes. It hit her with sufficient force that she tipped back in her chair and went down on the ground, instantly dead. Jason backed up against the window, raising his hands and trying to stop me. "Stacey, wait."

"Au revoir, motherfucker," and I fired a round into his chest. He staggered, his eyes wide with fear and surprise, but as I had hoped, he wasn't quite dead yet. "Just so you know, when I get out of here, I'm going to find your Peon whore of a mother in that internment camp. I'm going to take with me a dozen sex-starved veterans and let them fuck her motherfucking brains out." It was a lie. I wouldn't do that even to a damn Peon. I wanted him to suffer for not only betraying us but also for humiliating me. I fired my final round, messing up that handsome face, and he went down. I turned around and quickly locked the door because, within seconds, the Peon guards were pounding on it. Their own security measures screwed them as I stood safe and sound behind their steel security door. I stepped over to the bodies and searched the commander, and removed her standard-issue officer's pistol from its holster. Then, for good measure, I strapped the holster to my thigh and slipped the weapon inside. It gave me just twelve rounds. Not much, but it had to do.

I pulled the radio off the back of Jason's belt and spat in his face for good measure. His dead eyes stared up at me; they no longer had that dreamy sparkle.

"Eagle to Mama Bear," I said, making up the names on the spot.

Jen came on the radio, and I breathed a sigh of relief that she hadn't already been picked up. I could tell from her tone that she was concerned that I was breaking radio silence. "Go ahead, Eagle."

"Richards betrayed us. He was working for the Peons. We've been made, and they're coming for you."

All she said in reply was surprisingly calm. "Roger and out."

I had no fucking clue how I was gonna get out of here. Two walls had windows. And I looked out of both, deciding which was the best possible ascent. I was on the third floor, so I couldn't exactly jump. While I'd most likely survive it, I wouldn't be unscathed. Plus, there were a hell of a lot of Peons down there, even if I couldn't see them from this vantage point.

So, I shot the window and dived to the ground as it ricocheted off. Obviously, they had toughened glass in an environment where decompression could occur at any time. I started to study the frames. I noticed they had emergency seals that would pop out in case of a fire within the office. The pounding on the door stopped, which scared me more than anything. It meant they had thought of something because they certainly wouldn't have given up. I wondered if there was any possible way to start a fire, but there was nothing, so instead, I climbed on a chair, whacking one of the sprinkler devices with the butt of the gun, hoping it would at least set off the alarm system and disorient those motherfuckers outside. It did better than that.

Soft, white, soapy foam spread over me and made me fall from the chair, which probably saved me from injury, as the windows popped out of their frames and some fell inward, one just missing where I had been standing moments before. I grinned, but not for long, as I heard the door's bolts automatically unlock. In a second, I was up on my feet and running to the window, and I jumped out onto the ledge just as a bullet whistled past me from inside. I spun around and looked up. Up was the way I had to go because only death awaited me below. I jumped up, grabbed onto the edge of the roof, and pulled myself up as I felt a bullet hit my sneaker. I prayed to whatever God that it had not gone through my foot, and I just couldn't feel the pain yet. As I hauled myself up onto the roof, I looked down at it. It had just grazed the rubber on the side, fortunately. Unfortunately, the roof was convex, and I had difficulty finding any grip with my shoes. But, after a lot of scrabbling, I managed to make it to the top, where it was a little more flattened out. A shot rang out, and I turned to see a Peon scrambling up on the roof to follow me. I pulled out my gun and fired. I missed, but he lost his footing and quickly disappeared. I heard him scream, followed by a distant thud.

I didn't wait around for more. I ran along the roof and jumped the small gap between two buildings. I found a ventilation shaft, but it went straight down, and I wasn't stupid. A drop down a ventilation shaft or drop off the side of the building, same difference – I'd go splat. I looked up, but above me was just the closed dome that opened out onto the Pallas sky. Behind me, I saw two Peons in pursuit, but they were too unbalanced to take aim and fire at me, so I ran and jumped to another building and another vent. This time it was slanted, but only slightly, and I'd still go down too fast.

I climbed in. Pushing my feet up against one wall, my back against the other, I very carefully tried to 'walk' down. I pressed my back against the wall and slowly moved down. About ten feet down, the wall curved even more, making it a little easier to navigate. It had the added benefit of preventing anyone from shooting down at me from above as I moved out of sight of the opening. Then all hell broke loose, and my heart leapt into my mouth as I lost my footing and began sliding rapidly down. I held my breath as I waited for impact at the bottom. Fortunately, it started to curve more sharply, and I began slowing in my descent until, finally, I slid to a stop. I waited momentarily to catch my breath before turning onto my hands and knees and crawling along the shaft.

I looked through various vents as I passed them, but they all led into warehouses or factories. I continued along, hoping for something less entrapped. Eventually, I heard voices and grew nervous as I approached the vent. I saw what looked like a Parisian street. Or rather, an alley that led out into a main street. People were passing by the alley, but no one was actually in it. I pushed my back up against the back of the shaft and drew up my legs, ready to kick out the vent. No matter what I did, it would be heard, but people might be unsure where the noise came from if I got it all at once. It was a gamble, but I had nothing to lose. Getting lost in a crowd of people would be the best cover I could find. I took a deep breath and held it, then slammed my feet as hard as possible. It buckled and popped out, and I swiftly climbed out of the shaft. I cursed as I saw that the vent cover was now twisted. I'd wanted to put it back so they didn't know where I'd come out, but here it was, practically a neon sign showing exactly where I had gone. I unfastened the holster from my leg and strapped it to my arm, inside my jacket, to hide it from view. Then, sinking my hands into my pockets, I strolled out casually into the street.

It looked like any street in Paris, except that the sunlight was artificial. When I looked up at the sky, the large dome was black as night, and the stars shone brightly. I could even make out the dim and distant sun. People were going about their day just as if they were on Earth, enjoying this little replica of their home. I walked past a couple of streets, trying not to move too fast but not so slow that I stopped putting distance between myself and my exit. I turned down a smaller road and emerged onto another large one. This time, it had a row of bars and clubs. I had no clue where I was or where I should be. I was lost and alone.

Chapter Twelve

Starbourne

I wanted to call up Jenna. I didn't know what situation they were in. Had they been captured? Would my call reveal my location or theirs?

I couldn't keep wandering around the streets until someone picked me up for vagrancy or something and found out who I was. I headed down another alleyway and hid in a recessed doorway. I pulled out the radio and switched the sender/receiver button on and off, knowing it would register a noise on the other side. I felt such relief when Jenna's voice returned, and she whispered, "Be brief."

"I'm on the run. I'm hiding in plain sight in some sort of commercial district. I don't know where to go."

"Head north. Contact me again when you can't go any further."

"Which way is north?" I asked, perplexed.

"Follow the stars."

I looked up at the sky. "Follow them where?

"You are an interplanetary pilot who didn't study astronomy? Never mind. If a road has an even number, it is heading north or south. If the numbers go up, you're heading north, and if it's an odd number, you're heading east or west. Contact me the same way you just did now when you can't go any further north. We will attempt to rendezvous with you."

I desperately wanted to ask about Harper and Trisha. Instead, I clipped the radio back onto my belt at the small of my back, under my jacket. I stepped out of the alley and looked up at the road sign. It was odd, so I turned around to head to the nearest junction, only to find myself a couple of yards from two gendarmes. I was about to turn the other way immediately, but realized that would draw their attention. Instead, I walked straight past them. One of them glanced at me but paid me no mind beyond that. I turned left onto Fourth Street and started checking the numbers – yes! I was finally going the right way. I continued along casually for about ten minutes, crossing at the intersections until I came to a dead-end that ended in a T-junction that intersected with Twenty-First Street. I reached behind my back as if I was scratching it and toggled the radio a couple of times. I walked further up Twenty-First Street until I was alone.

"What intersection are you at?" came Jenna's voice.

I pulled the radio out and said quickly, "Fourth and twenty-first."

"Okay. Continue along twenty-first, heading toward fifth. We aren't near you, so we cannot meet up, at least not without you waiting a long time. As you hit fifth, click the radio again. If you don't hear anything, continue to the sixth and so on." The radio went dead, and I slipped it back on my belt. Then the siren went off, and as a voice boomed out, everyone started ducking into shops and other buildings. Speaking French over a city tannoy system, I didn't understand it, but I was sure it was something to do with us. The way to get caught now was not to follow suit. I dashed into a doorway, opened the door, and found myself inside a designer clothes shop. A woman in French ushered me toward her, then passed me to pull the shutters down. She then turned back toward me again, and I found my accent once more and said, "I am sorry. I am Norwegian and do not speak French."

"They are looking for infiltrators. You must report to the High Command. All foreigners must be accounted for," she said in broken English as she looked at me nervously.

"But I'm too scared to go out there. What if I run into these bad people?" This seemed to alleviate some of her tension.

"Very well, you will stay here with me. I will call the High Command. I will let them know that you are here. What is your name?" She stepped over to the communication system, but when I didn't answer her question, she turned back to me and found she was facing my drawn gun. "Sit down, and you won't get hurt. There on the floor," I pointed in front of the counter with my weapon. As she nervously complied, I pulled the radio from my back and clicked it several times. No reply came, and I clicked it a couple more times.

"I see they've got a lockdown," Jenna said eventually. "Where are you?"

"I did what everyone else was doing and ran into a store. I'm somewhere between 4th and 5th."

"Okay, you have to get out of there and take your chances. That store will eventually be searched."

"I have another problem. I'm not alone."

"How many?"

"Just the one."

"Take her out."

"Take her out? How?" I asked uneasily.

Jenna responded coolly. "Aren't you armed?"

"Yes, I have a gun."

"Then shoot her, Stacey," Jenna said calmly.

"You're kidding, right?" I snapped back. "She's an unarmed civilian."

"I know it stinks, Stacey, but you cannot take any chances now. Despite everything, we are not aborting this mission. If this Starbourne goes online, thousands of lives will be at stake. We cannot leave anything to chance. Shoot her, Stacey. Shoot her now."

I released the button on the radio and looked at the terrified woman. "I'm sorry," I said weakly. Closing my eye, I fired a single round into her head. I quickly turned away, unable to look at her. I felt like throwing up on the floor then and there. I raised the radio again and clicked the button, "It's done."

"Okay, I have Tracker currently trying to hack into the camera system. We should be able to see where the search is going on. Be ready to move on my mark." Once more, the radio went dead. I found a nearby chair facing away from the dead woman, sat down, and waited, and waited. It was probably only about fifteen minutes, but it felt like hours. You might think I'm a coward, but I was terrified about being caught. When you're in a fight, that all switches off, but just waiting to be captured is another thing altogether. Then the radio came on. "Okay, Stacey, leave now. Turn right and move out to the sidewalk's edge so we can pick you up on camera. Fortunately, you've managed to make it a considerable distance from where you started. They're still searching the area where you first entered the city block."

I threw open the shutter and stepped out into the street. I turned right and cleared the sidewalk's edge as she had instructed. "Good, we can see you." *Whoop-de-Doo*, I thought. "You're going to need to make it about two blocks and then go down an alley, and there'll be another ventilation shaft. You are going to get in it and turn left. Keep going past the first two grates. You will find us at the next," and the radio went dead once more. I followed the instructions, but this time I ran. I ducked into the alley and saw the vent ahead, trying to work out how I would get through it. I pulled out the radio. "I can't open the vent. I was able to kick the other one out from the inside, but I'm outside now. I'll never be able to kick it in."

"Wait there," and the radio went dead again. I paced up and down the alley as I waited, and the minutes passed. I went to the edge of the alley and peered out. Several troopers were coming down the road, coming my way. Suddenly, I heard a crash of metal, and I turned back to see that the vent was off. I tried to see into the darkness of the shaft, but I couldn't make anyone out as I ran back to it. As I bent down, McKenna grabbed me by the collar and pulled me in just as the sound of a gunshot rang out. It pinged off the wall just above me, and I scrambled faster as McKenna reached past me and fired several rounds at the two soldiers running up the alleyway. She pushed me past her, shouting, "Keep going up that way." I scrambled along on my hands and knees as fast as I could. I stopped to look back and saw McKenna coming up behind me, but she was still quite a distance away. "Keep going! I set a timed limpet mine." There was a sudden loud explosion, and she shouted, "Get down." I lay flat on the ground as flames flashed over me. The flames were followed by the sounds of grinding metal and collapsing masonry. Then came the screams of someone who'd obviously been trapped in the explosion. "Keep moving. It will take them a while to clear that." I got up again and scrabbled onwards until she told me to stop near an already open vent. I started to climb out and realized we were high up near the ceiling. Tracker and Jenna ran over to me and helped me down, but McKenna waved them away as she jumped into the room. "Where are we?" I said, looking around at the banks of the machinery in the small, squat room.

"We are inside the military wing of the Peon base, not far from where the Starbourne is," Jenna advised me.

"Where are the others?"

Jenna shook her head. "I don't know. After we got your warning, we split up. Now, tell me, what happened exactly?"

"It was a setup from the start. The Peons knew we were coming. They just didn't know when. It turns out that Jason Richards was a sleeper agent embedded in the Kennedy crew. When he found out we were coming aboard the Kennedy, he sabotaged the MET, knowing that he'd be the only French speaker left aboard, and you'd have no choice but to select him to replace them."

"I should have been more suspicious. I just thought it was sheer bad luck that we lost both our French speakers."

"Yeah, well, his so-called "date" was just his opportunity to return to his own side. But I managed to throw a spanner in those works with our plan to have me interrupt his date."

"Where is he now?"

"Where do you think he is? That traitorous bastard's dead. I shot the fucker in the face, and I don't regret it one bit," I replied as if her question was dumb.

Jenna smiled at me. "Now that's one story you will have to tell me sometime. Right now, though, we have to get out of here."

"In case you missed it, Boss, there's this little thing called a lockdown right now," I said.

"Tracker is working on that," and Jenna led me over to where she was busily working.

Tracker looked up from the console and gave me a quick smile, and just as quickly, she was back to work. "What exactly is she gonna do, change all the traffic lights to green or something?" I muttered.

"This may surprise you to know, but Helen Tracker is considered one of the best technology engineers in the solar system. She's currently uploading a virus she designed herself that is about to send this base into utter chaos. Hopefully, that chaos will give us the time we need to make it to the Starbourne."

"And if we can stay concealed for another thirty minutes, I will make it happen," Tracker responded.

"You know, there isn't all this waiting around in the movies," I pointed out.

Jenna laughed and patted me on the back. "You know what? I am starting to like you, Stacey Grant."

I turned to McKenna, who was sitting on a counter, clearly much more patient than I was. "Thanks for saving my arse back there."

"You can thank me by flying that damned ship and saving all our arses," she grinned at me.

"I'll do my best," I said, hopping up on a counter and sitting down too.

After some time had passed, Jenna stepped over to Tracker. Leaning over her shoulder, she asked, "What's the holdup?"

"Back off, please," Tracker said, and Jenna complied, albeit with an impatient grunt. "They must have upgraded their code recently. It means I have to rewrite mine."

"But you can do it, can't you?"

Tracker's hands fell to her sides, and she turned and smiled. With a flourish of drama, she lifted her hand, pointed her index finger, and slammed it down onto the enter button on the keyboard. Suddenly, sirens began blaring; every siren, everywhere. Fire, air leak, chemical release, and earth tremor, and at the same time, every warning message sounded all at once in a wall of gibberish sounds, giving instructions about what to do next. Suddenly, the lights in the room began flickering on and off, blinking in random sequences. Tracker grinned like a kid who'd just pulled the old "pull my finger" gag. "That's going on in every room, on every street, and in every corner of this colony."

"Fuck me!" I laughed. "Helen, I would bend you over this counter and shag you into next Tuesday if I played for that team."

She looked at Jenna with a raised eyebrow. "Do I want to know what that means?"

Jenna chuckled. "No, Helen, you really don't. Now, come on. Let's move out." Jenna went ahead, and Tracker and I followed; the other Marine and Anderson brought up the rear. We moved down the corridor until we passed a large window, and looking out, we saw her. The Starbourne gleamed white and was inlaid with red, a humongous fighter plane bristling with guns. Far below, guards were running here and there, confused by what was happening. Jenna stuck a limpet mine on the glass and said, "Stand back," as she blew the window out. McKenna, pulling up her shirt, started to unwind a cable wrapped around her waist as Jenna pulled out what looked like a flare gun from under her jacket. She pulled a cylinder from the barrel, and McKenna tied the cable through a hole in one end. Jenna then shoved it back into the barrel and fired it into a walkway high up on the side of the Starbourne. McKenna held onto the end and tied it off around the now glassless window frame. Jenna then pulled off her belt, wrapped both ends around her wrists, looked at me, and said, "Get your belt and throw it over the cable and wrap it around your wrists as I have."

She said it so casually that I looked back up at her and said a lot less casually, "You can fuck right off, mate." I leaned out of the window and looked down at the long drop below. "You need to get your fucking head read if you think I'm gonna go across that wire like I'm some sort of fucking ancient superhero who leaps tall buildings in a single bound."

Jenna glared frustratedly at me. "There are two ways we can do this, Grant. The first is you go down just as I explained, or the second option – and right now my preference – I strap you to it myself and throw you down there."

"You're serious, aren't you?"

"Want to test me?" she glared viciously at me.

"Why don't you go first and show her how easy it is?" McKenna suggested.

"Because I have no guarantee that she'll do it once I'm down there," Jenna replied, still glaring at me.

"Okay, I'll do it," McKenna shrugged and pulled off her belt. She went down the zip line so fast that it didn't ease my nerves. But she landed at the bottom seemingly unscathed, bringing her knees up to her chest to reduce the impact. I looked back up at Jenna, wide-eyed.

"Stacey, we have to do this; lives depend on it. I thought you wanted to be on the frontline when we go back into Australia?" I didn't respond. Instead, I just stared down at McKenna, who was little more than a speck in the distance. I sighed and gritted my teeth as I unfastened the belt from my jeans, threw it over the cable, and stood on the ledge. I closed my eyes, but I couldn't bring myself to move. "What's the problem?" Jenna asked.

"I think you're gonna have to push me, mate."

I heard her laugh behind me. "It would be my pleasure," and her hand shoved me roughly out of the window, and down I went, clenching my jaw so hard that I thought my teeth would break. "Oh fuck, fuck, fuck, fuck, fuck," I screamed. Then I hit something soft, and I opened my eyes to realize McKenna had caught me. She quickly pulled me aside because Tracker had followed me down almost immediately after I was pushed out of the window. She landed next to me, followed by Jenna, who showed no signs of being out of breath or even the jarring sensation as she hit the ground – Fucking lucky GenMod, I thought to myself. I turned around and faced the airlock of the Starbourne.

"And how do you expect us to open it?"

"Stand aside, please, Miss Grant," said Tracker, pulling off her backpack.

She smiled at me as I moved aside and muttered to myself, "I should have guessed."

She pulled a small device from underneath her hoodie and slapped it against the door. I thought we'd have another long wait while Tracker hacked the door, or whatever it was she did, but on this occasion, it swung open almost immediately.

"Let's go," Jenna said. But I stopped dead in my tracks.

"What about the others? I'm not leaving here without Trisha or Harper," I said defiantly.

Jenna sighed. "We can't go anywhere until you get everything ready for liftoff. But Stacey, if they're not here by then, they won't be coming. Am I clear?"

I was about to argue, but footsteps on the walkway made us suddenly spin around, and both Jenna and I had our firearms drawn. A huge sigh of relief escaped me as Harper came up and threw herself into my arms with the tightest hug; Trisha and one of the Marines followed behind her. "You're gonna be the fucking death of me, Harp," I said to her, my ear-to-ear grin softening my reproach.

"Where is Peterson?" McKenna asked the Marine, but he just shook his head. "No time for a reunion," Jenna insisted. "The three of you need to get inside now."

"What about you?" Trisha asked.

"The ship doesn't hold passengers," Jenna responded. "There's only room for the three of you inside the ship. We will have to climb in through the back and stow ourselves in with the ordinance."

My eyes widened. "You're gonna hitch a ride in the bomb bay?"

"Yes," said McKenna. "So we would appreciate it if you didn't do a bombing run," she winked at me.

A shout came as two Peon troopers climbed up onto the walkway. Jenna and I turned and fired, and one of us hit them.

I didn't know which one of us it was, but I have to assume it was Jenna – the United States Marine was a more accurate shot than I. McKenna pulled out her weapon and began firing as Jenna shouted for us to get on board. The Marine who had come with Harper suddenly flew back over the rail as he was hit. We moved in quickly, but soon found that it had turned into a crawlway rather than a corridor branching into three directions. I moved to the front of the ship while Harper and Trisha took the other two directions. My crawlway led to a hole in the cockpit's ceiling. So, I turned around, slid feet-first into the seat, and wondered how I was supposed to get out again, but that was a problem for later. It was odd not to be in my flight suit, but I was relieved to see a helmet hanging in front of me. I pulled it down onto my head, adjusting the mic to sit in front of my face. I then began studying the controls. Holy hell, this thing was a beast. I concentrated on launch thrusters, wondering what the computer system was telling me in French, and thought I'd worry about the rest once I got this bogey in the air. I heard Jenna on the radio, and I pulled it out and clipped it to the flight stick. "We're under fire, and Tracker can't get the bay door to open. Can you do something, Stacey?" I couldn't find any controls for the bomb bay doors, then remembered I had two weapons personnel for a reason.

I looked about for the ship's comms and, after a frantic search, finally found it. I asked desperately, "Do either of you have access to open the rear door of the bomb bay?"

There was another eternally long wait, then Harper replied, "I've got it."

"Make sure you don't drop the bloody ordinance on them," I muttered.

"Hey, you do what you do, and let me do what I do," Harper sniped.

"We're inside. You can close the door," came Jenna's voice through the radio. I relayed it to Harper, and she closed them.

"You know you being in there will severely limit what I can do. If I start pulling g-forces, you're gonna be more scrambled than the eggs I had for breakfast," I said earnestly.

"Miss Grant," Tracker's voice came back to me. "Can you launch without the aid of the D.E. compensators?"

"Sure, I can. With the gravity on this planet, we could probably jump off. However, using only thrusters will undoubtedly kill you. "

"Not if you reversed the polarity," Tracker sounded uncomfortable. No doubt because she was cramped inside. "Generate a dampening field within the ship, and we should barely feel it move."

"For fuck sake, mate, I left my engineering doctorate back in Wagga. Can you talk me through it?"

She did, and after opening a panel on the D.E. compensator control, I switched over a couple of wires. However, as I was closing the cover, I heard the sounds of rapid gunfire. "What the fuck is going on back there?"

Trish's voice came back to me. "Peons were trying to board us. It's okay, though. I've discovered this ship's got some handy antipersonnel guns, but I suggest we get the fuck out of here instead of sitting here like shags on a fucking rock."

"Bloody hell, I'm doing the best I can, mate," I said. At last, I think I'd finally worked out how to launch this damn ship, and as the engines burst into life, their roar almost deafened us. I activated the dampening field, and the sound rapidly reduced. When I looked out of the window ahead of me, I realized there was no runway ahead of me, or anywhere I could see, for that matter. It was at this moment that I realized this ship was supposed to launch using only the D.E. compensators in a vertical takeoff. But I had an idea. "Trish, Harp, is there any way you could take out the back wall?" Now you'd think they would have asked me why, but they knew if I was asking if it could be done, then it needed to be done.

Each of them launched a rear-firing missile at the target like it was any other firefight. When they confirmed it was coming down, I hit the reverse thrust. We flew back through the wall and tipped off the landing pad, falling backward with the ship's nose pointed upwards. I heard Harper and Trisha cursing, questioning whether I'd made some colossal cockup. But as I looked out of the dome above me, I could see the stars beyond it. I fired the forward missiles. They hit far above, but although the dome didn't break, it did crack. I heard Harper reporting the troops were running for cover, knowing that the dome above them and all their precious air could vanish at any moment. Then I saw it. The dome was opening; they were letting us go rather than risking losing the base. I pushed the flight stick forward, and we shot up into the sky much faster than I expected. I should have known it wouldn't be that easy. As we left Pallas behind us, the ship's computers sounded an alert, and as I looked down at the scanner, I saw two entire squadrons of fighters moving in to intercept us. This was about to become the most incredible fight of my life so far.

Chapter Thirteen

Fire Flight

In these extraordinary circumstances, engaging the enemy, unless there was no alternative, must be avoided. Dogfights did not usually last long, especially in space. As I described in the Battle of Cape York, you might think it's the same as aerial combat on Earth, but you'd be wrong. They are very different. To begin with, there is no up and down in space. Your need to keep your craft upright, as well as air resistance, is completely taken away, which means you can devote all of your energy to blowing fuckers out of the sky.

The two squadrons came at me from the rear, port, and starboard, and if I continued going straight, they would converge and intercept me together. Whichever angle I tried to avoid them, they'd still manage to get us at some stage. Unless I turned back, but that was hardly an option. This beastie could outrun them, but only after accelerating for a significant amount of time, meaning I didn't have enough time to do it before they intercepted me. I was left with one option. If I turned and flew into one of the squadrons on a direct intercept course, I'd have a bit of time up my sleeve before the second squadron could join them. I called Jenna on the radio. "Okay, Boss. I'm going to engage the enemy and pull some serious gees. I really hope Helen was right about those D.E. compensators."

"Your priority is to get this ship out of here. We are expendable to meet that aim," she replied.

"Bloody hell, sometimes I think you wanna die in space. Sorry, but no one is expendable in my book, but I get your point." I then spoke to Trisha and Harper. "Okay, ladies, we're about to teach these Peons that you don't mess with a mob of Aussie sheilas, especially if they're carrying bloody big guns."

"The weapons system on this thing is making me horny, Stace," Trisha said excitedly.

"Yeah, let's go, see how they hold up in a fight," came Harper's excited voice.

I grinned, and just for good measure, I opened up inter-ship communications so that the enemy could hear me. "Okay, you pack of bastards. This is for Cape York and for Wagga." As I sped toward them, I started to sing, "Once a jolly swagman camped by a billabong under the shade of a coolibah tree, and he sang as he watched and waited 'til his billy boiled, You'll come to a-Waltzing Matilda with me." Barely able to contain their laughter, Trisha and Harper joined in the chorus, "Waltzing Matilda, Waltzing Matilda. You'll come a-Waltzing Matilda with me, and he sang as he watched and waited 'til his billy boiled. You'll come a-Waltzing Matilda with me." As we reached the end of the chorus, I launched a swarm of missiles ahead of me.

The squadron started to break formation, and we roared between them, going straight down the line in an interplanetary game of chicken. Every single one of my missiles failed to make contact. But I didn't really expect them to. They did achieve exactly what I had hoped they would. As the enemy passed on both my port and starboard sides, my girls released a barrage of mines out of both sides of the craft. A cheer went up on our ship as several ships flew straight into them and erupted silently, breaking up in that surreal way ships did in an airless vacuum. As we reached the rear of the squadron, they began to turn around, and it was up to my girls – they didn't let me down. Harper opened up with guns on the port side, strafing up and down, left and right, taking out two more in the process. "Damn, this baby is good," I cried out with laughter. "Gotta give it to the Peons. They know how to design a good ship." Suddenly, we jolted, and alarms sounded in my cockpit. We'd been fired on, and the pack leader was on our tail. The solution to this would normally have been to open the rear bomb-bay doors and drop a bunch of mines on them. Since doing that would essentially open Jenna and the entire gang up to open space, it wasn't exactly a viable option. I know, I know. Jenna said earlier that they were expendable, but that would never be an option in my books. Thankfully, I managed to keep out of range because he swerved and then dipped, clearly expecting me to retaliate. When we didn't do it, he grew more confident. A klaxon went off, indicating one of our thrusters was out, but I laughed as I saw a readout saying that auto-repair nanobots had been dispatched. Fuck me sideways. This ship actually repaired itself in flight. Even so, it wouldn't be done fast enough to outrun the bastards on my tail. "Doing a 45 on starboard. "

"Roger on that, Stacey," responded Trisha, understanding what my intention was. I spun the ship on a dime until we were positioned sideways on our enemy, facing the starboard side. Trisha immediately opened up with her guns, and we ripped into his fuselage even as he tried to pull up. She then launched a dumb-dumb into his soft underbelly, and he disintegrated. I corrected our course and noticed the three surviving members of this squadron were now hanging back. With the thruster out, we currently couldn't outrun them, but they couldn't do anything more than match our speed, and they'd be unable to catch up. I started to relax, and the adrenaline began to subside. "Got any idea how many bogies we took out?"

"Fourteen. You broke your record, Stacey," Harper said, clearly proud of me.

"Does it really count if we're not in one of our own ships?" Trish asked.

"I'm sure it does. I'm certainly going to count it," said Harper.

I chuckled softly as I watched the scanner showing the ships behind us. Even if we couldn't outrun them, they'd eventually have to turn back. They were only short-range vessels, unlike the Starbourne. I was suddenly startled when a shadow passed over me, and I looked up through my starboard window. "Oh fuck. Oh fuck. Oh fuck, fuck, FUCK!"

"Ahh, Stacey!?" came Harper's shocked voice. "Another Starbourne is coming in on us."

"I can see it," I said as I pulled off to port. I looked down at the scanner, but it didn't show up. "The fucker has some sort of cloaking device."

"Doesn't that mean we have one too?" Came back, Trisha.

"No shit, Einstein," I said as I looked about the controls, desperately trying to work out which button would activate it. Suddenly, we buckled and went into a spin as a volley of missiles made an impact on the port side of the ship. Decompression alarms went off, and suddenly the cockpit entrance above my head slid shut. I attempted to conduct a damage assessment while also regaining control of the craft. That's when I noticed the controls for our cloaking device, and I hit them, but an alarm beep told me it was offline. My blood ran cold as I saw the damage readout. The port side of the fuselage was open to space. " Harper?" I said softly and then more urgently. "Harper! Respond, dammit!" But no response came. I tried again and again until Trisha came online.

"She's gone, Stacey. There's nothing you can do," Trisha's distressed voice concluded.

I sat there completely frozen, unable to move, unable to think.

I tried to blink away the tears that welled in my one good eye, and I cursed and punched the control panel. "Get a grip, Stacey. Otherwise, we'll be joining her." The switch came on in my head—the defensive one that allowed a pilot to keep being offensive. I knew the odds weren't good that we'd get out of this alive. I mean, our ship was severely damaged, and I was going up against a pilot who had a familiarity with the design of these ships that I didn't. He was on my tail and hanging on tightly. No matter how much I dipped, swerved, and dived, I couldn't shake him. To make matters worse, the damage readout indicated that we were heading toward a potential decompression.

There was only one option left – I had to release the rear bombs. I hit the radio. "I'm sorry, Jenna. If you want the ship to survive, I'm gonna have to release the payload where you are." Harper was dead. I didn't give a fuck about anything besides ensuring she didn't die for nothing.

"Do it," she said determinedly. Then, in a softer voice, she added, "Stacey, it's been an honor and a privilege working with you. Have one on me when you get back to Wagga Wagga."

I didn't say anything back as I reached down to the control that would jettison the payload, killing my three passengers. "Hold on," Trisha shouted, and I pulled my arm back quickly. "Look on the edge of your scanner."

I did, and I actually laughed. "It's a fucking American fighter carrier. Probably the Kennedy." Then I realized how close we'd been to safety when we lost Harp, and I didn't laugh again for a very long time. I turned toward it, trying to get as much speed as possible, swerving, dipping, and rolling around to avoid the ordinance that my opponent was launching at me. The other ships in the squadron appeared to have reached their limit as they started to turn away and head back toward Pallas. But the

Starbourne II didn't give up. "Get ready, Trisha. I'm gonna 45 again. Blow every single thing you have except the bomb bay. Save nothing. I want every last bit of ordinance going into that fucker of a ship."

"You got it, Stacey." I spun the ship one last time. I only wished that I could have seen the explosion and heard the tearing of the metal. Once more, in total silence, we launched multiple missiles, guns, mines, and flak. Absolutely everything we had to launch from the ship was launched. It was so much, in fact, that the wake pushed us away. The Starbourne II tried pulling up, but he'd made the rookie mistake to end all rookie mistakes. He'd come in too close and stayed there too long.

I saw the cockpit eject. Oh no, he was not getting away that easily. This fucker had killed Harper, and he wasn't going to walk away. "Shoot down that life capsule."

"You asked me to unload everything," Trisha said, exasperated. "I unloaded everything. I have nothing to shoot him with."

"I'm not letting Harper's killer walk away from this." I spun the kite around and started to accelerate. I pulled up alongside him. He looked at me and shook his head in disbelief. Taking out a life pod was considered the most despicable act a pilot could commit. But I didn't give a fuck. Slowly, I raised my middle finger at him, and he looked around desperately as if there was something he could do; there was nothing. Once you eject, the process is automatic, and you have no control over it. I jerked my craft to the left and slammed it into his cockpit. I had to repeat this several times before the glass began to crack. He held his hands desperately against it as if this could save him, but I slammed him several times more until the glass exploded. For good measure, I hit him even more until, finally, the cockpit fell apart. As I looked away, I glanced down at my scanner and set a course for the American vessel.

It turned out it wasn't the Kennedy. It was the Reagan. It had been pure chance that we'd come across it. It took quite a bit of discussion with the ship's Captain to stop them from blowing us out of the sky, but eventually, we were allowed to dock. As we landed, Trisha opened the bomb-bay door, but I just sat there with my eyes closed. I was more tired than I'd ever been in my life. My heart was broken. Harper was my best friend. Sure, she wasn't that bright and frequently irritated the crap out of me, but she was loyal. She loved me, and I loved her. I don't think I'll ever have a friend like Harper again. It was four years before I even allowed myself to feel something for another human being. It wasn't until I met Michael Phelkar that I learned to care again. And while Jenna became as close a friend as I could have, she didn't hold a candle to Harper Davis.

The ship's side was completely destroyed. I'd never know if she was just floating out there in space or if her body had been destroyed. I was just angry that we had nothing to give a funeral for.

FUNERAL

In time, the Starbourne project was scrapped. The Americans reverse-engineered it and developed countermeasures for everything, including radar invisibility. It was too expensive to put into production once it lost its edge. That was how things worked in this war, a game of measures and countermeasures.

"I'm sorry for your loss," Jenna told me when we met up a couple of days later. I hadn't wanted to talk to anyone after we landed; I just wanted to spend time with Trisha, one of my own. But Jenna kept insisting on meeting with me, and finally, I relented, and we met in a small office on board the Reagan.

"Harper Davis was a fine officer, and she will be remembered as a hero if I have anything to do with it."

"I got the impression you didn't like her," I responded curtly.

"There are lots of people that I don't particularly like, and I think they're still fine officers. There are also people I like who are lousy officers. However, credit where credit is due, Harper saved many lives. I hope that gives you some comfort."

"Meh, it doesn't. But I appreciate the gesture." I waved a dismissive hand in her direction and looked away.

There was a long, awkward pause, then I got up to leave.

"I want to talk about your future, Stacey." Jenna stopped me. "There is a lot of shit going on out there. I could use your help."

"I'm not really into this cloak-and-dagger stuff. I fly kites," I said dismissively. "That's all I do."

"And that's all I want you to do." It turned out it wasn't, but she meant it at the time. "The Pentagon has set up a new operations unit, and they asked me to lead it. I'm joining a ship called the U.S.S. Lewis Puller. It's under the command of a friend of mine. Its pilot is a guy called Neville Batty, but he doesn't have a tenth of the skills you do. I would like you to take over the reins as the pilot."

"What about Trisha?" I asked.

"If that's a deal-breaker, I'll make sure she is assigned as your co-pilot," Jenna responded.

"Let me talk to her, and I'll get back to you."

Trish and I met up later that day, but it was clear when I saw her in the American uniform that the time to part had come, at least for now. "There's only one thing I want more than to stay with you, Stace," she told me. "And that's to be the head pilot of my own ship. I hope you can understand that, but even without Oz, I've reached a stage in my career where I no longer want to be a co-pilot. Can you understand that?"

I smiled at her. "Of course, I do, mate. It's just that you and I are the last of Epsilon, and I kinda hoped we'd stick together."

"I promise we will keep in touch."

"Me too."

But we didn't. I'm not the type to have a pen pal, and we both moved on in different directions. It would be another four years before I saw her again after the fall of the United States. I briefly considered resigning my commission and trying to get a job as a commercial pilot, but that didn't last long. That desire to be on the front lines for the return to Oz was way too strong to consider anything outside of a military career.

As you already know, I accepted Jenna's offer. Unfortunately, I did it before I saw the wreck of the U.S.S. Lewis Puller. As you also know, Helen Tracker accompanied us, and so too did McKenna Anderson, unaware that we would be working together again four years later.

Jenna and I went on many missions together over those years. Maybe I'll tell you about them one day, but they aren't what this story is about. It's about how I met Jenna and how she rose to power. Those adventures play no part in that. During that period, Jenna and I became good friends. Sure, she was pretty stuffy compared to me, and we had little in common. The number of times that woman has saved my life, and although she'll never honestly admit the number of times I've saved hers, there's a bond between the two of us that can't be broken. I know Jenna Plural would die for me, and I would die for her.

It's time to move on to the time when we both met Michael Phelkar.

Chapter Fourteen

Phelks

Helen Tracker not only worked with us during those four years but also continued working on ideas to overcome Peon technology. The Phobos communication base had been in operation for about ten years, and the Pacific Alliance had attempted to assault it on numerous occasions, resulting in the loss of countless lives. Its satellite system defenses were second to none, and even then, if any of our troops made it to the ground, the Peons on Mars had long been alerted. Unbeknownst to us, Helen had worked on it in secret, trying to develop a program and device to overcome their satellite security. When she said she had succeeded, we were all skeptical because the only way to test if it worked was in the field during an assault – so I mean, you hoped she was right, or else we'd be as good as dead.

That's why we were back in Manassas that summer. Jenna and Tracker flew off to the Pentagon for briefings while the ship got an overhaul and its routine crew rotation.

Me? Well, I hadn't taken any leave in four years. So I grabbed the golden opportunity, packed my bathers, and headed to California for three weeks of sun and surf. I'll be honest. It wasn't exactly Bondi Beach, but I had a good enough time, and if I squinted my eyes just right sometimes, it felt like being back in Oz. Like all vacations, it was over all too quickly, and I got back the same day we were due to ship out again. It was only then that I learned that the powers that be had given the green light to Helen Tracker's plan.

It was then that I also learned of the change in command. I was a bit upset that I hadn't had the chance to say goodbye to the Captain and Claire Addison, who were already gone and replaced by James Royce and Stephanie Morris as the new Captain and First Officer.

As a GenMod, Jenna wasn't allowed to hold either of these positions. It was even frowned upon by some that she held the role of the Second Officer. She'd proven herself time and again, and anyone would be hard-pressed to criticize her achievements.

Jenna and Royce didn't get on right from the start. I didn't remember it at the time, but I'd already met Stephanie Morris when she was serving as the Second Officer aboard the U.S.S. John F. Kennedy.

The entire dynamic of the crew was set to change because both the former Captain and Claire knew they were merely fulfilling legal requirements. Jenna was in unofficial command from the start of our time onboard the Chesty.

That changed with Royce, who clearly considered himself the head of Theta Squad. His first action was to file a transfer order for Jenna, months before we even returned to Earth. They hadn't even met at that point. When it was denied, he appealed and had to attend a meeting to discuss the issue. I have no idea what happened in that meeting, but later Jenna told me he wasn't too happy when he returned.

This was Jenna's assignment, and there were only three people on the team that the higher-ups didn't consider replaceable. Jenna, Tracker, and yours truly. You see, Royce was what we call an antigen, and he truly despised Jenna and her genetic perfection.

When I next saw Jenna, she wasn't in the best of moods. We met up in the quarters she was using in the astrodome. "I don't know what our new Captain is thinking," she said as she tossed me a tinnie and allowed herself to fall back into an armchair. "He actually volunteered us to babysit some diplomat who's coming on board as an 'observer,'" she sneered at the word 'observer.'

"And observe what exactly?" I asked as I opened my beer and sat in the chair opposite her.

"Oh, I don't know," She waved a dismissive hand as if it didn't matter. "The Brits have been getting shitty ever since the Texas front opened up. They are pressuring their government to sue for peace with the Europeans. They are sending dozens of observers who are supposed to assess whether we have what it takes to win this war. It's insulting." She took a swig of a beer. Sadly, Jenna could never get drunk. Her altered DNA metabolism filtered out alcohol before it could have any effect. Personally, if I couldn't get well and truly shitfaced every now and then, I'd lose the will to live.

Before I could say anything, she continued her tirade. "A foreigner is not only assessing the United States Marine Corps but the *elite* unit of the United States Marine Corps."

"He's actually flying out with us on this mission?" I asked, having already finished my beer and glancing around to see if there was more.

"Yes. Can you believe it?" Jenna fumed.

"No, that's a liability," I said, getting up and going over to her refrigerator. "We're gonna have to expend resources keeping the damn Pommy alive," I finished as I helped myself to another beer and returned to my seat.

Jenna fixed her eyes on me. "That is exactly what I said, but is anyone listening? No, I'm just a damn GenMod."

I grinned at her. "I thought you didn't like that term?"

"I don't," she scowled at me. "I am just reflecting on their thinking. To make it even worse, he's not even military. He's a bloody civilian," she said the word civilian as if she was referring to dog shit on the bottom of her boot.

"Well, let's hope he's a beauty. There's a rare few of those around here," I grinned.

The anger dissipated from Jenna's face, and she grinned back at me, "You're such a slut."

"Fuck you!" I chuckled. "You know, maybe we should just retire."

"Here you go again," Jenna rolled her eyes at me. "You're not gonna retire until you're standing on Wagga Beach."

"Oh, don't get me started on that, mate," I said curtly, although I was still having fun with her. "Four years ago, you promised to get me back to Oz. Yet here we are, Virginia, in the good ole U.S. of fucking A."

Jenna knew I was joking, but she looked at me seriously. "I assure you, Stacey, I really do intend to keep that promise."

A couple of hours later, I was back on the Chesty, unpacking in my quarters. I was just putting the picture of Harper and me back into the bolted-down frame on my bedside cabinet when Jenna came over the intercom. "Stacey, are you aboard?"

I hit the intercom and told her, "No, I'm not."

She ignored my comment and continued. "We need to get to the control tower. Our diplomat has apparently been shot down by the Europeans just as they flew across the border."

"Hey, a great way to start. Is he dead?" I asked, almost hopefully. I just knew Jenna would make me his babysitter.

"No clue. I need you to take up a drone and look for him."

"On my way," I said with a resigned sigh. I was knackered and just wanted to have a kip, but I pulled my coat back on and headed out.

The rear cargo entry was the fastest way out of the ship when we were planetside. We met up at the entrance at the same time. She was dressed in shorts and a hoodie, her hair tightly pulled back into a ponytail. Phelks said she had a tank top, but I'm calling bullshit on that. Like, can you imagine Jenna wearing a tank top? Anyway, she appeared to have been working out when the call had come through about the shuttle going down. As we raced down the ramp, we almost knocked over a couple of troopers who were storing supplies on board the ship. "Sorry, mate," I shouted back as I raced on with my commander.

We ran over to the air traffic control tower and into the operations room. Jenna made her way over to the radar operators while I slipped into one of the four drone simulator cubicles. As I activated the camera, the screen lit up in front of me, and it was just as if I was in the cockpit of a plane, except much smaller. I could just make out what Jenna said as she spoke to the radio operators while I started taxiing the drone toward the runway. "Got anything better for me than somewhere between here and the coast?" she asked with frustration.

Eventually, Jenna called back the grid pattern coordinates, and I keyed them into the computer. "That's a very general area," I sniped back.

"After flying over the European blockade, the shuttle was still running its defense systems. It's deliberately designed to send out false readings, allowing it to be anywhere within a ten-square-mile area. I guess he didn't have time to deactivate it like regulations state they're supposed to."

As the drone took off into the air, I advised her, "I'll run the grid pattern and look out for signs of smoke or fire. You need to signal out clearances as I fly over the cities, so I don't create a panic."

"Already on it, Stacey," she stated.

"Thanks, Boss." I took the drone out over the city of Manassas and continued until I reached the rural area where the craft was supposedly located. Then, I dropped it to a low altitude, about twenty feet off the ground. I flew over farms and adjusted the craft's altitude to fly higher over the wooded areas, then switched to infrared.

I was almost an hour into the flight and starting to get concerned. This drone hadn't been fully fueled before takeoff, and stupidly, I hadn't noticed that fact until a few minutes earlier. I got excited as I saw smoke, then debris, before finally spotting the shuttle half-buried in the ground. "I've found the shuttle," I called out to Jenna. She ran up to stand beside me. "Any sign of our diplomat?

"Sorry, Boss. I don't think he made it," I said as I finished a scan of the wreckage. "I'm not picking up any signs of life at all."

"We cannot assume that. We don't know if anyone managed to walk away. Keep looking."

"He would have to be a deadset moron to leave the shuttle where we could find him," I muttered.

"Indeed," responded Jenna and returned to the radar guy.

I grew uneasy as I watched the fuel gauge drop, and I decided to raise the craft higher, taking a longer view when I saw the main road. I took a gamble that someone would follow it as night loomed closer.

As I passed over a small cluster of trees, I thought I noticed someone sitting on the road. I wasn't sure, so I slowed the drone and turned it around. As I hovered a small distance away, I turned the light directly toward him. He stood up and covered half his face as I pulled up his file to make sure it was who I was looking for. I turned on the drone's speakers. "Hands by your sides, mate. I gotta see your face," I told him.

"Are you with the Americans?" he asked like an idiot.

"Ah, don't be a fucking dick, mate," I replied irritably and sighed impatiently. "Now, arms by your side. I won't repeat myself a third time. This thing may look like a toy, but it can make your day go real bad, real fast. And let's be honest, you've had a pretty shit day already."

I gotta fess up here. I don't have an eidetic memory chip like Phelks, and I don't recall the exact wording, so I assume he was correct and using his own words. I won't always do that. If I remember things differently, then I'll say so. Fuck his eidetic memory chip.

I took the drone over to him, but followed protocol and stayed out of his reach. "Well, g'day, mate. I'm Stacey Grant of the United States Navy. Would you care to identify yourself?"

"I am Michael Phelkar of the British Ministry of Defense. Liaison to the United States Marine Corps."

I grinned. I'd found him. I turned and leaned out of the simulator. "Oi, Boss. I found your missing Pom – he's alive." As Jenna hurried over to me, I returned my attention to him. "Okay, mate, we've got your location."

"Tell him to stay there. I am on my way." She looked at my screen and noted the coordinates, muttering them under her breath.

"You just stay right where you are. We have a car coming to pick you up." I told him as she ran out of the control center. "Are you injured?"

"No, Ma'am. I'm a bit shaken up, but that's about it."

"What about your pilot?"

"I'm sad to say he didn't make it."

"Geez, I'm sorry to hear that, mate." Of course, I was used to death, but the death of a pilot had a special place in my heart. "We are dispatching a cleanup crew. We'll make sure he gets back to Blighty. The boss is leaving now and should be there in about fifteen to twenty minutes. I gotta get this baby back in the dock

– she's running on fumes. Keep your chin up, mate. I'll have a nice cuppa and some tucker waiting for you when you get here."

"That would be most welcoming, Lieutenant Grant."

I was not exaggerating when I said the drone was on fumes. The alarm was already beeping away on the console in front of me. I had just made it down onto the runway when the engine died, and I lost control in the V.R. It spun onto the grass, settling nose down. Fortunately, it wasn't damaged, although I couldn't say the same for my ego. As I climbed out of the simulator, one of the officers laughed. "Nice parking, Grant."

Obviously, he got the one-finger salute. "Up yours, Patrick. You'd have trouble keeping a quadbike upright," I said as I left the room.

Instead of returning to the ship, I headed down to the officers' mess. I didn't usually go to segregated bars, but this one was the closest, and I was feeling lazy. I had a few drinks and played a round of cards with the boys and girls. As per usual, I lost my money and left when I heard Jenna had returned. I wanted to check out the Pommy wanker, who was already proving to be a pain in the arse.

Jenna had parked right by the docking ramp of the Chesty, and the Pom was staring at it in horror.

"She ain't as bad as she looks," I said with a chuckle as I walked up to him. He looked around at me and offered me his hand.

"Lieutenant Grant, I presume?" he said in that pompous yet cheery Brit manner.

"Got it in one, mate."

Jenna called me over to where she was dealing with his luggage. "Mr. Phelkar of the British Ministry of Defense Liaison, please meet Second Lieutenant Stacefield E. Grant, our senior pilot."

"You can call me Stacey," I said, but before our conversation could continue, Jenna joined us.

"Is everything ready for launch?" she asked me.

"As ready as she'll ever be," I shrugged. Jenna glared at me because she knew I was trying to freak out the Pom.

"Wait a minute," Phelks interrupted. "When exactly are you shipping out?"

Jenna glanced at her watch. "In about two hours, Mr. Phelkar."

"Wait a minute. I am here to do a review. How can I do that if you are off base?"

"You weren't told we were shipping out today?" Jenna asked, slightly amused by this turn of events.

"I most certainly was not. I have no intention of shipping out anywhere."

Her smile widened. "Why, Mr. Phelkar, how can you possibly assess us without accompanying us?"

"That is not part of my brief. Where pray tell are you so urgently going?" he blustered, and I have to be honest, he was starting to bug the fuck out of me.

"To Mars, Mr. Phelkar."

"I was not told of this."

"We generally don't share mission details ahead of time."

"You are going into combat?" I thought he was about to shit his pants.

Jenna was exasperated. "That, Mr. Phelkar, is what United States Marines do," she looked at me and half concealed a wink. "Lieutenant, show Mr. Phelkar around the ship. He should also check in with Dr. Archer for his preflight medical." I glared daggers at her for palming the Pom off on me. She struggled not to grin – Phelks was oblivious to the entire exchange.

"You got it," I replied with a forced smile, and she turned away quickly, struggling not to laugh. "Come on, Phelks," I instructed him and led him up the cargo platform. I tried to show him around the ship, but all he did was fucking whine about launching with us. In the end, I just took him to the medical center to get it over with as quickly as possible.

I had to go through the whole rigmarole of putting the Tracker into his skull; I must admit, though, when a tirade of profanity flowed from his mouth when I did so, I was taken aback. Maybe he wasn't the stiff upper-lipped Pommy wanker I thought he was.

I'd only met a couple of Poms in my life, but never actually spent much time with any of them. Well, not unless you counted that bitch Charlotte Kensett.

Once we'd finished with the doctor, we headed back out to the corridor where he now spent his time complaining about the M.E.T., and fortunately for me, we ran into Jenna. After waiting long enough for her not to be paying attention to me, I slipped away and returned to my quarters. I finally finished putting away my stuff and decided to head to the mess to grab a coffee.

I passed Harlow and Tracker on my way, and the Chief Engineer gave me his usual grunt of acknowledgment. I smiled at him. "G'day, Mr. Harlow, what a delight it is to see you again," to which he grunted something about 'stupid kids' and shuffled off, leaving me grinning at Tracker.

"Did you meet the English guy yet?" she asked me.

"Yeah," I said unenthusiastically.

"He seems quite nice."

"Yeah, well, you didn't just have him bending your ear for the last hour," I complained.

Helen shook her head at me. "Cut him a break. His country has been taking quite a pounding recently. If something doesn't give soon, they could very well end up like Australia, and you know better than anyone how that feels."

She hit me where it hurt, but I had to admit that she made a good point. It didn't mean I wasn't gonna stop picking on him. He's a Pom. I'm Australian. The natural rivalry and disdain are just something we've come to expect. "Yeah, yeah, I'll try." I don't know what it was about Helen, but I liked her. Maybe it was because she reminded me of Harper, although they were complete opposites in many respects. I couldn't help thinking they would have made a cute couple.

Chapter Fifteen

The Voyage to Mars

I headed into the mess where he and Jenna were having lunch. Like the completely incompetent knob I assumed he was, I found him trying to move his bolted-down chair. Finally, after giving up the futile endeavor, he looked up at Jenna and said incredulously, "You don't generate gravity on this ship?"

"It's too small," I told him. "The Captain won't let me spin her either."

"My zero-gee certification is long expired," he said, looking eager as I handed Jenna and him a coffee before pouring my own.

"We operate personal dark energy generators. I will show you before we lift off," Jenna told him. She scowled at me as I moved behind him, giving her a wicked grin and a wink as I placed a hand on his shoulder. "Don't pick on him, Boss. It's nice to have some eye candy on board."

Jenna tried not to laugh, and it came out like a snort. "I would hardly call me that," he said, color filling his cheeks and spreading down his neck.

I massaged his neck and leaned into him. "Take a look around, Phelks. There isn't exactly a plethora of men on this ship to choose from."

He was not amused. On that note, I gave him a swift kiss on the cheek, and I left the room with my coffee.

Back in my quarters, I turned on my small TV and settled down on my bed with my coffee and a couple of cookies I'd snagged on my way out – they were no Tim Tams, but it was all I had in the absence of those Aussie faves. It'd been a while since I'd had a chance to catch up on my favorite American soap, and I thought I could get a couple of episodes in before we launched, but that thought was short-lived. My internal intercom buzzed, and the captain's voice crackled to life and ordered me to report to the bridge. I climbed sluggishly out of my bed, downed as much of the still-hot coffee as I could, and loped off to the bridge.

I didn't like James Royce; I don't think anyone did except possibly Stephanie Morris, the no-good whore. Both of them were on the bridge as I entered. Royce greeted me with that weird smirk of his. I may not have liked him, but he clearly liked me. To be honest, I think he probably jacked off to pictures of me from my personnel file. My real animosity toward him, though, was the way he treated Jenna. Now, it wasn't like she couldn't stand up for herself, but she was a mate, and nobody messed with my mates and got away with it.

"Ah, Miss Grant. We are ahead of schedule and have been given clearance to leave."

I raised an eyebrow at him. "Don't you mean you've been given permission to depart? I think I'm the only one who gets clearance. Clearance means I have been granted permission to get this ship out of here without further discussions with traffic control."

"Just get us ready for launch, Miss Grant," and although the smile did not leave his lips, I saw it leave his eyes.

The agreement I had with Jenna when I signed up with the U.S. military stated that I wasn't obligated to follow any of the protocols they still had in place. James Royce tried to put his foot down with me, but it came unstuck. The bigwigs in command had told him that they couldn't override that agreement (upside of being friends with Jenna, there wasn't much that went on that I didn't find out about one way or another). They couldn't override the agreement I had signed, but they could replace me as the pilot. Now, I'm not one to blow smoke up my own arse or anything like that, but when you're as good a pilot as I am, no Captain in his right mind is going to have me fired. My exploits had made the rounds, and many commanders had tried to headhunt me for their ships. As far as I was concerned, though, I worked for Jenna Plural and nobody else.

I slipped into my chair and hit the chimes that rang out through the ship, signaling that we were preparing to launch. This gave the crew fifteen minutes to prepare and strap down. Royce left the bridge during that time to do whatever he was doing, leaving me alone with Morris. I sat back in my chair, and she slipped into the co-pilot seat that my colleague, Neville Batty, normally occupied. However, as this was a routine launch, he had already been uploaded to the MET. As I waited for the fifteen minutes to pass, I found my mind drifting once more to thoughts of my home, Australia. I still wanted to be at the front of the invading force, but it had been four years now, and rather than moving forward, the Pacific Alliance had been steadily losing ground. For the first time in its history since the Spanish-American War, enemy troops marched through the U.S.A.

"Are you all right, Stacey?"

Even though she was sitting next to me, I was so deep in thought that Stephanie's words startled me. In hindsight, I'd like to tell you how much I hated and despised that bitch. The reality is, though, if I am being fair dinkum with you, I actually liked her, which is one hell of a conundrum, let me tell you. Like

Jenna always complained, she was not what you would consider 'officer material,' but she was a decent person, or so I thought. I looked at her and pondered. "I'm thinking of retiring after this mission. I originally signed up for a six-year term with the Australian Air Force. I'll be past that by the time we return, and although I haven't specified how long I'll stay with the U.S. military, I still technically consider myself A.A.F."

Stephanie chuckled. "And what exactly are you going to do, Stacey? Fly cargo planes from Chicago to Indianapolis? What about your big plan to 'storm the beaches of Sydney'?"

"I guess you're right, but...." I never got to finish my sentence, as the second beep came just as Royce re-entered the room and took his seat. "Let's get out of here, Miss Grant."

I buzzed the tower. "G'day, Control. This is Lieutenant Stacefield Ellen Grant of the U.S.S. Lewis Puller, requesting departure clearance." I glanced back at Royce as I said this, but he stared back at me expressionless.

There was a brief pause, and then Control responded. "Confirmed Lewis Puller go for immediate lift-off. Clear skies to you, Stacey."

"That's a roger, Control. Keep a brew on 'til we get back. Igniting thrusters." I fired up her engines, "External gravity compensators at twenty percent. Compensators at thirty percent and rising." The ship began to rise slowly, the wave of invisible dark energy making us lighter than air. "D.E. compensators are at one hundred percent. We're in ascending freefall and increasing thrust." I could have let the ship float up into space, but that wasn't my style. As I activated the secondary thrusters, they forced us to accelerate even more rapidly until the sky went dark. "We've left Earth's atmosphere. Switching off the D.E. compensators." I conducted a quick scan for junk littering the near-Earth orbit and then updated the crew. "The skies are clear, and the stars are shining bright. At this time, you are free to unfasten your seatbelts and move about the cabin. Drinks will be served in the cocktail lounge in half an hour." If this were any other world, I could have just plotted the course to Mars and called it a day. Gone back to my bunk, put on some porn movie, and spent some special time with myself, but this was Earth, and behind every piece of junk was a potential enemy combatant lying in wait—anything from automated bots to limpet mines and small scout ships. Leaving Earth was the most dangerous aspect of a pilot's career. When I thought we were almost clear, I spotted it – the most minor of anomalies on the scanner. You could pretty much cloak everything these days, but when the cloaked device moves between another object and yourself, it hides that other object. It isn't always easy to spot, but on this occasion, I managed to catch it. "That's a motherfucking limpet tracker. It'll light us up to every Peon scanner from here to Mars."

"Must you always cuss, Stacey?" the captain admonished.

"Fuck yeah, I must," I said and hit the shipboard alert. "Tactical Alert Seven. Tactical Alert Seven." I tried to send a wave of dark energy at it to push it away, but the automated alarm came on instead. "Oh, for the love of..." and I hit the ship-wide intercom. "Whoever has their D.E. belts active, turn the fucking things off. You know they screw with the maneuvering thrusters."

Jenna floated into the doorway a couple of minutes later. I didn't see her, though, as I was too damn busy trying to get us away from the thing. I could hear her talking to the captain, but I hadn't realized that Phelks was still tailing her like a bad smell.

"What's happening?" she asked urgently.

"Damn Peon probe," Royce said, acting like he was an expert on the subject rather than merely repeating what I'd just finished explaining. "One of the limpet kinds is trying to stick to us. They'll be tracking us to Mars if it attaches. Any element of surprise we have will be gone if it succeeds."

"We should return to base and have it removed," Phelks said as I shot another burst of dark energy at the probe.

"Do you know *anything* about planetary movement, Mr. Phelkar? Those limpet trackers bury themselves very neatly and deeply into the hull, and it'll take several days, maybe even weeks, to remove them. In that time, Mars will have moved thousands of miles further away."

"Hold onto your seats, ladies and gentlemen," I interrupted as I spun and twisted the ship in a one-eighty spin, lurching backward and forward repeatedly before we suddenly accelerated at full speed.

"Everyone can relax now," I cheerfully announced. "I lost the little bastard. Damn, I am *good*."

I turned to see Phelks pressed up against Jenna in a most compromising position. I grinned at her, and as she pushed him back, he flailed as he grabbed the back of the captain's chair. She shook her head and rolled her eyes at me.

"Indeed, you are, Miss Grant," the captain said appreciatively. "Now, take us to Mars."

"Setting course," I responded as I spun back around to face my controls. "We'll rendezvous with Phobos in seven weeks, three days, and thirteen hours."

"Close the shields," Royce ordered. I hit a couple more buttons, and extensive exterior shielding came down over the glass screens.

"Let's go get our molecules broken down," I said as I turned and grinned at Phelks, watching him turn positively green. He raced out of the cockpit like he was about to chunder.

We met up again when we were all at the MET, and as I was getting ready to upload, Phelks seemed out of touch with military life and appeared quite bashful about getting undressed in front of a bunch of women. Just to tease him, I started taking off my top, but I never got undressed in front of anyone I didn't know. I didn't like to take my eye out in front of anybody except for Jenna and Tracker. While he waited outside, I shoved my eye into one of the lockers, stepped up onto the circle, gave Jenna a wink with my one good eye, and said, "See you on the other side, ladies."

In a flash, it was several weeks later.

From the look on Helen Tracker's face, I knew something was wrong the moment I rematerialized. "Incoming!" she said as I put my clothes on and inserted my eye. I was still tucking my shirt into my skirt as I ran down the corridor to the bridge.

I was pumped by the time I ran into the cockpit. Jenna, who was standing beside the captain in his command chair, stepped aside so I could drop into the slight well and the pilot seat. Morris sat in the co-pilot seat. My eyes swiftly scanned over the systems telling me the trajectory of the Peon frigate. "E.T.A. twenty-three minutes," I reported. "I can probably gain you seven more minutes with some maneuvers."

"There's no point," Jenna said, her kick ass ready for battle voice deep and commanding. "It'll only delay the inevitable. We could be ready well before that."

"Morris, get your troops ready to repel boarders," the captain ordered.

"Sir, how do I do that?" Morris responded, fear in her voice.

Royce sounded horrified. "You're my first officer and a United States Marine."

"Sir, before coming here, I was the second officer on board the John F. Kennedy. My duties consisted of supply lists and crew rosters." Morris stated defensively.

"We are wasting time, Captain," Jenna snapped. "You know I'm the only person here who can deal with this. Get past your damned bigotry and give me the go-ahead."

Royce pondered a moment, sighed, and said, "Go for it, Plural."

As she and Phelks left, I looked at Stephanie with a contemptuous glare. She just blushed and slipped into the chair beside me. She wasn't going to help Jenna at all. I rose to my feet, but the captain raised his hand toward me. "Stay where you are, Miss Grant. This is a job for the Marines. "

"That's not usually how we work. Jenna prefers..."

"Lieutenant Plural is not in charge of this ship, Miss Grant," he said coldly. "It is what I prefer that counts, and I prefer you stay in that seat until your piloting services are needed." I sighed and sat back down and stared straight ahead. I heard the stamping of feet and the shouts of "oo-rah," and then everything fell silent. Minutes passed until the enemy ship hit us, the impact reverberating throughout the ship. I made to get up again, and again, Royce shouted me down, growing more irritated this time. Then the gunfire started. I felt impotent and frustrated, but I couldn't come to my friend's or my team's aid. I closed my eye and fought the frustration and anger brewing in me.

Then I got the worst call of my life since Cape York. The Emergency Interplanetary Line came on. The one line used by the highest authorities, including the President herself. The voice that came over the line sounded dispirited, broken even. "Ladies and gentlemen, officers and enlisted personnel, this is Major General Martin Hernandez. It is my sad duty to inform you that as of ten hundred hours this morning, the President of the United States signed an unconditional surrender with the European Union. All operations are to cease immediately. You are to lay down your arms and, where possible, surrender them to E.U. forces. For those in transit, you want to set course for the nearest U.S. or E.U. base for decommissioning."

The three of us in that cockpit sat in shocked silence. I don't know how long it was until James told me to open up the ship-wide intercom. "Lieutenant Plural, stand down. Purple sky, I repeat, purple sky. Stand down." Again, we waited in silence, and when no reply came, he barked louder, "Lieutenant Plural, confirm order received. Report to the cockpit."

"Stand down, confirmed," her voice responded aggressively. About a minute later, she burst into the cockpit once more, shadowed by Phelks. "What the hell is going on?" I looked up at her desperately. "It just came over the Interplanetary Emergency Broadcast. The United States had surrendered – Britain, Canada, and Japan were expected to follow suit with the other Allies."

"What in the hell are you talking about?" Jenna practically screamed at me. I had stopped listening. I just sat there in numb disbelief. Was this it? Was it really over? Would I really never see Australia again? At least not as the free and vibrant country I remembered.

The beeping of the inter-ship communications drew me from my dark thoughts. "There's an incoming call from the Peon Captain," I told him.

"Put it through, Miss Grant," Tsarevich said dejectedly.

"This is Captain Matis of the Force d'Action Navale ship Jauréguiberry. I wish to discuss your surrender with your captain." His accent was thick, and there was obvious joy in his voice.

"Go ahead, Jangweberry. This is the Captain of the U.S.S. Lewis Puller."

"Bonjour, mon Capitan. Can I assume that you've heard instructions about the ceasefire?"

"You can. I am willing to discuss the terms of our surrender to your authority."

The Peon Captain laughed. "Oh, mon Capitan, there are no terms. Your President has agreed to an unconditional surrender. You will disable all of your weaponry, disconnect your automated systems, and prepare for my Second Officer to take command of your vessel. You will be towed to the nearest E.U. base and turned over for processing. Don't worry, mon Capitan. I am sure you will soon be home watching baseball and eating hot dogs."

"Give me a few minutes."

"I give you no more than ten minutes, captain. I hope you do not intend to resist."

"I have no intention of resisting."

"Ten minutes then... And captain, if I do not hear back from you, I will assume hostilities have resumed."

As I cut the feed, the captain muttered, "Frog bastard."

The argument between Jenna and the Captain continued for several minutes until he finally said, "You are out of line, Lieutenant. Prepare the main airlock to receive company."

"This is fucking bullshit!" Jenna returned less than ten minutes later with the Peon Commander.

The Peon smiled as the captain stood up and saluted him. "Captain, you will power down all ship systems except life support and your matter converter. You will proceed to put all of your crew into storage."

Royce nodded to me, and once I had shut everything down, I turned and looked at Jenna; she gave no indication of her intent.

"I require medical attention before I can be uploaded," Jenna said determinedly.

The Peon looked her up and down, "You look fine to me, Madam."

"Thanks to Mr. Phelkar's field dressing, it looks that way. There is still a bullet lodged in my abdomen. I can't go through the MET with a foreign object embedded in me."

The Peon sighed. "Very well, Madam," and he turned to one of the guards and spoke in French, which was all blah, blah, blah to me. As they made their way to the door, Phelks stepped up to the Chief Peon and jabbered away in his language. Their back and forth went on, and all I understood was the word Australia and Phelks' name. When they finished, he was allowed to leave with Jenna.

The Peon Commander then turned to me. "Would you please call my ship, Mademoiselle?"

"Call them yourself," I snapped and turned away.

"Miss Grant!" the captain snapped with equal vehemence.

I turned to the controls, "Okay, okay, I'm doing it."

"I thank you, Miss Grant," the Commander said.

I looked up at him, "You know me?"

He chuckled, "No, ma cherie, your Captain just said your name."

I switched on the inter-ship comms, feeling like a complete dumbass. The Commander jabbered away in French, and someone at the other end jabbered back at him. This went on for several minutes, and they were most happy. Finally, he nodded to me to switch it off, and I did. "Don't look so sad, Miss Grant. You will soon be going home to America, yes?"

"I'm an Aussie, mate."

"Ah, Australia. A beautiful country. I was there just last year."

"Yeah, well, I haven't been back since you set your garlic-soaked boots on it."

"Stacey!" the captain snapped, reprimanding me yet again.

The Commander raised a hand to silence him. "Do not concern yourself, mon Capitan. We all carry hard feelings from this war, and I do not begrudge Mademoiselle Grant's need to vent her feelings to her enemy. Now is the time to heal, and in time, we will be friends, yes?"

"Will you be getting out of Australia?" I asked with a sarcastic smile.

"I am sure in time we probably will, but not before we have secured all of your armaments so that you cannot use them to rise up against us," he smiled back at me.

"So, we will be free as long as we do as we are told?" I said as patronizingly as possible.

"That is the privilege of the victor," he replied, and I said no more. I could tell he was growing tired of me, his warm smile gone.

He turned toward Stephanie, who Phelks swears had already left, but I remember this clearly. "You are the First Officer. Are you not, Mademoiselle?"

I couldn't believe it. Was she about to deny it? She looked terrified. She nodded slowly. "You will go arrange ze upload of your remaining crew, oui?" She nodded again and headed rapidly for the doorstop. He turned back to me, "I am sorry, Mademoiselle. But I must ask you to accompany her – all crew except the captain must be uploaded." I said nothing in response as I slipped out of my seat and followed Stephanie out.

Chapter Sixteen

Mutiny on the Chesty

I tried to catch up with her. "What are we going to do? I asked.

She looked at me like I'd just said something idiotic. "You heard the man. We're going to start uploading the crew."

"You're just gonna jump into the M.E.T. – what's to stop them just shutting it down and deleting us all?"

"I am quite sure they will act with integrity," she said, her words sounding more confident than her tone suggested.

"Since when have the Peons ever acted with integrity?" I blustered. "Hell, when has either side acted with integrity in this war?"

She stopped and glared at me. "Oh, just stop it, Stacey. Don't cause trouble. Follow your orders, and do not try any of your shenanigans."

I just stood there staring at her, and as she turned and carried on, I felt my jaw hit the floor. Then slowly, I headed toward the M.E.T. room where Peon soldiers were rounding everyone up. There was already a line when we arrived; Stephanie went to the front and entered the room, where I assumed Helen Tracker was.

Everyone was talking until the guard told them to shut up, and a hush fell over the room. I leaned against the wall and closed my eyes, even my cybernetic one. Could this really be the end? Was I really never going to see Australia again? Eventually, I opened my eyes and looked down toward the end of the line. I was completely startled to see Jenna and Phelkar standing there, just chatting casually as if this was all perfectly normal. She turned her head in my direction and gave me a single nod; that was all I needed to know that she was up to something. I attempted to delay entering, but one of the guards suddenly pushed me with the butt of his rifle, and I stepped inside. I feigned a problem trying to get my eye out, and Stephanie stared at me with irritation. She knew full well that I was deliberately stalling.

As the guard went back outside, Stephanie, who looked ready to turn on me, was pulled up short when Jenna and Phelks stepped in. "Surely you are not going to accept this, are you, Morris?" Jenna rounded on the First Officer, who couldn't even look her in the eye.

"Plural, this isn't the time for your patriotic fervor. Get over it. We lost."

"You just give up like that?"

"It's not my call, and it's not yours."

Two Peon guards came in to see what the delay was. They were behind Jenna, and she suddenly took a step back and thrust her elbow back into the gut of one of them. As he doubled over, she grabbed his gun and whipped him on the back of the neck, sending him to the ground. The other guard was already aiming for her head. I deflected the guard's aim by knocking his arm away just as he was about to shoot Jenna. His gun went off, and Helen jumped back as sparks flew up from her control panel. Jenna grabbed his gun and pushed the weapon's barrel into his stomach to suppress the sound and fired. As he expired, Phelks gently lowered him to the floor. Just then, the other guard tried to get up, but Jenna pushed him back down to the ground. Stephanie tried to protest, but Jenna was having none of it.

I bent down and pulled the handgun out of the holster of the dead guard, and I pointed it at Stephanie. I was seriously pissed when I realized that Jenna had doubts about whether I would back her up. I don't know if I was more hurt or offended, but Jenna has since apologized multiple times.

I didn't consider this as taking a side. As far as I was concerned, there was only one side – the alternative was completely and utterly unacceptable.

Jenna had her uploaded, but I'm sure she would have preferred to shoot her right then and there. To be honest, if she had, it would've saved us a lot of trouble later. As Phelks has already told you, I did indeed question whether we could trust him or not. Four years working in secret Special Ops isn't conducive to one being particularly comfortable around people you don't know in dangerous situations.

"I'm only obeying my orders, Plural," Stephanie screamed. "Just as you should be."

"Semper Fi," Jenna said softly. "Get undressed," Jenna ordered. "Helen, get ready to upload her," Jenna ordered.

"Don't listen to her," Morris' voice broke, and there were tears in her eyes. "She is acting contrary to orders."

"Six years, Tracker. When have I given you a reason to doubt me?" Jenna said coolly.

Tracker hesitated momentarily, then, with a nod to Jenna, she looked at Morris. "Sorry, Ma'am, but would you get undressed and step onto the circle, please?"

"I'll wait outside," Phelks said, but Jenna gripped his arm.

"Stay where you are, Mr. Phelkar, and stop being such a goddamn idiot," Jenna barked. "You're working with the United States Marines now."

Stephanie's wavering voice conveyed her tears as she undressed. "You will all be court-martialed for this."

Jenna smirked. "By who? The Peons?"

Tracker hit the upload button before she could reply

Jenna turned and looked at me, then Tracker. "Thank you, ladies. I'm glad I could rely on you."

"What flying fuck, mate. You had doubts about that?" I responded with offence.

Jenna looked at me sheepishly and shrugged. "I don't know. Never asked you to commit mutiny before."

I looked at Phelks, who stood by looking very scared. "Can we trust him?"

"I think so." Jenna looked him up and down. "He has already proved himself several times today."

"I'm standing right here, you know," He said with irritation. "Whilst I cannot imagine the consequences of our actions, I have already committed acts of mutiny and treason. I'm a dead man for killing officers I had technically surrendered to. However, I think I have proved my loyalty and ability, so really—"

"Wow, you're such a long-winded pommy wanker," I said, wanting him to shut the fuck up. "Maybe you should go talk the Peons to death. You're certainly killing me, mate."

"Helen, I need Harlow and Sakamoto downloaded now." Jenna turned to the tech.

"I'll do my best, but there's a dirty great bullet hole in my console now." Tracker replied I almost lost Morris uploading her."

She tapped in the commands. I closed my eyes before the flash of light blinded me once again. When I opened them, the surprised, elderly chief engineer, as naked as the day he was born, was standing looking at the group of women surrounding him. "If you have woken me up for some weird sex party, I warn you, girlies, you may not be able to handle me," he said with a snort.

Jenna grinned. "I can't speak for the others, but I think you're a little past that, old man," she said, passing him a towel. "Get off the circle, and we'll explain what's going on in a minute."

He stepped off, and almost instantly, the short figure of Sergeant Tomiko Sakamoto appeared. I unwrapped a towel and passed it to her.

"What's going on, Lieutenant?" she asked grimly.

Jenna quickly explained the situation, and both looked shocked at the news of the surrender, but they had different reactions when they learned of Jenna's intentions.

Harlow leaned back against the wall, folding his arms. "I have worked with you for thirty-plus years, Jen, and still, you surprise me. You've always been straight with me, so I'll be straight with you. I'm not happy about this, not happy at all. But you know you're my gal, and I've got your back."

"That's appreciated, Rocky." Jenna smiled at the old man.

Sakamoto's reaction offered more outright support. "You know you can count on me, lieutenant. Maybe now we can do things properly."

Jenna grinned. "The one thing I knew I could count on was your loyalty, Tomiko. Now there is much to do." She turned to Tracker. "Start bringing people we have worked with for some time—ones you think we can count on. We have a fight ahead."

Tracker looked down at the console and shook her head. "The M.E.T. has started fluctuating. I can no longer stabilize anyone's patterns. We can't bring anyone else out without some workaround."

"Is everyone safe in there?" I asked with concern.

"Yes, but I can't promise it will stay that way," the tech advised.

"Fuck!" Jenna snarled. "Okay, I guess it's up to us. Helen, is there any way you could block transmissions from the Puller to the Peon ship?"

"I can cause some temporary interference by networking into the primary computer," she said. "However, we can only make it permanent via the systems in Environment and Life. Security lockdown."

"Do it. We can't have the Jangle Berries captain informed of what's going on." As the tech began working, Jenna turned back to the Japanese officer. "Get Harlow to engineering. Rocky, get ready to give Stacey all the power you can as soon as she needs it. The rest of you are with me. We will stop by the armory, then head for the Environment and Life room. I have an idea."

We were about to leave the M.E.T. room when the Peon soldier, bleeding out from his gut wound on the floor, groaned. Jenna went to withdraw her firearm again, but mine was ready. I popped him in the back of the head. Phelks gasped, stepping back against the wall.

"What's the matter, mate? You look like you're about to chunder." I smirked.

"It's... It's nothing. You just startled me, that's all," he said, all flustered.

"You're with me, Mr. Phelkar. We need to make for the armory," Jenna said as we headed back out into the corridor. "We will go ahead."

"Wow, you sure I'm the best choice?" He looked quite pleased.

"You're the only choice, Mr. Phelkar," Jenna said casually as she chambered a round in her snap pistol. "We can't risk losing either Grant or Tracker."

"Well, thanks," he said dejectedly.

She looked at him and shrugged off his comment. "Well, you did ask, Mr. Phelkar."

And at those words, she pointed around the corner, and we stepped out and opened fire on two startled guards who were dead before they could get as much as a look at us.

Just as we stepped into the armory, the ship-wide intercom came online with an irritated captain. “Lieutenant Plural, what the hell are you doing?”

Jenna couldn’t resist, and she hit the intercom on the wall. “I’m doing my duty, Sir, as an American and a United States Marine.”

The Peon commander’s voice came on next. It was sickly sweet. “I understand your patriotism, lieutenant, but this is a hopeless fight. Stand down now, and you will be treated fairly. If not, I have the authority to execute you and your entire crew.”

“Listen to reason, girl,” the captain added. “They know what you’re doing. They found the bodies in the M.E.T. room. Why are you doing this?”

“Because I’m Semper Fidelis, *sir*.” Her tone was now bitter. “Some of us haven’t forgotten what that means, *sir*, but I’m about to educate you, *sir*. Plural out.” She switched off the intercom. She turned to Tracker. “Anything you can do about our transponders? It is most likely the captain has given the Peon bastards our codes so they can find us quickly.”

“I can hit them with a disabling pulse, but the nanobots in your system will immediately start repairing it. We will have an hour, two at the most.”

“It will have to do,” Jenna responded. “Go for it.”

Tracker slipped a small device off her belt and held it up to each of our ears. There was a slight irritating buzzing, but otherwise no apparent effect.

During this exchange, I keyed in my code to unlock the weapons and armor lockers. I pulled out a couple of flak jackets and handed them out. Jenna swapped the Peon guns for our own and gave us each four extra clips. Turning to the field ordinance, she grabbed some limpet mines and handed them around. I stuffed them into a backpack I had grabbed out of a locker.

"What do you plan to use these for?" Phelks asked.

Jenna shrugged. "We will board the Peon's ship eventually and might want to blow stuff up."

"Second rule of a military life, mate," I smirked. "Always take what you don't need just in case you need it."

He frowned. "And what is the first rule?"

"Always make sure you know which of your teammates has the biggest dick," Jenna said, chuckling as Phelks turned a beetroot colour. "Hey, it's Stacey's rule, not mine." She said innocently.

"You're learning well, my young apprentice." I laughed before looking at Phelks. "Spot check." He tightened the fasteners on the back of the breastplate. Jenna did the same for Tracker.

"Okay, listen up," Jenna said, all business again. "They know we're fighting back and will be looking for us. Any ideas on how we can get from here to Environment and Life without fighting our way there?"

"I can scan for nearby heat signatures so we can tell who's in the vicinity of wherever we go," Tracker suggested, pulling such a device from one of the shelves.

"That only gives us a heads up on who we are about to get into a fight with, but it's better than nothing. Anything else?" Jenna looked at Phelks, and when he stared blankly at her, she just rolled her eyes and looked at me.

"There is always the ventilation shaft. It will get us two rooms down from the Environment and Life room." I advised.

Jenna grinned at me. "Yes, you're the expert on ventilation shafts. You can lead the way."

It was my turn to blush. She knew I had a penchant for getting rooted in ventilation shafts near the engine room ... what can I say... vibrations are... Hmm, let's just get back to the story.

Jenna then handed out a set of night-vision goggles to everyone except me. My cybernetic eye had me already covered for that. Since my hair hung over my fake eye, and he hadn't seen it, Phelks looked at me quizzically.

I shrugged, "I eat a lot of carrots, mate."

We moved some furniture so we could climb it, and I climbed up, pushed out the ceiling vent, and nimbly disappeared into it. We were soon crammed together in a line. I stopped as I reached another grate.

Jenna called ahead to me, "What's the holdup?"

"There is one snag when you enter the vent via the armory. They seal off the bloody ends with more grates to stop people from getting in that way."

"Here, let me deal with this," said Tracker. It was too tight to swap places conventionally, and I had to lie down while Tracker climbed over the top of me and lay upon me as she worked.

"Fucking hell, have you put on weight, mate?" I gasped.

For the first time since this affair began, Tracker laughed. "Fuck you, Grant." She pulled out a tiny device that made a slight buzzing noise as it magnetically unfastened the screws. Then with a gentle push, she popped it out. She scrambled back off me, and I pulled myself up to my knees and continued on.

After about fifteen minutes, I stopped and pointed to the vent below me. I gave Jenna a thumbs up, but then put a finger to my lips. The vent was larger here, and one could pass another, so Jenna scrambled up next to it and looked down into the room below. It led into a dunny, and a peon was taking a shit. Jenna stared for a long moment, then gave me a most disgusted look. She then scrambled back and whispered something to Tracker that I couldn't hear. Tracker moved up next to me. She, too, looked down, then rolled her eyes at me as she pulled the little device out again. However, this time she left one final screw. Again, she scrambled back, and once more, Jenna went up and gave me a final dirty look. I just shrugged with an innocent stare. Then we both turned around and placed our feet on the vent. Jenna did a count-off with her fingers, and when she got to three, we both slammed our feet down hard.

The cover fell, and we followed. The Peon was on the ground, and Jen quickly twisted his head, snapping his neck. Jenna waved for the others to come down. Then we both left the cubicle to give them room.

"You couldn't find somewhere better than a bathroom?" Jenna was saying.

I shrugged. "I know it sounds weird, but it didn't occur to me that the Peons would need to use the loo."

Jenna just rolled her eyes, shook her head, and headed towards the bathroom door. She peered out at first, then stepped out, waving us along with her. Just two doors down, we were outside the Environment and Life room.

Jenna tapped out the code, and the door slid back. The Environment and Life room was filled with row upon row of computer banks, occupying every possible space in an area that wasn't designed for it. Tracker immediately stepped over to a screen and keyboard and logged herself in.

"Isn't that a little outdated?" Phelks asked her.

"Huh?" Tracker grunted as a reply, not looking up at me as she worked.

"The keyboard. Why aren't you using voice activation? It's a lot faster."

"Voices can be recorded and imitated. The keyboard remains the best device for security."

Jenna hit the intercom once more, calling down to the engineering department. "Sakamoto, give me good news."

The Japanese officer's lightly accented voice returned. "We had a minor encounter but made it safely." In the background, we could hear Harlow complaining about getting blood all over his uniform.

"Good work, Sakamoto. We hope to seal you in there so you don't get any interruptions. Ensure Harlow is ready to fire up those engines if needed. Plural out." She then turned back to Helen Tracker. "Cut the inter-ship communications so the French commander cannot contact his ship."

Tracker's hand darted over the keyboard once more. "Done."

"Are you sure there are no crew members other than us, the captain, and in the med bay presently out of dematerialization?" Jenna stepped up beside her.

"Yes, Ma'am."

"Fine, start shutting down all the air systems everywhere except this room, the med bay, and engineering. Do it fast. They will know where we are even without our transponders once we start shutting things down." Helen Tracker's hands hesitated. She looked up at Jenna, her face filled with concern. "He has given us no choice, Sergeant. If you know of another way, any of you, tell me now." The silence spoke volumes. "Stand aside, Sergeant. Tell me what to do."

Helen Tracker showed her, and then Jenna's fingers nimbly dashed over the controls. The intercom crackled into life with the captain's voice less than thirty seconds later. "What the hell are you doing, Plural? You stupid bitch."

She looked at me and nodded to the intercom as she worked. I turned it on. "You haven't given me much of an option, Captain." She said bitterly.

"What the hell do you expect to achieve, girl? Fight a war on your own?" He sounded almost hysterical now.

"I hope I won't be alone, sir. I hope there are patriots like me who want to fight back."

"Mademoiselle," came the silky voice of the French commander, "you're achieving nothing here. I have dispatched troops to your location. We will be out of here, and you will be dead in a matter of minutes. You will be remembered as an idiot if you're remembered at all."

"Hey, at least I'll be remembered as an *American* idiot.

"Zut! So be it." The intercom went ship-wide, and he ordered in French.

Jenna looked at Phelks, and he quickly translated. "They are coming."

Chapter Seventeen

My First Command

She nodded in acknowledgment and said to the group, "This is it, boys and girls. It will take some time to open that door."

"They won't get a chance to," said Helen Tracker. "I have run a bypass through the defense systems using my back-door password. I can turn on the automated internal weapons right here, but there is a problem. It requires an officer of a command rank to authorize it."

"That is not a problem," Phelks said, confused by what she said. "Lieutenant Plural is of command rank."

Helen Tracker flushed bright red, and Stacey looked the other way. There was a moment of silence before Jenna spoke in a cold, bitter tone.

"I'm a GenMod, Mr. Phelkar. I cannot be trusted with weaponry that could be turned on our own troops. Even as the second officer, the government won't allow me to do certain things."

He pondered this a moment, then looked back to Tracker. "But surely there must be emergencies where Lieutenant Plural can take command in the event of the death of Royce and Morris?"

"Yes, but neither of them is dead," she replied, confused.

"But does the computer know that?" He asked intently. "Can you update their records to say they are deceased?"

"I can, but Lieutenant Plural will still have restrictions based on her rank and genetic modifications."

"So, that's a start. Change the record to indicate that she's been promoted."

Helen Tracker looked uncertain but simply shrugged. "I can but try."

She tapped on the keyboard, and there was a long, nervous pause before the ship's computer came online on the intercom.

"Attention all personnel," it stated in its melodic male voice, "with immediate effect, First Lieutenant Jennacia Louise Plularian has assumed command of the U.S.S. Lewis Puller with orders to return to the nearest U.S. base immediately."

"Bloody hell," I laughed.

"Don't start celebrating yet," Tracker muttered as she continued to tap out on the keyboard. "If you went to the cockpit now, you would find that you could only set the ship to the coordinates of the nearest base. We probably have less control now than we had before."

There was a long, silent pause, and then a grin crossed Helen Tracker's face, and she stepped back. The computer intoned once more, "Attention all personnel, with immediate effect, Major Jennacia Louise Plularian has assumed command of the U.S.S. Lewis Puller."

"Well, that scared me for a moment there," Tracker said with relief. "It kept refusing to allow me to enter the rank of major. So, I told it there was an error in Lieutenant Plural's file and deleted the fact that she was genetically modified. Then, bingo, it let me update the rank as easily as that."

"Helen Tracker, I could kiss you," Jenna said to the chief tech. I heard Helen mutter that she wouldn't complain about that.

Jenna pulled herself together and instructed Tracker to engage assault weapons at her leisure.

Tracker's fingers darted nimbly over the controls as she encoded the weapons system to target all life forms not currently wearing a Marine pin.

We heard gunfire followed by the cries of dying troops. The sound was coming from all over the ship. Silence eventually fell once more, but still, we waited. It had been a desperate decision. The risk to the vessel's integrity, although small, was still a threat.

"Open up engineering and let Sakamoto and Harlow out, and let's go," Jenna commanded.

As we headed back into the corridor, the walls, floor, and ceiling were shredded by gunfire. The ship looked like a giant cheese grater with gouges on all the walls. We encountered bodies of French troops whose remains were barely recognizable as human. We stopped at the mess hall, and Jenna led us in.

"So, how do we take the cockpit?" I asked as I flopped into a seat.

"We don't," Jenna said firmly as she took a seat between me and Tracker. "If we take the Lewis Puller now, the captain of the Jangle Berry will become aware. To succeed, we must take the Jangle Berry."

Phelks was making a pot of coffee at the counter as Jenna said this, but he turned to her with wide-eyed disbelief. "So, how exactly do you propose to take the Peon ship?" he asked as Sakamoto and Harlow came in. "These are insurmountable odds."

"Bloody hell, Phelkar, don't be such a gloomy guts." He was really pissing me right off.

Jenna looked at me. "Stacey, you must have some ideas. Didn't you study Peon ship design as an air intelligence officer in the Australian Air Force?"

"Wow, that's bloody eons ago now. But yeah, now let me think about it. The Peon ship is a light cruiser of the Lafayette class. This means waking a crew that could be as many as forty-six, not counting troops that are probably in an M.E.T. However, it is most likely that most were deployed in boarding the Chesty. She doesn't have internal defense systems solely relying on manpower to repel boarders."

Phelks had been passing around coffee whilst I spoke. "The six of us against forty-two? I don't like those odds."

"Oh, do shut up, Mr. Phelkar," Jenna ordered irritably. "Carry on, Stacey."

"The pom is right, major. We don't have a chance in hell of assaulting that ship, not without downloading a lot more Marines." I replied honestly.

Jenna looked to Tracker. "What're the chances of getting the M.E.T. back online?"

Tracker shrugged. "Honestly, I'm not even sure I can. I'm a programmer and an operator, not a repairman."

"You're a repairman now," Jenna advised. "But I'm sure Harlow can help you."

Harlow grunted but nodded.

"We're still talking several days." Tracker looked exasperated.

"That's your sole priority now, got it?" Jenna insisted.

Helen gave up the fight and, with a weary sigh, said, "Got it, Major."

"Oh, that's one less person," Phelks muttered.

"Mr. Phelkar," Jenna snapped, "you know I know how to break bones?"

"No, but it would be a reasonable assumption, given that you're a United States Marine," He replied.

"Well, if you don't knock off the negative crap, I'll start breaking yours. Do you understand me?"

"Yes, Ma'am," he said meekly.

She turned to the others. "There must be some way we can take that ship."

She looked at me again. "Well, the ship does have one weakness that could compromise everyone inside," I told her. "But, fuck, you're not gonna like it, major."

Jenna's eyes narrowed. "Tell me."

"If we blow all six airlocks at the same time. The environmental defense systems cannot respond in time to sudden decompression. Unless someone is sealed somewhere, they're gonna be dead."

"So," Jenna said, looking confused. "Let's just do that."

I hesitated a moment. "As soon as they secured the Chesty, they would have disconnected to take both ships wherever they wanted. There will be some distance between us and the Peon ship now."

Jenna went pale and leaned back wearily in her seat. "You're talking about a spacewalk."

I glanced at Sakamoto, who immediately averted her eyes. I looked back at Jenna. "Yes, boss."

"What's the problem with that?" Phelks asked, somewhat bemused.

Jenna sighed and colored a little. "There is only one thing that I hate, Mr. Phelkar, and that's leaving a ship in the middle of space."

"You're a Space Marine, and you're scared of space?" He chuckled. Jenna punched him in the side of the head, and he went crashing to the floor. She was already talking with us again by the time he recovered.

"That's our only option?" she asked dejectedly.

"No," I shrugged. "But it's the only one I know of that leaves us with an intact ship to use afterward."

Sakamoto shook her head. "If we are aware of this, then the French are aware of this. It would be a standard tactic for taking out the ship."

"We have the elements of surprise," I said. "They believe that we are currently under their control."

"They will know by now that communications between the two ships are down," Jenna replied.

"We can render the E.M.U. Suits scanner invisible," Tracker said.

"The Peons cracked that technology more than ten years ago," Sakamoto said, frowning.

"Yes, but it still takes a couple of minutes for anyone to be detected, and that's after they start looking for them," Tracker said. "I would trust that the French will not be looking for us."

Jenna let out a long, weary sigh. "Very well, if that's what we have to do, let's do it."

"Don't get pissed at me, Jenna," Sakamoto said intently. "But are you sure you can do this? I have been out there with you before."

"I'll be fine." But the tremor in her voice did not instill confidence in the assembled group. "Sakamoto, I want you to take point on this one. We can't risk my issues getting in the way of the operation."

Tomiko Sakamoto nodded. "No worries, Major."

Jenna looked around the room. "We need six. That gives us a problem. I don't want to risk Tracker or Stacey, and Mr. Phelkar is bloody useless."

"Hey, that's not fair. I think I've played a good part so far," Phelks protested.

Jenna ignored him and continued. "That means I have to take you, Mr. Harlow. It's a toss-up between you and Tracker, and I need her working on getting my Marines out of storage. Are you up to it?"

The old man grunted and shifted in his seat. "I was doing spacewalks before you girlies knew where to stuff a tampon. Of course, I'm up for it."

Jenna grinned. "I'm older than you, you grump."

Harlow snorted. "I was supposed to retire to a little farm in Kentucky after this mission, and now I've got a goddamn GenMod making me do a spacewalk."

"That leaves just three more spaces." She leaned back and reached the intercom on the wall. "Doctor Archer, I need three Marines. What have you got for me?"

"I'm willing to release Kelsey Anthony, and you can now have Dodgson, but that's it," the doctor stated firmly.

"I need one more, doctor. If they can walk and hold a gun, patch them up and send them to me." Jenna ordered.

The doctor started to protest, but a man began talking to her in the background. We could not make out the words. The doctor returned to us with a sigh. "Sergeant Hardy will join you, too. However, I will note that he has discharged himself against my advice."

"Noted, Doctor, thank you." Jenna turned off the intercom and turned back to us. "Okay, Marines, I want everyone ready in one hour. Stacey and Sakamoto stay with me to go over the ship plans. Tracker, keep working on the M.E.T."

"What do you want me to do?" Phelks asked.

Jenna pondered that a moment, then raised her empty coffee cup and, with a smile, said, "Be a darling and refill this for me, would you, Mr. Phelkar?"

He sighed and took the cup.

I can't tell you much about the mission to take Jangle Berry because I wasn't there. I couldn't even sit up in the cockpit, where I felt most at home as we waited, since the Captain and the Peon Commander were locked in there.

Instead, I went to the little cabin that had been converted into Helen Tracker's office. I took a bottle of Scotch, but I didn't end up drinking anything when she declined to join me; drinking alone looks terrible when you're not alone. "So what do you make of all this, Stacey?" she asked me.

I pondered her question before answering truthfully. "Well, it'll more than likely end with us all dead. I think the chances of success are slim, but if anyone can pull it off, it's Jenna. I, for one, will be damned if I accept Australia will become some permanent European puppet state."

Tracker pondered this, staring off into space before suddenly coming back to the conversation at hand and saying, very unenthusiastically, "You are probably right."

"Honestly, mate, I don't know anymore. I've never been one to think with my head, but rather my gut, and that has been chewed up since The Cape. "

"I can understand that. But it's hard for us to comprehend peace. We've never known it in our lifetime," she said, sitting back and pondering.

"Well, I'm a little older than you, and I can just about remember when it started. There was a lot of panic and fear because everyone thought they'd start firing nukes. Turns out even our own governments weren't dumb enough to engage in mutually assured destruction." I laughed, but Helen was clearly not amused. "We were one of the last to get involved. We had intended to remain neutral. However, when trade supplies to the outer worlds started to become affected, and we started running out of things, we threw our lot in with the Pacific Alliance. My dad tried to get us visas to go to the Martian colonies; my brother and I didn't want to leave, though, so we were pleased when the planet closed itself to immigration due to the conflict." I changed my mind about that drink and took a large swig from the bottle. "It's all a bunch of shit, really, isn't it?"

"Pretty much," Helen chuckled before quickly becoming serious again as she looked at me and said, "But you sound anti-war."

"Everyone should be anti-war. If you're not anti-war, you're a fucking psycho. But it's a question of trade-offs, isn't it? You have to decide whether or not you are so opposed to the war that you're willing to roll over like a dog and let others tell you how to live your life." A silence fell between us, one of those awkward silences where neither of us knew what to say. Both Tracker and I liked each other, but we had nothing in common, and as a consequence, conversation between us had always been difficult. It was almost a relief when Jenna eventually came online and told Tracker to meet Phelks at the airlock to the Jangle Berry. She headed off, and I took the opportunity to return to my quarters, still wondering how it was going but knowing better than to call Jenna during an operation. I was relieved when I finally got the call to crossover onto the Jangle Berry. Climbing into my EMU, I crossed over the umbilical, making sure to deactivate my personal D.E. device as I stepped out into the gravity of the Peon ship.

I made my way up to the bridge, where I found Jenna and Phelkar, along with Tracker. I don't remember Dodgson being there, but she's such an unassuming girl that she's easy to miss.

Jenna didn't waste any time on pleasantries. "Can you fly this thing?"

"I don't see why not," I said, sitting at the console and studying the controls.

"Fine, once we have dealt with our captain and the French commander, I'm putting you in command of this ship. I'll send some help to get rid of these bodies as soon as I can. Sakamoto, you stay with her. Do whatever she needs. You'll hear from us once we regain the bridge of the Chesty," and with that, they returned to the Lewis Puller, and I assumed my first real command. I was starting to feel a little annoyed at being left out of everything. The rigid Sakamoto wasn't exactly the warmest company.

Nevertheless, we were friendly. I overlooked the fact that she didn't like anime, which to me seemed weird, considering she's Japanese. She eventually headed back over to the Puller for the night since there was nowhere for us to sleep on board the new ship.

Chapter Eighteen

Fun with Phelks

After a couple of hours on my own, knowing we weren't going anywhere. Thus, my services as a pilot were no longer needed, and I wandered back over to the Lewis Puller. Heading to my room, I grabbed one of the last three remaining flasks of ambrosia from my mother's distillery. Jenna had gotten them for me as part of my payment for the Pallas mission four years prior, and I pulled them out on the rarest of occasions: Harper's birthday, Anzac Day, and the anniversary of the day Cape York fell. Right now, it wasn't any of those days, but I decided that in spite of that fact, a depressed Stacey was reason enough for me to crack open a fresh one. I headed to the mess, sat back in a chair, put my feet up on the table, and crossed my legs. I unfastened my military-issue bra and slung it into the corner of my chair. I hated those fuckers.

By the time Phelker walked in, I was already half-cut.

Yeah, yeah, I know you've been dying to hear my version of events about the night I fucked Phelks. Hell, you probably skipped through this book just to get your jollies. Well, go back to your porn channels, boys and girls, cos it isn't as exciting as he made out. I don't care if he has an eidetic memory chip. His version of the following events was, let's say, a little more skewed in his favor.

"Heeeeyyyyy. If it isn't our resident Pommy hunk," I was taking the piss; I was definitely *not* flirting. Phelkar didn't actually become attractive to me until I was really shitfaced. Sorry, but he honestly wasn't my type with his soft hands, and that accent just didn't do it for me.

Phelks just grunted at me and threw himself into a chair – something was up for sure. "Who pissed in your cornflakes?" I was a little irritated that he was bumming me out with his downer.

"I'm not in the mood for it, Stacey," he replied like a sulky kid.

"Wow, I'm just messing with you, Phelks. Something's sure got your goat, though. Come on, tell your Auntie Stacey all about it." To be honest, I didn't really care. I just felt obligated to ask.

"How come you're not on the Jangle Berry?" he asked, ignoring my question. Of course, he'd actually used the correct French pronunciation because he's so irritatingly clever and worldly.

I couldn't help but laugh. "Well, I don't like seeing a mess hall with dead Peons lying around, plus the lack of air makes it hard to drink."

"Ah, yes, sorry, that's next on my list of things to resolve. I'll get Dodgson on in the morning. "What's that?" he pointed to my drink.

Now that was more like it. "This, my good sir, is pure Australian ambrosia, the nectar of the Aussie gods," I said as I picked the flask up from the floor. "This right here is Portobello Brandy. One of the very last bottles from Oz."

He stared in amazement. "Wow, how much did that set you back? I heard they auction it nowadays!"

I smirked. "Never cost me anything. Jenna got it for me."

His eyes widened. "Wow, that costs thousands, literally. Even before the annexation, it was beyond the average person's means."

"Oh, the American taxpayer picked up the bill on this. After the Battle of Cape York and the fall of Oz, the boss wanted to recruit me. I asked for this as part of my sign-on bonus."

"She must have really wanted you," He said, surprised.

"What can I say? I'm good at what I do, Phelks." I chuckled.

"You could've just asked for the money."

"What's the point in money if you can't go surfing on Bondi Beach?" I shrugged.

"Well, I haven't had the fortune of visiting Australia, and I'll certainly never get to surf." He sighed.

"Well, I'll make you a promise. When we kick the Peons out of Oz, I'll take you surfing, but only if you wear a pair of budgie smugglers." I winked as I poured him a drink.

He flushed again and said, almost stammering. "Oh, my dear Stacey, I'm sure a delightful young man is waiting for you."

I shrugged and gave him a sideways look as I handed him the glass. "Maybe, but he ain't here right now, and as I said, there's a big shortage of men on this ship." I yawned and stretched my tight white shirt, showing off my boobs, and as intended, he didn't fail to notice. "I plan on getting absolutely smashed tonight, so, hey, I might even end up fucking you," I said as if he'd have no say in the matter. He looked startled and downed his glass in one. "Hey," I said irritably. "That's not some cheap Russian vodka."

"I'm sorry," he rasped, the heat of the drink in his throat. "I guess you should pour another and let me try again."

I refilled his glass, and let my legs slip off the table and onto hislap. He didn't know how to respond, acted like it wasn't happening, yet rested his hand on my shin.

It was only then that he noticed the bra in the chair, and his eyes were instinctively drawn back to my tits. "Enjoying the view, Phelks?" I laughed.

"I have no idea what you mean." He lied. I could feel the pressure of his donger building against my calf.

"You're so full of shit, Phelks!" I chuckled, bit my lower lip provocatively, and rubbed my leg against the growing bulge in his trousers. He made some sort of stifled whimper and started massaging my calf. "Oh, that feels *so* good." I closed my eyes and let my head fall back. He nervously moved his hand up to my knee, then hesitated.

I like forplay as much as the next Sheila, but this was like trying to fuck a forty-year-old virgin, and I was way too toey for this shit. I put my glass down, slipped my legs off his lap, and stood up. Standing astride his knees, I sat down upon his lap, my wrists crossed behind his neck. I plucked the glass from his hand and knocked back the remains. His hands went to my hips and then grabbed my backside. He pulled me closer. I giggled at his awkwardness and leaned down. His lips met mine, soft and gentle at first. But as we kissed, the intensity grew. I pulled back and whispered. "Get up, mister." I pulled him up, pulling him to his feet. "Come on. I can think of one place where you can root me that doesn't stink of greasy food and United States Marine armpit sweat."

We ran down the cramped corridor towards my quarters. I was so sure we were louder than we meant to, but that didn't seem to bother us at the time. I clicked the door open and grabbed him by the shirt collar, pulling him through the door and into my quarters. Looking into his eyes, I said softly, "I want you, Phelks."

He smiled, looking down at me, and he reached up to push aside the pink hair that covered my right eye. He suddenly tensed and let out a startled gasp. I'm not exactly vain, but as you have seen, I am a little sensitive about my artificial eye, with its deep scar running over it, which looks like something out of a cheesy cyborg sci-fi flick.

I backed away, but he pulled me back."Hey," He said gently. "It's okay. I was just startled. It doesn't bother me, honestly."

I hesitated momentarily, but then my smile slowly returned, and we kissed once more. "You know, Phelks. I have never fucked an Englishman before."

He chuckled, "Well, there is a first time for everything, and hey, if it helps, I have never slept with an Australian before."

"Then you have never lived, Phelks." I grinned. "It's a known fact you can't get better than an Aussie girl. Especially one from Wagga." He chuckled again as I undid my belt, pulled it through the loops with a swift flick, and tossed it behind me. Why, Phelks, I do believe you have gone right past boring and blushing and straight to bold," I whispered in his ear as my hands slid his shirt up over his head. He squeezed his hands on my hips, letting out a low grunt as his daks came down. "Wow. So that's what you were hiding under there. I'm impressed." I crossed my arms over my stomach and took hold of the bottom hem of my shirt, inching it higher before removing it completely and throwing it among the heaped clothes in the corner.

His hand went to my breast, causing me to lean my head back. I suddenly lost balance and, grabbing onto him, we tumbled down onto the bed, me on my back and him falling on top of me. It was the perfect accident. Without hesitation, I brought my hands up to either side of his face, and we started kissing again, lips and tongues going every which way with a fervent passion as my hands explored his body. I'm not exactly a missionary girl, and I rolled him over and climbed on top, taking charge of the situation.

As I guided him in, he looked like an excited schoolboy, which was such a turn-off, so I closed my eyes. Now I can't say

Phelks was a great lover. I had had better plenty of times, but he was adequate to what I needed right then.

There's one thing that made this encounter different from the other blokes I'd been with before. He was so giving and caring. He treated me with gentle respect. I'd been looking for some tension relief, but as I lay there in my post-coital bliss, curled up against him, I felt scared. I felt close to him in a way I never had with a man, and it unnerved me. Before today, I'd never really given him much thought beyond him being that whiny brat, but now... I'm not sure what I thought at first. I certainly couldn't allow myself to have feelings for this man.

I don't know why, but I felt the need to clarify the situation. "This doesn't make you my boyfriend or anything." I wanted to make it very, very clear.

"If that's what you want," he said. I read it as a sign of his disappointment. I feel kind of confused now. I can honestly say I've never really gotten into a steady relationship. The nature of my life has meant people I've gotten close to often died, and I've kind of had a barrier up against getting into long-term, or even short-term relationships, for that matter. Yet, there was a guy who gave off a vibe that he genuinely cared about me. Ironic, really, because after reading Phelkar's account of this incident, he didn't see me as anything more than a fuck toy either. This confusion I felt led to complications in my relationships with both Jenna and him.

"This was just a bit of fun. If I led you on to believe it would be more than that, I'm sorry."

"It's fine. I'm glad I shared this experience with you."

I thought he was into me really badly. "Oh shit, don't go mushy on me, Phelks. It was just a root."

He kissed me ever so gently, and my heart literally fluttered. "Don't worry. I know where we stand." Good for him, I thought, because I had no fucking clue.

He fell asleep with me in his arms, and apparently, he thought I was satiated and ready for sleep, too. I wasn't. I carefully detached myself from him, and I dressed as quickly as I could. I headed out of the room and slept in one of the crew bunks that night, giving him space to get up and leave the next day without it getting awkward. I was severely pissed off with myself. He had been so caring to me, and that was something I wasn't used to. For me, sex was just something you did from time to time to blow out the cobwebs, so I seriously did *not* want to develop feelings for this guy. For fuck sake, he was old enough to be my dad, for one thing!

Chapter Nineteen

The Lady Liberty

I'd like to take time out to introduce you to the Lady Liberty. I don't think she was called the Lady Liberty by this time, but since I can't say Jangle Berry properly, I'm gonna start using it from now on. I hope that's okay with you. Truth be told, even if it isn't, I don't really give a shit. It's hilarious just thinking about anyone possibly listening to this or reading it if they print it out. Come to think of it, it's weird how you're gonna know all this stuff about me, and I don't know a damn thing about you. Well, that is, unless you're in my group of friends here, but here I am going off on a tangent.

Now, where was I?

Oh yeah, the Lady Liberty.

I want to talk about her because she was my first command. Even though my time with her was short, you can't deny she was a beaut. Now I know she wasn't an American or Aussie ship, but rather she was 'spoils of war.' As was typical with the light Peon cruisers, she was all shiny and chrome, both inside and out. Her corridors were wider than on any American ship, and the officer accommodation was about twice the size. Even though enlisted personnel shared bunkrooms, the beds were little cubicles that could be closed, giving you a modicum of privacy. Like the Chesty, she had no external armaments or fighter craft – thanks to countermeasures that now made any type of intelligent missile weaponry redundant. However, that didn't stop either side from trying. A vast amount of GDP was thrown into researching new and exciting ways to eradicate human life.

No, the exciting thing about the Lady Liberty was in her engines. She didn't have just one quantum thruster. No, this baby had two. You see, there's the Einstein problem. In a nutshell, the faster you go, the slower time becomes. Now don't ask me to explain it. That's something to ask someone like Tracker about. I think by now, you know I'm no science nerd. Even trying to wrap my mind around the concept makes my head feel like it's about to explode. Just accept it like I do, and we'll move on. Right, so we measure speed by what we call standards; you'll often hear me refer to standard by two or standard by three. With both engines going, this little Peon beauty could hit standard by five. Breaking that down, how fast is standard by five? In a nutshell: fucking fast. However, going that fast, well, that does all sorts of squishy things with time. You can find that your flight takes any number of months on your ship. Yet, an entire year could've passed outside of your ship. That is crazy fucked up. As a result, ships are fitted with the Einstein compensator device. Now I can't tell you how that works either; let's just say it ensures your watch still shows the same time as the planet you're landing on. The Lady Liberty's two engines and fast speeds had the potential to outrun the capacity of Albie's compensator. This meant the second engine was a complete waste of time. You could not hit those maximum speeds without the universe shooting you in your snatch and time getting all fucked up.

While that is all interesting, the biggest problem we faced was that, despite being able to recycle air, we couldn't create it, at least not outside a colossal production facility with a team of eggheads messing with molecules. Having blown out all the airlocks, we'd pretty much expelled almost every pocket of air possible. In the end, we had to siphon some off from the Chesty.

Doing this meant we were forced to seal off vast sections of the Lady Liberty to the point I could barely leave the bridge. I didn't even have access to the dunny! I managed to set up a porta-potty in the Captain's ready room – not ideal, but it solved the issue temporarily. Now that you know that, you can understand why I devoted a lot of my time to working out where we could pick up new air supplies.

I was given a skeleton crew. Harlow assigned one of his assistants, Lucas Tarrant, as my Chief Engineer, but he was locked away at the other end of the ship with no way of getting to me without an EMU suit. Sakamoto stayed on the bridge with me, but we didn't have much to discuss. My only genuine interest in Japan was in anime and manga, and apparently, she found those childish – the nerve! Tell me, whoever heard of a Jap that doesn't like anime? Weird huh! And there was a Techie called Daisy Bell. And in case you're wondering, yes, I did have fun with that name! But alas, she didn't give me her answer do.

As the repairs of the two ships were underway, I spent my time with Daisy going over charts that listed nearby allied and enemy resupply depots. It was no surprise that none were on our side. The Peons had dominated Martian space sectors for a couple of years. Multiple nations had colonies on Mars, but we were pretty well cut off from them. Daisy did point out that a large station orbited Demos. Since we weren't going down onto Phobos with the others, we started to work on a plan to try to get the much-needed oxygen supply from the Peons themselves. "Although the base is large," Daisy said to me. "It's mostly automated and is only manned by three or four people."

"That sounds a little too good to be true," I said skeptically. "They wouldn't leave such a valuable base unguarded."

"Absolutely. They rely on fighters from Mars to respond to any incoming foreign ship."

"And, there's the rub. We can't respond to that sort of force."

Daisy rolled her eyes and looked exasperated. "Captain!"

"Call me Stacey," I said, not looking up from the plans as I tried to work out another possible option.

"Stacey, we *aren't* a foreign ship to them."

I looked up at her. You know that feeling you get when you realize you've just done something dumb? Don't lie; you know you do. "Well, clearly, I'm the big dunderhead for once."

Daisy grinned. "It's an oversight anyone could make, Ma'am."

"Do you think you could stick your nose any further up my arse, Daisy?" I replied, but with a smile."You don't have to worry about my ego. It's big enough and hard enough that it isn't easily bruised. Now, tell me more about this base and what you have in mind."

"Well, although it's a major base for the Peons, it isn't a strategic target. It will probably have only the basic protocols and, like I said, three or four personnel."

"How much 'probably' are we talking about here? I really don't do 'probably' very well," I asked warily.

"I'm quite confident," Daisy nodded.

"And 'quite' is as good as I'm gonna get, right?" I said with a dejected sigh.

"Sorry, Ma'am... I mean, Stacey. We should have no problem approaching the base. Heck, we may get them to replenish us without even needing to leave the ship," she said hopefully.

"Yeah, well, I've never been that lucky," I said with a tone of irony, running through the scenarios in my head before continuing. "I think we need to get Jenna on this. Maybe she can give us some personnel just in case the shit hits the fan." I went over to the ship's controls and called the Puller. "Boss, you got a minute?"

"You can have all the time you need, Stacey. Go ahead."

"I've come up with a possible solution to our issue, or rather Daisy here has."

"I'm listening," Jenna responded cautiously.

"While you're down on Phobos, Daisy and I are gonna hop over to a Peon base. She thinks we will be able to pick up some air supplies from there. She thinks we could even do it without engaging the enemy; however, I'm not quite so convinced about that part."

"Yeah, I don't think you can count on that," Jenna sighed, and there was a moment of silence before she came back. "Do you want me to send you over some Marines?"

"That's what I was hoping for," I chuckled lightly.

"Are you sure you're gonna be back in time for our departure from Phobos?"

"Honestly, I have no idea. But we're gonna give it a red hot go," I laughed. "I don't think three Peons are gonna give us too much hassle, though."

"Even so. You're not going in there without any backup.

"Thanks, Boss. Just one more thing?"

"Go ahead."

"Make sure you send over some good-looking blokes. I'm getting kind of tired of all the estrogen over here."

Jenna laughed. "Sorry, Stacey, I'll be sending troops over based on their ability, not their looks or gender."

"You're killing me, Boss. You're absolutely killing me."

She chuckled. "Hey, I just don't want you to end up pregnant and then ask for maternity leave. Plural out."

I pulled up every schematic I could find on the small station. Daisy and I spent the next hour going over it. We only stopped when we received the request to open the airlock. Jenna had sent us over four Marines – two females and two males. Sadly, the females were better looking than the males.

One of them was clearly unimpressed that she'd been pulled off the Phobos mission, and she somehow thought it would be appropriate to complain to me about it – this wasn't uncommon. You see, many enlisted Yanks didn't consider us, foreign U.S. Officers, to hold any actual authority.

Corporal Taggart was an older woman, much taller than me, who looked down at me, both literally and figuratively, from the moment she stepped aboard the Liberty. Behind her, she was trailed by three Privates. "I don't know why I have to come over here. We've been training forever for this mission, to be passed over to..." her voice trailed off as she stared at me.

I folded my arms and tilted my head slightly, fixing her with a steely gaze. "Please continue to speak your mind. Come on. You may as well get it out of your system while you can," I said to her.

"Well, Ma'am, I mean no disrespect, but..."

"Hold up," I raised my hand and put it in front of her face. "Starting a sentence with 'I mean no disrespect' means the next words that are about to come flying out of your mouth are going to, without a doubt, disrespect me, Corporal."

She looked flustered at this, but as I turned away and led them up to the bridge, she grew more emboldened. "It isn't right to have a United States Marine under the command of a foreigner."

"I get that. Hell, I wasn't particularly chuffed when I was placed under the command of a foreigner myself."

She paused, seeming to ponder this for a moment. "I never really thought of it like that before. It must be just as bizarre for you."

"Now it's even more bizarre for me."

"How so?"

"I've had to work for fucking Yanks for years now. You're lucky. You now have the absolute privilege of working for an Australian."

"I don't think you're very funny, Stacey."

"Now, wait up a minute," I turned on her. "That's Ma'am to you, Corporal."

Taggart frowned. "My understanding was you don't like all that formality!"

"Oh, everyone else can call me Stacey. Only you have to call me Ma'am from now on."

"Oh, is that how it's going to be?"

I stepped up chest to chest with her, my eyes mere millimeters from hers. "You fucking better believe it, you stuck-up bitch," she blinked as spittle from my mouth hit her cheek. "I've invested four years with the United States Navy, and I have fucking earned your fucking respect," I finished and stepped back. "You step out of line. Question a single order, or disobey a single command of mine, and I will fucking shoot you myself. Am I clear, Corporal?"

She stood to attention. "Yes, Ma'am."

I turned to the other three and looked them up and down. "Which one of you has the biggest schlong?"

They stared blankly at me, and I stared back until the second woman said, "What's a 'schlong'?"

I rolled my eyes. "Penis, dick, cock."

"That would be Cartwright, Ma'am," she responded without thinking, and the two men looked uneasy.

I couldn't help but laugh as she realized what she had done, and her face went crimson. "I was gonna give the command to the guy with the biggest schlong, but you clearly have the biggest balls. What's your name?"

"Pentauk."

"First name?"

"Audra."

"Well, Audra, you're going to be the Acting Corporal for the rest of this mission. This bitch just got herself demoted, and if she doesn't pull her weight on this mission, I'll be talking to Major Plural about making it permanent." I then looked at the two men, "Which one of you is Cartwright?"

"That would be me, Ma'am," one of them said.

"When this mission is over, we have to swap contact details," I gave him a wink, and he blushed. "You'll all have to use the Captain's ready room as bunk quarters. Thanks to our limited air supply, we can't open up the crew cabins, so we're all gonna sleep in the same room. And just so you know, if any of you snore, I will put you out of the airlock. Dismissed." Without another word, I turned away and moved back to Daisy and the plans while they settled in. Eventually, I called Audra out of the ready room to join us for a military perspective. "How did Miss Uptight respond to her field demotion?" I asked.

Audra looked at me nervously. "She is plenty pissed, Ma'am," she told me. "Permission to speak freely, Ma'am?"

I gave her a feigned, bewildered look, "Is someone keeping track of what we're saying that you need to ask?"

Audra just smiled and gave a weak laugh. "Taggart is gonna make my life a living hell when this mission is over."

I shook my head disbelievingly. "That's another reason she's not fit for her rank. You didn't do anything. It was my doing, but I'm beyond her reach, so she's gonna take it out on you. But I don't want you to worry, Audra. I'm gonna do what I can to see that this change sticks, and if it doesn't, I'll make sure she stays on the Chesty, and you can stay here with me. Fair enough?"

"Fair enough, Ma'am," she smiled.

"It's Stacey, okay."

"Okay, Stacey."

We spent the next couple of hours going through the plan in case we had to board and take the station by force. When the other Marine heard that I would be boarding with them, he protested. "Nothing personal, Ma'am, but you aren't a Marine. We cannot guarantee your safety."

"Keep calling me 'Ma'am,' and I can't guarantee *your* safety, Corporal." Then I explained, "I may not be a Marine, but you're not a pilot. Do you know how to refuel and siphon air into an interplanetary ship?"

He processed what I said before replying, "You make a good point, Ma'am... I mean, Stacey."

At that point, I realized I was getting hungry, and I wrapped up the meeting. I had my Marines go through virtual drills over the next couple of days, while Jenna prepared her Marines for the Phobos mission. When I say 'virtual,' we didn't have space to practice physically, so instead, Daisy had set them up with computer screens displaying the ship's blueprints. I made them study every part of that station intensely. They had to know it as if they'd been there regularly.

Finally, one morning, I received the call I had been waiting for. Every day, I'd meet up with Jenna for about 20 minutes to update each other on our progress. On that day, she told me she was ready to go. I called Batty, who was taking over my role as Chief Pilot of the Lewis Puller. It was just a courtesy call to wish him well, but part of me didn't like that someone else would be flying my kite. Batty was a really nice guy. Sorry, I should say he is a nice guy – it's not like he's dead or anything. However, he has come close a few times. He's an okay pilot, and I trust him, but he's too by-the-book and doesn't think outside the box when it's needed. So, with that, I was kind of nervous about leaving my team's lives in his hands, but I didn't let on that I was concerned.

When it came time to continue on our way, Jenna and the senior officers transferred to us.

"G'day, Major, welcome aboard the Lady Liberty," I said, getting up as she entered the bridge.

Jenna smiled back and nodded, "Let the record show I'm assuming transferring authority to the Lady Liberty at this time."

I nodded and returned to my seat, and Jenna took her place in the command chair. "How about those engines, Miss Grant?" Jenna asked. I fired them up, and the delicate hum of the engines grew louder.

"Engines online and purring like a kitten, Major."

Jenna grinned. "Well, Stacey, let's get this kitten to Phobos."

As we continued toward the minefield, I spent some time with Helen Tracker. She worked out how to ultimately change the transponder from the Jangleberry so the Lady Liberty was marked as an American vessel. Jenna wanted us to be able to switch over the moment the Phobos mission was over.

The plan was that I would drop them off, but once the base was secured, the Chesty would come in for the pick-up since it could land, and we couldn't. Slowly, I managed to bring them to the edge of a minefield as close as possible. It was then up to Sakamoto to spacewalk over to the satellites and reprogram them using a kit supplied by Tracker. There was a tense moment when the Phobos base called us to find out what we were doing. Phelks managed to talk us out of the situation with his perfect French. Mission accomplished, Sakamoto returned to the Liberty. I then took the Liberty onto Phobos. At this point, Jenna moved her people down into the rear docking bay in EMU suits, ready for me to attempt to take them in for the jump. I broke all protocols by taking the ship down to about thirty meters above the surface, kicking up dust in my wake. I skimmed over the small moon, trying to reduce speed to the slowest possible while still maintaining my set altitude. Then I hit the green light, and over the intercom, I heard Jenna give the orders to go. She was the last to leave, and her parting words were, "Stacey. If I don't make it back, keep up the fight."

"Just make sure you make it back, Boss. I don't wanna take command of a bunch of inbred Yanks." I heard her laugh, and then there was silence. I pondered for a moment whether I would see them again, and I closed the hatch before pulling up back into the darkness of space and laid in a course for Station de Ravitaillement Mimas. Wow, that was a bloody mouthful!

Chapter Twenty

Raids and Rescues

As the hours passed, they seemed to relax and understand what had happened. When we got close enough, we knew there was a possibility of the starbase contacting us. I had Cartwright come and sit next to me. "You feel up to this, mate."

"Well, I'm not really into all this cloak-and-dagger stuff. Don't blame me if they start shooting."

"I'll be keeping my hand firmly on the 'get-the-hell-out-of-dodge' button, so don't you worry your pretty little head about that." He laughed at this, but his laughter was cut short as the inter-ship communications went off. It was a brief, high-pitched squawk, affectionately known as a handshake. The clincher – we had to reply with the correct code. "Okay, Tracker, I really hope you haven't let me down," and I sent back the signal that Tracker had installed before she'd headed off to Phobos. When the voice communications came on, I knew that we had succeeded. The voice that came on sounded cheerful and bizarrely relieved. I sat back in my chair and turned to face Cartwright straight on. He looked equally surprised, but both were laughing after another back-and-forth exchange. A few more words were said before Cartwright ran a finger across his throat to get me to cut the channel – I did so. Then I turned back and stared questioningly at him. "Stephanie

Morris contacted the base and told them exactly what we were doing."

"Bloody hell. So what was all that laughing about, and why aren't they on alert?"

"When we sent the correct signal, they concluded that she was lying and trying to play some trick. They sent out a scan and picked up the Chesty and us. They assumed we were aware of them and intended to pursue."

"Were they suspicious when you said no?" asked Audra.

Cartwright smiled at her. "Well, I didn't say no. I said we'd intended to, but we needed to refuel first. That we weren't worried because that hunk of junk couldn't outrun us even if we spent the night using their recreational facilities. Which, I might add, they have offered to let us use."

"Cartwright, I could root you right now. You bloody ripper!" Cartwright, with a look of utter bewilderment, looked at Audra as if asking if she could translate what I'd just said, but she just looked at him equally as confused and just shrugged. I began guiding the ship through the docking maneuvers that would connect us to the docking port on the side of the outcropping, which was specifically designed for docking.

It took about 20 minutes to complete the docking procedure and ensure we were securely latched on. The tricky part was following instructions from the Peon controllers. I couldn't understand what was being said, and Cartwright was pretending to be the pilot, so he couldn't suddenly turn around to me and speak in English. Ultimately, I had to rely on my experience and make an informed guess about what they wanted. At worst, I hoped they'd just think he wasn't a very good a pilot; and to be honest, that was the truth.

Automated drones began exiting the space station – some connected a fuel line to us, while others began searching all over the fuselage, inspecting for damage. They concluded that some work was required on one of the thrusters and set to work repairing it. Then the Peon technicians came back online. This time, their voices sounded wary. After a minute back and forth, Cartwright turned back to me. "I think the jig is up. After we requested such a large amount of air, they sent out the probes to check for a leak. And well, they want to know why all of our airlocks were blown."

"But they were already repaired by the ship's automated systems."

"Yep, they were, but those same automated systems communicated with the base's automated systems and alerted them to what happened. I mean, they didn't say that a bunch of United States Marines blew them up, but the fact that they had been blown up... They don't understand why we hadn't reported it, and they're wondering why there's no report of an attack on the Jangle Berry."

"Fuck! It would've been cool to have gotten in and out right under their noses."

"Can't we just open the door and let the air in?"

"No," said Daisy. "Suddenly opening up a vacuum on a ship of this size, the air would be pulled in so fast. I hate to think what sort of damage that might cause."

"Okay then, listen up, young whipper snappers. We're clearly gonna have to deal with this the 'Jenna-Plural-Way' – with extreme prejudice. Lock and load."

All of us except for Daisy headed down to the airlock. At this point, I'd delegated mission command to Pentauk as the combat specialist. She immediately made me stand at the rear behind Cartwright and the other guy. Yeah, yeah, in case you haven't already guessed, I can't remember his bloody name. I could go and look it up, but I can't be arsed – his name isn't important. Audra Pentauk took the lead, and the exit door slid open. A big white ball with a multitude of tooled arms greeted us in French.

Cartwright started translating, "It's saying it's looking forward to serving our needs." Audra stepped toward it, and it moved aside for her. "It's instructing us to put our weapons away."

I thought quickly. "Do it. This is unlikely to be an Artificial Intelligence soldier, but it may have an automated response to our weaponry." The Marines slung their rifles back over their shoulders, and I slipped my handgun back into the holster on my side. "Nice and easy now. We're all friends here," I said through my teeth, a smile plastered on my face as I tried to act casual. We walked on through the base, following the directions we had memorized from the floor plan; gleaming white walls matched the gleaming white floors. Robots of all kinds were coming and going, but none seemed bothered with us since the white ball that had welcomed us and continued to follow us to our destination, it would seem. It didn't try to speak to us anymore until we reached the outside of a door that read 'Central Control Room.' It babbled away again, and Cartwright told us, "It's telling us that we are not authorized to proceed any further."

"Ask it if it'll try to stop us if we continue," I said.

Audra looked at me with a raised eyebrow. "Seriously?"

I shrugged at her with a wide grin. "Nothing to lose, mate."

So Cartwright asked it my question. "It says that its programming will sound the alarm and lock down the base."

I thought about that for a moment and then said, "Ask it to show the other guy where the dunny is." Of course, I didn't say "the other guy." I used his name, whatever it was.

Cartwright raised an eyebrow at me. "The *dunny*?"

I rolled my eyes and put on an awful posh American accent, "The lavatory."

"Ah, right, you mean the head," he turned and translated for the bot. I nodded to the other guy to follow it as it happily led him away. We continued up to the control room. The door wasn't even locked, and, despite having been suspicious of us, the occupants didn't expect us to walk in wearing our American uniforms. As expected, there were three of them, but they remained surprisingly calm as they raised their hands before we even finished drawing our weapons again. "Tell them to start filling the Liberty's oxygen tanks."

Before Cartwright even spoke, one of the Peons said, "I've got it. There is no need to translate. I speak your language."

"Well, that's bonza," I smiled appreciatively. "Start the transfer."

He stared at me blankly, and this time, Audra translated my Aussie slang to American English. He looked at one of his colleagues and gave the command in French. His colleague nodded and began tapping controls. Audra moved to the window to see the Liberty and another fueling tube being carried out to the ship. I pulled out my radio and called up Lucas in the engineering section. "G'day, mate. We've got some lovely jubbly air coming your way. Open up the tanks and start venting into the ship. Once we're at a hundred percent, close off the tanks, and we'll refill them too." After acknowledging my instructions, he turned the radio off and took a seat, waiting patiently. Then I remembered the guy I'd sent to the dunny. I radioed him and told him to return to the ship. Cartwright stood over the guy operating the controls while Audra covered them with her automatic rifle.

"We're at eighty percent," Lucas called over the radio. I walked over to Cartwright and the guy pumping the air into the Liberty. It was a dumb mistake. One of the other guys jumped over to some controls, and although Audra opened fire, it wasn't until after he'd managed to press some buttons. As he slid down to the floor, he coughed up blood and laughed soundlessly as the klaxon blared out. The computer spoke, and

Cartwright's eyes widened. "He's activated the base's self-destruct system. We have five minutes before this place goes up."

I looked at the Peon guy we'd been speaking to. "Can you turn it off?"

"No, Madame. The man you just shot was our commanding officer, and he was the only one who had the deactivation codes."

"Okay, everybody moves out. Leave the air pump in so we can get as much as possible." I had intended to take the two Peons with us, but he just stood there, stoic and refusing to budge. "I do not relish the prospect of interrogation by your security services. We will not be leaving."

"Oh fuck, don't do this to me!" I said earnestly. "I can't just leave you here. Not when you could tamper with the connections to the ship."

"I understand, Madame. Do what you must." I sighed. Turning away, I nodded to Audra, who opened fire on them.

We ran as fast as we could down the corridor. However, only two minutes had passed since activation. I still had to fire up the ship and disconnect it from the fuelling tubes. I knew I'd taken a risk by allowing it to continue to pump air into the vessel for the last five minutes. If the station went up before we detached, it would ignite the air in the tubes, which would lead straight into the filled oxygen tanks, and then the whole ship would explode. I ran up to the bridge with Audra, leaving Cartwright to seal the airlock. Before I arrived, I heard the engines coming online, and I rushed in, looking bewildered. Daisy was no pilot, but clearly, she knew enough to start us up.

"You're one brilliant and surprising Sheila," I cried out gratefully as she jumped out of my seat, and I dropped into it, checking my watch – one and a half minutes until self-destruct. I called Lucas and told him to seal off the oxygen tanks. I barely heard him as he reported that we were at 99.6% capacity.

I released the clamps that held the oxygen in place, and then the fuel line, just as a rumbling began within the center of the base. I didn't even take the time to set a course as I detached us from the docking station. The locks had barely opened when I pulled on the speed. I heard metal grinding and prayed it was the station, not the ship. I would find out that was indeed the case as I slammed her hard to port as the station went up in the throes of death and destruction. The Liberty jostled slightly as the invisible wake from the explosion hit us, but I had already put some distance between Demos and us.

As I looked back at Phobos, my thoughts turned back to Jenna, and I wondered if she was even aware of the predicament she was now in, thanks to the betrayal of that bitch, Stephanie Morris. I apologized as I gave Audra and the two men the unpleasant job of removing the remaining bodies from the rooms that we'd been unable to reach due to the air situation. They were no longer in a vacuum, and decomposition would become a rapidly growing problem.

I did take one indulgence before returning to work. I took the First Officer's cabin as my own. He was the guy who had led the boarding party onto the Lewis Puller. The one Jenna had shot outside the Chesty's cockpit. I threw most of his stuff into the garbage chute, keeping only minor things that I found useful. I avoided looking at the family pictures on his desk and bedside cabinet, picking them up fast and throwing them away before the images drew me in. I felt a pang of guilt, but not the guilt you're thinking of. I felt guilty that I felt bad about the families of the Euros I'd killed. The Euros were scum, but any feelings for their families could become a weakness. Any hesitation, any doubt, could mean the end of my life or the lives of those I cared about.

My task was complete, and I headed up to the bridge once more. I met with Daisy and discussed the problematic situation of trying to pick up the Phobos team without a ship that could land. We were barely into the conversation when an inter-ship communication reached us. I turned it on and heard Jenna Plural's voice. The signal was strong. I realized she was using the advanced communication relays of the Peon base. "This is Major Jenna Plural of the U.S.S. Lewis Puller, contacting all free Americans throughout the solar system. We have chosen not to recognize the President's treason against the United States of America in signing a surrender to the European Union and its functionaries. We call on all Americans and our allies to rally to our cause and to fight the oppression of European imperialism. We will rendezvous at a coordinate that will be encrypted and transmitted after this message. My fellow Americans, we must unite and continue this battle in whatever way we can. The fifty-two stars of the American flag will fly over a free people once again. The time has come to decide – to live under European Union oppression or be a free nation once again. Please acknowledge this communication. Plural out"

"Bloody hell, she actually did it," I clapped my hands in a triumphant cheer. It quickly subsided as I realized I had to relay some difficult news. I then called the base with a priority alert. Helen Tracker came online and sounded pleased to hear from me, but that quickly disappeared. "Morris' done a runner. She's taking the Chesty and is heading for Earth. She tried to sabotage my mission. "

"You have to be kidding me."

"I wish I were, mate."

"Let me get the Major."

The line went quiet for a while, but when Jenna came on the line, it wasn't me that she was speaking to. A tirade of brinkmanship went on between Jenna and Morris for some time before, finally, Jenna told her, in no uncertain terms, that she was going to come after her and then take her life.

I began calculating what we needed to do for a fly-by pickup. I hoped my figures were wrong because we clearly couldn't slow the Liberty enough. I got Daisy to double-check the numbers, and she concurred with me. "Although it's not impossible," I said unconvincingly, even to myself.

"Even if you could achieve it perfectly, it will ultimately come down to the ground coordination," Daisy said. "Get the timing wrong by so much as a second, and you could be killing them yourself rather than saving them."

"I have to give them the option. It might be their only chance." I called down to the base again.

Tracker came online, quite distressed. "The Major is in the gym – they're going to execute the prisoners to give us more time."

I readily admit I was horrified at this. Even though I knew there wouldn't be any survivors once we destroyed the base, I guess it was a bit of a case of 'out of sight, out of mind' at its best. "Put me through to her. Now!"

Tracker did as I demanded, and I explained the plan Daisy and I had devised to Jenna. She was hesitant at first, but in the end, I managed to convince her.

About an hour later, I alerted them that we were above Phobos. If they had been outside, they would have been able to see us orbiting overhead. I began to slow the craft down, but I was still completing an entire orbit in under a minute. I pondered a solution and then turned off the engines. Daisy looked at me as if I were completely mad, and maybe I was. However, it was clear that only a madwoman could solve this issue. "You now have no control over this vessel."

"That's not true," I grinned at her. "I can still descend."

"With no way to pull up if you run into a problem."

"That's fine. I don't plan to run into any problems."

"Stacey!"

"Yes?"

"You are a fucking lunatic."

"Ah, that's the nicest thing anyone has said to me in the longest time," I grinned and began the descent.

Jenna signaled to me that the ground team was now outside and waiting. "Be ready. I'm coming in for my first pass." I got us down to thirty feet, but I was still going too fast. To Daisy's horror, I hit the retros, something that could easily have sent us into a spin, but I managed to hold on. I saw the base approaching fast. I could barely make out the specks that were the team on the ground. I would not be able to see them jump as I passed over. I relied entirely on them to let me know whether they were on board. I let out a little cheer as the first two troopers confirmed they were in the forward docking bay. I circumnavigated the moon once more, and Daisy tapped the screen in front of me, which read that I had dropped to twenty-eight feet. "Don't piss your pants, mate. I can do this." We passed over them again, and again I got the confirmation. After three or four more attempts, and with the indicator showing we were now down to twenty-four feet, I started to feel nervous. So far, everything had gone perfectly, and I feared that my luck would run out before we got to Jenna and Phelkar.

After I passed over them and no report came, my blood ran cold. Internal communications came on, and I heard Hardy call up to me. "They missed the jump, Lieutenant Grant. Go around again." I complied, but looking down this time, I saw that we were at nineteen feet. This would be my last run before ditching into the moon's surface, where we'd end our days.

I came in for the last time, and after passing over them, I reignited the engines. Looking down, I saw that we were only eight feet above the ground, so I pulled up and took us away from Phobos. I let out an enormous sigh of relief as I heard

Hardy call me to tell me that all were aboard. I closed the cargo hold door, and we re-entered space.

A few minutes later, Jenna entered the bridge. Both Audra and Daisy went to stand up, but were waved down by Jenna as she slipped into the command chair.

"Let the record show Major Jenna Plural has assumed command of the U.S.S. Lady Liberty at this time," I stated.

"Stacey Grant," Jenna said, and I turned to look at her. "You were damned amazing."

I just grinned and said, "Yep." I then introduced her to Daisy and Audra."By the way, I gave Audra a field promotion. She's now a corporal, so ignore those private stripes."

"I thought I had sent over a corporal?" Jenna asked with curiosity in her voice.

"Yeah, well, that's a long story, Boss," I said sheepishly.

"In that case, I look forward to reading your report," Jenna said with a tone of amusement.

"Yeah, like I'm ever gonna write a report," I muttered.

Chapter Twenty-One

Complicating My Life

The pursuit of the Chesty was like everything in space – long and arduous. We closed in slowly; the bitch had dared to transmit a distress signal saying she was under attack by enemy forces.

Jenna and Morris engaged in more testosterone-filled banter, which was kind of strange considering that both of them were sheilas. Jenna wanted to head up the assault, but Phelks persuaded her otherwise because she was now the face of the resistance.

At Jenna's recommendation, we performed what was known as a bounce maneuver. It was perilous but negated the need for umbilicals. In essence, you grapple onto the sides, push your hull up to theirs, and go straight through to the other side with your troops.

They tried to stop us from getting ahold, but he couldn't outmaneuver me. I fired the grapplers, and we slammed into the side of the Chesty, which caused us to shudder and jerk slightly. We probably messed up the paintwork a bit, but beyond that, everything else was fine.

"Wowzer, the Lady Liberty and the Chesty are attached," and I cut the engines; the larger mass of the Lady Liberty began to slow the Chesty. "Come on, Batty," I muttered. "You know you have to cut your engines, or you'll burn them out." When he didn't, I started getting quite frustrated. We wanted that ship intact, not with blown-out engines."Cut your engines, Batty. Even a rookie would see sense in doing it. You're gonna burn up if you don't. Now don't be stupid."

Surprisingly, a cheerful voice spoke. "Good to hear your voice again, Lieutenant. Morris just left the bridge and can't hear me. Tell me now if there is anything I can do to assist you."

Jenna looked at me, her eyes wide with surprise, and then she grinned and turned back to the commlink. "You are a true patriot, Batty. Can you shut yourself off in the cockpit?"

"Aye, Major," there was a pause before he came back. "I'm sealed in the cockpit. Morris is going to be so pissed."

Jenna chuckled at the co-pilot. "I bet she is. Don't worry, Batty, you're not going to have to put up with her for much longer."

She transmitted an order at Phelks recommendation for the crew to stand down and take Morris into custody. To our surprise, a nervous stammering voice came online a few minutes later.

"This is Private Emma Dodgson. We have taken Commander Morris into custody, and she's furious at us."

"I think I love you, Private Dodgson," Jenna said with a laugh.

"Umm, thanks, I guess, Ma'am," Emma replied with a nervous laugh.

"Clear the portside. We're coming aboard."

"Aye, Ma'am."

Jenna came up behind me, and in a rare moment of sentimentality, she placed an arm around me from behind and hugged me. "Thank you, Stacey," she said softly.

I was surprised how much that meant to me, and it got even better when she boarded the Chesty as a cheer went up. I learned later that Jenna had Stephanie Morris killed, I think Phelks told me, but he wouldn't go into details for some reason. Then I started receiving the signals and responses to the message she sent out across the solar system. Admiral Baines of the U.S.S. Constitution kept demanding to speak to the Major.

When Jenna was next on the bridge, I told her about the calls. "Boss, I'm pleased to report that we now have forty-two confirmed ships heading toward the rendezvous point. However, an Admiral Baines reckons he's gonna 'assume command upon arrival.'"

"Oh, he is, is he?" Jenna almost growled.

"Yeah, and he's constantly demanding to speak to you, Boss," I said.

"Well, inform him I'm busy, but you're happy to take a message. Where is he coming from, and what's his ETA to the rendezvous point?"

"He's coming from the moon of Uranus. ETA is a couple of weeks."

"So we'll arrive before he does?

"Definitely," I responded.

When Jenna announced that we were going to have a celebration, I was really looking forward to it. The peons love their grog and had left us plenty. That was not the same on the Chesty. I was on duty on the bridge of the Lady Liberty. I was alone and really bored, so I decided to call Batty. Jenna had told them to have a party too, but he was clearly not as impressed with the idea. "You know, Stace, we have a total of two bottles of whiskey and enough beers for three apiece. And it's mostly men over here."

I pondered this a moment. "Well, I can't exactly send you any Sheila's mate, but we can do something about the grog. What if I were to stack some up on an escape pod and launch it? Think you can scoop it into your hold?"

With that planned, when I was off duty, I headed down the cargo bay and pulled out an antigravity cart, which I took up to the stores. I stacked it up with several cases of liquor and added a couple of cases of beer. It was late-night ship time, and I managed to avoid most people. Not that it mattered. One of the benefits of being an officer is that enlisted people don't generally ask you questions about what you are doing. I got to the emergency evacuation area of the ship and stacked it up into a life pod. And with the press of a couple of buttons, I jettisoned the fun time into space for the crew of the Lewis Puller. As the alarms sounded and the ship's computer notified the bridge in French, presumably about what I had just done, I felt my blood run cold. I wasn't exactly doing anything *that* wrong, but I hadn't exactly asked permission to do it. Within seconds, ship security rushed in with guns raised. Of course, as soon as they saw me, they immediately lowered them and looked at me, bewildered. "Um! G'day, mates," I said sheepishly.

They called up Jenna, and within minutes, Phelks arrived, soon followed by Jenna herself. "What have you done now, Stacey?"

I felt like a kid with a hand in the candy jar. "I just wanted them to have a good time. I didn't mean any harm by it."

"What did you do?" Jenna scowled at me.

"I sent over a bunch of our liquor for the crew of the Chesty. Batty has the scoops on to pick up the life pod."

Jenna sighed. "Give me the room, gentlemen," she said, dismissing everyone else within the room, including Phelks. As they left, I thought she was about to reem me off. But a grin quickly crossed her face. "When you first came aboard four years ago, and I told you that I was making you the head of the entertainment committee... You know I was being sarcastic, don't you?"

I grinned at that, "Do you honestly expect me to have a good time knowing that they're over there sharing a tinny between five of them?" Sure, it was an exaggeration, but I thought it was funny.

Jenna laughed, "Your insanity keeps me sane, Stacey Grant." And I laughed along with her.

The party took place about a week into our trip. I dressed in this slutty little tartan skirt and translucent shirt, hoping to get lucky. I went round to the service side of the bar to get a drink, and somehow, I found myself enlisted to serve drinks. But I didn't mind, and I continued to do so for most of the evening – it was kind of fun deciding how heavy a pour some would get over others. Audra and Daisy both turned up, as did Tracker and Dodgson. Sakamoto was on the Lewis Puller, who were also having a party. Let's be honest, though. A party led by Neville Batty wasn't my idea of a fun night. Don't get me wrong, I love the guy, but he's as straight-laced as they come. Phelks arrived looking totally out of place, which kind of made him look cuter. I'd been thinking about him a lot lately, and I have to admit, it bothered me. He was such a nice guy, the complete opposite of the type of guy I usually went for. The music was really cool. They were playing the latest stuff from the U.S.A. Well, the latest music from before the collapse, anyway.

This was the first time I met Bridget, the young French girl that Jenna had brought back from Phobos and who was now in the care of Phelks. She entered the room and made a beeline straight for me, and pointed to a fancy liqueur on the shelf behind me. I didn't think much of it when I poured it out for her, and no sooner had she reached out for the glass. Phelks approached and took it from her the moment it touched her hand.

I pondered, hitting on Phelkar again. Lately, I'd had a tingly, butterfly feeling in my stomach every time he was around.

Maybe a relationship with him wasn't such a bad idea, but then I saw how he looked at Jenna; the guy was smitten, and I gave up on it as a lost cause.

She went through the entire Marine routine, which apparently was a tradition since the Marines first entered space. There was a rousing chorus of the Star-Spangled Banner, and I followed it up with my own rendition of 'I Still Call Australia Home." Yes, I sang it a cappella and, according to others, I don't have a bad voice.

She walked up to him, and they talked for a bit. When the slow music started playing, they began dancing together, and that old pang of jealousy rose up again.

When the song came to an end, he headed over to me. I composed myself and gave him one of my trademark grins. "Hey there, Phelks. You trying your luck with the good Major there, I see?" I said, trying desperately to hide the jealousy that coursed through me against my will.

I was serving Neuman at the time, and he grinned at Phelks, who blushed as he gave him a dirty look. Neuman hurried away, and Phelks looked back at me. "Don't be silly."

I decided to have some fun with him. "Ah, come on, Phelks. Even you have to admit she has a great pair of legs, hell, even I get tingly looking at them, and I'm as straight as a damned arrow. Could you just imagine them wrapped around your back? Or better still, your neck?"

"You can be pretty crude, you know?" he sneered at me, and to my annoyance, it hurt. "Pour me a couple of brandies, if you please."

"Just telling it as I see it, mate," I grinned as I poured out two large shots and noticed Malcolm Hardy sidle up to Jenna. "Anyway, looks like you've lost your chance," I said, inclining my head and enjoying the moment as I handed the glasses to him. As he turned back to her, his face went white, and I'm sure his hands were shaking as he stepped closer to hear them; I wasn't amused anymore. I was instead thinking how cool it would be if he looked at me that way, or any half-decent guy, for that matter, looked at me like that. I noticed Dodgson was watching Phelks carefully, occasionally glancing at me. She was dancing with some guy she clearly wasn't into. Jenna was flirting with Hardy, but it confused me the way she kept glancing over at Phelks, too.

Phelks turned away, and grinning, I simply shrugged. "Oh, never mind, Phelks. Hey, there's always Dodgson; I mean, she's been checking you out since you got here," and I nodded toward Dodgson. Both Dodgson and Phelks flushed before hurriedly looking away from each other.

He downed one of the brandies, then placed both glasses on the counter, "I don't think it would be considered appropriate to fraternize with an enlisted, do you?" He said coldly.

I shrugged, thinking, here we go again with that old line. How's a girl supposed to get a root if she's a million miles from Earth, with no civvies in sight? "You're not military, mate. You're free to root whoever you like."

He looked at Hardy and Jenna one last time, then strode from the room.

About a minute later, Jenna looked over at us again and appeared startled to see that Phelks was no longer standing there. She walked over to me, surprising Hardy, who was in mid-sentence. "Hey, Stacey, having fun?" She said distractedly.

I shrugged nonchalantly. "Sure am," but Jenna didn't seem all that interested in my response as she looked around the room as if she was looking for someone, and I could only assume that person was Phelks. "Did Mr. Phelkar leave?" She asked quietly.

"Yep. About a minute ago."

"Shit!" she muttered under her breath. She then glanced down at her watch and looked around the room again.

"Something wrong, Boss?"

"Hmm?" she looked back at me as if she'd forgotten I was standing there. Then she looked a little flustered. "Oh, it's nothing." She looked down at the brandy on the bar and said, "Phelks was supposed to be getting me a drink. Is that It?"

"Yep," I said. She picked it up and downed it in one go, then looked at her watch again and around the room. Looking back at me, she smiled. You know, the smile someone used when trying to pretend everything was all fine. "Thank you, Stacey. Carry on," she stepped away, and Hardy again made a beeline for her. This time Jenna didn't seem as interested as before, and now she spent the next hour circulating the room, checking in on everyone, but mostly checking the time on her watch. Eventually, she glanced around one last time before heading for the door. I didn't know what to make of it until I read Phelks' book. Honestly, I had no clue she was interested in him. However, I was left frustrated. I spotted Cartwright and decided to hang up my bar wench hat as I left the bar and sidled over to hit on him, pulling him away from the girl dancing with him. "Come on, Cartwright, let's see if Audra was exaggerating or telling the truth." Fuck the stupid fraternization regulations. He looked bewildered as I dragged him out of the mess by the hand. For the record, though, Audra definitely wasn't exaggerating.

I returned to the bridge with a hangover and a satisfied glow the next day.

There was another boost to ship morale when Daisy informed me that she had detected the new armada's first ships coming into scanner range. I told Jenna at once, but her joy quickly evaporated when she and Phelkar joined us on the bridge later that day, and I had to inform her of some comms chatter. "Boss, I'm picking up transmissions from the U.S.S. Constitution to most of the fleet,"

She took the headset from me and listened in. She turned to Phelkar, "That Iowan pig fucker is trying to convene a meeting over the comms without us." Damn, I hadn't heard her that pissed off in a long time.

Phelks outdid himself as I put him through to Admiral Baines, as a brief war of words was exchanged. As the Admiral disconnected, Phelks carried on rallying the ships, and soon, all but a few signaled their support for Major Jenna Plural.

"Was one of the ships that signaled its transponder code the U.S.S. Los Angeles?" Phelks asked me.

I looked at the list on my screen, "yup!"

"Would your old friends be willing to host us?" he asked Jenna.

"What have you got in mind?"

"Arrange a strategy meeting. Not to discuss your leadership, although that will undoubtedly come into play. Set it up as an inter-ship discussion on the way forward as if leadership is already decided."

She nodded, "Stacey, give me a secure line to the Los Angeles if you please."

"Encrypted and secured. You have a line," I replied.

It was good to hear Claire Addison again, and there was no doubt that our former First Officer would give us the support her successor had refused, as a meeting was quickly arranged aboard the U.S.S. Los Angeles.

So, I know I said this recording is supposed to be about my part in Jenna's rise to power. The truth is that, at this point, I was pretty much out of the loop. I didn't even attend the ship captain's meeting, as I wasn't technically the official captain of the Liberty at the time. Nor did I hear the details from the after-meeting meeting where they came up with their plans to take out opposition and capture the U.S.S. Constitution. I was a little pissed when the attack on the Constitution started, and

I hadn't been included. A little paranoia had begun to well up within me, thinking that Jenna was pushing me out. The truth is, she was just too damn busy to worry about the little Australian pilot who was now on what was really quite an insignificant ship in this new fleet. However, I did end up getting to pilot the Los Angeles into battle against the Constitution, which was bloody awesome. Phelks has already filled you in on the details of that stunt. So I won't repeat it here.

The actual case, as it stood, was that Jenna Plural emerged as the most powerful individual amongst the Free Forces.

Over the coming days, I fell into a kind of funk and found myself drinking even more than usual. The surrender meant any hope of liberating Australia was gone, so to cope, I found myself drinking more often. When I drank, I missed Harper, and when I missed Harper, I drank. On that particular night, the night you'll come to realize, changed my life forever. I decided I wasn't going to drink alone again. I headed down to a bar, of which the Los Angeles had several, and by chance, this one was frequented by Dodgson and Phelks. I saw them sitting in an alcove. Phelks was on a couch, and Dodgson was sitting opposite him in an armchair. She was looking at him as if he were the greatest invention since the Hills Hoist clothesline. Again, that annoying jealousy washed over me as I saw how she looked at him. She clearly had it bad for Phelks, too; my bitch mode switched on. I might not be able to have him, but she sure as shit wasn't going to either. I jumped over the back of the couch and slipped in beside him, much to the apparent annoyance of Dodgson.

It turned out to be quite a pleasant evening – Dodgson was kind of cute and easily embarrassed by my brusque manner. I teased both her and Phelkar to the point that any flirtation between them became uncomfortable. Yep, full bitch mode really worked. Despite this, I was clearly getting nowhere with Phelks either, even after he became intoxicated from the copious amounts of Melbourne firebombs. In the end, he excused himself and left me sitting with Dodgson.

"Well, I guess I'll call it a night, too," I told her after we had sat for a long time in a very long, awkward silence.

She simply nodded as I got up, and as I headed for the door, I glanced back to see her heading over to the bar. She was a sweet kid, but jealousy has no time for compassion.

I pondered, going back to my room, but I was still thinking about Phelkar. I almost staggered to his room in a drunken haze. I had enough sense to realize I needed my wits about me if I was going to face him again. Instead, I popped one of those pills that sobered you up. My heavy drinking lately meant I'd started carrying them on me, so I didn't risk turning up still intoxicated to duty. I popped one of the pills and waited outside his room for several minutes, waiting for it to take effect. I wasn't 100% sober when I finally hit the buzzer on his door, my own impatience getting the better of my judgment.

Chapter Twenty-Two

Trouble in Deep Space

He looked surprised to see me as I leaned against the doorframe and said casually, "You could have had both of us tonight."

"Maybe. But I would have regretted it in the morning and had a complicated relationship with someone working as my aide."

"Life is complicated, Phelks. Like, it makes no sense why I'm interested in you again." I took the plunge and reached up to him, and as he responded to my kiss, my heart began to flutter. I became lost in the moment. He made to pull me into the room, "No, not here. I want to show you something. Something you can only do on a battleship of this size."

He looked confused, and I led him down the corridor toward the engineering section, hoping to find a ventilation shaft – I did, and he looked somewhat bewildered as I opened it.

"What the hell are we doing?" he asked nervously as I made him climb in. The design of most ships is pretty similar. I determined the direction I wanted us to take and provided him with directions as he proceeded ahead of me, until I found the sweet spot where the engine vibrations in the ventilation shaft were just right for what I had planned.

He lay on his side, and I crawled up and lay next to him. "Do you feel it, Phelks?"

"Feel what?"

"The vibration of the ship."

"Of course I do. What of it?" he raised his eyebrows.

I chuckled, "Have you never fucked in a vibrating ventilation shaft before, Phelks?"

"You want to do it here?" he looked at me incredulously.

"What can I say. It's the Navy Way."

He laughed, "Is everything the 'Navy Way'?"

"Oh, my dear, Phelks. The rules of the Navy Way are very simple," I said in my best come fuck me voice and pushed my mouth against his, entwining our tongues tenderly, gently exploring each other. Then pulling back, I said softly, in little more than a whisper, "Rule number one, The Navy way is any way a Navy girl wants it." I slowly unfastened his belt and released his erection from its confines as I spoke. "And what this navy girl wants, she gets." He jumped in surprise as I wrapped my cold hand around him. "Relax, mate," I said and slid down from his view and enveloped him in my mouth, listening to him moan softly. I stopped when I thought he would finish prematurely and slid back up to him. We laughed as we struggled to get our clothes off in the ventilation shaft, but it didn't kill the mood.

I learned something that day – there really is a difference between fucking and making love. When we had finished, I knew without a doubt that I was in love with this man. We had tried to keep the noise down, but it was so good I couldn't help myself. I had never experienced anything like it. I had never really believed that sex could be better when you had feelings for the person you were with, but it was so true. When I finally came, I let out a scream, and Phelkar, almost laughing, put a hand up to cover my mouth to avoid drawing attention to us, but as you know, that failed.

He pulled out and lay beside me, panting softly. It was then that I started to doubt whether he could possibly feel about me the way I felt about him. Was this nothing more than just a stress-relieving fuck like it had been for me the last time we'd met up? I was twenty-seven years old, and I can truly say I had never been in love before, although I had come close a few times. Not having felt like this before, I didn't know how to deal with it. Men had just been entertainment all my life, and I had never considered anything seriously since I'd almost fallen for Jason Richards four years previously.

Since the death of Harper, I'd never been truly happy. And this fucker made me happy. To both my surprise and humiliation, I found a tear running down my face. To make it worse, he turned and saw it.

"Oh, sweetheart, what's the matter?"

His look of concern only made it worse, "It's nothing, don't worry about it."

"Please tell me. If I've done something wrong, I would like to know."

"You haven't done anything wrong, mate. You make me happy. That's the problem." He looked so confused as I turned and lay on my back, staring up at the roof of the ventilation shaft. "Did you want to be with me tonight, or the Major, or Dodgson?"

"There was nobody on my mind but you. And that's the truth."

"You're full of shit, Phelks. But thank you," I smiled and kissed him gently.

"So what has got you in this negative frame of mind?" he asked.

"Just been thinking about home a lot lately. And the last day I saw Oz."

"Want to tell me about it?"

And for the first time in four years, I opened up about the loss of my country and the heartbreak I still felt about the loss of Harper.

Oh my God! Harper, I miss you so much! Even now, I wish I could see you. I wish I could hug you. I wish I could protect you. I'm so sorry I let you down. I am so sorry I let you die. It was all my fault. Jenna offered to keep you safe, but I chose to keep you at my side—you, wonderful, crazy girl. Jenna was right. Jenna is always right, and I say to you, whoever you are, reading or listening to this. Listen to Jenna. Follow Jenna. She is our leader. She will never steer you wrong. She will prevail for all our sakes.

"I swore that day I would never be happy again until the Australian flag flew over Canberra once more. But you make me happy, Phelks. " Tears now streamed down my face as they had never before, and for once, I didn't feel embarrassed about showing such emotion. I felt comfortable with him. "Can you understand that, Phelks?"

He was about to reply when we heard a voice, "Whoever is in there, come on out. You have ten seconds to comply before we flood the vent with neuron gas."

It broke the tension, and I actually laughed as I scrambled for my clothes. We headed out of the ventilation shaft, and in the act of pure chivalry, Phelks offered me his hand to get down. Normally, I would have taken the piss out of someone doing this, but his proffered hand felt really nice. As you know, about an hour later, we were getting reamed out by Claire Addison, Jenna's new First Officer. But I left that office on a high, not realizing what a dumb bitch I truly was.

I finally had a crew. At least enough to fill the key positions on board the Lady Liberty. It was skeletal, but it was my crew. It was gonna to take us several weeks to reach a point in the middle of nowhere between Mars and Jupiter's orbits. I had never truly understood the bureaucracy that came with running your own ship. Audra had stayed with me, and I made her my First Officer with Jenna's approval, even though she wasn't technically an officer. The lines of rank became blurred in those days. We were no longer an official military force, and people were expected to fill roles where replacements couldn't be found. Routine crew rotations were now a thing of the past. It came down to me to decide who would fill each post. This involved reviewing personnel files and the tedious task of weighing the pros and cons of each individual. I know I make it sound worse than it was for my skeletal crew, which consisted of ten people, but bloody hell. The mindless, unending tedium of reading boring personnel reports often found me asleep with a datapad on my lap. Ultimately, I decided to delegate the task to my First Officer. She thanked me for the opportunity, but I'm pretty sure she was being sarcastic.

The oddest thing about the Lady Liberty was that we had no formal role. We had no troops aboard. We had no medical facilities beyond what was required for our own use. We had nothing. The new fleet added more ships every day, but they lacked spare personnel for a confiscated Peon light cruiser. Sure, in time, something would be sorted out, but in the interim, each day was just as dull as the one before it.

I wasn't too bothered as I understood that Claire and Jenna had a lot of logistics to work out, but running this big empty ship was kind of boring. I even went so far as to rig up the forward monitors so we could watch movies to pass the time. Unfortunately, with nothing new coming out of the U.S., even that eventually grew dull.

Cartwright's request for a transfer and subsequent sexual harassment charge against me was the only vaguely interesting thing that happened during those days. To be honest, I kinda thought that he would have said no if he hadn't wanted to.

That's a pretty serious charge, which can ultimately result in dismissal from service and a prison term of anywhere from five to twenty years.

A hearing was set, but a couple of days before it, Cartwright withdrew his complaint, even stating that he was jealous of Audra receiving the promotion over him. It didn't sound right to me, but you don't look a gift horse in the mouth. It did curb my ardor for jocks with big dongs. A period of celibacy appeared to be looming.

Then the Peons came – we picked them up on the scanners. The enormous armada was set to be a major headache for us, and we prepared for the Battle of Deep Space.

It was another waiting game, and one that I wasn't going to be participating in. We moved the Lady Liberty to the center of the fleet, but again, I was excluded from the game plan. I was surprised when Claire took the best ships and headed away from us at full speed. I was concerned she was indeed fleeing the fleet. The Claire that I knew wasn't a coward. That wasn't her style at all.

Everything became apparent, though, when we received an inter-ship transmission. "This is the U.S.S. Seattle. We can confirm the Peon fleet is now directly between us and the Addison flotilla. It's now or never, Major."

"Thank you, Seattle," came Jenna's reply. "Plural to Beta Fleet: this is it, boys and girls. Engage your engines, full thrust toward the Peons. Captain Addison, about turn, prepare to engage the enemy.

"Aye, Major," came Addison's voice. "Alpha Fleet one-eighty on my mark." A pause for all ships to plot the maneuver, then. "Mark!" The legendary Battle of Deep Space had been joined.

With no troops to drop and no fighters to launch, I just sat there like a dummy, growing more frustrated. The only excitement I got was moving my ship farther away whenever any friendlies showed interest in me. When I saw the Lewis Puller under heavy attack by three cruisers, my frustration reached a boiling point. When I saw huge chunks flying off of her, I knew she wasn't gonna make it, and I started to bring my ship back in, at which point I picked up communications between Jenna and Sakamoto.

"That is a negative, Sakamoto. I repeat. That is a negative," Jenna was shouting. "You are to abandon ship, do you read me?"

"That is not protocol, Major. My duty is to ensure that this ship does not fall into enemy hands."

"Fuck protocol, Sakamoto. You are more valuable to me than that shitty piece of junk. They can grow damn tulips on it, for all I care. I want you alive."

There was a long pause before Sakamoto responded. "The ship's Captain is the last to leave."

"Damn it to hell, Micky; I am not going to continue to repeat myself. Get off that ship, and that's a damn order."

"What about the rest of the crew?"

"Evacuate as many as you can in the life pods and eject the M.E.T. Anyone who doesn't make it, I'm sorry, it's tough luck, but I need you, Batty, and Harlow off that ship. Now, enough talking. Just do it."

"Harlow is already dead, Major."

I winced at this. I knew Harlow and Jenna had a history, and I hoped that wasn't gonna distract her. I'd worked with the old coot for four years, but he wasn't someone you could get close to.

"Get yourself off that ship," Jenna said in response to this news.

"Yes, Ma'am," and the line went dead.

About fifteen minutes later, the place I'd called home for the last four years went up in a violent, silent explosion. I said a silent prayer for the young Batty.

Claire was running much of the show, which surprised me. It was then that I realized Jenna wasn't actually on board the U.S.S. Los Angeles, which was the current acting flagship of the fleet. I had no clue where she was, but clearly, she was somewhere without access to tactical computers, meaning Addison had to coordinate.

It looked like a mess, like chaos, as tiny pinpricks of light flew between ships; the pinpricks were actually men and women crossing the void to attack their enemies.

One thing that quickly became obvious to me was when the Peons started to retreat. My heart pounded with adrenaline as I realized we were on the verge of victory. Audra again spotted the imminent danger of two Peon cruisers not joining the retreat but instead heading directly to the U.S.S. Constitution, which sat limply, drifting in space.

I hit the communications switch. "The last two Peon cruisers are heading directly for the U.S.S. Constitution."

Seconds later, Jenna came online. "Tracker, you've got Peon cruisers coming your way. Can you get anything online?" There came no reply. "Addison, disengage now and protect the Constitution."

"Major, all ships are in the process of picking up troopers. We've got thousands of shuttles out there in space. If we stop now, we will lose most of our men and women."

"Damn it to hell! I will not lose that ship," Jenna practically screamed.

I didn't hesitate. I hit the internal ship communications. "All personnel begin evacuation procedures. Abandon ship. I repeat, abandon ship." I plotted a course directly at the nearest cruiser and accelerated the Lady Liberty.

"Stacey, what are you doing?" Daisy asked me urgently.

"Get the fuck off this ship," I shouted back at her, and without another word, she got up and left the bridge. I was alone, and I was gonna damn well make sure that at least one of those cruisers didn't reach the Constitution.

I almost hit this shitty little garbage hauler that was chugging along for all its worth toward the Constitution as I overtook it. I had no idea that it held the precious cargo of Jenna Plural.

I had no time to think about it as I slammed the Lady Liberty into the side of the Peon cruiser at full in-system speed.

"Suck on that, you motherfuckers! That's for Harper and for Wagga."

The grinding of metal within the ship was so loud it hurt my ears. Even the seat I was buckled into threw me off. Parts of the ceiling began to come down, narrowly missing me. I crawled on all fours back to the control console, which had twisted into a bizarre angle. I climbed to my feet and hit the communications again.

"Ok, you pack of flaming galahs, it's time to disembark this joy ride. Abandon ship, I repeat, abandon ship. Move your arses. That's a fucking order."

I must have still been on inter-ship comms because Jenna's voice came over. "Stacefield E Grant, I love you. Don't you dare die, or I'll bring you up on charges."

"Ahh, you only get all kissy kissy when I save your genetically designed arse from hot water. Love to chat, but Mama's got to get her sheep moving to the shearing sheds, I mean escape pods." I cut the line and left the bridge.

Nearly all of my team had managed to get into the escape pods. However, there was still plenty left for me, even with an entire crew on board. I climbed into the tiny capsule. After taking one last look back at my short-lived command, I ejected myself into space. Being a pilot in a craft over which you have no control is very disturbing. While I sat in a comfy seat, all I could do was look out the transparent door and watch space spinning around me, filled with tiny ships. I was surprised at how quickly

I was picked up, and it was only later that I realized Jenna had made my rescue a priority. While I appreciate that that does leave one with a little bit of survivor's guilt, I was grateful that all my crew was picked up, and I had no fatalities from my first command.

Chapter Twenty-Three

Betrayed and Bewildered

I was picked up by the HMS Manchester, which took me over to the U.S.S. Constitution with the other Americans, where a medic patched up my cuts and bruises. I was exhausted and took the opportunity to spend the rest of the day in that med bay bed, but part of me wishes I never had.

Jenna had taken time out of her schedule to visit me. She said nothing as she came into my room, stepped over, and kissed me hard on the forehead, then hugged me. I couldn't help but laugh.

"Officially, Stacey, I have to tell you that that was damn stupid, and you put all of your crew at risk," she flopped back into the chair beside my bed. "Unofficially, I have to tell you that was a 'bloody ripper' move." Once again, her positively woeful Australian accent made me want to cringe.

"It was dumb," I laughed. "I wasn't thinking. I just saw red that I couldn't do anything, then I saw an opportunity to get amongst it."

"You saved the Constitution. Once Tracker has that backup online, it's going to be the best chance we have to hit the Peon bastards hard. "

"I'm gonna miss our missions together, Jenna," I said with a note of sadness.

"Hey, what's with the downer? Now's the time to celebrate. Anyway, I'm gonna have Addison put you in as Chief Pilot on the Constitution."

"It won't be the same. The truth is, you're gonna be a desk jockey now," I grinned and slipped into a moment of nostalgia. "Remember that time on Mars when we picked up those couple of fellas who didn't know what a GenMod was, and they thought you were an android?"

Jenna laughed. "What was it he called me again?"

I cracked up at this memory. "A pleasure bot."

Jenna laughed harder. "That's right. Is there even such a thing?"

"Nope. But he wasn't exactly the brightest spark."

"No, but I recall you telling me he was pretty good between the sheets." We both erupted in raucous laughter. Suddenly, Jenna went quiet.

"What's wrong?"

She sighed softly. "Stacey, you are the closest thing I have to a best friend. I want to tell you something strictly between us."

And at that, I sat up, looking eager. This made her chuckle, but she grew serious again. "Despite everything going on, I'm considering trying a serious relationship again. To be honest, I'm kind of scared."

This surprised me, and my one good eye widened to its extreme. "Good on you, mate. You've let that GenMod thing hang over your head for far too long. You got someone in mind?"

My whole world went into a tailspin at her following words. She flushed slightly as she said, "Mr. Phelkar."

My brain spasmed as it tried to work coherently, and even Jenna noticed. "Is something wrong with that?" I saw fear in her eyes.

I gathered my thoughts together quickly and composed myself. "No! I'm just surprised, that's all. I didn't think the two of you got along."

Jenna smiled. "He can be frustrating at times, but there's something about him. The vulnerability, the devotion."

"There is that," I said, grinning yet desperately wanting to ask one oh-so-important question. "But there is also your penchant for guys who are submissive to you."

Jenna grinned yet flushed slightly. "Yes, there is that. I've kind of gotten used to being in control of everything in my life over the years. Including men."

"So, how long has this been going on?" I tried my best to sound casual, but this was the most important question I'd ever asked her. I could deal with him choosing her over me; that's just the way of it. The question was, *had* he chosen her over me?

"Well, the attraction has been there for a while, but we never expressed it to each other until the night of the party."

My head exploded, and I struggled to maintain my composure. I didn't want her genetically superior observation skills to notice the slightest hint of the stress I was now feeling. The time Michael Phelkar fucked me on the U.S.S. Los Angeles, he'd been in a relationship with my best friend. That goddamn motherfucker! Maybe I was mistaken, though. Perhaps they hadn't committed to each other then. It could well be that he'd still been a free agent when he was with me. Honest truth – at that moment, I was more concerned about Jenna than myself or him.

"So it's serious, is it?"

"Well, we agreed we were gonna try for a committed relationship that same night, but no promises about the future were made."

No promises about the future made no difference to me; he had committed to Jenna, and he had lied to me. He'd fucked me, knowing full well he was Jenna's man.

"Do you even have time for a relationship right now?" I tried to sound casual, but I knew something about Michael Phelkar that she didn't, and I didn't know whether to tell her or mind my own business. Perhaps if he had cheated with someone else and I knew about it, the answer to that question would've been much easier to come to. But I didn't want to have to tell her that I'd rooted her man soon after they'd committed to each other.

"Well, it's not going to be easy, and I'm not even sure that I want to go down this path, but I care about him a lot."

I didn't tell her. At that moment, all I was concerned with was the prospect of losing my friendship with a woman whom I cared deeply about.

A couple of days later, I was heading to the new quarters assigned to me on board the Constitution. I hadn't spoken to Phelkar since that night in the ventilation shaft, and when I saw him coming toward me along that busy corridor, I didn't want to talk to him then. I turned and headed in the opposite direction, hoping he hadn't seen me. It was clear I wasn't going to be that lucky.

"Stacey," he called out to me. I pretended not to hear him, and I picked up my pace. Suddenly, he grabbed my arm, and I snatched it away. "No, Phelks, don't make this any worse." I looked up at him and found that my anger had turned to sadness, which frustrated me immensely.

"What are you talking about?" he asked. I don't know if he was genuinely stupid or just playing the fool.

I looked around to make sure no one was listening before looking back up at him and saying in a lowered voice, "I know about you and Jenna."

"What about us?"

Ohh, that bastard. "I know I joked about you being with her, but I didn't realize it was true. I would never have..." I was genuinely lost for words

"Stacey, what's the problem?" he asked.

"Seriously!" I glared at him. "Do you realize what that makes me, Phelks? Do you? At best, it makes me your mistress. At worst, it makes me your whore."

"It's not like that, Stacey. Truly, it's not," He said, flustered.

"Really? Then explain to me exactly what I am to you."

"You're one of my very dear friends, and I care about you greatly."

"Is that all?"

Moments passed, and he gave no answer before eventually saying. "No, no, that's not all. But it is the way that it has to be."

Was he playing me for a fool or playing Jenna for sport? "Fuck you, Phelks," I whispered angrily. "You let me fall in love with you when you knew nothing could come of it."

He looked confused and responded. "I'm sorry, I had no idea. Honestly, I just thought you were letting off some steam."

This hit me for a loop, and my fury fizzled out. "The first time, yes. That was just something between comrades, but there's something about you, Phelks; you never treated me like some conquest. In so many ways, you're a total wanker, but you did something most men don't."

"And what is that?"

"You treated me with respect. It's been a long time since any bloke's done that. At least, that is what you had led me to believe."

"That's because I do respect you, Stacey. I respect you a lot. I'm sorry for any hurt I've caused you."

I found myself saying something I'd never wanted to. "I knew it was too good to think you may feel the same way about me.

I guess I'm just making a complete arse of myself." At this, he had the fucking gall to step even closer to me.

"No, don't," I shook my head. "You're the Major's man. And I love her too much to mess with that."

"Does it help if I told you I had feelings for you?"

This completely floored me. The man I thought was the decent one showed me he wasn't. "Don't be a cunt."

He looked startled. "What?"

"Don't fucking mess with me."

"I assure you, Stacey, I'm not. I'm confused, yes. But I do know my feelings for you are more than friendship, even if I tried to deny it myself."

I admit my head was a whirlwind of thoughts and feelings. My sense of logic was at odds with my emotions. No matter how bad a guy treats you, you still go through that sense of loss even when you realize he's bad news. "Well, you sure know how to confuse a girl."

"I'm sorry. I just didn't want you to think you're meaningless to me."

"And you also told Jenna this?"

"Not exactly," he said uneasily.

I laughed ironically. "So, what you're saying is instead of being a cunt to me, you're being a cunt to Jenna?"

He actually shrugged and said, "I guess so."

"Do you have any idea of how much I respect that woman? She gave me the chance to give those Peons some payback for my country. She's had my back more times than I can count. If it weren't for her, I would have been cashiered a long time ago. She gives me hope that I will sit on Bondi Beach again one day. Have a barbie on Christmas Day that I'll return to the land that I love. No, Mr. Phelkar, I'm never going to hurt her."

"Nor do I expect you to." There was a long, uncomfortable pause. "So, where do we go from here?"

"We don't," I said coolly. "We stay apart from each other as much as possible and make sure we're never in a room alone together. We put this down to some bad decision-making on both our parts."

"But."

"No buts," and I shook his hand. "It has been a pleasure, Mr. Phelkar."

"Likewise, Captain Grant. Clear skies to you."

"Clear skies to you too, Mr. Phelkar," and I smiled and turned and walked away, not looking back. Damn it, Stacey. Don't you dare cry, I told myself.

The celebrations went on for days. Many were unsure about the newly announced Solar Confederation. However, the fact that we'd been victorious was enough for now. In the past few weeks, I had gained and lost my command, and lost two ships on the same day. To be honest, I wasn't going to miss the dreary U.S.S. Lewis Puller. I had sat at the helm of the U.S.S. Constitution, the flagship of the United States fleet, and now the flagship of the Confederation. I thought that would be like a dream come true; however, it wasn't for me. Piloting such a large vessel relied on multiple people and didn't feel like "my ship." I sent Jenna a message saying I preferred not to assume the role, and I was severely pissed when the response to my request came from Claire. It felt as if Jenna was now too good for the likes of me, but when I met with her, the first thing she did was clear that up.

"Before we discuss your position, I have a message from Jenna," she said as she let me into her office. She didn't go and sit behind the desk. Instead, she led me over to the more casual seating area where she had a couple of armchairs and my favorite thing in the world – a drinks cabinet. She indicated for me to sit, then she opened it and said, "She doesn't want you to think that she now has some superiority complex and that she isn't dealing with this matter herself. She's tied up with discussions with the Japanese Fleet Command. She said that she would prefer to be sitting here chewing the fat with you. I have been ordered to state this next part verbatim, 'Stacey, I do not mean to offend you. But if you are offended, well, you can just go stick your head in the dunny.'" I snorted with laughter. I realized that nothing had changed between us by that comment. Claire grinned at me. "Can I get you something to drink?"

"I'd love a Scotch if you have some. But don't tease me with it," and she looked at me questioningly. I elaborated, "Be generous with your pour." She pulled out a bottle of genuine Scottish Scotch and poured me the equivalent of at least four fingers of Scotch. To my surprise, she poured herself the same and then took the seat opposite me.

"You have impressed me, Stacey. That stunt you pulled with the Lady Liberty saved the U.S.S. Constitution, the most powerful weapon in our arsenal. And you did it without a single loss of life of your crew."

"Well fuck, if we're gonna be honest. I didn't think I was gonna walk away from that, let alone my crew."

"Then I'm even more impressed that you are willing to admit that."

I shrugged that off, too. "I've got no reason to hide it. It's not like I'm after a medal or anything."

Addison sat back in the chair and took the first sip of her drink. I looked down at my glass and noticed I'd already finished mine. "Let's talk about your future. Jenna really wants you at the helm of the Constitution."

I couldn't hide my look of disappointment. "If that's what she wants, then I'll do it. But I won't be happy."

"She understands that and isn't going to compel you to do it. I am here to discuss what you want to do, and I'll try to accommodate you."

I looked at her disbelievingly. "So you're telling me that Jenna says that I can have any position I want."

"Anything besides the command of the Constitution or my job. So, pretty much."

"Mind if I get another drink?" I asked.

"Be my guest," and she waved a hand at the cabinet.

I went over and poured out the Scotch, and as I filled my glass, I said, "So if I were to ask for the command of the U.S.S. Los Angeles, you'd give it to me?"

Addison sighed. "Well, I'd strongly discourage you. I don't believe you have the experience to command a battle cruiser, and it's the Major's opinion that you wouldn't ask for something you knew you couldn't handle. However, the Los Angeles does need a new commander now that I am Second in Command to Jenna."

"Right, but if I insisted that's what I wanted, you'd actually give it to me?" I asked as I sat back down and swirled my drink.

Addison sat back and looked at me for a long moment, weighing me up. Eventually, she said, "Yes, my orders are to give you any position you request."

"Well fuck me sideways. That's quite a position to be in." I downed the second drink in one. Placing the glass on the table, I sat back. I could see that Addison was looking nervous that I would indeed request command of the Los Angeles. Before telling her, I let the moment linger. "I want to get back behind a flight stick again. I want to pilot a fighter."

I expected Addison to agree immediately, but she didn't. "If that is your wish, I will arrange it, but please, hear me out."

"Sure."

"It's an honorable choice for sure. However, you are part of what is unofficially considered Jenna Plural's inner circle. Your name is becoming legendary amongst both our people and the enemy. I feel that the position you hold should be more prestigious."

"But that's all I want to do. It's who I am."

"How about this? We promote you to Senior Flight Major, and then you can take control of the Constitution's fighter command?"

I immediately shook my head. "That's a desk job. It's sitting around coordinating attacks without actually participating. But give me command of one of the Constitution's twelve squadrons, and I'll consider it."

Addison looked unsure about this, as if it wasn't good enough. Instead, she came back with another idea. "How about this? You form a new squadron picking whoever you want, and you'll have full autonomy. You'll lead Special Ops missions exclusively."

A grin crossed my face. "Now that's something to get my knickers wet. Do you really think Jenna would go for that?" I'm not even sure why I asked the question. I knew she would. After all, I knew Jenna better than Addison did.

"Absolutely. Give me a couple of days to discuss it with the current Head of Fighter Command. It needs a softly softly approach. We don't want anyone feeling undervalued."

"Do I get to name it?"

"Within reason."

"And what's that?"

"Nothing crude, vulgar, or profane, and nothing that can be considered nationalistic to just one nation. And I request, though not demand, that you consider people from every nationality in the alliance. I don't want this to become political."

"Oh, bollocks. That rules out the Australian Flying Arseholes," I said jokingly, but also to get a rise out of her.

It didn't work, but she did reply. "I can see working with you is still going to be a challenge, Captain Grant."

And that was how I learned of my sudden promotion, skipping several ranks.

Chapter Twenty-Four

Hannah

A few hours later, I was in my quarters, which were sadly sparse because I'd lost everything on both the Puller and the Lady Liberty. The paperwork came through confirming both my new rank and my transfer to the new Air Force. I pondered going through personnel files to look at pilots, but there were just too many parties going on to waste my time on that shit. I did find out where Phelks was gonna be just to make sure I could avoid him. My head was still screwed up over my feelings about him, but I was determined not to tread on Jenna's territory.

Fortunately, the Constitution was so fucking big that it had several bars and mess halls. Naturally, I chose to head down to what they called the all-rank mess, which was exactly as advertised: officers and enlisted could mingle. I'd changed into civvies for the occasion, my typical white skirt, stockings, boots, and buttoned-up sleeveless colored blouse. I even put on a bit of makeup, which was rare for me since losing my eye. I intended to get wasted, but blokes were off the menu this evening.

It was kind of weird going into a bar where I didn't know anyone. I hadn't done that in a long time. I think the last time I did was back in Wagga. The lights were dimmed, the music was blasting, and bodies were gyrating and swaying to the rhythm in the center of the room.

I made my way up to the bar, squeezing through the crowd and then slipping my arm between people to place it on the counter in an attempt to get some service. It took a while, but I managed to get myself a beer and a large tequila shot. I downed the shot and went looking for somewhere to sit down and drink my beer. There wasn't a hope in hell of finding an empty table, so I just looked for somewhere that had no blokes on it. I found one where three girls were sitting, and there were a couple of spare chairs. "Mind if I sit here, mate?" I asked.

The woman looked up at me with surprise. "Yeah, sure. Go ahead." As I sat down, she leaned in and started whispering to one of her friends. It was pretty bloody uncomfortable when they all started gawking at me.

I placed my beer on the table and looked back at them."Is there some sort of problem?" I asked quite loudly to be heard over the music.

One of the girls leaned over to me and, in a thick Australian accent, asked me, "Are you from Down Under?"

A grin crossed my face, "Fucking oath, mate. Good to see another fellow countryman."

"Where from?"

"Wagga."

"No shit. I'm Billie from Alice Springs. This is Eleanor from Sydney and Hannah from Melbourne. What's your name?"

"Stacey. If you don't mind me asking, you all look a little too young to have been serving in the military when we lost our country. How'd you end up on the Constitution?" I asked.

"We weren't in Oz when she went down except for Han over there. Our parents worked for the mining consortium out on Io.

"Well, Ellie and I are civilians. I'm working logistics. Han over there, she's Air Force."

I looked over at Hannah, who was smiling proudly. She was a young girl of about nineteen, with straight black hair with a single pink stripe running down it. She was dressed in one of those teeny 'come fuck me' little black dresses. But out of the three, she seemed the most shy.

Her hair was perfect, long, dark, and luxurious. Her skin tone – flawless. Her face – perfectly symmetrical. She was either a GenMod or her surgeon was nothing short of an artist. I guessed the former as she was clearly a rival for Jenna in the looks department. The truth was, though, that there was only one question I wanted the answer to, and I looked at her before yelling out, "Are you a pilot?"

She chuckled in a rather adorably innocent way. "Oh, I wish. Unfortunately, I'm just a ground crew member; there's nothing really exciting about it. I'm just a Maintenance Engineer."

"Don't sell yourself short," I said rather too harshly. "Maintenance Engineers are the lifeblood of the Air Force. Pilots wouldn't have the first clue if it weren't for you making sure their kite was flying."

Hannah chuckled again. "You almost sound like you're Air Force yourself."

"Sure am," but for some reason, I didn't want to tell them that I was a pilot. So I added quickly, "What d'you sheilas say to a round of shots and a jug of brew?"

"Let me get them," said Ellie. "It was my round anyway," and she slipped away to the bar.

"Do you know many other Aussies around here?" Billie asked me.

"Nah, mate. To be honest, I just got posted here after my last ship was destroyed in that last battle."

"So, what is it you do?" Hannah asked.

I don't know why I was so reluctant to tell them. I was just enjoying being one of the girls again, and I thought if they knew that I was an officer, that'd come to a swift end. "Oh, I'm between postings right now," I said, deliberately misinterpreting the question. Fortunately, some bloke came up and asked Billie to dance at that moment. Saved by the skin of my teeth. One of his friends came over to ask me, but when I looked up at him, he saw my 'not a snowball's chance in hell' expression, and he asked Ellie instead. Unfortunately, that left me alone with the hot flight mechanic. So, I gave up the charade and went with it. "Have you ever thought of going through flight school?"

Her expression changed to one of disappointment. "Unfortunately, it's not an option. You have to be a commissioned officer to be a pilot, and Australians don't get commissions in the United States Air Force unless they've already got some skill or another that the Yanks decide is useful."

"Maybe that will change now," I said, even more uneasy about revealing my status as a very newly commissioned officer. "Did you hear Jenna Plural's speech?"

Her eyes lit up, and she smiled. "Did I ever! Isn't she just amazing? She makes you feel like our flag is already flying over Brissy again. And she's so beautiful that she looks like a GenMod. She's perfect."

I wanted to say, "Yeah, well, you haven't heard her in the dunny after eating a bad kebab." Instead, I said, "Well, the military will no longer be based on national lines. The new fleet is going to be completely integrated."

"You know, I hadn't thought about that. You have a point, and I have the grades to take the aptitude test. But will there even be things like flight schools? We're now just this big, ragtag fleet of ships. We don't even have a homeworld anymore or even a place to land a ship."

Billie returned at that point without her dancing partner. "What happened to the hunk?" Hannah asked her as Billie flopped into her chair, looking annoyed.

"He had an issue with his ability to control his hands. I told him I'm not that kind of Sheila. I hope the slap I gave him leaves him with a nice big handprint across his face tomorrow."

Both Hannah and I laughed at that, and we spent the rest of the evening getting drunk. I'm talking good old Australian munted. By 3 AM, we were standing on a table, entertaining those around us with a rousing rock version of Waltzing Matilda.

I don't even remember getting back to my quarters that night. I woke late in the morning, fully dressed, on the couch. As I made myself breakfast, I pondered my conversation with Hannah, and something occurred to me, and the spark of an idea lit up in my fast brain. I went to my desk and switched on my computer. I began researching records of men and women in the Navy and Air Force who were born abroad. I didn't have access to the records for Mother Nations within the alliance, or, rather, should I say, the Solar Confederation, as Jenna had recently announced we were to be called in order to distance ourselves from the traitors of the Pacific Alliance. So I filed requests from each national flagship. I wanted to find Hannah's personnel record, but I didn't get her last name. However, there weren't exactly many Australian Hannahs around who'd served in the United States Air Force. It didn't take me long to find her personnel file. When the name popped up in front of me, I was struck dumb with shock as I read "Hannah Grant."

I couldn't calculate the odds of running into my sister. When my parents divorced, my mom remarried and had more children, and yes, I knew one of them was named Hannah. However, I never had anything to do with my mom; therefore, I had no connection to these new siblings.

At this point, I wasn't even sure it was my Hannah Grant. Neither Hannah nor Grant was an unusual name, and it doesn't automatically make you related to me. There were probably thousands of Hannah Grants. However, a closer look at her personnel file revealed that it was a done deal, for we had the same mother. I sat back in my chair, trying to digest this new revelation. I never thought of my other family, and on the rare occasions I did, it was when they were on the news. Something now tickled the back of my brain, and I did a quick search on the net for Hannah Grant. News videos came up – old ones. Over four years old before the fall of Oz. There she was, surrounded by paparazzi, the daughter of the wealthiest woman in the Solar System. The closest thing we'd had to a queen since we left the Commonwealth. Princess Hannah, in designer clothes that matched her designer genetic profile.

My baby sister, eight years younger than I am, and... I froze. If she were only nineteen now, then she couldn't be a GenMod. Genetic modification was always illegal in Australia. Even if you went abroad, the child would be denied citizenship Down Under. Aside from that, it was outlawed worldwide by treaty for over fifty years. Holy fuck! My sister was an illegal GenMod. I hurriedly researched some more because I was sure that I wasn't the only one who could see it. Yes, there had been a scandal about it, but Mother had brushed it off. She even released her DNA profile, which proved that Hannah was natural. Bullshit! My mother could prove she was the King of Siam with her money. The story had died, but it had started to surface again when she was sixteen, and she'd begun to become more publicly visible. Then came Last Day when Australia fell, and she was never heard of again.

I resented that side of my family, considering I'd practically grown up on the breadline, but that wasn't my sister's fault. She was still my blood, and that mattered.

I called up Addison's adjutant to arrange for a private office I could use. I wasn't the world's most professional individual, but even I wouldn't conduct business in the same place I slept. He immediately assigned me a room, and it only took me forty-five minutes to find the damn thing. It had been unused for some time and was devoid of any form of personalization or decoration. It was a simple grey office with a desk, computer screen, and the obligatory American coffee maker. As I sat down, I felt the annoying weight of being a bureaucrat come down on my shoulders. Once I got going, though, I could pass off all that boring stuff to someone else. I may not have been into all that rank-and-file stuff, but bloody hell, I was gonna use my position not to do anything I didn't want to.

I pulled up Hannah Grant's file again and studied it before hitting my intercom and requesting someone be sent to bring her to my office. A little while later, I heard her come in. She was clearly nervous and utterly clueless about what was going on. She spoke to Delaney, my newly assigned PA, concerned about why she was there. I couldn't help but get up from my desk and look through the crack in the door as he told her why "Captain Grant" wanted to see her. She looked amused to have the same name as the officer who had asked to see her, but she didn't think anything of it beyond coincidence. Well, it was a doozy of a coincidence, but not in the way she was thinking. I hurried back to my desk and looked as if I was busy at my computer when he let her into the office. "Hannah Grant, Captain."

I looked up at her and smiled at the amazement on her face when she realized I was the woman she had just spent the night drinking and getting drunk with, not to mention a particularly loud and obnoxious rendition of Waltzing Matilda.

"Come in, Hannah, and take a seat."

"Hey, Stacey, I mean Captain Grant," she said, suddenly turning crimson.

"I'm not big on formalities. Stacey's fine, mate."

"You failed to mention that you were an officer last night," she looked almost chastising as she took the seat in front of the desk.

"Well, it would've kind of ruined the night, don't you think? I just wanted to celebrate our victory with a couple of sheilas from Down Under," I grinned.

"I can understand that," she smiled, a perfect smile reminiscent of Jenna. "It's funny, but I have a sister called Stacey Grant. I've never met her, but I know she's an officer in the Air Force." Great. My sister was a moron, and I just kept smiling at her and said nothing. After an awkward silence, the lightbulb went off in her head, and her jaw dropped. She was lost for words as I looked at her impassively, letting it sink in. Eventually, she said almost breathlessly, "Stacey?" I nodded. "Oh fuck me!" she exclaimed. Oh, she was my sister, all right. "Why didn't you say anything last night?"

"I only found out myself a couple of hours ago when I pulled up your personnel file."

"Why were you looking at my personnel file?" she asked with genuine curiosity.

"For a position working with me that I wanted to discuss with you. So I want to be clear, what I'm about to talk to you about has nothing to do with our relationship."

"Okay," she said uneasily.

"I'm starting a new squadron, and I want you to be part of it. "

"I'm not due for transfer for another year. I really don't think they will let me out of my current position."

I smiled. "Don't worry about that. That's my problem. I was hoping you could join my team as soon as possible, although it may take a couple of weeks to finalize all the details. The position is voluntary. You are not obligated, nor am I ordering you to come over to us."

"I really appreciate it, but I'm in line for promotion to a mechanic position. I don't want to miss out on the opportunity."

"I am not recruiting you to be a mechanic. You said you wanted to fly, and the only thing stopping you was the fact that you're Australian. Like I said last night, that doesn't apply anymore."

Hannah's eyes widened, and I could see myself reflected in them. The smile featured a prominent row of slightly overextended teeth, perfectly aligned by genetics. "Oh, are you serious?" she smiled.

"Well, I have to get permission to start teaching new pilots, but I don't think I'll have a problem with that, and you'll have to begin training as a gunner. If I think you have the chops, we can start working on flight training."

"Oh my God, that would be amazing," she said like a kid being told that she was about to go to Disneyland.

"Don't get too excited. As I said, I need permission first. However, I can tell you that you'll begin gunnery training as soon as your transfer is approved. So, what do you say, Hannah? You wanna join me?"

"Absolutely," she said positively, beaming at me.

I smiled back at her. "Then let's make it happen. Leave the paperwork to me, and when the time's right, you'll hear from your CEO about your transfer."

It was a dismissal, and she rose to her feet. "Thank you for this opportunity." I just smiled and nodded, and she headed toward the door. Before she went through it, she hesitated and turned back to me. "Would it be inappropriate to say I'd like to get to know you as my sister?"

"Why would that be inappropriate?"

"Well, you're an officer and all that. And well, there's our obvious family issues," her voice trailed off.

"Well, I don't think it'll be the first time someone outranks their sister, but they can still share a prawn or two on the barbie."

"Let's do lunch sometime. Can I call you?"

"Anytime you want, sis." With a smile, she positively bounced out of my office.

I pushed the thoughts of Hannah out of my head and turned my attention to looking at the plethora of other personnel files. I selected promising candidates who had applied for flight training but were turned down for what appeared to be no other reason than their national origin. I took a call from a Russian Logistics Officer who interrogated me about why I wanted the files I had requested, but he finally agreed to send them over. I repeated the process after running them through a translator. By the end of the day, I had the names of fourteen potential recruits, of which I would ultimately choose just eight to form a new squadron. I also picked out the ground crew I wanted. I was deliberately poaching the best from other squadrons.

Chapter Twenty-Five

Sisters

I then made an appointment with Addison and took my list with me. She wasn't too pleased. "This does not look like an elite squadron to me?" she said.

"Yeah, about that. I've been doing some thinking," I said a little sheepishly.

"Yes, well, I do wish you'd stop doing that," Addison said coldly. I'd like to think she was joking.

"We're gonna need new pilots. We lost a lot of good people during that last battle, and there will be no more crew rotations from Earth."

"I see where you're coming from, but these names, they're not even the ones with the most potential."

"No, but I think their potential was overlooked because they weren't raised with stars and stripes on their nappies."

Addison sighed. "Let me talk to Jenna about this. At the end of the day, it will be her call. Okay?" She was staring at her screen, and then, slowly, her eyes raised to meet mine. "Hannah Grant?"

I felt slightly uncomfortable and replied relatively weakly, "I was considering her before I found out. Honest."

Addison sat back and looked at me for a long moment. "That could well be true. Honestly, I don't care. Whatever the case may be, it absolutely reeks of nepotism."

"Be fair, Claire. My getting this position reeks of nepotism. Jenna and I may not be related, but we are closely associated. I wouldn't even be considered for half the posts Jenna has offered me if I were back in Oz."

"That's different."

"Really? So you can say to me you're the most qualified to be the Chief of Staff of the entire military?" I said incredulously.

Addison was startled but eventually just grinned. "Get out of here."

When I returned to my quarters, a message from Phelkar was waiting on my intercom, requesting a meeting. I deleted it. When I went to bed that night, I didn't sleep very well. Thoughts of Hannah rambled through my fucked up brain. Epsilon Squadron would be my family. Automatically, I looked over to where I would normally have kept the picture of myself and Harper, but it wasn't there. It hadn't been beside my bed since I lost it with the Lady Liberty. I'd never been interested in possessions, but that was the one thing I'd never wanted to lose. Of course, I now realize how stupid it was that I didn't make a copy of it and carry it with me. I'd never been one for those modern electronic holo pictures. I love the look of old-fashioned paper with a flat image. But right now, I was regretting it. I had never really thought of Harper as my best friend until she was no longer there. What I would give for one more day, an hour, just to see her again. Just to give her a big hug and tell her how much I love and miss her.

It was about another week before all the paperwork was completed and my personnel requests were approved. During that time, I avoided calls from both Phelkar and Hannah. I felt guilty about the latter, but not enough to do anything about it. I simply didn't know what to say to her. Despite coming from the same semen of the same man, we had nothing in common. I almost regretted offering her a position in my new squadron.

I didn't get to name the new squadron after all. That privilege was decided upon by a committee that made up the provisional government of the new Solar Confederation, with, of course, Jenna at its head. We were simply to be known as the Plural Squadron. We soon became known by a nickname, Grant's Grunts, which is pretty much what we went by, but I'm getting ahead of myself. My eight squadron members were raw recruits. So Addison assigned instructors from the other squadrons. They tried to assert their authority over me; I'll let you guess how well that went.

I avoided Hannah for the most part, with her only attending mission briefings. I really didn't know what to say to her. One evening, as I went back to my quarters, I found her standing with her back against the front door, legs crossed and arms folded, waiting for me. Just like a Grant, she cut straight to the point. "If you don't want to see me, I want you to tell me. If that's the case, I'll never speak to you again. Hell, I'll even ask for a transfer."

"Well, I will deny the transfer," I grinned, but she was unamused at that, and I couldn't blame her.

"You are my Captain, so should I stand and salute you now?"

"I don't expect anyone to do that even when we're on duty. Do you wanna come inside?"

"That depends. Do you want me to?"

I indicated for her to move aside from the door, and she complied slowly and deliberately. I opened the door and indicated for her to enter. "Wow!" she said as she stepped inside. "For big and fancy officers' quarters, you certainly keep them bare."

I slipped off my flight jacket and threw it on my armchair. "I lost everything I had on board the Lady Liberty when it was destroyed. I just haven't gotten around to getting anything. To be honest, there's nothing I really want."

"Nothing? Nothing at all?" she sounded surprised.

"Not really. I lost a picture of my best friend and me that meant a lot to me, but I can do nothing about that now."

"Can't you take another?"

"No. She died."

"I'm so sorry. How did it happen?"

"Four years ago, on a mission, but I can't talk about it. It's still classified." I shrugged it off as if I was over it.

"I understand."

I headed over to my small drinks cabinet. "Want a drink? I got scotch, and I've even got Portobello Brandy."

Hannah grinned. "Seriously? I've never even tried the stuff," she said as she stepped over to look at the bottle.

"How come?" I asked with surprise.

She shrugged, "I was sixteen when Oz fell."

"Sixteen, and you hadn't started drinking? Are you sure you're a Grant?" I chuckled.

She laughed and gave me a wink. "Well, I never said that. I just didn't have access to Portabello Brandy."

I grinned as I opened the bottle. "I guess your life is very different than mine,"

Her face fell, and she looked down. "I'm sorry, Stacey. I know that Mum was a shit mum to you," she said uneasily.

"Was? Is he dead?" I asked, very much hoping so.

"To be honest, I don't know. I didn't see her on that last day. I was in school when it happened, and I never went home. Do you mind if we don't talk about this?"

"Not a problem." I handed her a glass with a generous pour of the brandy. "I grew up in Wagga. Dad never remarried and died when I was sixteen. I was shit broke. My brother, or rather our brother, was killed during his national service. So I lived on the streets for a couple of years before joining the Air Force. After the Battle of Cape York, Jenna recruited me, and I've been working with her ever since."

Her eyes widened. "You've worked alongside Jenna Plural?"

I laughed at her reaction before giving her a friendly warning about the brandy I poured her. "You're gonna want to sip that. Don't just gulp it now."

She took a sip and then looked down at the glass. "That... It's bloody amazing."

I chuckled and took a sip of my own before saying, "That's why we call it Ambrosia. Take a seat."

We both sat back in armchairs in companionable silence as we sipped our drinks.

"So, what is she like to work with?" Hannah asked.

"Who?" I said, amusing myself by being deliberately provocative.

"Jenna Plural, of course," Hannah said wide-eyed.

"To be honest, she's one of the finest people I have ever met," I smiled.

Hannah's eyes opened wider. I saw the excitement of someone clearly with a case of hero worship. "I bet she is. And you're actually friends with her?"

"I thought I was, but I haven't seen her since she assumed her new position," I shrugged. "I think she's far too important for the likes of me now."

"Well, I'm sure she's very busy with all that's going on now. When I saw her and heard that speech, I knew we'd found the right leader to get us out of this mess," Hannah smiled.

"Now, that is something we can agree on. I honestly wouldn't trust anyone else. However, I do miss hanging out with her," I said regretfully.

A moment of silence fell between us again. This time it was a little bit awkward. I could see there was something on her mind that she wanted to get out. "Whatever you're thinking, just say it," I said casually, although, in reality, I was nervous about what the issue was.

She tilted her head thoughtfully as if trying to find the right words. "Stacey, I just wanted to say I'm sorry about what happened with the family."

I laughed that off with a dismissive wave of my hand because it was a subject I was uncomfortable with. "No worries, mate. I got over that years ago," I lied as much to myself as I was to her.

Hannah sighed and slowly shook her head. "Please be honest with me. I really don't know what happened. Growing up, the subject of you and our brother was off-limits."

I sighed and downed the rest of my drink. Did she really want to go there? "I didn't fit into her perfect world. In her eyes, I was flawed, and that simply wouldn't do for Marcia Grant." I smiled and added unkindly, "And that, my dear little sister, is why she replaced me with a GenMod."

It was Hannah's turn to look uncomfortable. She glanced away from me, "I'm not a GenMod. They're illegal. At least any that were designed after the Prague Convention."

I raised an amused eyebrow at her. "You asked me to be honest, and yet you won't do me the same courtesy?"

She looked up and fixed her eyes on me. "Well, your story can't get you killed. Mine can."

I shook my head. "Not anymore, little sister. Jenna Plural is in command now."

Hannah frowned, looking a little confused. "Jenna is accepting of GenMods?"

I laughed out loud at this, and the irony was too funny not to. "For someone who's got perfect eyesight, you seem incredibly blind. Have you not seen Jenna Plural? A veritable walking goddess of perfection?"

The way Hannah's eyes now widened was almost comical as her jaw dropped open. "Jenna Plural is a GenMod?"

"Born and bred in a tank just like you, albeit in a time when it was legal."

Hannah still looked unsure, and in the long pause that followed, I could almost see her brain taking over. "You mean I no longer need to live a lie?"

"While you're never gonna be free of the prejudice, and I assume the laws are still in place back in Australia, which would mean you'd lose your citizenship, I can assure you as long as Jenna prevails, you are as safe as safe can be."

Hannah looked at me again, but something was lurking behind her eyes. "If you don't mind me asking, what was supposedly so wrong with you that our mother did what she did?"

I laughed, but it was without humor. Instead, it was filled with resentment. "Ironically, it turned out to be a totally fucked up misunderstanding," I said as the memories returned to me. "I was a klutzy kid. I could never sit down and be quiet when there were so many things to do and see. I enjoy talking and interacting with everything around me. My mother didn't think this was normal. She said I was hyperactive, and that was a problem. She took me to see a specialist, a pretty dumb one," I sighed as I poured myself another drink and offered one to Hannah, which she declined. "They made me take this test. There were shapes on the screen, and every time one appeared, I had to press a button. I was eight years old, and it was just boring as fuck. So I made it more entertaining when I pressed the button. I made little exploding noises," I laughed genuinely. "I guess even back then, I was considering a career in the military. Well, after what seemed like an eternity, the medical dickhead came back in. She gave me this little pill. I can still see it, a little blue one, but I had trouble swallowing it. It tasted like shit. She then made me wait a while, sitting there alone, before coming back in and asking me to repeat the test. This time, she didn't leave. I felt so uncomfortable. In fact, I was pretty well scared stiff because I didn't really understand what was happening. This time I concentrated harder on the test because she was watching me, and I didn't wanna do anything wrong. Her conclusion was the little blue pill had calmed me down when in reality, it was the fact that she scared me shitless."

Hannah didn't need to say anything. The look on her face said it all. She was horrified. "So what happened?

"Well, I am sure you're aware of Mother's desire for that perfect public family. I didn't fit in with that, and when my father objected to her medicating me, there was a fight about it. He took me away rather than have me medicated. This embarrassed her. It was okay for her to leave her partners, but it wasn't okay for her partners to leave her. She used her power and influence to ensure my father wouldn't be successful in any career. She initiated legal proceedings to get me back, but then suddenly stopped. Six months later, you were born. The perfect Grant."

I saw a tear run down Hannah's face, but she quickly wiped it away and steeled herself. "I'm so sorry this happened to you. If it makes you feel better, my life with our mother was not a pleasant one. I was more of a prize pig on display than an actual daughter. Everything was about appearances, and my own father left when he discovered we weren't genetically related. She had told him she was using the DNA of herself and him to create me, but she didn't. I have no clue who my father is, other than that he's some genetically superior donor, possibly even a GenMod himself. I doubt I will ever find out, and to be honest, I don't really care. " Another long silence fell between us, and we just looked at each other. "Stacey, we come from a pretty fucked up family, but you and I are still family, and I want to get to know you as my sister. I want to be part of your life."

A multitude of emotions was flowing through me. Hannah Grant was not just my sister. She was my replacement. Could I get past that? Could I look into that perfect face, with those perfect eyes, that perfect mouth, and perfect hair, and see her as a sister instead of a memory of an early life that I wanted to forget?

Just as I was about to respond to her, the buzzer on my door went off. I sighed, put my glass down on the small table beside my chair, and pulled myself up. "Don't worry. I'll get rid of whoever it is, and then I'll take you to the officer's mess, and we'll have one of their fancy dinners." I paused, contemplating what I had just said. I shrugged. "Well, it's fancy for me."

Hannah laughed. "Oh, you have no idea what I ate trying to escape Last Day in Oz. But I'd like that."

I went out of the room to the front door, and as it slid back, I had quite a shock. Leaning on the doorframe was the lady herself, Jenna Plural. She had no guards, no sycophants, and thankfully no Phelkar. "You don't call. You don't let me know how you're doing. Nothing," she grinned at me. "Instead, you make the Admiral of the Fleet have to ditch some very conscientious guards and come down to find out if you're okay for me."

I grinned back at her, "Well, I just thought you were too important for that girl from Wagga."

"I am never gonna be too important for you, mate," she said 'mate' with an awful Australian accent, and I cringed at her.

"You got time to come in, or are there too many people waiting to kiss your fat arse?"

Jenna raised her eyebrow, "Calling my ass fat is now officially treason, Stacey Grant. Of course, I have time. After all, that's why I'm here."

"You'd better come in then. There's someone I'd like you to meet."

Chapter Twenty-Six

Downtime

I wish I had a camera for the look on Hannah's face as Jenna and I stepped back into the room. It was priceless. She jumped out of her seat, stood rigid at attention, and gave the sharpest salute I think I've ever seen. Jenna smiled and returned the salute quite neatly and said, "Careful there; you might pull something."

"Yes, Ma'am. Sorry, Ma'am," Hannah said, her voice quivering as she spoke.

I grabbed another glass and poured a drink for Jenna. As I handed it to her, I noticed Hannah hadn't moved and still stood rigid at attention. "Jenna, this is my sister Hannah."

Jenna smiled at her, but she didn't look surprised, and I realized then that she'd already found out about her. "Nice to meet you, Corporal Grant," she stretched out a hand to her. "You can relax now. You're Stacey's family, and I don't expect Pomp and circumstance when we're alone."

Hannah took the hand and shook it, but remained standing at attention. "For fucks sake, Han. Sit down, ya drongo," I said as I flopped back into my chair and picked up my glass again. Hannah nervously retook her seat.

"I have to be honest," said Jenna. "When Addison gave me the list of your recruits, and I saw the name Grant, I was curious enough to look up and see if there was a relationship. Though I'm sorry, it looks like I'm interrupting you tonight."

Hannah sat on the edge of her seat, still rigid. I grinned. "I'm sorry, Boss. My sister appears to be having an attack of hero worship."

Hannah blushed. I guess she must have gotten that from her donor's side. "I'm sorry. It's just when I heard your broadcast... Well, it was so inspiring, and I really became convinced that we're truly going home...." Her voice trailed off, and she flushed slightly again. "I'm sorry," and she made to stand up again. "I'm sure you two want to be alone. I'll get going."

"No, it's me that's intruding," Jenna moved to get up too.

"Oh, for fucks sake, will you two knock it off and sit the fuck down?"

They both complied with looks that could kill me, but I just continued sipping my drink. I looked over at my sister and said, "Whatever Jenna is, she's still just a person. But I can guarantee you. There are only two things she'd judge you on – your patriotism and your ability to kill Peons."

Jenna laughed, "I can't deny this. Tell you what, have you eaten yet?"

"We were about to go out to the officer's mess and get some dinner."

"If you don't mind, may I take you up to my mess and get you both dinner?" Jenna asked.

Hannah looked at me eagerly, and I shook my head disparagingly with a wide grin. "You planning to pick up the bill? Hell, I won't say no to a free feed," Jenna and Hannah chuckled at this.

"May I be permitted to go change quickly?" Hannah asked.

"Sure," Jenna smiled. "Tell you what, you go change, and I'll have one of my people come down to escort you up to the command section."

Hannah stood up and saluted again, which meant Jenna got up and saluted her back. I rolled my eyes at the pair of them. Hannah raced out of my quarters, and Jenna finally allowed herself to laugh out loud. "I am so sorry, Stacey; I mean no offense to you and your sister, but she is rather extreme."

"I don't really know her," I replied. "We weren't raised together. I literally just met her a few weeks ago, but you've certainly made a lasting impression on her. "

"Stacey," Jenna became quite serious. "You know she is an illegal GenMod, don't you?"

I immediately became defensive. "Under whose law?"

Jenna raised a defensive hand. "Relax, you don't have to worry. She has my personal protection. I'll have Kennett assign people to a protection detail. She won't even notice them."

"No," I said intently. "She needs to live a normal life. No guards, no watching her."

Jenna looked doubtful but relented, "As you wish. Are you sure I'm not interrupting you from getting to know your sister?"

"No, I'm pleased you're here. I was starting to think you were too high and fucking mighty for me these days," I chuckled.

Jenna did not smile. "Stacey, you do realize that it's you who has isolated yourself. You never come up to see me, and you don't return any of Michael's calls."

I felt uncomfortable, but I wasn't about to tell her why. "Well, I've been busy."

Jenna held me in her gaze, "I miss you!"

I rolled my eyes. "For fuck sake, Jenna. When did you turn into a pile of mush?"

She didn't laugh as I had intended. "When I know my best friend is in pain, and I don't know why."

I smiled weakly. "I'm gonna be okay, Jenna. You know me. I'm Teflon – nothing sticks."

Jenna sighed. "I can't make you tell me. Just know I am always here for you."

I forced a grin. "It's all good, Boss. Just keep me flying."

"Well, I do actually have a mission I wish to discuss with you."

"What's that?"

Jenna smiled. "Oh no, I'm not discussing that with you tonight. I don't want you thinking I came down here to talk shop with you. This is a social visit."

I laughed again and finished my drink. "Fair enough, mate. Let's go have some of this fancy tucker of yours."

"Let's do just that."

I thought she would take me to the Captain's dining room, which would be all formal and Pompous, but clearly, I'd forgotten who Jenna really was. We went to the officers' mess, which was reserved exclusively for the higher ranks. "This is the only public place I can go to now where people aren't trying to kiss my ass," as a steward showed us to a table that was clearly permanently reserved for her. It was more elegantly set and could sit six or seven people. We took the seats in the corner adjacent to each other. "So what's been happening? I mean with the team, not the whole ruling the universe thing," I asked as I declined the wine list and ordered a sambuca shot and a beer.

"Well, Tracker is in her element as Head of Technical Services. Oh, and you remember that Private Dodgson who stopped Morris? I gave her a commission. She's now training up her own unit of Marines. In fact, she's part of the mission I'd like to discuss with you tomorrow. Kensett is doing a sterling job heading up my personal security operations, and Phelkar, well, he's just Phelkar. I have set him up as head of civilian affairs."

"It's funny how much things have changed. All those missions, all those worlds on planets we visited, taking orders, doing the jobs no one wanted to do. Now we're the ones giving the orders.

Jenna smiled. "I can see the irony of it. But I want you to know I'm going to make a promise." I looked at her questioningly, but I said nothing. "We are going back to Earth one day, and the first front to open will be the retaking of Australia. I said I would make sure that you are on the frontline of that, and I won't go back on my word. You've been one of my most loyal supporters. I owe you, Stacey Grant. I owe you a lot."

"What the fuck is all this mushy stuff? Fuck! Are you gonna try and kiss me next?"

For the first time ever, she looked flustered, but only for a moment, and then she grinned. "Hell, it's only been a few weeks since I last saw you, and I've already forgotten what you were like."

"Yeah, well, I haven't even got my tucker yet, and you're already making me want to chunder. "

Before discussing it further, a young, good-looking Marine approached the table and stood by Jenna with a snappy salute. She saluted back as Hannah stepped up, "Airman Grant, present as ordered, Ma'am."

"I asked you to escort her here, not place her under armed guard. She is my guest, not my prisoner."

"I'm sorry, Ma'am."

"You are dismissed, Lieutenant." As he hurried away as fast as humanly possible without raising an alarm, Jenna turned to Hannah. "I'm sorry. Come and take a seat, Hannah."

"Yes, Ma'am," as she made to sit by me, but Jenna patted the seat beside her.

"Hannah, I want you to think of this as a family dinner. We're off duty in an informal setting. So, while we're here, please call me Jenna."

Hannah nodded meekly and slipped into the seat next to her. I was pleased that she dressed in a smart, casual style. I was worried she would turn up in some sort of evening gown or another 'come fuck me' outfit.

I must admit, it was a pleasant evening. As the night wore on, Hannah began to relax, and while she remained completely professional with Jenna, they managed to converse on a more even keel. I actually stayed sober that night watching my sister, and honestly, I saw some of myself in her. The better part of me, obviously. The part of me that was all about honor and integrity.

As the evening concluded, we bid farewell to Jenna, declining her offer of an escort back to our quarters. I didn't want the evening to end, so I asked her to come and spend the night in my quarters. I only had one bed, so I got a steward to set up a spare bunk in the living room. I poured her another drink and shared with her my luxury indulgence – a cheesecake dessert. I curled up in the armchair with my feet tucked underneath me, eating it one little piece at a time to make the pleasure last longer. We talked about nothing and everything into the small hours of the morning. I had a sister, and I loved every minute of it.

I got up early with only about two hours of sleep under my belt. I had to go to that meeting with Jenna. I dressed quickly and went into the living room, where Hannah was snoring softly. I wrote her out a chit to excuse her from reporting for duty that morning. Just before I left, I checked my messages and found Jenna had rearranged it for the afternoon. I went back into my bedroom and threw myself onto my bed. I woke up to a smell coming from my small kitchenette. It was something I hadn't smelled in four years. I rushed out of my room and saw Hannah making toast. "*You* have Vegemite?"

Hannah grinned conspiratorily at me and held up the small jar of black gold. "I have Vegemite."

"I will give you a thousand dollars if you make me a slice of Vegemite toast, and I'll chuck in a fifty for a cuppa."

Laughing, she pushed a plate over to me. I grabbed the slice as if I hadn't seen or tasted food in days. I savored the beautiful smell and sighed in complete ecstasy. Then slowly, I took a bite. "Bloody hell. Now, if that's not a little slice of heaven."

"It's all I have left. I only have a scoop or two."

I put the slice back down on the plate and looked at her guiltily. "I'm sorry. I don't wanna pinch your Vegemite stash."

She smiled at me and handed me a fresh cup of coffee. "I got it out for you."

"Why?"

"Because you're my sister." This was so alien to me. "Go on, keep eating. It'll make me happy. Just think of it as nineteen years of birthday presents I never got the chance to give you."

"Oh, you can't do that."

"Why not?"

"Because I can't afford to find nineteen years' worth of presents that could possibly equal Vegemite on toast."

She laughed, and after we finished the last remnants of her jar of Vegemite, we headed out; her to her training and me to the mission briefing with Jenna.

It was good seeing the old gang together. I took a seat opposite Jenna. Tracker was seated on my left, and Emma Dodgson was on my right. Also present were Kensett, Addison, and Phelks. I didn't know the two other people – one was an older Asian man, the other a young Marine who appeared to be taking notes.

"Ladies and gentlemen, we cannot maintain a fleet, especially one of this size, without ground support. We need supplies and maintenance tools. Most of us can achieve at least some of that out here, but we're going to find ourselves dwindling if we continue trying to be self-sustaining as a fleet. We need a homeworld, or at least a temporary one, until we return to Earth. We've decided that we should retake an old allied base.

We may get a little resistance. We may get a lot. Our target is the moon, Enceladus. Most of its communities were only recently constructed, and they're not yet fully populated. It's in full production, mining very valuable ore. Our attempts to communicate with the base on Enceladus have proven fruitless. We have no idea what is going on there, nor do we know whether the Americans who run it have remained loyal or whether they have conceded to enemy control. I intend to drop a unit of Marines onto the moon under the command of the newly commissioned Emma Dodgson here. It's not going to be easy – scouts have reported a heavy presence of European ships in the area. To avoid possibly drawing unwanted attention, we will use a Peon shuttlecraft that we commandeered from one of the ships taken during the Battle of Deep Space. Miss Grant will pilot the craft, and Mr. Phelkar will accompany her. We still have the upper hand in communications, thanks to the successful mission on Phobos. It could be months, maybe even a year, before the froggies get their communications working effectively again. This means that the usual updating of their code systems will likely experience disruptions, so we can use the codes Miss Kensett has extracted from the Peon prisoners in our custody. Phelkar will try to bluff his way through any European encounters the team may have. "

"Bloody hell, Boss. This whole thing sounds like it hinges on a wing and a prayer, doesn't it?"

Jenna smiled at me. "That's why you're the pilot, Stacey. It'll be your job to get them out of there if things go sideways."

"Oh yeah," I said unenthusiastically.

"Stacey will drop Dodgson's team a few miles from the main Enceladus complex. She will continue her mission and, once complete, return to the fleet.

"What type of shuttle am I getting?" I asked.

"It's a German Delta Class flyer. They're standard issue on Peon heavy cruisers, Helen Tracker informed me.

"At least that baby's got some teeth. Even though it's only got fixed forward position guns."

"You didn't think I'd send you in there unarmed, Stacey?"

"I would bloody hope not."

"Well, that's about the size of it. You'll have access to more details of your individual objectives from your personal terminals."

There wasn't much else to learn regarding my part in this operation. Fly in, drop them off, and fly out again. The hardest part would be trying to avoid conversations with folk. I met up with Hannah one last time that evening to let her know that I would be gone for a few days, but didn't tell her why. I had to assume that the mission was classified, so I couldn't have shared any of the details with her, even if I wanted to.

We made an early start the following day. The Delta flyer had been flown over to the Constitution, and as per usual, I went through the safety checks on the craft with the ground crew. It was in reasonably good condition. It had seen some minor action – the paintwork on the hull had been patched up here and there. Despite the cosmetic issues, the techs reported the Delta was sound and cleared for the flight, which was good enough for me. Dodgson arrived with about fourteen Marines and a shitload of equipment. And since this was an ice world, they would have to trek along the wastes, facing obstacles like chasms and cliffs. I'm not a big fan of the cold, and I was pleased that I wasn't going with them.

As they boarded, the moment I had long avoided came. Phelkar was in a cheerful mood and greeted me with a warm smile. I told him to get on board and prep for the launch. I wish I had an excuse to make him sit in the back with the Marines, but he needed to be upfront in case communications were required, so, much to my own discomfort, the Pom sat next to me.

It was supposed to be an off-the-books launch in case there were any spies among us. As a result, we couldn't go through the usual protocols that took place when any ship left another. Instead, we just had to sit and wait until another shuttle, any shuttle, launched. Then I was to follow them out without requesting clearance, hiding in their wake to avoid many scanners that might be watching us.

Chapter Twenty-Seven

Starship Down

It took about an hour for a suitable craft to be ready to take off. During that time, I responded to any attempts at conversation from Phelkar with grunts and one-word answers as much as possible. Eventually, he gave up and actually went to sleep – given it was four o'clock in the morning, it didn't look overly suspicious. I took off behind the shuttle and gave one small burst of the forward thrusters before cutting them off and allowing the forward momentum to carry us out. We simply drifted onward with nothing to slow us down in the vacuum of space. The dots of lights of the assembled fleet were barely distinguishable from stars, and I marveled at the sheer amount out there. Even more, ships had arrived to join us recently. Some of them were simply too slow to have gotten here in time for the rendezvous, while others, I was sure, had deliberately hung back to see which way the solar winds were blowing. After a reasonable distance had been maintained, I plotted our course toward Enceladus and set off another burst of the engines, accelerating us to a more reasonable speed. I would not fire up the engines properly until we were out of scanner range.

During the first part of the drop-off journey, nothing challenged us. I tried to call the Enceladus base, but just like Jenna, I received no response.

"Okay, Em. Have your team ready," I shouted to the back, and she came forward.

"We're all set, Captain Grant," Dodgson replied. "How close can you actually get us to our objective?"

I checked the terrain's visual as I came down toward it. "I'm sorry, it's gonna be at least three miles away, and you're gonna have quite a nasty trek. If I drop you any closer, you risk falling down a chasm or landing on a mountain.

Dodgson seemed remarkably relaxed about it all and just shrugged, "We'll manage." The casualness of the remark concerned me. However, it was not my concern.

She headed to the back and rallied the troops, getting them ready for the jump. I dove down to the surface, on alert for any anti-aircraft fire, but nothing came. I was a little surprised by this, given that it was an American base and we were in a Peon vessel with a disabled transponder. "Getting you in as close as I can." I sealed off the cabin to protect us, as Dodgson had opened the outer doors, since we weren't wearing protective thermal suits fitted with an oxygen supply. I heard the door open and saw the indicator lights on my dashboard and over the intercom. I told Dodgson she was cleared to go. "Good luck." I was kind of pissed that she didn't even reply and simply started counting out her men. She was the last one to go, and I closed the door automatically from the cockpit, immediately pulled up, and headed up and away from the small moon."Well, that was easy," said Phelkar, settling back into his chair.

"Yeah, I'm not used to things being that easy. It's making me nervous. If the Yanks are still in control of that place, they should have fired upon us. I was even ready to transmit the Constitution's transponder codes if we detected any weapons powering up."

"Just enjoy the fact that this mission went smoothly. Well, for us, at least. I am rather worried about Dodgson, though. She was just a private a few months ago, and now she is leading an elite assault team."

"Yeah, I sometimes wonder about Jenna's tendency to put loyalty before experience. But I guess she knows what she's doing."

"Honestly, I have never been more confident in command than I am of Jenna Plural." I never knew how he would have responded to my statement because, at that exact moment, the shuttle's alarms suddenly blared out a proximity alert. My eyes dropped to the scanners and then widened. "Oh fuck," I stared down in disbelief. "We have twelve Peon interceptors coming at us from all directions."

"How did we fly between them?" Phelks asked – a great question that even I was pondering.

I frowned, confused. "We couldn't have. The odds of that would have to be astronomical. We were out of range of each other, yet coming in on an intercept formation? They couldn't possibly be doing that unless they knew we would be here."

"That's impossible. Even if they knew about this mission, they wouldn't have known our flight plan to set this up."

"Exactly, Phelks. Which means somebody told them our flight plan."

"But who would do that?"

"We'll worry about that later. Right now, I'm more concerned with how the fuck we're gonna get out of here."

No matter which way I turned – up, down, left, right, or loopty loop. I would meet an interceptor. With the speed those bastards could maneuver, the chances of me making a decent hit on them with the forward guns would be next to impossible. I hit the inter-ship comms. "Delta flight to fleet, we're under attack. Prospects aren't looking good." I was about to ask for assistance, but there was no way in hell I'd get any. "This is gonna be the end of the road, Phelks. I'll try and take as many of them with me as possible, but that'll pretty much get us cornered."

"Stacey, you're the best pilot in the galaxy. I know you can get us out of this. I'm not giving up as long as you are at the helm of this ship."

"Well, I'm sorry to let you down, Phelks. But we're up Shit's Creek, and we're all out of fucking paddles." The first interceptor came into firing range, but it was beyond my ability to fire back. I tried pulling away, but doing so just put me within range of another interceptor. Every which way I turned, the same thing happened. The more time passed, the worse it got as more came into range. "Phelks, they're gonna get us. If I blow this ship up, though, I might be able to take some of them with us."

"Stacey, have you noticed they aren't firing at us?"

Phelks was right. I was completely confused. All of a sudden, a burst of light erupted from the front of one of the interceptors. It was the stuff of science fiction – laser guns or something. Then the others fired at us that same burst of light. Suddenly, I realized what they were doing just as they were about to hit. "Hands off the console, Phelks. Now!" He knew better than to disobey my order, and we both lifted our hands off anything metal. The full force of an electromagnetic pulse coursed through the ship. Sparks erupted from the consoles in front, overhead, and behind us as the engines cut out instantly.

Alerts rang out as the life support system went offline, then they, too, suffered the force of the charge as the lights blinked out. We continued our forward momentum despite the ship's sheer mass, but it was dead, and there was no way in hell I was going to be able to start it up again. Any chance of using the ship to take out some of the enemy by intentionally blowing it up was now completely gone. Looking out the window, we saw the interceptors forming a perimeter around us. As they circled, they came in closer and closer. They clearly wanted to make sure we were indeed incapacitated. Then there was a sudden thump to the back of our fuselage, and I couldn't work out what it was. Then there was another, and we suddenly jerked forward in our seats as something pulled against the ship's forward momentum. A ship appeared on our port side, as another appeared on our starboard, and finally, we saw two craft in front as they fired tethers from their vessels into the front of our ship with the same thumping sound we'd heard at the rear. They'd never planned on taking us out. No, they intended to take us alive all along, and at that moment, we realized the Peons had us captured.

With the communications out, they couldn't send us instructions on what they wanted us to do or whether they expected us to assist in any way. It didn't really matter, though. With the systems fried, we couldn't do anything. I couldn't see Phelkar's face, but I could hear his breathing, and I heard the anxiety in it. I reached out to find his hand, and he gave it to me, squeezing it tightly. We were speechless. We didn't know what to say. Becoming a Peon prisoner was possibly the worst thing that could happen to us. Neither of us was in uniform. The ship didn't carry the insignia of any nation or fleet, which meant the standard rules of war did not apply, and even if they did, neither side was known to follow them. I couldn't help but admire the skill of the interceptor pilots as they managed to turn around and take us with them without causing any damage to us. We couldn't even feel the motion of our movement. It was as if we were suspended in space. Only the lights of the interceptor propulsion gave us any indication that we were even going anywhere.

Thinking on it now with hindsight, I should have just opened the airlock, taking us both out then and there, rather than face what was coming."

"When they take us off this ship, they're gonna separate us. So, if there's anything you want to say, you better say it now." I hadn't meant anything by that. It just came out.

There was a pause, and then he said it. "I love you, Stacey."

"Oh fuck! You could have said just about anything besides that, Phelks." But my heart skipped a beat, which only irritated me all the more.

"I know you feel the same," he said softly.

"Oh, you do, do you?" I snapped back and pulled my hand from his. "I'm not even going there. Say something else. I don't want those to be the last words I hear from you."

He sighed, then he gave a little laugh. "It has been an honor and a privilege to serve with you, Miss Stacey Grant. And if these are to be my last days, then I want you to know I would not change a thing."

"Oh, to have the benefit of hindsight," I chuckled. "But the truth is, there is one thing that I would change if I could."

"Oh, what is that?"

"I'd tell Jenna to fuck off when she asked me to go on this mission." We both laughed genuinely, but then we fell silent as the interceptors pulled us onward.

Even though I said I wasn't going there, his words reverberated around my head. "I will admit, Phelks, I cared about you. Maybe I still do. But you're not the guy I thought you were. You not only cheated on my best friend, but you sank to a new low when you cheated on her with me."

Phelkar sighed. "I know that was wrong. I was drunk. I was enamored by you, but I never lied to you about how I felt. It doesn't really matter now, as we're probably not going to survive this encounter."

"It does matter, Phelks. You've put me in the worst position I could imagine. If it had been anyone else who cheated on Jenna, the first thing I would've done was tell her. But I can't do that because the one you cheated with was me!"

"I am truly sorry, Stacey. I'm sorry to you, and I'm sorry to Jenna."

I paused and bit my lower lip as I tried to work things out in my fogged-up brain. "Do you love her?" I asked softly

"Yes, I do, very much so," and he sounded genuine, but that didn't mean anything. Hell, he sounded genuine when he was fucking my brains out on the Los Angeles, and look how that turned out.

"Yet you can say the same thing to me? You do realize how that makes you look, don't you?"

"One of the few upsides about impending death is you can say all the things you know you shouldn't, but are true all the same."

"True or not. Nothing is ever gonna happen between us again. Let me be very fucking clear on that, mate. Not only because you cheated on my best friend, but because I can't trust a man like you." I know, right now, you're thinking I'm a hypocrite because, if you know me, you know I've never really let the relationship status of my latest root stop me. And that was true until now. Before, I never knew how that behavior really felt, but I do now.

Suddenly, the forward interceptors released their tethers and peeled off. I sat up and tried to see where they'd gone. A minute or two later, the sounds of more tethers releasing could be heard. "What the fuck?" I muttered. I leaned forward to try to see more, but whatever was happening was behind us. Then we heard it as the last tethers released, and we drifted. "This is weird."

"Is there a chance we can get the engines back online?" Phelkar asked.

"They might come back eventually if they're not completely fried." Then the stars began listing to the left. Now that shouldn't be happening. We shouldn't be falling sideways. If anything, we should be continuing straight on with inertia. Then Enceladus slowly came back into view. "Oh fuck, oh fuck," I muttered.

"What is it?" Phelkar asked urgently.

"Gravity, Mr. Phelkar. We're going to crash."

"Please tell me you're kidding me," Phelks said, fear in his voice.

"Brace yourself, Phelks. This is no joke." I strapped myself into the seat and heard Phelks do the same. We sat in silence for about ten minutes as Enceladus got closer and closer. I kept looking down at the console, hoping we would see some life in it again so that I could pull off a last-second, heroic Stacey Grant last-second save.

And then we hit. We smashed into the side of the moon and kept going. Shit! Fuck! Shit! We had plowed into the surface and were now buried deep beneath the snow. Only for the low gravity had we been stopped from turning into a pulpy mess. We came to rest relatively intact, but we were now buried deep under the snow-covered surface. One saving grace was that we had come down somewhat upright with only a slight gradient to the floor.

We sat in silence for nearly ten minutes, just pondering in a state of shock. "Are you okay?" I asked.

"I appear to have survived," he said weakly. "Should we get up?"

"We won't even be able to get a flashlight to work, so moving around in the dark is gonna be pretty dangerous for you."

"Don't you have some sort of light-intensifying capacity in that artificial eye of yours?"

"Light intensifying being the operative words, it doesn't work if there's no light to be intensified." Again, we sat in silence until finally, I announced, "Bloody hell, I need a piss."

I started to unfasten my straps, and Phelkar asked, "Do you need any help?"

"I don't have a dick, mate. So no, I don't need you to hold it for me," I muttered. He had no response. I climbed out of my seat and headed toward the back, fumbling my way as I went. When familiarizing myself with the shuttle, I worried about the controls, not the layout, and after banging into a few things, I gave up, dropped my daks, and peed right there on the floor.

"Stacey," Phelks said quietly.

"Hmm?" I said, now realizing I had nothing to wipe with.

"I'm probably not supposed to talk about this, but I need to trust someone, especially with what's happened to us."

"I'm no blabbermouth, Phelks. You know that. Come on, spill it."

"Charlotte Kensett came to see me the other day. She told me she had discovered that someone unknown had given the fleet's coordinates to the Peons. She's currently investigating."

"So, what made you wanna tell me this now?" I asked.

"You said earlier someone must have divulged the details of this mission. We were cautious. Very few people knew what we were doing."

I hadn't thought of it since I'd said it. Crashing into a moon generally distracts you from thoughts of who might be a traitorous bastard, but he was right. "The list of suspects is small, Phelks. And that list leaves a nasty taste in our mouths because it can only mean one thing. It has to be one of our friends."

"Exactly what we were thinking."

"I guess Charlie Kensett's taken you off the list. Otherwise, there's no way she'd be talking to you about it."

"She doesn't think I have the technical ability to have transmitted the code."

I laughed at this as I made my way back to my seat. "Conversely, I guess she hasn't ruled *me* out because she didn't tell me," I said, strapping myself back into the chair.

"Indeed."

"But *you* have because you're telling me this?"

"I trust you, Stacey. Charlotte Kensett doesn't."

"Charlotte Kensett doesn't trust anyone," I sighed. "I advise you to be careful around her, mate. Don't ask her to do any favors for you because she will come looking for the debt to be repaid." The silence that followed made me rest my head back and roll my eye. "For fuck sake, you've already asked her for a favor, haven't you?"

Another long silence before he said, "Yes."

I sighed and shook my head. "You're a deadset dickhead, Phelks." The conversation didn't go any further as a light came on on the console. It was small and dim, but it was nearly blinding after all that time in darkness. I sat up, trying to work out what it was. I grinned as if I had just won first prize in the Wagga Show's pie-making competition. "We've got power, Phelks. I don't know if it's gonna do us any good buried down here, but let's start rebooting everything." I ran my hands across the console, just as I had when practicing the boot-up procedures blindfolded, and the lights came on. We both cried out in pain – the sudden flooding of light burning our eyes. We sat there, our eyes closed, until we were sure the glare had diminished and we had grown accustomed to the light again. I looked ahead of us at the wall of ice that covered the window. I turned my attention to the scanning equipment and restarted it. "Oh fuck. We're almost two miles down, and we've been sinking deeper since we got here. If we go down any further, we're gonna hit the underground ocean, and then we'll never find our way out."

Chapter Twenty-Eight

Interrogation

"Can you get the D.E. compensator back online?"

"No good, Phelks. The ice has collapsed on top of us. It won't be powerful enough to get us to rise."

"Yes, but it may stop us sinking further."

I shrugged. "I'm no physics expert, but I guess it's worth a shot," and I activated the D.E. compensators.

"What would happen if we put the burners on? Could we blast our way back up there?" he asked.

"I want to leave that as an absolute last resort. It may get us out of here, or it may just heat the ice around us enough that we plummet even further down."

"What about communications? Could we call for help?"

"Well, there's the rub, Phelks. The Peons were trying to take us prisoner, but something distracted them. Hopefully, that distraction was someone attacking and destroying them, and now they're looking for us. But given our luck at the moment, the Peons could be the ones looking for us instead, and activating the comms could just signal to them where we are."

"We don't really have a choice," Phelks said impatiently.

"Maybe, but we have at least six days of air in here, and there's a sufficient water supply. We're gonna be bloody hungry, but at least we won't die from a lack of water. In the meantime, we can look for an alternative solution." I unfastened my seatbelt again, got out of the chair, and went to the back to find the survival gear. Just great – we didn't have any EMU suits. There was no way we'd be leaving the ship on foot. Enceladus might look pretty, but it was instant death to anybody who wasn't wearing the right gear outside. There was a flare gun, which was useless since we couldn't go outside to use it. We had some blankets, so we could at least make up some beds on the seats if we had to stay here overnight, which was highly likely. So I made up a couple of beds, and then it occurred to me that Phelkar wasn't talking. He hadn't even gotten out of his seat. There wasn't anything wrong with him. He was just sitting there, subdued and already defeated. "Snap out of it, Phelks, we've been in worse shape than this, and we got out of that."

Reluctantly, he climbed out of his seat and came over to join me. He placed a hand on my arm, "I'm so sorry for everything, Stacey. I wish I could change it."

I sighed and said, "Let's just forget about it, okay?" I was genuine this time. I meant it. I just wanted us to move on, but then he leaned in to kiss me. I stepped back, and before I knew what I was doing, I punched him hard in the face. "You are fucking unbelievable. Do you know that?" I said as he started to get up. "You really are the bastard I thought you were."

"What did I do?" he asked, genuinely bewildered by my actions.

"You tried to kiss me," I replied weakly.

"I did no such thing," he blasted indignantly. "In case you haven't noticed, we're on a slight slant here. I was just trying to regain my balance."

"Oh!" I blushed. "Sorry, mate."

"Bloody hell, Stacey," he said as he wiped the blood from his lip.

I'd made a stupid mistake, but it was still bloody funny - no pun intended. Before I could say anything else, I heard a sudden banging on the roof above us. I looked up, trying to decide whether it was just ice falling from the roof or someone out there. The noise stopped, and I climbed up onto a chair, grabbed a rifle, banged back, and shouted, "Hello? Is anyone there?"

The banging repeated. I was still unsure what the source could be. By this point, I couldn't fathom what could be making that noise besides a person. I banged three times, and three more came back in response; I knew it – someone was out there. Then everything went silent. I wasn't sure whether to be happy that there was a possible rescue or worried that the enemy had found us. It all came down to who was outside the shuttle.

"Will they drill their way through?" Phelks asked.

"Let's hope not, because we'd be dead within seconds of them opening us up if they do. Maybe they'll try to pull the shuttle out?"

It turned out to be neither when, about an hour later, the outer airlock door hissed open. We ran to the window to look through and saw two people in American EMU suits, and we breathed a sigh of relief. When the outer airlock closed, I opened the inner one, and a man and a woman stepped in. When the woman turned to face me, a big grin crossed my face. "Well fuck me, if it isn't McKenna Anderson, I thought you'd be dead by now."

McKenna grinned at me. "And I thought you'd be cashiered by now, Stacey." Then the grin faded, "I have a bit of a good news/bad news situation for you."

"Well, don't keep me in suspense."

"The good news is we're here to rescue you. The bad news is that in the name of the Pacific Alliance, you are under arrest.

You are hereby charged with treason against the United States of America."

"You're fucking joking, aren't you?" But I knew McKenna Anderson well, and I knew she wasn't. I hadn't even considered the need to arm myself when I saw the American uniforms.

"Sorry, Stacey. But you have openly aided and abetted a terrorist who ignored a lawful order to stand down. The war is over. You must realize that."

"That 'terrorist' is Jenna-fucking-Plural, you stupid bitch," I snapped. "Your friend!" I shook my head in disbelief. "Never did I ever believe that I would see McKenna Anderson bow down to the Peons."

McKenna tensed at this and looked at me angrily. "I work for the United States government, Stacey. The lawful government, not a GenMod with Grozny-level delusions of grandeur."

Her companion, a large, burly guy, stepped forward. "Turn around and place your hands behind your back, both of you. "

They had tunneled through the snow and attached an umbilical to the airlock outside. We were able to walk, handcuffed, into a waiting shuttle. Although we were supposedly on a United States vessel, there was an unusually large number of French accents around us.

We were transported to the U.S.S. James Garfield, where, as expected, Phelkar and I were separated. I was led to a small room with a rather scary-looking chair. I was made to remove my shoes and strip down to my underwear. McKenna and her partner strapped me in, fastening buckles around my wrists and ankles. "Proud of yourself?" I asked coolly, looking up at McKenna.

"Just tell him what he needs to know, and everything will be fine. I promise you," she replied softly.

They left the room, and a short time later, another character appeared in the doorway, reading from a datapad. He didn't look up, nor did he step further into the room. He simply said, "For the record, please state your full name, rank, and identity number."

"That's a good question, mate." I smiled at him. "Because that's one of the few things I am allowed to tell. My name is Stacefield Ellen Grant. My current rank is Captain, and did you want my Australian number or my American number?" He didn't reply. He just stood there, continuing not to look at me or step inside the room. Mr. Black, as I named him, stood silhouetted against a very bright background, and I couldn't make out his features. "Of course, I'll probably be issued a new number as part of the new Solar Confederation. Let me give the C.O. a call, and I'll find out."

"Oh yes, you are a comedian. One that doesn't like following proper military protocol."

"Fuck me. I take it my reputation precedes me, mate? You little ripper!" I grinned at him.

"I learned classical English, Miss Grant. Not that backward, guttural dialect you call "Australian English." Please refrain from using your vernacular," he sighed.

"Oi, get fucked, mate. That's not nice, and here I thought we were all getting along."

"There is no longer any such thing as an Australian, Miss Grant. We are now members of the European Union. You are, therefore, guilty of treason against your homeland, given that they are at peace with us."

"Well, if that's the case, you can go ahead and shoot me now."

"Oh, trust me, Miss Grant, we will shoot you," he paused before adding, "eventually."

"Wow, did you practice that dramatic effect? You know..." Suddenly, he stepped forward lightning-fast and pushed my head back against the chair. He grabbed my artificial eye and yanked it out without disconnecting it. I screamed. The pain was beyond anything I've ever experienced, as the tendons and nerve endings felt like they were on fire because of the sudden and vicious trauma. He tossed it aside, and I heard it land on the floor, and I felt the blood running down my cheek from my eye socket. The pain continued to rip through me. He just stood there, waiting patiently. Although breathing heavily, I managed to compose myself somewhat and looked up at him. I could now see his face. It's a face that I will never forget. He was young and handsome with a lightly tanned complexion, flawless skin, and designer stubble. "What are the transponder codes of the U.S.S. Constitution?" he asked. I said nothing. "What are Jenna Plural's plans?" Again, I said nothing. "Who are her most loyal advisers?" Yeah, you can guess what I did, nothing. "How bad is Jenna Plural's fear of space?"

Now to that, I responded. "Oh, someone in our circle has been very naughty," I grinned. "Very few people actually know that. So, come on, you can tell me. It's not like I'm going anywhere."

"Not everyone is a sycophantic zealot of your whore mistress."

"Oh, we're gonna resort to using nasty names now, are we? Isn't that a little childish?" And he slammed his fist right into my front teeth. Being rather prominent, they don't tend to react well to such treatment. I screamed again as my two front teeth snapped and cracked inside my mouth. I spat them out as that awful, metallic taste of blood filled my mouth.

You often think about capture. You think about how heroic it would be to resist revealing anything amid relentless interrogation and torture. The reality of it is not as heroic as you imagined. I was well aware this guy had barely started. I had a feeling he could do things to me that I'd only imagined in my nightmares. I wanted to tell him what he wanted to know so it would end before he really got started. I wouldn't give in that easily. I've been trained to resist interrogation, and while, in time, none of that would matter. He'd asked me something that suggested he was under pressure. As soon as Jenna realized that I wasn't coming back, all the codes on every ship I had so much as looked at would be changed. They wanted those codes to sneak up to the fleet without arousing suspicion, which meant he only had a day to break me, and I only had to resist his torture for a day. Okay, so they could torture me for weeks about a number of other things, but I could be sure that he was going to put the screws to me for the next 24 hours or so to get those codes while he could.

"I'm going to cause you a lot of pain before you die. Even if you don't tell me anything, you will suffer for your crimes against my people, and then I will shoot you in the back of the head."

"Mate, you're not giving much incentive to be helpful."

He smiled for the first time. "Oh, but I intend to give you a great incentive, Miss Grant. Your friend Mr. Phelkar is not of much use to us. He does not know any codes, and he probably doesn't know any of Plural's plans. I find it highly unlikely she would trust an English dog with her secrets."

Of course, he was utterly wrong on that, but I thought that he might be spared what I was about to go through with a sense of relief. Oh, how wrong I was. He turned back to the door, summoning two guards. I looked up at McKenna, who looked startled when she saw me sitting there, toothless, blood running from my eye. She glanced at Mr. Black, then bent down and unfastened my leg. "Proud of yourself, Mac?"

"You think this is any different from what Charlotte Kensett does? Just tell him, Stacey." She glanced up at me, and I took advantage of her distraction. I managed to kick her in the face with my bare foot. Her partner, who was working on my wrists, grabbed me by the hair and slammed my head several times into the back of the metal chair. I closed my eye and stopped resisting. I heard McKenna tell him to stop. There was concern in her voice.

They pulled me up onto my feet, and with a final act of defiance, I spat into the guard's face. He punched me in the stomach, and as the wind was knocked out of me, they let me fall to the ground, where I curled up, clutching at my stomach and groaning. They each grabbed me by an ankle, and I was dragged out of the room with no concern about me hitting the door as I was taken down a corridor to what turned out to be a small cell. I was dragged inside, and they left me there.

When I eventually raised my head to look, my tormentor stood silhouetted in the doorway once again. "When you have had enough, call me. He threw a radio down onto the ground and closed the door. I was confused about what he meant by 'having enough'. I picked up the radio. It was locked into a single channel and had a single working button that I was sure was linked directly to him. I dropped it back down and sat against the wall, hugging my knees up to my chest. I began searching for any sign of escape. There was nothing. The thick metal bars stretched fifteen feet above me. The door had no handle. There was also no window, not even one of those little slots to push food through. There was just a camera above me that I could never reach. I sat and waited patiently, and that waiting was probably the worst torture. Or so I thought.

Then I heard it. A scream that broke the deafening silence. It was a man's scream, a tortured, agonizing scream. I couldn't imagine what they were doing to that poor man for the life of me. Then the lightbulb went off in my head, and my one good eye widened. I pulled myself to my feet and leaned my forehead against the door, resting my palms against it. Phelkar. Those bastards. Those motherfucking bastards. I closed my eye, trying to shut it out of my head. A single tear ran down my cheek. The screams went on, and I couldn't bear it. I wanted to die right then and there. If I were dead, then maybe they would stop. I sank to my knees and sobbed for the first time in my adult life. "Leave him alone, you fuckers," I muttered.

"You can make it stop, Stacey." The voice startled me, and I turned to see the radio on the floor. I scrambled to my knees and picked it up. "Please stop. Do it to me. Leave him alone and do it to me. He's a fucking civilian."

"What are the transponder codes for the U.S.S. Constitution?" That was all he asked in reply.

I closed my eye and squeezed it tightly shut, and I cried. "I can't tell you."

"Mr. Phelkar will be most sorry to hear that." The screams started again. I tried to cover my ears with my elbows as I lay on the floor and curled up in a ball, my arms wrapped around my head. Silence fell once more, and the voice that would haunt me for the rest of my life returned. "I am tired, Stacey. I intend to go to bed. This is your last chance before the morning to tell me the U.S.S. Constitution's transponder codes. I will not be back for eight hours. Do you want to listen to this for eight hours? Just tell me the transponder codes, and I'll make sure the pain stops for both of you."

He'd won. I couldn't bear to hear that again. At that moment, I was going to tell him. I'll admit it. I was about to betray Jenna Plural and usher in an era of an unchallenged European empire. "Okay, let me think."

"Think fast, Stacey. I don't know how much longer I can stay awake."

"I'm trying to remember," I said honestly. My brain was a foggy mess. I had been beaten both literally and figuratively. The man I cared most about in the entire universe had been tortured just to get me to talk. "One, seven, nine, six.... " I stopped. Hannah. Hannah was aboard the Constitution. I couldn't let them kill Hannah. Hell, I couldn't let them kill any of them. Was I really about to sacrifice everybody I loved for the life of the one man I loved?

"The rest of it, Stacey, there are four more numbers I need, and then all of this will be over."

I lifted the radio to my mouth again and said coldly, "One, two, fuck, you." I threw the radio against the wall hard enough to smash it. Then I picked it up and, still sitting down on the floor, I slammed it over and over and over and over again into the floor.

The screams began again.

I don't know how long they went on, but I'm sure it wasn't for eight hours. I didn't know if he had passed out or if they'd killed him. I just prayed that his suffering didn't continue. I was exhausted, and despite everything, I fell asleep only to be woken sometime later by the sound of the door opening. I looked up, expecting to see my tormentor, but it was a woman. She came and crouched down beside me. "Can you get up? We don't have much time."

I looked at her nervously, and it was only then that I recognized McKenna. "How do I know this isn't another trick?

Chapter Twenty-Nine

Escape

She pushed a gun into my hand and said, "Come with me if you want to get out of here. We don't have time to sit here and debate. If you think I'm here to betray you, then shoot me now."

I pondered doing that and trying to make my way out on my own, and although I'd seen the schematics of this ship, I still didn't have an eidetic memory chip like Phelks. I climbed to my feet and followed her out into the hallway. I saw a guard unconscious on the ground, and I could smell the remnants of some type of gas.

"This whole block has been put to sleep, but it won't stay that way for long. Additionally, we still need to pass through areas of the ship where other people are present. She took me through another corridor, and a female guard was lying on the floor as well. "She looks about your size. Put her clothes on." I hurriedly dressed, but unfortunately, her shoes were too small for me. Instead, I pulled a pair off of one of the men. They were too big, but they were lace-ups, and I managed to tie them around my feet. As she made to move out of the prison block, I stopped and put a hand on her shoulder. "Phelkar?" I asked.

She shook her head. "He's been moved to the medical wing, which is on the other side of the ship. We have no chance of getting there."

"I am not leaving without him," I said aggressively.

"Then you aren't leaving," McKenna shrugged. "I simply ask that you return to your cell so that I don't get killed for nothing. I'm not doing this because I believe in your cause, sweetheart. I'm doing it for you." Before I could protest, she placed her hand on mine and said, "I know you have no reason to trust me. But hear me out. He is being tortured to get information from you. The thing is, Beleg has been ordered to bring him back alive. He'll be taken to Earth to stand trial as an example."

"I can't let that happen," I insisted.

"You cannot help him if you're dead!" McKenna said, exasperated. "Beleg hasn't got the same instructions about you. When you prove useless or when you give him the information he wants, he'll shoot you in the head. At least if you get away, you might still be able to do something to help Phelkar."

The decision was the hardest one of my life, and it felt like an eternity passed before I finally said weakly, "Fine. Let's go," and I followed her into the docking bay. I felt as if all eyes were looking at me as if they knew who I was, but it was just paranoia and fear. Nobody could see my disfigured face with the guard cap pulled down low over my face. We walked up to the side of an interceptor. McKenna climbed in, and I followed, grabbing the helmet off the floor in front of the seat and slipping it on my head. I heard someone shout something in French that I assumed was 'stop,' but I just looked ahead. There was another interceptor in front of me, so I couldn't use the fast launch option. Instead, I activated the dark energy compensators and lifted the craft into the air. Alarms were already sounding, and the launch doors were sealed instantly. I shook my head and shrugged, launched every last warhead into that doorway, and lit up the engines, putting on speed and flying through the newly created hole as it was still exploding open. I instantly locked in the coordinates of our fleet and set us to full thrust forward. It would take a couple of hours to reach maximum speed, but the same went for any of my pursuers, and pursue they did.

They couldn't catch up. Unlike me, they had a point of no return. If I ran out of fuel, I could continue onwards with the momentum I had generated. There's nothing to slow you down in space. They would have to turn back at some point if they hoped to get back home. It reminded me of when I flew the Starbourne, only this time, I had lost Phelks instead of Harper. I tuned into an encrypted fleet frequency and called out, "This is Stacey Grant making an emergency broadcast. I repeat. This is Captain Stacey Grant making an emergency broadcast. I'm in a stolen V8 Interceptor with Peon markings on a Peon's transponder code. I'm heading back to the fleet, but I'm being pursued."

At first, there was no response. Then a voice responded. "Please do not approach the fleet until you have transmitted the appropriate codes."

I laughed. How ironic, he asked for the same codes I was beaten up for.... Or was it? I had been about to tap them in when a cold shiver of suspicion ran down my spine. McKenna was silent behind me. I lifted my hand from the keypad, "Can't do that, mate. They've been trying to get the codes from me, and I don't know if they're listening in right now. I am not in an American vessel."

"Do not approach the fleet. You will be fired upon," the fleet officer stated firmly.

"What the fuck, Stacey?" snapped McKenna. "I didn't get you out of there to get blown away by other Americans. Send them the damn codes."

"No!" I said firmly.

"You're on an encrypted frequency, aren't you? No one could be listening. Send the fucking codes."

I ignored her. "Put me through to Jenna Plural, now," I demanded.

There was a long pause. "You expect me to put you through to the Admiral?" he said disbelievingly.

I laughed. "I am Stacey Grant. I'm supposed to be a fucking legend or something. Yet I get the one moron in the solar system who doesn't know who I am? I'm that girl from Wagga, you drongo."

"Ma'am, you are coming in too close. Send the codes or turn back. We *will* open fire on you."

I saw the heavy cruiser HMS Liverpool turning toward us. "If you won't put me through to Jenna, put me through to Addison or Tracker or even that bitch Kensett."

"The Liverpool is powering up its fighters," McKenna shouted at me from the gunnery position where she had access to all the readouts.

"Hold the line, interceptor," the fleet officer said.

The wait was intolerable. Then a voice I recognized came on the line. "Please repeat your identity," said Addison.

"For fucks sake, you're taking the piss now," I said, frustratedly.

"Yes, that is Stacey Grant," she said with a sigh. "What happened, Stacey? We had ships out there looking for you. Dodgson reported that you left Enceladus safely, but then we heard nothing from you."

"Got captured. Long story," I replied.

"Well, you will be pleased to know Dodgson's mission was successful. We are moving the fleet to the Enceladus base. However, there is a Peon flotilla waiting for us."

Yet another silence hung between us as I thought it out, then finally replied, "What can I do to help?"

"Dock with the Los Angeles. It still doesn't have a commander. Take command of it."

I almost asked her to repeat herself. "Are you serious?"

"No. I'm crazy, Stacey, but I need that ship flying ASAP."

"At your command, Addy," I grinned.

"Saints preserve us," I heard her mutter before the line went dead.

The moment I managed to dock with the U.S.S. Los Angeles, I was met by the First Officer. "Welcome aboard, Captain Grant," the First Officer said as I jumped down and tossed the helmet to a tech.

"Thanks," I nodded and half-heartedly returned his salute as he stared wide-eyed at my injuries. "Call security," I told him, and he waved over to two guards just as McKenna climbed out. "Place McKenna Anderson under arrest."

Mckenna's eyes widened. "You bitch! I just saved your ass!"

"Oh, come on, Mac," I glared at her with my one swollen eye. "The party's over. We just escaped from an American cruiser like we were making a break from a nursery school. Conveniently, no American ships were available, and we had to take a Peon interceptor. You knew full well that I would be expected to give the transponder codes."

"Stacey, I just gave up my commission to save your life. This is how you're going to repay me?" she implored as one of the guards started to cuff her.

"So you're telling me that if I get a full diagnostic of this ship, I won't find it transmitting back to the Garfield?"

McKenna hesitated. She was about to say something, but stopped herself, and a wry smile crossed her face. "You know the Peons considered you to be the stupid one. I tried to convince them otherwise, but they seemed to think they knew better than me."

"Why McKenna? We served together for three years. We were friends."

"I'm sick of war. I'm sick of watching my friends die. When the surrender came, I was relieved. I just want to go home and live in peace. That will never happen as long as Jenna is starting trouble out here."

"We are all sick of all war, McKenna," I said coldly. "I don't side with Jenna because I like war. I do it because I want to return to my country as an Australian, not some European flunky." I turned to the guards. "Take her away before she makes me chunder." They started to lead her off, and something else occurred to me. "Hold up!" they said, turning to face me. I smiled at her. "McKenna, I'll let Charlotte Kensett know that you're here and would love a reunion."

McKenna's face turned ashen white. "Fuck you, you bitch. You're dead, Stacey Grant. You are so fucking dead," but I just winked at her and turned away.

We went up to the bridge. "They've had us sitting out because of the command issue," the First Officer told me.

"Why didn't you take command?

He looked confused. "Because you'd already been assigned as Captain. Addison ordered it weeks ago. We have been retrofitting everything in readiness for you. The Los Angeles will become the training center for the new fighter pilots. You didn't know?"

"This is the United States military, mate. No one tells you anything," I grinned, but I realized Addison did have a sense of humor.

I was barely through the doors when I ordered the pilot to set a course to catch up to the fleet. "Standard by twelve," I said.

The pilot turned and looked at me, confused. "Ma'am, standard by twelve isn't possible for any ship."

I grinned at him. "Oh, I'm gonna have so much fun with you, mate. How about this... Fly real fucking fast... We've got Peons to kill."

The pilot looked at the First Officer as if to say, 'Is this really our Captain?'

"You heard the Captain, Mr. Marshall, fly real fucking fast."

"Aye, aye." He spun back around, and the ship hummed as it began a rapid acceleration. "Flying real fucking fast, *Captain*."

"Do we have a Cybernetic Med-tech on board?" I asked the First Officer.

"Yes, a Chief Tech was just assigned here. She's a grade three in cybernetics."

"Is that good?"

"Well, the max is six. So, I'd say about average."

"Tell her to get up here with the fastest cybernetic eye implant she can install," I said and sat down in the Captain's chair. Minutes later, and to my total surprise, Daisy Bell came onto the bridge, and I gave her a beaming smile. "Daisy, good to see you again. Can you fix me up with something fast?" I pointed to my eye.

She stepped over and stared into the socket."There's a lot of damage and swelling in there. I can spray it now, and then we should wait for the swelling to go down. Once it has, I can fix you up with something."

"How long will that take?"

"About thirty to forty minutes."

"Do it," I said, and she sprayed a chemical into my socket, which stung like a bitch, and I tried not to wince in front of my crew. "Okay, Daisy, stay here with me." I turned around to the pilot and said, "What's our E.T.A. to the rest of the fleet?"

"About three hours from now, Ma'am."

"And how long before the enemy's able to engage them?"

"About two hours."

I sighed and sat back. "Fuck! We're gonna be late to the party." I looked up at the First Officer. "Do you think you can handle things here while I go take a quick shower?"

He nodded, and I indicated to Daisy to follow me. I headed out to the Captain's ready room next to the bridge. All these larger battleships had sleeping and shower facilities for the Captain near the bridge, and it only took me a few moments to find them. I stripped off the Peon uniform and my filthy clothes. "If you get a chance, get a steward to burn those or something. I don't ever wanna see them again," I said to Daisy. "I'm gonna take a shower. Can you go see if there's any alcohol here? Then we can do something about my eye." I didn't wait for a reply and stepped into the bathroom, turned on the shower, and stepped inside. I finally felt the adrenaline wash off of me as the pain of my injuries and the weariness in my heart swept over me. All I could think about was Phelkar telling me that he loved me and how I'd refused to say it back. I turned the water up in the shower so Daisy couldn't hear me crying.

As I composed myself and walked back into the main room, I saw that the steward had come in. He quickly turned away from my nakedness. "Sorry, Ma'am! I was told to come in with a clean uniform for you."

"That's cool. Hope you got me some clean undies in there too."

"Umm, yes, I think you'll find everything is in order, Ma'am. I've laid it out on your bed. Is there anything else you need?"

"No, mate, you're good to go. Thanks." He hurried out as I walked into the bedroom. There was a new set of underwear still in the cellophane wrap waiting for me.

Daisy came in as I was slipping them on, and she checked my eye again as I fastened my bra. "I think I can work with that now."

I turned around and sat on the edge of the bed while she knelt in front of me, and with a small device, she cauterized something or other in my eye socket. Dunno what it was because, after all, I couldn't see what she was doing, and I'm no Med Tech. She then opened a small box that she had placed beside me, and inside it sat a smaller, neater, and more human-looking eye. "I got this from the Japanese with you in mind," she told me. "It's their latest design, and it won't irritate you as much as the other one did. Plus, it won't cover your face as much as the previous model did. She lifted it out and slotted it into place. There was a moment where it integrated with my nervous system, going through its booting-up sequence, before suddenly, twice as much came into view. "Daisy, you are one damn fine lady."

Daisy smiled. "Come by and see me tomorrow, and I'll fix those teeth. It'll just be a quick injection, and a new pair should grow back in a couple of weeks."

I pulled on my clothes as we were talking, and as I buttoned up the jacket, I noticed my name was embroidered on the breast. Captain Stacey Grant. U.S.S. Los Angeles. Addison had gone out of her way to spoil me. Just a damn shame I was gonna change the ship's name.

I pulled on the boots and tied the laces. "Look, I have to go command this big spaceship. Maybe we can catch up later over a few tinnies."

As I headed back to the bridge, my thoughts returned to the information I had learned from my tormentor. He knew things about Jenna that he shouldn't have known. There was a traitor among us. I had no idea who, but I didn't have much time to think about it. None of it made sense.

The Solar Confederation had a new home. Jenna put out the message, and this was now the provisional capital of the Solar Confederation. If you were hoping for a grand battle, I'm sorry. The Peons turned and ran when they saw the size of our fleet. Normally, I would have been disappointed, but there was something else on my mind, and I needed to see Jenna Plural as soon as possible.

As we brought the Los Angeles in, we went into orbit around Enceladus. Well, I say orbit, but with a moon that size, you can't put four hundred battleships in orbit around it. So let's just say we parked the Los Angeles in space nearby.

I took a shuttle down just behind Jenna, who departed from the Constitution, and I landed just after she did. I exited, and crowds of people were already milling outside the astrodome, desperate to see their official liberator. It had clearly been set up as a media event with cameras everywhere, both stationary and flying around. Jenna made straight for me. "What happened to Mr. Phelkar?"

"The Peons have him. Actually, the Americans working with the Peons have him. He's on board the U.S.S. Garfield." I couldn't read anything in her features as I spoke. She was as impassive as the day I met her. "It's quite heavily armed, but there's only one ship. Give me a couple of hours, and we can go and get him."

"You have no idea how much I want to do that, Stacey. I cannot justify the loss of personnel for just one man, regardless of who they are. I hope you can understand that."

I stared at her, and a lump came up into my throat. "I understand it, mate. I just don't agree with it. You didn't hear him scream." As soon as the words came out of my mouth, I instantly regretted them. Jenna closed her eyes just for a moment, but her face was still impassive. When she opened them again, I looked at her apologetically and said, "I'm sorry," and I meant it. "I shouldn't have said that."

"No, Stacey, you really shouldn't have." I watched as a single tear ran down her face. She made no move to wipe it away. I'd never seen her cry before. Hell, I'd have sworn on a stack of Bibles that she didn't know how to. Without another word to me, she turned and walked off. It was only then, with her back to me, that I saw her lift her hand to wipe her face as she left me feeling like complete shit.

Chapter Thirty

Confession

I didn't stay on Enceladus. I did not want to be any part of any celebration because there was nothing for me to celebrate. Instead, I felt like there was something else I had to do, so I took a shuttle up to the Constitution. A couple of hours later, I was outside the new SCSS office, which stood for Solar Confederation Security Services but was better known to me as Chuck Kensett.

I didn't knock; I just walked in. She was clearly just moving in, with assistants setting up furniture and unpacking boxes. I just looked at them and told them to get out. They looked at Kensett, who nodded, and they left the room. "Good morning, Stacey. It's been a while. What brings you to my office?"

"I want to be kept apprised of everything you find out about Phelks," I said, not interested in perfunctory greetings.

She raised an eyebrow. "There's nothing more that I would like to do. However, my remit is to answer to Jenna Plural and Jenna Plural only."

"Yeah, yeah. All the same, you'll keep me notified about everything you find out about him. In return, you can call upon me once to help you in your work, no questions asked."

Charlotte's eyes widened. I think it was the first time anything in her life had ever taken her by surprise. A thin smile crossed her face, "No questions asked? Now that's a phrase I really love. He's already on his way to Earth. The Euros are already planning a big showy trial. He's to be used as the poster boy of treason."

I found it positively ludicrous, and I shook my head disbelievingly. "You're shitting me. Even the Peons aren't dumb enough to charge him with treason when he isn't one of them."

"No, he's not being tried by the Europeans. The British are trying him. They're hoping to break the resolve of our resistance forces on Earth by making an example of Jenna's right-hand man."

"So, how do we get him out?" It wasn't really a question. It was a demand.

"I'm sorry, Stacey, but we don't. We can't. The best thing we can do is to try to take him out before he becomes a public spectacle or before they break him and he blabs to the Euros."

At that, I stepped over to her, grabbed her by the neck, and slammed her against the wall. "Listen to me very carefully. That is not going to happen, mate. I'm not gonna let it happen, and I'm going to make damn sure Jenna doesn't let it happen."

She simply straightened her dress as I let go, looking completely unfazed by what I had just done. "Yes, I suppose it's most unlikely Jenna will let me pursue the most sensible course of action on this." She sighed. "I have nothing more to tell you now, but I will keep you apprised of anything passing my desk."

"Make sure you do," I growled.

As I turned to leave, she stopped me. "I will be in touch when I need that favor, Captain Grant." I didn't look back. I just stepped out, slamming the door behind me.

I avoided Jenna like the plague over the next week. It wasn't just the comments I'd made to her when I got back, but that strong feeling of guilt I had because of the situation between myself and Phelks.

When Hannah was transferred to the Los Angeles, I was really happy. We spent a lot of time together, but we didn't really talk about anything serious until one night when she said, "Why is there such a big deal about this, Michael Phelkar? We've lost so many people in this conflict, but rumors are going around about plans to rescue him."

We were sitting in the lounge of the Captain's suite, finishing off a bottle of wine after dinner. Not really my taste, but it was Hannah's preference, and it was kind of rude to expect her to drink what I drank all the time. "Well, they keep it on the down-low, but Phelks and Jenna are an item. And we really miss him."

Hannah raised an eyebrow as a slight smile crossed her face. "We?"

I think I actually blushed at that, and Hannah's grin widened. "Looks like you have a thing for him, too."

I sighed. The grin fell from her face as I couldn't hide the sadness in my eye. "We were involved."

"He dumped you for Jenna?" Hannah placed a hand on my knee, reassuringly.

I laughed at the irony of that statement. "No, he saw me again after he became involved with Jenna. Although I didn't know they were involved at the time."

Hannah screwed her face up in disgust. "Oh, my God! The man's a pig."

I laughed, amused by her reaction, and I explained. "Therein lies the real problem. He really isn't a pig. Sure, that was a fucked up thing to do, but I don't think he intended it. In every other way, he's probably the nicest guy I've ever met." To my surprise, Hannah looked startled. "What's the matter?"

"You're in love with him, aren't you?" she said softly.

I chuckled softly, but there was no mirth in my laughter, and I ended it with a long sigh. "I wish to fuck I wasn't," I choked out.

Hannah got up from her seat and came over to sit next to me. She pulled me close, and I buried my head on her shoulder. "Hey, sis. You're gonna get him back. I don't know how, but I promise you that you will get him back if I have anything to do with it." It was really sweet, but what the fuck could she do? She had no power, influence, or particular skills that could help, but I appreciated the sentiment nonetheless.

Of course, I couldn't avoid Jenna forever. I expected her to call me over to the Constitution at some point, but to my surprise, I was summoned to the bridge one morning and informed that a shuttle from the Constitution, bearing the Admiral, was in the process of docking. As protocol demanded, I went down to meet her alongside my senior officers. Her face was grim as she stepped off the shuttle. I felt uneasy, and I saluted her for the first time in my life. She looked startled by it and raised a curious eyebrow as she saluted me back. She had her usual retinue of flunkies, but no one I knew was there. "Captain Grant, it is good to see you again."

"Likewise, Admiral," I responded most formally and totally out of character.

"Is there somewhere where we can talk privately?" she asked, maintaining a business-like tone.

"Of course." We walked back to my ready room in silence. I seriously thought that she was about to take away my command or something like that. I'd never seen her this formal with me. Not since the first time we'd met. Even then, when she'd barely known me, she wasn't this cold. She entered the room first, stepped past the conference table, and stared out of the window into space and at her fleet. I stepped in behind her and steeled myself for whatever was coming. The moment the door closed, she turned back around and stepped over to me. To my astonishment, tears were streaming down her face. "I've missed you, Stacey Grant. I've missed you so much." And as she pulled me into her arms for a tight embrace, the floodgates opened in the one eye I could still cry out of. We stood there for several minutes, saying nothing.

When we released each other, we composed ourselves before speaking again. Jenna took a seat at the table while I went to the drinks cabinet I had installed and poured us out a couple of whiskeys. "You should know, I had asset recovery go over the wreck of the Lady Liberty," Jenna told me as I handed her a glass.

"I didn't leave much of that ship to go over," I chuckled. "Did you find anything interesting?"

"Oh, just a couple of things that might interest you," she grinned mischievously at me.

"Oh, for fucks sake, Jenna, just tell me, would you?"

"The rest of your Portobello Brandy, for one. And probably most importantly, they found the picture of you and Harper."

"Seriously?" The truth was, I didn't really give a shit about the brandy. Sure, I was very disappointed to have lost those remaining bottles. But the picture? The loss of that picture had cut me to the core.

"Seriously. Bunker has it. He'll bring it over to you later."

"Bunker?"

Her face fell. "He's my new adjutant. I worked with him about ten years ago, and I trust him."

My stomach turned over. Phelks had moved on from working as an adjutant to become some kind of Chief of Civil Affairs Minister, but it was still his replacement.

I made a decision then and there to tell Jenna the truth. It could end our friendship completely, but I felt it was the honorable thing to do rather than have her find out another way because these things always have a way of coming out.

"Jenna," the smile dropped from her face, and she looked at me intently, hearing my tone had changed so drastically. "I have to tell you something," I hesitated. This was much harder than I thought.

"Go on," she said, sounding a little nervous, which only made it harder.

"Me and Phelks. We... We slept together."

Jenna's expression didn't change, and she said softly, "I see." She then sat back and sighed. "I'm assuming this was not before he was involved with me. If it were, then there'd have been no reason to tell me."

"I didn't know, Jenna. I only found out when you told me about your relationship when I was in the hospital after the Battle of Deep Space. He never said anything to me."

To my surprise, Jenna smiled at me. It wasn't exactly a big, beaming smile, but a smile nonetheless. "Well, that's a relief. I don't think I could handle losing both of you."

I stared at her. "You're not mad at me?"

"Why should I be? He cheated on me. You didn't. But tell me the truth, you love him too, don't you?"

Tears welled in my eye again as I said, "I'm trying not to, but it's really hard."

Again, Jenna surprised me by smiling. She shrugged and sighed once more. "He's not difficult to love."

I laughed lightly. "Yeah, but I don't even know why. Even you have to admit, he's a moron."

Jenna laughed. "He is quite the idiot."

I grew serious again. "Look, Jenna, it doesn't matter how I feel. I promise you that I'm not gonna make things difficult when he's back. I will stay out of the picture."

"Stacey, I have to be honest with you," Jenna said grimly. "I really don't think we're going to get him back."

I was about to argue, but truth be told, I knew she was right. It would take a full-scale battle to secure his release from European custody. "Yeah," was all I said in reply.

The next few weeks were spent turning Enceladus Base into a home. Once again, there was a round of personnel moves as people were pulled off the fleet to maintain the new base, so the ships that could land could get much-needed repairs that were difficult to perform in space.

The Peons had a field day with the arrest of Phelks, and under the guise of British broadcasts, lists of his crimes, both real and completely fabricated, started to come out from the so-called investigation. On top of treason, they added mass murder to the charge—basically, they were pinning the deaths of the Peons who died in the Battle of Deep Space on him. Then they added a larceny charge for the theft of the Lewis Puller, stating the ship was not returned after peace was declared. Then the Peons' protests started over the deaths of the Peon crew on the Lady Liberty. I got to see him just once before his trial. It was just a brief snippet on the British news as he was transferred from a truck into the courthouse. He was manacled at both hands and feet and shuffled along, unable to take a proper step. At least he looked healthy. They weren't stupid enough to put him on TV looking like a sympathetic figure. Then, the news we had all expected arrived. He was found guilty. They didn't want to make a martyr out of him, so he was spared a death sentence. His sentence was much worse – life plus a hundred and fifty years to be served on an undisclosed penal colony. They didn't want us to find him.

I tried not to think about it and came up with an idea to boost my spirits. However, I would need help to pull it off.

"No, Stacey. Absolutely not." Helen Tracker looked horrified by my suggestion. "It's totally illegal and against regulations."

"Oh, come on, mate. Whose law? Whose regulations? America's? Japan's? Maybe Canada's?" I said imploringly.

"I think all of them will have a law against what you're asking," she snapped back."Why don't you just ask Commodore Addison or Admiral Plural?" she said, using their new ranks.

I sighed and responded frustratedly. "Because they might say no. Have you never heard the term 'it's better to seek forgiveness than ask permission'?"

"Of course I have, but the answer is still no."

"Look, mate," I put on my best sad face in a last-ditch effort to get her onside. "I haven't asked for anything since I joined up after losing my country. There aren't many of us out there who are independent. I just want to give them something. Something to remind them of home."

Tracker sighed. "Fine!" she said irritably. "But if I end up in the stockade, I'm taking you with me."

I grinned at her. "You got a deal, mate."

And so it was, just twenty-four hours later, I got a call to the bridge. Most of the crew were huddled around the Communications Officer as I entered. The First Officer looked up at me as I entered, looking very confused. "Ma'am, something's gone wrong with that transponder. It's gone offline. We're no longer beaming out that we are the U.S.S. Los Angeles. Do you think the Peons are hacking us?"

I shook my head. "No, I think you'll find it's just been reset. That's all. On my orders."

He looked confused, but before he could say anything more, the U.S.S. Constitution called, saying they had Admiral Plural on the line. "Well, g'day, Admiral," I said cheerfully.

"What the hell is going on over there, Stacey? My security personnel are having fits thinking that the Peons are hacking you. Tracker is telling me not to worry, but refuses to tell me any more. So, unless you want me to charge her with disobeying orders, I think you'd better explain yourself."

"I must ask you to be patient, Admiral. All will be clear very soon, but I assure you it's nothing to worry about."

At that moment, the transponder came back online. The First Officer's eyes opened wide as he read the readout in front of him, then turned to look at me questioningly.

I waited nervously for a reaction from Jenna, but suddenly we heard her laughing louder than I'd ever heard her laugh before. "You are by far the craziest woman I have ever met, Stacey Grant. But if that's what you really want, I'll let you have it. Plural out."

I looked up at the crew, who were all staring dumbfounded. "Welcome aboard the Republic of Australia Ship 'R.A.S. Wagga Wagga', guys and girls."

Unfortunately, the joy didn't last very long as Addison came online. "Captain Grant, we have a problem."

"What's going on, Commodore?" I asked, a little miffed that my fun moment had just been interrupted.

"McKenna Anderson has escaped."

"What the fuck? How?"

"It appears she had help. You're not going to like hearing this." My blood ran cold, but whatever I thought was nowhere near as bad as what she said next. "It was your sister, Hannah."

I was seated in an office with Jenna, Claire, Charlotte Kenzett, and Helen Tracker just two hours later. "You know this is quite a serious accusation," I said, not allowing myself to believe it even though I realized I really didn't know Hannah that well. "You better damn well have solid proof."

"We have her on surveillance cameras," Kensett said casually as if she were reading off a shopping list. "She used your security ID to get into the Constitution's cells. They then made their way to an airlock and spacewalked out to a shuttle that was apparently waiting for them. They were out of range before we even noticed it had happened. Unfortunately, we are unable to track them."

I sat open-mouthed. "Well, I guess that evidence is pretty fucking conclusive." I looked up at Jenna with considerable distress. "I'm so sorry. If I had any idea...."

Jenna interrupted me. "No one's blaming you, Stacey. It's not like you were close."

No. Hannah and I were not close, but we were starting to become so. Or at least I thought we were, but I'd been played for a fool once again.

My sister. Hannah Grant had betrayed me and everything I stood for. But what was worse? What cut me in half? That bitch had betrayed Australia. She's a dead woman walking. When I finally find her, she's going to die.

Epilogue

I was late.

Nothing new about that, right?

On this occasion, that had a whole different meaning.

I had returned to my duty on board my ship.

I'd been meaning to do this for several days, but to be honest, I was frankly quite scared too.

I slipped out the small packet I had hidden in my pocket and read the instructions carefully before taking out the contents.

I looked in the bathroom mirror, took a deep breath, then dropped my undies and squatted over the toilet.

It was hard to believe that you still had to piss on a stick with all this technology around us.

The deed was done, and I placed it on the side of the sink to wait. I flushed the toilet, washed my hands, and once more, I picked up the stick and looked at it.

Nothing!

That was good, right?

I thought I would feel relieved, but my hands still shook.

Then I finally let out a sigh of relief and turned to throw it into the garbage can.

Then I saw it change.

The thin line was turning pink. I looked down in disbelief.

Unable to move, unable to think straight, I finally raised my head and looked into the mirror again. My artificial eye stared back at me as if judging me.

I let out another sigh, but it wasn't one of relief this time.

I stared at my face in the mirror again and said, "Oh fuck!"

END

www.ingramcontent.com/pod-product-compliance
Lightning Source LLC
LaVergne TN
LVHW041924090826
845145LV00015B/295

* 9 7 8 1 9 5 9 1 3 8 5 0 1 *